BEAUTIFUL
CREATURES

Lulu Taylor grew up in the English countryside, was educated at Oxford University, and has lived all over the world. She is married and lives in London.

D0762798

Also by Lulu Taylor

Heiresses
Midnight Girls

Praise for Lulu Taylor

'Nothing lifts the winter blues quite like a glam bonk-buster, and *Heiresses* is one of the highest pedigree . . . Addictive, decadent and sexy, it'll easily see you through the depths of winter's most depressing month. *5 Stars*'   *heat*

'If wealth and glamour turn you on, then turning the pages of this epic blockbuster will brighten the credit crunch chill for you'   *Best*

'Well-written and fresh'   *Mirror*

'Pure indulgence and perfect reading for a dull January evening'   *Sun*

'Such great escapism it could work as well as a holiday'
Daily Mail

'Wonderfully written and bursting with greed, sex and money, this indulgent read is totally irresistible'
Closer

Lulu Taylor

BEAUTIFUL CREATURES

arrow books

Published by Arrow Books 2011

2 4 6 8 10 9 7 5 3

First published in Great Britain in 2011 by
Arrow Books
Random House, 20 Vauxhall Bridge Road,
London SW1V 2SA

www.rbooks.co.uk

Addresses for companies within The Random House Group Limited
can be found at:
www.randomhouse.co.uk/offices.htm

The Random House Group Limited Reg. No. 954009

A CIP catalogue record for this book
is available from the British Library

ISBN 978-0-099-55045-7

Mixed Sources
Product group from well-managed
forests and other controlled sources
www.fsc.org Cert no. TT-COC-2139
© 1996 Forest Stewardship Council

The Random House Group Limited supports The Forest Stewardship
Council (FSC), the leading international forest certification organisation. All
our titles that are printed on Greenpeace approved FSC certified paper carry
the FSC logo. Our paper procurement policy can be found at
www.rbooks.co.uk/environment

Typeset by Palimpsest Book Production Limited,
Falkirk, Stirlingshire
Printed and bound in Great Britain by
CPI Bookmarque Ltd, Croydon CR0 4TD

To Fiona Alexander
With love and thanks

Part One

1

Spring 2008

The night was balmy, one of those gold and petrol-blue evenings when the day seems to take its time slipping away, turning softly and slowly from light to dark. A silvery moon hung low in the night sky, glowing benignly over proceedings.

Below was a scene that might have come from three centuries before. In the exquisitely manicured gardens, people promenaded elegantly between the privet hedges and herbaceous borders, gliding past statues and fountains as they talked and laughed. The gentlemen were in white stockings, buckled shoes, breeches or pantaloons, and gorgeously embroidered coats worn tight across the shoulders and to the waist, before billowing out in extravagant folds. The ladies were a truly splendid sight: on their heads were towering wigs of white and silver, some halos of powdered thistle-down, others masses of intricate curls and ringlets. In their locks were velvet ribbons, sprays of crystal flowers or other magnificent adornments. One lady had the proverbial galleon in full sail perched on her ocean of hair; another wig was encrusted in jewelled sea creatures, with crabs, lobsters and oysters nestled among mother-of-pearl shells and crystal rocks. Below the sumptuous wigs were powdered and painted faces, with spots of rouge in doll-like circles and velvet beauty spots worn on cheeks, at the corners of eyes or on the curve of a pretty jawline. Each dress seemed more lavish than the last, encapsulating the extravagance of the *ancien régime*: heavily embroidered silks and satins, edged with stunning laces, glinting with gold and silver thread, in a rainbow of beautiful colours.

Diamonds sparkled and pearls glimmered softly in the moonlight or in the beams of the delicate Chinese lanterns suspended at intervals from bamboo poles. The women moved slowly, held back by the weight of their costumes, waving fans in front of their faces as they talked and flirted with the gentlemen, their merry laughter ringing out across the stately garden.

A few clues revealed that this was not a night of pre-Revolutionary jollity at the court of Versailles: some of the dresses were scandalously low-cut and rather short, with the slim legs visible beneath clad in fishnet tights and feet on towering platform heels or sharp stilettos, or even, in one case, magenta biker boots with chrome buckles up the side. More than one hand was holding a cigarette, and more than one breast, back or shoulder sported a tattoo.

This was no eighteenth-century soirée, but rather a twenty-first-century party where the rich and privileged of society had gathered to play. *'Fête Champêtre'* the invitation had proclaimed in gold engraving on the stiffest card, to celebrate the twenty-first birthdays of

Octavia and Flora Beaufort. Dress: Marie Antoinette and Louis XVI.

A group of girls sat on two semi-circular stone benches in the rose garden, dressed in a riot of silks, petticoats and wigs.

'Why aren't you wearing a wig, Amanda?' asked one, who had a peroxide-white tower on her head with fat ringlets falling on to her snowy bosom.

'Because, Suze,' said Amanda sweetly, putting her head on one side, 'I've come as Madame de Pompadour.'

'Oh.' Suze looked blank, her round eyes wide. 'But didn't the invitation say Marie Antoinette? Who is Madame de Pompadour?'

'She was a royal mistress,' Amanda said, her nose in the air. 'One of the people who held *real* power at court. Do you like my dress?' She looked down at her costume with satisfaction. 'I sent my pet dress-maker to look at the portrait in the Wallace Collection, and then had her make it up. It's come out rather well.'

The others gazed at the splendid confection. It was a beautiful shimmering sea blue, cut low, with a rose-pink silk bodice adorned with large pink silk bows that narrowed towards the tiny waist. The full skirts below were like something from a fairy-tale princess's gown, festooned with ruffles and miniature pink roses. The sleeves were tight to the elbow, then billowed out into a cascade of silk and lace, with tiny bows stitched wherever a tiny bow could be put. Amanda wore no jewellery but round her neck was a delicate chiffon fichu in the same pink as the roses. On her feet were rosy silk slippers with bows on their high stiff fronts. She looked magnificent.

5

'I'm not David Starkey or anything,' drawled another of the girls sitting on the benches, 'but wasn't Madame de Pompadour the mistress of Louis XV, not Louis XVI? You're about fifty years out of date, sweetie.'

Amanda smiled condescendingly. 'Don't split hairs, Claudia darling. I'm in a bloody costume, aren't I? Besides, you can talk. You're covered in fake tan and wearing sunglasses! Was Marie Antoinette satsuma-coloured? I can't remember.'

'Piss off, sweetie. No one comes between me and my sunnies.' Claudia smoothed out her own candy-pink taffeta dress. 'Anyone know the time? I'm not wearing my Cartier.' She looked over at the sundial near the centre of the rose garden. 'That thing's useless at night. Not that I'd know how to read it in the daytime anyway.'

'I'm surprised you can see it at all, with those sunglasses on,' murmured Amanda.

'Ten o'clock,' piped up someone else.

Amanda pouted and looked sulky. 'Ten o'clock? For God's sake, how long do you think we're going to have to wait? I only came to see those girls. I can't think of any other reason for coming out here to the back of beyond. How long are they going to hide away? This is their party, for fuck's sake.'

Just then a voice said loudly, 'Joan Fish, as I live and breathe! Joan Fish, is that you?' and a man at the tail end of middle age, with white hair, bright brown eyes and suspiciously unlined skin, appeared on the path leading to the benches. He went straight to Amanda and bent to kiss her.

'Gerry darling.' Amanda offered him one smooth

cheek and then another as she pursed her own rosy lips and touched the air with a kiss. 'I'm not Joan Fish, I'm Madame de Pompadour.'

'Same difference.' Gerry Harbord gave a flourish of his wrist, flicking out the waterfall of lace ruffles that emerged from his startlingly tight frock coat. 'La Pompadour was just a sexy little parvenue, sweetheart. She may have died a marquise but she was born plain Mademoiselle Jeanne Poisson. Or Joan Fish, as I call her. Still, one can't fault her taste. She was exquisite – and so are you.' He looked around at the others politely. 'You *all* look fabulous.'

Suze twirled a ringlet round one finger and said, 'What I don't understand is why everyone's making such a fuss anyway. Who are these girls? I've never heard of them.'

Gerry breathed in sharply. 'Never heard of the Beauforts? What on earth are you saying?'

Claudia laughed. 'Oh, Suze, you are an idiot. Surely you know about the Beaufort money. It all came from steel, I think. A couple of generations back at least.'

'And you must have heard of that divorce,' chimed in Amanda.

'The custody battle,' sighed Gerry. 'Two little girls, fatherless, left with their feckless mother, then taken in by their aunt after a vicious court case.'

Suze seemed puzzled, her small face looking rather comical under the great wig she was wearing. 'But that must have been years ago.'

Claudia tossed back her long dark curls over one shoulder. 'I remember seeing that court case all over the news like anyone else, though it didn't mean much to me at the time. Suze is right, it was fifteen years

7

ago, wasn't it? And I haven't heard anything about them since.'

'Hardly anyone has,' Gerry said mysteriously. 'They've been protected like little princesses in purdah. Who knows why? But all that's about to change.' He smiled at the little group. 'Now, I'm going to steal my darling Amanda away, I simply can't go a moment longer without her. Do excuse us, ladies.'

He offered his arm to Amanda, who stood up and took it, and they walked away together along the path, leaving the other girls staring after them. They made a striking couple, with Gerry outfitted in a magnificent cream coat and matching breeches, the shimmering silk embroidered with golden birds sitting in twisting golden vines. He had attached a curling white tail of hair to the back of his head, tied with a black velvet ribbon. 'You're very out of fashion, darling,' he murmured. '*Scandalous.*'

Amanda smiled at him mischievously. 'I know what I'm doing. Everyone else was going to come in huge white nylon wigs, all struggling to outdo each other.' She put her hand to her head. 'So this is my take on Madame de Pompadour . . . a little modern twist.' Her hair, usually a rich brown and cut into a full, wavy bob, had been dyed a colour that was almost silver until the light caught it in a certain way and then it glowed the softest lavender. It was pulled back into a simple chignon, and pinned with a few more miniature silk roses to match the ones on her dress.

'Now, I *love* that,' Gerry told her. 'It ought to look pure Mrs Slocombe but somehow it doesn't. So clever. I might have known you'd do something a little special, Amanda. You never let *one* down.'

'And if I know you, Gerry, you'll have the same colour by Monday morning, and claim it was all your idea,' Amanda retorted, although she smiled at his compliment. They progressed up the long walk towards the splendid Queen Anne house that dominated the night skyline. The strains of a Haydn string quartet floated out from the terrace on the night air. 'Now listen, I want to know when these blasted girls are going to make an appearance. If anyone knows anything, it'll be you. There are furious rumours going around that you planned this whole bash. You always get Chloe de Montforte on the harp – and there she is, strumming away by the grand staircase. I'd guess the guest list is your work too. All your pals are here.'

Gerry looked pleased. 'Of course I did, my dear. Frances called me. She's an angel . . . a bit stiff perhaps but a darling at heart. She knows no one, though. Just think – all that money and not a friend to call her own, only that crusty old husband of hers. She told me about her scheme to launch the girls in society, and I simply clapped my hands with joy. It was just too adorable! Two little nuns, never been seen out of the convent, and here they are, making their debut as no one does any more. If a girl retains much of her unworldly innocence beyond thirteen these days, she's probably a simpleton. So refreshing to find two of them so unspoiled.'

'Oh, spare me,' muttered Amanda, rolling her eyes. 'And have you actually met them? They've been under lock and key for so long, I've begun to think that they don't really exist at all.'

'Well . . . no, not really. I spied a couple of portraits

in the house when I visited but one never can tell how true to life they are.' Gerry looked a little shame-faced, as though he had failed his own high standards of social spying. 'But it was my idea that they should appear at just before midnight, like a pair of Cinderellas. And it was my idea too to have a *fête champêtre*,' he added happily.

'Yes – it has your queeny old fingerprints all over it.' Amanda giggled.

He raised an eyebrow at her. 'I forgive you for disobeying the dress code and coming out of period,' he declared nobly. 'Isn't that nice of me? Now, here comes a footman with some champagne. You clearly need a drink. I decreed gallons of vintage Krug and the old girl didn't bat an eyelid. There are cases and cases and cases of it. And there's a special surprise later too.' He lifted two flutes off the footman's tray and passed one to Amanda. 'Are you hungry? I'm starving. Let's go to the Orangery. There's a supper laid out there and, if I say so myself, it's *inspired*.'

They moved through the crowds. The revellers had by now been drinking and eating for a couple of hours and there were already signs of dilapidation among them: some wigs were looking distinctly askew, velvet ribbons and silk stocks were no longer crisply tied but hung down loosely, and some of the carefully applied make-up was a little smudged. The younger crowd had disappeared inside to the ballroom, which had been transformed with black velvet drapery and twinkling starlit cloths into a modern dance floor, the whole room pounding with the beat from the sound booth. The Orangery was quieter, with the strains of Haydn floating in from the terrace, and an older crowd relaxing among the armchairs and chaise-longues that Gerry had arranged be put there: their rich damasks and silks, laden with cushions, looked theatrical and stylish among the great stone pots, pedestals and statues that adorned the room.

It was certainly an amazing feast, with everything displayed as elaborately as possible: towers of seafood decorated with seaweed and oyster shells full of caviar, ice sculptures of cupids dancing in the middle of exquisite jellied terrines, whole salmon scaled in the tiniest, whitest slivers of cucumber, curling about ice waves. Lobsters, oysters, smoked chickens, foie gras, sides of beef and glistening hams studded with cloves . . . it was a riot of plenty and, in the manner of the period, focused predominantly on meat, which suited most of the society ladies who were on high-protein diets and refused to touch potatoes or bread.

Just then, Gerry was collared by an elderly dowager so Amanda went to admire the buffet table. She leaned over and plucked a langoustine from a tower of *fruits de mer*, dipping it into a jug of rich, yellow mayonnaise. While she ate it, she studied the table opposite where the puddings were laid out. They were just as marvellous: marzipan castles decorated in crystallised fruit, baskets of raspberries, blueberries and candied currants; towering, wobbling milk blancmanges swathed in cream, champagne jellies with violet and rose petals suspended in them, vast pillowy meringues drenched in vanilla-flecked cream and studded with scarlet strawberries. All was exquisitely beautiful, displayed on Meissen, Sèvres and Venetian glass, like a banquet from a fairy story.

Gerry returned as she was finishing her third

langoustine, unable to resist their delicate sweetness. He looked apologetic. 'Sorry, my darling, the countess insisted on talking to me about her party. She wants me to organise it but of course she wants all this' – he waved a hand about – 'for a fraction of the price. I don't think people really understand how much a bash like this costs.'

'Go on, tell me. How much?' Amanda said mischievously. 'Daddy spent fifty grand on my twenty-first and it wasn't a patch on this.' She licked a finger delicately and smiled at Gerry.

'Fifty grand?' Gerry raised an eyebrow. 'Hardly, my angel. But, shhh! I'm not saying another word, and don't even try to get it out of me because you won't. Discretion, discretion, that's my watchword.'

There was the sound of a gong booming out over the terrace and grounds. Gerry jumped, the startled expression on his face swiftly replaced by a smile of anticipation and a sparkle in his eyes.

'Look at the time! It's almost midnight. I think the moment of the unveiling is here.' He hurried out of the Orangery. Amanda stared after him for a second and then followed, heels clattering and skirts swishing on the stone floor, eager to see what was about to be revealed.

In the kitchen of Homerton House, Maggie the housekeeper was bashing things about crossly, swearing under her breath at the hired caterers who'd invaded her realm for the evening and who swarmed everywhere in their chic black outfits, carrying trays of food and stacks of plates. They had overrun the place, which was now in a kind of organised chaos – and they were politely but insistently ignoring her and overruling all the usual systems.

'Best to let them be,' said Jo the cook. She hadn't been needed for the night, not with the professional caterers on hand to carve flowers out of courgettes and peel the artichokes and do whatever else had been decreed for the special event, but she'd come up from her cottage to see what was going on. No one wanted to miss this, after all. 'No point in getting riled about it,' she said wisely.

'Maybe,' Maggie said with a sigh. 'But I don't like it, and that's a fact. I like things the way they're supposed to be.'

'We're not used to this kind of fuss,' Jo pointed out. 'Nothing much ever changes here, does it?' She picked up a tea towel and started polishing a champagne glass. 'We usually know exactly what will happen from one day to the next.'

'Yes, well . . . not any more,' muttered Maggie. She frowned. 'This place looks like a bomb site! And they've taken over the breakfast room too.'

'They'll be gone in the morning,' Jo said comfortingly. 'I know what these outfits are like. It's a terrible mess at the time but they'll have sorted it before they go. You won't know they've been here.'

Maggie sniffed. 'I doubt it.'

'What's bothering you?' The cook put down her towel and laid her hand gently on Maggie's arm. 'You're not happy, are you?'

Maggie said nothing for a minute, staring at the stone flags on the floor. Then she sank down on to a chair and clasped her hands round her knees. 'No,' she said at last. 'I'm not.' She looked up at Jo. 'Like you said, we know how things work around here. We know how it is. It's always been the same. But that's all going to change after tonight.'

'Is it?' Jo's eyes widened and she looked startled. 'How?'

'Can't you see? This night's going to be the end of everything here. Those girls . . . she's releasing them at last. Do you think, when they've got their freedom, they're going to stay here? In this big old house in the middle of nowhere, with that crusty old couple? I don't think so.'

'Oh.' Jo let out a long breath. 'I hadn't really thought about that but now you say it . . .'

'There's been plenty going on lately,' Maggie said sharply. 'I haven't wanted to say anything because . . . well, I try to keep my mouth shut. I don't like gossip. But there's been people coming here – lawyers, accountants, people in suits carrying briefcases. Something's about to happen, I just know it. And it'll change life for all of us.' She shook her head, her mouth turning down and her eyes filling with tears. 'I don't know how we'll survive without those girls. They're all that makes this place live.'

'But you wouldn't want them to stay here forever, would you?' Jo asked quietly. 'They're young. They have to spread their wings. Besides, it's not . . . healthy, them being here all alone. You know it isn't.'

There was a pointed pause and the two women exchanged glances.

'Course I do,' Maggie replied gruffly. 'And I know it's right they should go. Doesn't mean I have to like it, does it?'

The distant sound of a gong boomed out. They listened and then looked at each other.

14

'This is it,' said Maggie breathlessly. 'They're coming. Come on, we can't miss this.'

The small party began to descend the grand staircase from the upper floor: first two footmen leading the way, then the two girls and behind them the elderly couple. The Brigadier was in his mess uniform, a wonderful scarlet jacket with brass buttons and gold braid, medals displayed across his chest. His wife, Frances Staunton, majestic and elegant in navy blue satin and a sapphire necklace, glided beside him, her bearing as upright and soldierly as her husband's. With her silver and gunmetal-grey hair she looked every one of her sixty-two years, but with a regal quality that made her transcend age: her skin was soft, the lines in it as delicate as the creases in tissue paper.

No one was looking at the elderly couple, though. Below, in the main hall standing on the black-and-white chequered marble floor, Maggie and Jo tried to conceal themselves behind a statue of a Roman god, and gasped as they saw the twins.

'Don't they look lovely?' sighed Jo. 'Like film stars!'

'Beautiful,' whispered Maggie. 'Oh, I feel quite choked up! Oh, my goodness. Poor wee girls. What's going to become of them?'

The two women scuttled off to bag the prime viewing spot before the party arrived on the terrace.

The crowd streamed up the garden, along the formal walks, past the hedges and rose gardens, back from the rockery, the carp pond, the boating lake and the summer house. Others came from the Indian silk tents that had been set up on the croquet lawn, where they'd been lounging on cushions while drinking rose petal cocktails and feasting on exotic delicacies. It was late now, and the mood was relaxed: the night air was full of chattering and laughter, fragrant with cigarette and cigar smoke, and alive with curiosity.

The colourful throng gathered at the foot of the stone steps that led to the terrace. A line of footmen stood facing out, each one impassive, stopping anyone from going up to the house, its windows blazing with electric light that seemed somehow harsh and blinding after the gentle lanternlight and flickering torches that illuminated the garden. The string quartet stopped playing, and the crowd gradually quietened down as it watched with interest.

For long moments nothing happened.

'Hurry up!' shouted one woman from the back, and then screeched with laughter before she was hushed by her friends.

'Someone get that hag out of here,' hissed Gerry crossly. 'I won't have anyone spoiling the moment.'

Amanda watched the empty terrace. They had managed to get an excellent place near the edge of the crowd and could see perfectly.

Suddenly the house was plunged into darkness. Spotlights mounted somewhere high above flashed on and a single pool of white light appeared on the terrace, everything around it sinking into contrasting blackness. There was a hush of anticipation. Then into the pool of light stepped two figures.

The crowd drew in its breath and released a gentle 'Aah' at the sight. In the glare of the spotlight stood two identical girls, each with platinum-white hair set in a mass of curls that formed a glittering halo about her face, while a few wide soft ringlets were allowed to drop on to bare shoulders beneath. They wore strapless silver silk dresses, simple yet exquisite, an utterly feminine silhouette that skimmed every curve to the waist before floating down in a full skirt, with over it the softest dove-grey net embroidered with hundreds of crystals that sparkled and glinted as though the dresses had trapped a miniature galaxy of stars.

'They're not in costume,' murmured Amanda to Gerry.

'Not strictly,' he said, happily, 'but it *works*, doesn't it? The hair is the real nod to Marie Antoinette. The gowns are, I admit, more modern. But utterly classic. And those sweeping skirts and that dreamy netting . . . Aren't they magnificent?'

The two slender platinum blondes stared out over the crowd, each one shimmering in the white light they were bathed in. Their wide blue eyes blinked as they tried to make out the garden beneath, which was lost in shadow to them. One sister turned to the other and reached out a hand. Her scarlet mouth moved as though she were speaking but no one heard what she said. The other sister seemed oblivious, her lips curved up into a cherry-red smile, her expression expectant and happy.

Then, at some invisible signal, the string quartet began to play the tune of 'Happy Birthday' and a moment later everyone joined in singing heartily. The old couple joined the girls in the spotlight as the song reached its crescendo, then the lights widened to encompass the whole terrace. The aunt led her nieces to one side of it where four spindly gilt chairs waited, and they all sat down. A moment later the crowd

17

gasped as acrobats appeared as if by magic from the surrounding trees and hedges, from the battlements and windowsills and balconies of the house; they rolled, jumped and flew through the air, landing at last on the terrace where they performed a series of magnificent circus manoeuvres of such skill that the crowd laughed and applauded in delight. When their routine was finished, the acrobats disappeared as gracefully as they'd come.

As they vanished, music filled the air: eighteenth-century courtly music, strings and harpsichords in elegant fusion. From the French window, a troupe of dancers in period clothes and wigs made their entrance on to the terrace, stepping out in perfect time in the manner of a court dance. When they were all on the terrace, they performed a delightful minuet. It was graceful and enchanting but, just as the audience began to tire of it a little, the music changed: a deep insistent beat emerged and there was the harsher note of an electric guitar. The dancers tugged at their costumes and within moments the girls were dressed only in corsets, tutus and ripped fishnets, the men bare-chested with tiny biker shorts covering their modesty. The strains of a famous song began to pound out and, as the crowd screamed in recognition and excitement, one of the world's megastars strutted out from the French windows wearing hot pants, a corset and thigh-high lace-up boots. She adjusted her head mic, struck a pose and began to sing. Everyone went wild as the dancers twisted and writhed through a complex routine, the singer moving with them in time, stunning them all with some gracefully executed yoga moves.

As the song reached its end to ecstatic applause, the star shouted, 'Ladies and gentlemen, I give you . . . Octavia and Flora!' She gestured to the girls sitting at the side of the terrace. 'Happy birthday, honeys. You girls have *arrived*!'

Just then, a huge birthday cake was wheeled out from the house, a staggering tiered confection covered in white icing and ornamented with crystallised white rose petals, pushed along on its stand by two footmen. Forty-two candles burned on the tiers. The girls stood up and walked forward. Another chorus of 'Happy Birthday' broke out. At the last note, the sisters blew out all their candles, the singer helpfully stepping forward to blow out a few herself when they seemed to be struggling with the task.

The moment the last candle was extinguished, columns of golden sparks shot up from all along the edge of the terrace and a magnificent firework display began, exploding above the house, bathing the crowd of onlookers in red, blue, green and gold light. The birthday girls watched too, their faces tilted up to observe the show. They seemed in awe of the magnificence around them, as though they had not quite grasped that all this fuss was for them.

'Well, that was quite a coup,' Amanda said at last, turning to Gerry, who was grinning broadly, obviously satisfied with the way everything had gone. 'I thought she never did private performances.'

'If the price is right, my sweet, if the price is right . . .' Gerry rubbed his hands together. 'I'm not allowed to tell you how much it cost. Let's just say that each second of that song could pay off a substantial chunk of Third World debt.'

'So, those are the Beaufort twins,' Amanda said, staring at them. 'They don't look much. Beautiful, obviously. But plastic. Barbies.' A pleased expression came over her face. 'I don't think we've got much to fear from them.'

Gerry said nothing but raised his brows, and continued to stare beadily at the two shimmering figures as they watched the display in the night sky.

2

Frances Staunton made her way through the house, her eagle eye catching sight of everything that was out of place. The chaos of the previous evening had been worth it. The party had been a success, that was certain. The last task she had set herself had been achieved. As she walked down the hallway towards the breakfast room, she stopped in front of a portrait of a young man, a pen-and-ink sketch that looked as though it had been hastily dashed off while its energetic subject was uncharacteristically still for a brief moment. There were better portraits of Arthur – the Lucian Freud was wonderful and, of course, hugely valuable – but this was her favourite. It had caught her brother when he was at his peak: young, vibrant and full of promise. Before he married *that* woman. Before all the disasters that followed.

Frances stood in front of the sketch for a moment, filled with the bitter melancholy she always felt when she thought too long about him. Then she said aloud, 'Well, Arthur, I've done it. I've done what you wanted me to. I've brought them up the best way I could, and

I think I've done a good job. But now my work is finished. There's nothing more I can do. I've fulfilled my duty to you, my dear brother.'

Then she turned on her heel and continued on to the breakfast room, stopping on the way to glance out at the gardens where people were clearing up the mess.

'How could one party cause such havoc?' Frances said to herself as she watched them carrying sackfuls of litter and trays of discarded glasses. God only knew what the Orangery looked like, with the remains of the demolished supper still there, or what state the croquet lawn was in. 'Never again,' she told herself firmly. 'Once is most certainly enough.'

The strain of planning the great event had been very wearisome. And what it had cost . . . well, the bills would come in soon enough. No doubt it would be a lot, but sometimes it didn't do to watch the pennies and Frances was quite sure that this was one such occasion. *We can afford it after all*, she thought with a shrug. *And I had to make sure that people noticed.*

She saw one of the housemaids walking towards her, keeping her eyes downcast as ordered. 'Where are the girls? Have you seen them?' she demanded.

The maid shook her head, her eyes frightened. 'No, mam,' she said in a small voice. 'They're still in bed, mam, I think. No one's seen them yet anyhow.'

'I see.' Frances nodded at the maid, who scuttled off, and consulted her watch. It was after 11.30. Well, the party hadn't ended until five a.m., although she had been in her own bed by three. The girls had probably stayed up until the end. That party fellow,

Gerry, had darted forward at the end of the firework display, introduced himself to Octavia and Flora and then whisked them away, saying he would chaperone them very carefully.

They certainly weren't in any danger from him, she was sure of that. A small smile twisted Frances's rather thin lips. A confirmed bachelor, as the saying went. Anyway, he'd certainly done a splendid job on the party, and had charged plenty for his services, more than likely getting commission from all the people he'd recommended as well.

'Madam, madam . . .' It was Hobbs, the butler, approaching along the thickly carpeted corridor.

'Yes?'

'I've had word from the lodge. The lawyers have arrived. They're on their way up the drive.'

'I see.' Frances thought for a moment. 'Show them into the library, Hobbs. Offer them coffee. Give them the papers and ask them to wait. I'll be there to see them when I can.'

Hobbs bowed, the top of his bald head glimmering in the hall light. 'Very good, madam.'

Frances turned back the way she'd come.

Outside one of the main bedroom suites, Frances rapped hard on the door and waited. There was no answer, so she opened it and went in. Inside was a large but still cosy sitting room, decorated in a young, rather pretty style with vintage floral prints, soft armchairs and a saggy sofa covered with cushions. Frances walked quickly through, noting with disapproval a pile of glossy magazines on a coffee table, and knocked at another door on the far side of the sitting room.

23

'Octavia?' she said loudly. 'Are you awake?'

There was a stirring behind the door and a light moaning.

'Octavia!' Frances rapped again, then opened the door. She looked at the large four-poster bed that stood directly opposite the door, hung with swathes of rose-printed chintz. 'Octavia!' she repeated sharply.

'Oh!' A tousled white head popped up from among the pillows, blue eyes wide and blinking, smudges of mascara under each one. 'Yes?' Then she sighed and flopped back down. 'What *time* is it?'

'It's almost noon. You must get up.'

'But I've only been asleep for about five hours! I'm *exhausted*. That man Gerry made me dance and dance . . .'

'You heard me,' Frances said in her strict voice. 'I want you and Flora downstairs in thirty minutes. I'll have some breakfast sent up to you while you dress. I shall expect you in the library no later than twelve-thirty, do you understand?'

There was a muffled moan from under the bedclothes.

'Good,' said Frances sharply. 'I will see you then.'

She walked across the sitting room to Flora's bedroom door. The girls had shared a bedroom until they reached eighteen when Frances had decreed that they should have separate bedrooms and sitting rooms, and had planned to put them at opposite ends of the house. But the twins hadn't wanted to be apart and had put up a surprising show of resistance to her plans. In the end it was agreed that they would share a sitting room but have separate bedrooms and bathrooms on either side of it.

She knocked on Flora's door, to give her the same message, but Flora was not in her bed, a four-poster identical to Octavia's but swathed in delphinium-printed chintz. The sound of water coming from her bathroom indicated that she was showering.

No lazy lying about for Flora, Frances noted. She was always the more diligent of the sisters. Frances turned and left. The maid bringing up their breakfasts would make sure that Octavia had alerted Flora to the meeting in the library. *Dear Flora, so sweet, so unspoiled,* Frances thought to herself as she returned to her own rooms to tidy her hair and powder her nose. *Always so quiet and obedient. Quite unlike headstrong Octavia. If I could, I would keep Flora here . . . she would make the perfect companion.* Frances sighed. There was little chance of that. She was sure that once set free the little birds would fly away like the dove to dry land, never to be seen again.

At 12.30 Frances was sitting in the library, her least favourite room in the house. It was dark, lined with untouched leather-and-gold volumes, and furnished in burgundy leather and mahogany. It smelt of the Cuban cigars the Brigadier smoked, and the side table was covered in heavy decanters of whisky, brandy and port. On the darkest side were those grisly cabinets, covered in their protective green baize cloths. No, she didn't like it at all. This was her husband's territory, where he got up to his own masculine pursuits and drank his whisky. As a rule she preferred to sit in her own morning room, where she could listen to the radio and do her sewing and her painting in peace. Peace was all she'd ever wanted, after all, and if that meant closing her eyes to some of the less pleasant things that happened, so be it.

The Brigadier stood over by the window, in his casual clothes of baggy cord trousers, a soft brushed cotton shirt and a grey cardigan – less distinguished now that he was out of uniform. He was silent, as usual. He rarely spoke, but simply watched everything that went on. The lawyers were sitting a trifle stiffly on their chairs, shuffling papers and talking quietly to each other.

'I take it all is ready?' Frances asked.

'Yes, Mrs Staunton,' answered Challon, the senior lawyer present. He was rarely seen out of his office. Clients tended to go to him except in rare circumstances. This was obviously one of them. 'We only require the principals now.'

Frances looked down at her watch. It showed 12.30. There was a knock on the door.

Good. The girls were well trained, after all. They knew what standards were expected and the consequences of not meeting them.

'Come in!' she called.

Everyone turned to look as the library door opened. A young woman put her head round it and then came in. She was tall and slender, with a rangy coltish look and platinum-white hair that reached down past her shoulders, falling in a glossy curtain that curled slightly at the ends. Her face was dominated by wide blue eyes that had a violet tinge to them and were made even more dramatic by long dark lashes and the straight dark brows above them. Her most overwhelmingly attractive feature, though, was her air of unself-consciousness, as though she hadn't the faintest idea of how stunning she was. Certainly she wasn't dressed like a sultry sophisticated woman, but rather girlishly in a plain grey dress that looked almost like a school uniform, although she had belted it at the waist with a wide three-buckle twisted leather belt. She walked into the room in flat black ballet slippers, looking about her with interest, clearly curious about the men in their dark suits sitting opposite her aunt.

She was followed by another young woman, and the combined effect was almost supernaturally strange. This girl had her hair scraped back with an Alice band and wore a white jersey top under her grey dress and no belt. Apart from that, the two of them were identical. They had the exact same blue eyes, with those remarkable dark lashes, and high cheekbones that curved down to a small neat chin. The lawyers shifted in their seats: it was startling to see two separate human beings who so closely resembled one another, even though they'd known they were to be meeting identical twins.

Frances stood up. 'Good, you're here. Gentlemen, may I introduce Octavia –' she gestured to the girl wearing the leather belt '– and Flora.' She waved her hand at the other. 'Sit down, please, girls.'

The sisters went silently to the chairs she had indicated and sat down neatly, feet together and hands folded in their laps. They waited expectantly.

Over by the window, the Brigadier lit his pipe and puffed out a cloud of tobacco smoke that smelt like a mixture of vanilla and burnt leaves. No one paid any attention to him.

'Now,' began Frances, 'you are probably wondering what's going on. Girls, yesterday you turned twenty-one.

27

That is a remarkable moment in anyone's life – the transition to true adulthood. But it's more remarkable for you than most. I don't need to remind you that you are the children of a special young man, one who was cruelly taken from us in the prime of life, before he had achieved even a tenth of his destiny . . .' Frances walked over to a grandly framed oil portrait of her brother that stood in place of honour on an easel in the middle of the room. 'Here he is, Arthur Beaufort, the great hope of our family.'

Octavia looked bored while Flora gazed down at her hands. They had clearly heard something along these lines before.

Frances reached out to touch the painting. The young man in it also had startling blue eyes under thick, straight black brows. He was sitting formally by an open window that showed a Cambridge college in the background. One hand was resting on a degree scroll and over the back of his chair hung a mortarboard.

'He was brilliant, you know,' Frances continued, her voice mournful. 'This was painted to celebrate his first-class degree from King's. The tragedy was that he never lived to fulfil his early promise. Dead before he was thirty. My poor, beautiful Arthur . . .' She bowed her head momentarily then turned to face everyone in the room. The girls immediately snapped to attention. 'But he left us this legacy. You, Octavia and Flora, are his living bequest to us. His children.' She allowed herself a smile. 'He would be very proud of you if he could see you today. And . . . he left you more than that.' She looked over at Challon. 'If you would please explain?'

'Certainly.' The elderly lawyer coughed lightly and looked down at the green leather folder he was holding. Then he said, 'Young ladies, today you come into your inheritance. The terms of your father's will were that your fortune should be guarded for you in trust, with your guardian having main control of that trust, along with a few other trustees. You received the first portion of your inheritance when you turned eighteen . . .'

At this, the sisters looked surprised and shot quick, covert glances at one another.

'. . . but under the guiding hand of your guardian, who had total discretion over what you should receive.' Frances's face remained impassive as Challon spoke. 'Now that you are twenty-one, those restrictions are removed. The money becomes yours to do with as you wish. I will need you to sign some papers, and there will be some further formalities. I also wish to put at your disposal certain financial advisors who will endeavour to explain the situation to you and give you some pointers as to how to guard and maintain your inheritance.'

The two girls stared at him for a long moment and then Octavia frowned and said, 'Are we free to leave here?'

Challon looked puzzled. 'Of course. You're free to leave at any time. There haven't been any restrictions on your movements, except the usual discretionary rules laid down by your guardian – your aunt.'

'Oh.' The girls looked at one another again.

Flora spoke up next, in a soft, almost wispy voice. 'H-h-how much? I mean, how m-m-much is our inheritance?'

Challon coughed again. Frances raised her chin and stared up into the murky darkness of the ceiling.

'Your father's total legacy amounts to two hundred and eighty-five million pounds. To be split between you equally. So you have each come into your inheritance of one hundred and forty-two million, five hundred thousand pounds.'

The sisters gaped at him, unable to believe their ears. Even the hardened lawyers, used to enormous sums of money, raised their eyebrows and exchanged looks.

'Congratulations, young ladies. You have just become very rich indeed. Now, Mrs Staunton, shall we witness the necessary signatures?'

3

Octavia whirled about the room, tossing books and pictures on to the sofa, her eyes bright and her cheeks flushed with excitement.

'Tavy, Tavy!' cried Flora, trying to calm her sister down. She had a strange nauseous feeling, as though the bottom of her stomach had dropped away, or she had just plummeted a hundred floors in a lift. 'What are you doing?'

'Doing?' Octavia stopped whirling for a moment and clutched the back of the sofa with one hand, the other arm flung wide. 'Don't you see? We're free! We're free at last! Oh my God . . .' She clambered over the sofa and collapsed on its soft cushions, giggling and breathless. 'Didn't you hear what they said? We're rich. We can go anywhere we like, do anything!'

'But . . .' Flora blinked, bewildered. All this had happened so fast. First there had been that party. Only last night. That had been terrifying enough – she'd been sick for days beforehand thinking about it, horrified by the idea of so many people watching her. Only Octavia had been able to give her the strength to face it. Octavia always had so much strength herself, there was plenty left over for her sister. 'But where are we going to go?'

'Who cares?' Octavia's eyes were burning brightly. 'Anywhere. Out of this prison.' She sat up and held out her hand to Flora. Her sister went to her and took it, and they clutched one another tightly. 'Don't you want it too?'

'You know I do,' Flora said in a small voice.

'Then let's go tonight!'

'But how? I don't understand how it's going to happen. Some men have told us we have money, but how are we going to get it? Nothing seems any different to me.'

Octavia sighed. The fervour in her eyes died down a little. 'You're right. We can't go tonight. There will be masses to sort out, I suppose. But we will go. As soon as we can.'

Later that night, after a solitary supper eaten without a sign of their aunt and uncle, the girls went about their usual bedtime ritual. After their baths, they dressed in their pyjamas and then sat on Octavia's bed, slowly brushing out one another's hair. When they were very little, a nanny had taught them to brush their fair hair with long firm strokes, telling them it would make the hair strong and healthy, and ever since they had done the same thing every night, finding comfort in the routine.

Flora pulled the Mason Pearson brush through Octavia's locks. Their whiteness was unfamiliar. It was symbolic of how everything had changed overnight, she thought. Yesterday they were themselves. Today they were possessors of fabulous wealth, platinum-haired heiresses, about to strike out in the world on their own.

'I'm going to telephone that lawyer tomorrow,' Octavia was saying as she knelt on the bed, her legs tucked up underneath her. 'Aunt Frances will have to let me. Did you hear what he said? We got money on our eighteenth birthdays, and she never told us. If she tries to stop me, I'll tell her we'll sue her or something.'

'Do you think we could?'

'I'm sure we could. I've read in plenty of books that concealing that sort of thing from someone is criminal. I bet I could frighten her into letting me. Besides . . .' Octavia shrugged. 'She can't stop us any more. I bet she's just like a pussy cat from now on.' She turned to look over her shoulder at Flora. 'Her powers have been melted away. She's like the witch in *The Wizard of Oz* when Dorothy threw the water over her.' Octavia did an imitation of the witch's screech. 'I'm melting, I'm melting!'

They both laughed.

'But where will we go?' Flora asked, unable to stop the waves of worry that kept rippling through her. 'This is the only home we know.'

'We'll go to London. Where else? Don't worry, I know exactly what we should do,' Octavia said firmly.

'We'll always stay together, won't we, Tavy?'

'Of course we will.'

Flora pulled the brush through her sister's hair, softly dragging it from the scalp to the very ends which she held in her palm. 'Nothing will change, will it?'

'Only for the better.' Octavia squirmed round so that she was facing her sister. She grabbed Flora's

33

arms. 'Nothing will change between us, I promise. How could it?'

Flora felt comforted. She smiled. 'Good. We'll stay the same. That's all I need to know.' She hugged Octavia back, finding the comfort she always had in the warmth of her sister's nearness. *As long as we're together, everything will be all right.*

4

Two months later

Octavia walked through the house, almost high with excitement, as the estate agent, crisp-looking in a black pinstripe suit and sharp white shirt, led them from room to room and floor to floor.

'The cinema,' the agent said, opening the door to a windowless room dominated by a huge screen and two tiers of purple velvet chairs so wide they looked like small sofas.

'Oh, I absolutely *adore* this one,' Octavia said happily. 'A cinema, Flora, look!'

Flora came up to her and gazed into the room. 'Mmm,' she said.

From the moment they had walked into the building, Octavia had been overwhelmed and starry-eyed. 'It's like something from a magazine,' she'd breathed, as they entered the great bold space with its polished plaster walls and smooth wooden floors. It ought to have seemed cold and soulless but the masterly design made it endlessly interesting, from the banks of celadon-green lacquered cupboards in the kitchen, along with up-to-the-minute dishwashing and fridge drawers – no old-fashioned stand-alone appliances in this place – to the bathrooms that seemed carved out of single great pieces of grey marble. The whole place was light but with the warmth of a smaller dwelling, not the chill of a bare loft.

'This house was originally a warehouse that was later converted into artists' studios,' explained the agent. 'That's why there's so much light and space. You don't normally find rooms this size in properties of this age.' She opened another door. 'The owner uses this as a gym. It was obviously once one of the studios.' She led them into a large, light room full of fitness equipment, a long mirror running along one wall.

'Is the stuff included?' asked Octavia, running a hand along a black-and-silver treadmill with all manner of complicated-looking gadgets on its handlebar.

'I'm sure the owner will be open to any offers,' the agent replied.

Flora spoke to the agent for the first time, her voice almost a whisper. 'W-w-what's that?' she asked, pointing. 'It looks like some kind of m-m-medieval torture instrument.' There was a big contraption loaded with weights and pulleys and a sliding platform on which one was clearly supposed to lie down.

'That's a Pilates reformer,' explained the agent. 'They're the latest thing. They cost a fortune but apparently they're marvellous.'

Flora stared at it, her mouth open.

Octavia bounced up and down excitedly. 'Come on, show us the rest!'

'This way.'

They went back out along the wood-floored corridor. A flight of stairs curved away to the upper floor. The whole house was a graceful amalgam of straight and curved lines with no hard edges, a simple yet sophisticated design that made it seem amazingly easy to live in.

'The owner got a top-name designer to do this place. Everything – and I mean everything – is bespoke,' said the agent as she led the way. 'It's all hand-made and meticulously finished.'

'It's wonderful,' Octavia said sincerely. She was enchanted with the house. She'd always spent hours poring over fashion and design magazines, and could see at once that this was up-to-the-minute modern elegance of the kind she had always craved.

Flora pulled at her sister's sleeve as they climbed the stairs to the top floor. 'I liked the other one best – the one on the square.'

They had seen a much more traditional house, almost a cottage, done up in muted pinks and whites, with a large front garden that opened on to a private square. It had been more cosy than this house, decorated in an appealing shabby-chic vintage style, with faded floral prints, white-painted floorboards and even a baby-blue Aga in the kitchen.

Octavia wrinkled her nose. 'No . . . no . . . I can see why you like it but it's too twee, too . . . cute. I've had enough floral chintzes to last me a lifetime back at Homerton and everywhere else Aunt Frances was in charge of the decorating. Besides, we need to be where the action is. Look at this place, it's right in the heart of things.'

They emerged into a room at the top of the house,

a place to relax, read books and listen to music. It was the only room that had anything on display: white lacquered shelves that defied expectations of symmetry with odd-shaped and -spaced cavities full of books and CDs. State-of-the-art speakers and sound system were concealed behind bright red lacquered cupboards, along with a huge flat-screen television. Modern zigzag chairs, bean bags and long low sofas provided comfortable berths to laze on while listening to the music or watching TV.

'Oooh, the chill-out zone!' said Octavia happily. 'I adore it. Just the place to watch some telly, tucked away at the top of the house.'

'There's a lift here too, if you don't fancy walking,' the agent said, pointing to a small door at the back of the room. 'It goes all the way down to the basement, so you can come straight here from the pool or the underground garage.'

'Cool.' Octavia went over to the window and looked down over the Chelsea traffic and the people bustling about five storeys below. 'Look.' Her breath fogged the glass as she spoke. 'I love it here. It's so busy. This is the place to live, I'm sure of it.' She turned back to look at her sister, eyes sparkling. 'Don't you think so?'

Flora was standing by one of the low sofas, gazing at the perfectly matched and positioned cushions. She looked over at Octavia, her eyes anxious. 'Well . . . I did like the other place . . . or the Cheyne Walk house.'

'No way! That's for grandmas,' Octavia declared. 'All family portraits and antiques and enormous chandeliers. I don't want that, I want to live like it's *now*. We've spent long enough stuck in someone else's life.'

'We could always redecorate, make it the way we wanted . . .'

'No, I haven't got time for that. I want somewhere we can move into immediately. Besides, I love everything about this place. The dressing rooms are beyond amazing.' Octavia turned to the agent, who was standing patiently by the doorway, watching the sisters. 'How much is this place?'

'It's twenty-five million. You might be able to negotiate a little . . . the owner is a hedge funder who's been badly bitten in the crash. He wants a quick sale.'

'Perhaps he'll throw in the furniture and the gym equipment?' Octavia suggested. 'We don't have anything, you see. Just our clothes, and not many of those. His stuff would do to get us going.'

The agent looked bemused. 'Well, do you want me to make that a basis for an offer?'

'Octavia!' hissed Flora, grabbing her sister's arm. 'Twenty-five million pounds! Don't you think we should talk to someone about this?'

'It's nothing – twelve and a half mill each. It's hardly going to make a dent, is it? And it's an investment. Property in the heart of London . . . anyone would say that's an excellent buy.' Octavia spoke loftily, as though she'd been reading the financial pages all her life. 'I want this house, and if you don't, I'll just buy it without you.' She knew she was being high-handed and if Flora really dug her heels in, would certainly not buy the house by herself. The idea of their living apart was ridiculous. But she was certain this was the right place for them both. *We need to break free of everything Aunt Frances stood for*, she told herself. *And that includes her choice of wallpaper.*

Flora sighed. 'A-a-all right,' she said. Octavia noticed the stammer. It usually wasn't a problem when her sister talked to her. It must be a sign of the stress of the decision. 'G-g-go ahead if that's what you want.'

'Yay!' Octavia rushed over to her sister and hugged her, then jumped up and down with delight. 'Thanks, Flo-flo! You won't regret it, I promise. We're going to be really happy here!'

The agent looked thrilled as she realised that she had just made a cash sale, and that a percentage amounting to half a million pounds would be coming her agency's way.

Just then Flora scrabbled in her bag and pulled out her iPhone. 'I felt this thing move . . . someone's sent me a message. It's Vicky.' An expression of bewilderment crossed her face. 'How on earth do I read it? I can't get to grips with it.'

'Here, let me.' Octavia grabbed the phone and tapped the screen. She had mastered her phone much more quickly than Flora had. She read the message. 'She's in Lola's on Fulham Road, and says to join her there.'

'Right,' Flora said. 'Well . . . I'd better go. I'll see you back at the hotel, Tavy.' She smiled at the agent. 'Th-th-thank you.'

'You're *so* welcome,' said the agent feelingly. 'Any time . . . really, any time.'

'Say hi to Vicky for me,' Octavia said, then turned back to the agent. 'Now, can we go and see that cinema again? I'm so excited!'

5

Flora shut the front door behind her and ran down the stone steps to the pavement. *So this is going to be our new home,* she thought. It was a beautiful house, there was no doubt about that. The little library appealed to her most, a small, panelled room hidden away on the ground floor with a cosy sofa and a fireplace and lots of books. That was the only place where she thought she might be able to feel secure. The rest of the house was so wide and open, without the nooks and crannies she was used to.

I'm sure I'll grow to love it, she told herself. Octavia obviously did, and Octavia knew about things. Life was often organised by her more tempestuous sister and, because Flora trusted her absolutely, she would go along with whatever Octavia wanted. It had always been Octavia who'd broken rules and tried to run away, right from the time they were tiny, and Flora who'd complied with whatever she'd suggested. The first place they'd run to was the playhouse at the bottom of the garden. Octavia had persuaded Flora to take their bedding and some clothes out to the wooden house with its miniature furniture and pretend kitchen, little carved shutters at the windows and a ladder to the upstairs floor where they made their bed. Octavia had said Flora should take some cushions from the drawing room, and even though she'd known it was wrong, Flora had done it. Later, when the nanny, white-faced and frightened, had discovered them, they'd been marched to Aunt Frances. Octavia had declared that it was her idea and that she'd taken the cushions all by herself, and she took the punishment alone while Flora was sent upstairs to her room.

She always did that, Flora remembered. *She always tried to protect me.* She stood in front of the house, looking up and down the road, trying to orientate herself. She decided to retrace their steps, and set off towards what she hoped was the Fulham Road.

London was still a mystery to her. She knew she was on the border of South Kensington and Chelsea, in one of the most expensive areas in the world – there were probably more millionaires in the surrounding streets than you could shake a stick at – and that no doubt was why Octavia thought they would fit in here, but Flora couldn't see how she ever would. She was daunted by this enormous city, full of so many people. Aunt Frances had made sure that they had spent most of their lives so far in peace and quiet, removed from others, with only a few carefully selected people ever allowed into their world. They'd been educated almost entirely at home. When they'd travelled, it was in the seclusion of private planes and limousines, and when they'd arrived at another of their homes, the huge gates and electric fences had shut them in just as they did everywhere. Even when they toured places –

42

famous cities, historical monuments – it was in private, on specially arranged visits with guides and guards everywhere.

'I must keep you safe,' Aunt Frances had said solemnly, though she'd never explained the nature of the danger or what she feared might happen to them. Whatever the danger was, it needed to be kept at bay with locks, alarms, security guards, fierce dogs and panic rooms. In case the danger came inside the house, little cameras observed the corridors and main rooms, their tiny red lights glowing to show they were vigilant; sometimes they swivelled with a mosquito-like electronic buzz to follow whoever was walking past, their dark lenses like single glinting eyes.

The most adventurous event in the girls' lives was being sent to finishing school in Switzerland for a year when they were eighteen, but that had hardly been life in the fast lane. The school was designed for young ladies who required certain standards to be met, and most of the other pupils had been the daughters of billionaires or Saudi princesses whose reputations rested on the all-female staff, the constant chaperoning, and the school's promise that its wealthy pupils would be protected by bodyguards at all times. There were no mobile phones, only monitored access to computers and the internet, and any television programmes were carefully chosen for their educational content.

Still, they had learned to make profiteroles and a *sauce chasseur*, and how to embroider on silk. Apart from French, skiing, a little art and piano lessons, there was absolutely nothing else to do.

The repressive atmosphere had driven Octavia wild.

She'd been anticipating freedom at finishing school and the reality was a great disappointment.

'Out of the frying pan and into the *fucking* fire!' she'd groaned, throwing herself on her single bed. She'd hated the way they were constantly watched, and had loathed the docility of the other girls, who hadn't seemed to mind the curtailment of their freedom. Of course, she'd tried to break out, just as she always had at home, and she'd been lucky not to be expelled for rule infringement – the only reason she had not been sent away was Aunt Frances's money.

Flora hadn't minded so much, though even she had to admit that it was a restrictive way of life. She had heard the rumours about other schools in the area where the girls were permitted to go skiing alone, take trips into town, visit the local discos, even, it was said, bring boys back – though Flora hadn't believed that. Mademoiselle Estelle's was nothing like that. The only person in trousers was the chef, and no one ever saw him.

Flora had never confessed to Octavia that she had found being at the school a relief. She'd enjoyed the company of the other girls and liked the quiet pursuits she'd been given to do, and she'd always loved skiing since they were first taught at three years old. Most of all, she'd loved the anonymity of just being one among many. All her life, she and Octavia had been the only two – the only two in the classroom, in the playroom, at their riding lessons. She hated the constant attention. At Mademoiselle Estelle's, her stammer had disappeared almost entirely. It was only when they had to go back to Homerton that it had returned.

I ought to be happy that I'm free of the place at last, she told herself. So why did she feel so lost and frightened all the time?

She wandered along the streets of Chelsea, not sure of where she was going. Octavia had told her that her phone had some kind of fancy gadget in it that meant she could access a map if she needed one, but she had no idea how it worked. It was hard to believe the smooth black tablet even was a telephone; it certainly didn't resemble anything in any of the houses where she'd lived. But then, her aunt was not exactly up to date with the latest technology.

Flora stopped and looked about her. *Where am I?* she thought desperately. All the roads, lined with huge houses behind forbidding gates and severe hedges, looked similar and she recognised nothing. *Oh, God – I have no idea where I am, or how anything works . . . this is all just madness!*

The feeling of being overwhelmed – that buzzing sensation of things closing in that seemed to grip her more and more since they'd left Homerton – washed over her again and she felt tears burn in her eyes. The confusion was almost too much to stand. She felt wobbly and faint, and a sob started in her chest, shaking her shoulders and then catching in her throat. Reaching out, she held on to a gate post, determined to control herself, feeling that if she let herself begin to cry, she would not be able to stop.

Why is it so hard for me? she thought, agonised.

The phone in her bag began to ring and she scrabbled for it, picking it up and pressing wildly at the little screen before putting it to her ear. Somehow, miraculously, she had managed to answer it.

'Yes?' Her voice came out quavering and high.

'Where are you?' It was Vicky, sounding familiar and comforting. 'I'm in Lola's. Are you nearly here?'

'I don't know!' wailed Flora. 'I'm lost.'

'Hold on . . . I'll come and find you, don't worry. Tell me the name of the nearest road you can see.'

'Er . . . it's . . . I think I'm near Chelsea Square.'

'Okay, you're quite close. Don't panic, I'm on my way.'

'You've got yourself into quite a state,' Vicky said sympathetically. She'd found Flora only fifteen minutes later and brought her back to Lola's, ordering them both a restorative pot of tea.

Flora nodded and managed a weak smile. 'I feel so silly. Everything just got a bit much for me for a moment.'

'I'm not surprised.' Vicky shook her head, her dark red hair glinting as she poured out a cup of Earl Grey. 'You've had a lot to handle lately.'

'I know. I just feel so . . . at sea. I have no idea of how the world works. Octavia's different – she's rushing at everything and getting to know it all in moments. I'm not like that. I suppose she always knew something of life beyond Homerton – she was always reading books and magazines and watching the telly shows and trying to find out all she could.'

'It's a shock for you,' Vicky said adamantly. 'Aunt Frances kept you far too protected – we all knew that. But no one could do anything about it. It wasn't right, shutting you away like that. I mean, you hardly had any friends at all, did you? Apart from me and Laurence.'

'You know Aunt Frances. She only trusted people

she knew. She always said that you were the perfect companions for us – cousins our own age.'

'Well, we were,' Vicky said, with a smile. She still looked, Flora thought, very much like the girl who had come to visit them at Homerton all those years ago. The Staunton children, Vicky and Laurence, were the Brigadier's great-niece and great-nephew and therefore considered suitable companions for the twins; their background was safe and they posed no threat to the girls. All other children were suspect and very few of them were allowed into Homerton.

'You were a good friend to me back then,' Flora said warmly. 'Remember our Christmases when you all came to spend the day? So exciting! For once we were allowed to run around and play games and shout as much as we liked.'

'Of course I remember. We loved them too, you know.' Vicky grinned back. 'It was pretty different from the way we lived at home. You seemed to exist in a fairy tale.'

The girls smiled at one another. Flora remembered how Vicky would arrive at the house in her best dress, which was always a little shabbier than the twins' matching velvet frocks and white suede Mary Janes, her curly auburn hair brushed and pinned back with a bow, while Laurence's equally curly hair would be stuck down with water and he'd have a tie on, which he clearly hated. The Staunton children would always be wide-eyed at the twins' life at Homerton, and the way they were surrounded by every luxury, their rooms full of toys, books and puzzles, the stables stocked with bicycles, roller skates, trampolines and dozens of other amusements. From the others' gasps and comments,

Flora sensed that not every child had as much as she and Octavia did. Everything that she took for granted seemed to bowl the other two over; the Christmas tree, a giant Norwegian spruce dripping in decorations, was pretty enough but it didn't impress her the way it did Vicky and Laurence, and the piles of gifts underneath were simply what always appeared. Weren't all children taken to Harrods on a special private shopping expedition and allowed to pick out everything they wanted for Christmas? It didn't seem out of the ordinary to her, but the reaction of the other two led her think that perhaps it was.

'And there were our secret letters – remember?' Flora laughed. 'I can't think what secrets we had to tell each other, but we managed to think of some.'

'I bet you couldn't wait to find out that I had new shoes, or had pressed some flowers or something.' Vicky laughed too, and sipped her tea.

It had been Flora's only real act of rebellion; she'd written letters to Vicky, stolen stamps from the desk in the library and then hidden her little envelopes in the tray for outgoing post on the table near the front door, slipping them underneath the others. Vicky's letters back to her were always opened and read by Aunt Frances, so the girls had made a code to swap news without being understood – a simple thing where one sentence actually meant something else. Flora had not even told Octavia about the code; she had not thought her twin would be interested. Octavia had never warmed to Vicky. She'd preferred climbing trees with Laurence instead.

As they'd all grown older, Flora had seen Vicky and Laurence less and less. The Stauntons had gone to school, and during the long summer holidays the twins were away at the Connecticut house or at the seaside villa in France. Relations with Vicky had cooled slightly as they'd grown into teenagers, though Flora had no idea why, and the letters and codes were forgotten. Vicky no longer seemed as wide-eyed and impressed by what the twins had, but rather a little distant and pointedly underwhelmed. When Flora had tried to interest her in the boxes of clothes that had arrived from Harrods or Bloomingdale's, Vicky would put her nose in the air and affect total uninterest. After a while she stopped coming to Homerton altogether, except on family occasions.

It had been lovely to see her at the birthday party, a familiar face among the overwhelming sea of strangers. Vicky had been wearing a fancy dress costume in shiny fake silk that looked a little cheap next to some of the other marvellous outfits, but she still entered into the spirit of the occasion. She'd been affectionate and happy to see her cousins, eager to celebrate their twenty-first birthdays. When news of the inheritance had spread, Vicky had phoned to offer congratulations and then had visited for tea. Flora had loved rediscovering her cousin, someone who was a real friend with shared memories, and the two girls had hit it off wonderfully well. They'd seen each other again soon afterwards, and Vicky had been an amazing support to Flora ever since then. It was a sign of how comfortable Flora felt with her that her stammer virtually disappeared when they were together.

'Are you feeling better?' Vicky asked now. 'You've got your colour back.'

Flora smiled at her cousin. 'Much better, thanks. I feel safe with you, Vicky. You know about London and the outside world.'

Vicky grinned. 'Well, most of us have to. Besides, I've lived in London for a couple of years now. You'll get used to it, I promise.' She took another sip of her tea, staring at Flora over the top of her china cup. Vicky had become more sophisticated these days: her auburn locks were still curly but now were carefully dried into a thick straight mass of hair, and she'd learnt to use make-up to show off her chestnut-brown eyes to their best advantage. She dressed in simple but well-cut clothes in shades that flattered her colouring: dark greens, russet browns and rich purples.

'Looks like I'm going to have to get used to this place. I think Octavia's just gone and bought a house.'

'Really?' Vicky put her cup back, raising her eyebrows.

'Yes – not far from here. Near the Physic Garden.'

'Nice area,' Vicky said non-committally.

'So I'm told. And the house is gorgeous in its own way, even if it's not quite to my taste. But it seems rather expensive. Twenty-five million.'

There was a minuscule pause and then Vicky murmured, 'That *is* rather a lot.'

'Is it?' Flora laughed at herself. 'I mean, I know it is but . . . I don't really know how much other houses cost. Sometimes I feel as though I've just come back to civilisation after living on a desert island for years and years. Nothing makes sense to me.'

'I'm sure Octavia knows what she's doing.'

'Well, that's just it. Does she? She doesn't have much more experience of the world than me but she's running at it as though she did. She decided to buy the house and we'd only been in it five seconds. She's so impulsive.' Flora shook her head. 'But it's extraordinary to think we could live in a house like that. We have no idea how to do it!'

'What do you mean?' Vicky said, frowning.

'Vicky, we're living in The Connaught at the moment. We don't have to do a thing for ourselves, which is lucky because we can't. Imagine if we were living in a house on our own. I honestly don't think Octavia knows how to boil a kettle, or make a cup of tea, let alone cook a meal. And nor can I! We've never learnt. We don't know how. I might be able to make a profiterole if you put everything in front of me, but I don't know when that will ever come in useful. As for using a washing machine . . .' Flora rolled her eyes. 'We haven't so much as picked up our own clothes in our lives. Do you see what I mean?'

Vicky laughed. 'Yes, I think I do. Oh, dear, you really are like a couple of princesses, aren't you? I expect if I put a pea under your mattress, you'd bruise like a peach.'

'I know it's funny,' Flora said, smiling a little sadly, 'but it's also ridiculous. We need to be looked after but I haven't the faintest idea how to go about even finding someone to do the cleaning.'

Vicky picked up her cup again, put her head on one side and looked at the surface of her tea. 'It's a shame,' she said idly. 'I'm so busy at my job, I won't have time to help you. I know what you need to do – I even know of some good agencies where you can find a housekeeper and a cook and people like that. But I don't know how I'll spare the time.'

'That's a nuisance!' Flora said crossly. 'You're just

51

the person to help us.' She rubbed her hands together anxiously. 'I can't think of who else could. Perhaps the lawyers . . .' Then a wonderful idea occurred to her. She leant forward in excitement. 'Vicky, do you like your job?'

'Well . . . it's all right. Being a trainee accountant was never exactly my life's dream, but it will do for now, I suppose.'

'Then give it up!' cried Flora. 'Come and help us instead.'

'That's all very well to say,' Vicky said with a smile, 'and I can't think of anything nicer, but some of us do have to pay the rent, you know . . .'

'Oh, I'll pay you!' declared Flora. 'What are you earning now? I'll double it. I'll triple it! You can tell me what you think is right, and that's what it will be. It makes sense! And you could live with us too, so you wouldn't need to pay rent to anyone. You should see this enormous house . . . you could virtually have a floor to yourself. And there'd be a car, of course.'

There was a pause while Vicky considered, her forehead creased in a frown. 'What would Octavia think?' she said at last. 'I wouldn't want to put her nose out of joint.'

'Don't be silly, she'd be as pleased as I am. Besides, she's chosen the house. I think I should be allowed to make a decision as well. You're the perfect person and we'd simply love to have you with us.' Flora looked pleadingly at her cousin. 'Would you consider it? Please, dearest Vicky . . .'

Vicky laughed. 'Sometimes talking to you is like being trapped in a Jane Austen novel. You sound so old-fashioned, it's hilarious. Look, you won't have heard of things like handing in notice and P45s and so on, but I reckon I can swing it, if you mean it.'

'Oh, I *do*,' breathed Flora happily. This really was the ideal solution. Vicky knew how the world worked. She would make sure everything ran smoothly. 'I do. Thank you, thank you, thank you!'

6

The private apartment at The Connaught was a cool, stylish and relaxing penthouse, decorated in muted tones of dove grey and soft blue, high above the Mayfair streets. Self-contained and removed from the hurly-burly below, it was the perfect place to relax and be completely looked after.

Octavia was already in the drawing room when Flora got back from her tea with Vicky. She had clearly hit the shops again after she'd left the Chelsea house. The room was littered with carrier bags from smart boutiques, tied with all manner of ribbons, rainbows of tissue paper spilling out of them. Flora could see carefully wrapped packages and shoe boxes peeping from within.

'Who is that monster outside the door?' she said, throwing down her bag and going over to the sofa. She was glad to be back inside the safety and quiet of their apartment, but the great man mountain standing guard outside had given her the shivers, even though he'd stood back in a docile way to let her through.

'Oh, that's Jared,' Octavia said. 'The lawyers sent him. He's our bodyguard.'

'He looks very scary.'

'That's the idea, hon. He's supposed to deter any would-be kidnappers,' said Octavia, unwrapping a box from the Chanel boutique and taking out a camellia brooch in white tweed.

'But no one knows we're here, do they?' Flora cast a panicky look at the door as though she was expecting someone to burst through it that moment.

Octavia didn't hear her, she was too busy looking at a set of stacked rings, each decorated with a little enamel camellia or the Chanel interlinked double Cs. 'Aren't these pretty?' She slipped them on to her finger and held out her hand to be admired. 'I got you a set too. So we can match.' She grinned over at Flora. It was a tradition that they received identical jewellery at Christmas and birthdays – charm bracelets and necklaces with their names on when they were little, and then pearls and diamond studs as they got older. 'Would you order some drinks? I'm dying for a lime and soda.'

Flora sat down and picked up the phone to call the apartment's butler. 'Thirsty from all that shopping, by the looks of it.'

Octavia looked up at her with shining eyes. 'Flo-flo, it's amazing out there. You wouldn't believe the be-oootiful things that are everywhere! All these years I've only been able to see these things in magazines, and now I can actually go and touch them and buy them. I can have whatever I want! All those years of being controlled by Aunt – our clothes chosen by her, our diets dictated by her, all our friends, every minute of every day . . . I'm going to make up for it now, I can tell you that.' She watched as Flora gave the drinks order and when her sister had put the phone down, said, 'Why don't you do some shopping? You're still wearing your old clothes.'

Flora looked down at her clothes. They seemed fine to her: a white shirt under a plain navy cashmere V-neck, and a pair of bootleg-cut jeans worn with sensible flat penny loafers. Why would she dress up to look at houses? But . . . She glanced over at Octavia who looked fantastic in a jagged-cut navy-blue mini-skirt and a slouchy blue-and-white striped top, belted with a collection of twisted gold chains hung with gold discs.

Her sister considered every day an occasion to dress up. It seemed to Flora that there was barely a moment when Octavia wasn't either getting dressed or considering what she was going to wear the next time she got changed. She'd always devoured fashion magazines, clipping out her favourite pictures and sticking them up all over the walls, sometimes creating her own version of a paper doll and pasting different pictures of outfits over it, so she could see how a different top would look with a certain pair of trousers, or whether a pair of boots would transform an outfit in the way she wanted.

If she had ever gone missing – which she had, from time to time, even though she'd known what the punishment would be – she could be found in the nearest boutique or clothes market. And now she had her freedom, and her own money, it was quite obvious that one of the biggest spending sprees in history had just begun.

'By the way,' Octavia said, 'the lawyers want us to go in and see them tomorrow. Honestly, they never leave us alone for a second. It's all talking to this person or that person about investments and all that nonsense. Such a bore. I might not show up.'

'We ought to go,' Flora replied, feeling that she must be the sensible one. Octavia was still so enraptured with the world outside Homerton. They had stayed at their aunt's for only one week after receiving the inheritance while Octavia had arranged their departure. There were formalities that meant they couldn't leave before then, but that last week had been so strange: their aunt and uncle were barely to be seen. It felt to Flora as though the girls had simply been ejected from the only life they had known since they were tiny. Suddenly all the rules vanished. There was no timetable enforced; they could eat what they liked, do whatever they wanted. When the time came for them to go, it was almost as if Aunt Frances were relieved. There were no tears or pleas for the girls to stay in touch. Instead there were cool, almost stiff, goodbyes and a formal handshake. It was Maggie who'd cried and kissed them, and told them they would be missed.

As they were driven away with their few suitcases, Octavia had been full of excitement and hope. Flora had felt as though she'd been pushed from an aeroplane without a parachute, but she tried to hide her panic; she didn't want to spoil Octavia's pleasure. Since then they had moved from one hotel to another, wherever Octavia felt like going, until they'd settled here at The Connaught. Now the swooping terror only came to possess Flora from time to time, at night, and when she was alone. Only Octavia could make it go away.

It wasn't as if they were totally alone in the world, she reminded herself. There were plenty of people on hand to help. So far there had been several meetings with lawyers and accountants, and a trip to the private bank where the twins' money was deposited. It had been a bit like some kind of royal visit, Flora had thought, with everyone bowing and scraping and sucking up like mad. She had realised then for the first time that she and Octavia really did have a lot of money, an amount that the outside world viewed as important and impressive. They had been presented with their credit cards in beautiful leather wallets gold-stamped with their initials: pale pink for Octavia and pale green for Flora. Then they'd been introduced to their personal bankers who were available to them at any hour, just in case the girls wanted to manage their accounts in the middle of the night.

'We'll need to see the lawyers, and the bankers, I expect, so you can tell them about this house,' she reminded Octavia.

'I suppose so.' Her twin brightened as she thought about their new home. 'I can't wait to get there! How long do these things take, do you think? One week? Two?'

'I've no idea. Perhaps Vicky will know.' That reminded Flora of what she and Vicky had agreed that afternoon. There was a discreet knock at the door and the butler came in with a tray of drinks for them. Flora watched as he set them out on the table and said casually: 'By the way, I've offered Vicky a job.'

'Oh?' Octavia had pulled out her iPhone and was

scrolling through her messages. She glanced up at her sister and raised an eyebrow. She bent forward, picked up her drink and sipped it as she looked back at her phone.

'She's going to be our assistant. Is that all right with you?'

Octavia shrugged. 'Sure. I expect she'll be quite good at that.'

'I thought she could come and live with us, if we move into the new house. She's living in a poky flat miles away at the moment, and sharing with some people she says are really awful.'

Octavia made a face. 'Why on earth does she need to do that? Can't she just come in if she's needed?'

'I think she's going to be needed quite a lot,' Flora said, and sighed. 'I don't think you realise at all how difficult it's going to be for us to live on our own.'

'It'll be *easy-peasy*,' said Octavia with a wide smile, putting down her phone. 'Everything's going to be easy from now on, you'll see.'

It is *easy for her*, thought Flora. *Why is she so at home in the outside world, when I find it all so difficult?* She adored her sister, which was perhaps why these fluttering feelings of fright kept starting inside her. She'd only ever known life with the two of them together, and now she was anxious that Octavia was taking flight, about to disappear off into the great blue sky, leaving her alone.

Octavia stretched out one long leg. 'I'm so pale,' she muttered discontentedly. 'Everyone else is tanned and gorgeous. I must see what I can do . . .' Her phone beeped and she glanced down at it. 'Oh! Gerry is downstairs, he wants to go browsing with me.

Apparently I've got an embarrassing dearth of serious jewels and he thinks we should go down Bond Street and look at some sparkles.'

'Tavy, please be careful,' Flora said with a note of pleading in her voice. 'Don't go mad out there.'

Octavia laughed and tossed her long golden hair, now restored to its real colour since the party platinum had been replaced. 'Calm down! It doesn't matter how wild I go. Don't you understand, Flora? We're *rich*. We've got enough for several lifetimes. We can spend how we like, so let's just enjoy it. Why don't you come too?'

Flora shook her head. 'I don't really like shopping like you do. And that man Gerry makes me nervous.'

'Everyone makes you nervous,' Octavia said with a smile. Then she went over and gave her sister a hug. 'You'll be fine up here. Have some more tea and watch some telly, and I'll bring you back a nice surprise.'

'You'll be back for dinner, won't you? I don't want to eat on my own.'

'Of course I will. We'll have something terribly naughty off the menu and eat it cosily up here, just the two of us. Isn't Monday a green day? Well then, let's have steak!'

They both laughed and then Octavia straightened her skirt and patted her hair. 'Now, I'm off to bash my credit card . . . Got to give my personal banker something to think about, after all!'

She grabbed her jacket and bag and headed out of the door. Flora knitted her hands together and watched her go.

7

'You mean it's all going to be done by the end of the week?' Octavia said into her phone as she walked down the street. It had been almost three weeks since she'd made an offer for the house and she was getting impatient.

'Yes, we're confident we'll be able to complete,' the lawyer replied, his voice a little muffled by the traffic passing by.

'You said that *last* week.' Octavia sighed. 'Why is it taking so long?'

There was a short pause and then the lawyer said, 'It's been quite swift by most standards. But I do understand your anxiety, Miss Beaufort. We'll move heaven and earth to make sure you can move into your new property as soon as possible.'

'Thank you.' Octavia ended the call and frowned. Surveys, environmental reports, legal matters . . . It was all such a bore and she didn't understand it. She wanted her house now and she had the money, so what was the problem? They'd been living in The Connaught for a couple of months, and while she enjoyed it and liked being only moments from the goodies on offer in the West End, she also felt the need to put down some roots. Besides, Vicky had already started working for them while she finished up her notice at her old job, and had been coming round to the hotel in the evenings to show Octavia and Flora websites and magazines with furniture and household goods that they might like to buy for the new place. The owner of their house had agreed to leave a few things behind but now Octavia wanted lots of new ones.

We need a place of our own, she told herself as she continued walking down Beauchamp Place, stopping to stare into the windows of the smart shops there when something caught her eye. *A proper home. That poky little hotel apartment isn't big enough for us.*

It wasn't big enough for Octavia's burgeoning wardrobe, that was for sure, even though it had its own walk-in dressing room lined with wardrobes, drawers and shelves. Her things were already overflowing into her bedroom. For almost three months she'd been shopping to her heart's content. She only had to walk into Dior or Yves St Laurent now and the shop girls came scurrying over to her, practically prostrate in their eagerness to welcome her and present their most desirable goods. It was an amazing feeling to sit there and watch as they brought out the most exquisite gowns, shoes and bags, and then say, 'I'll take this, and this, and this . . .'

She could happily play dress-up for hours, oohing and aahing over the gorgeous things, putting a creamy silk pussy-cat blouse with a pair of skinny jeans, or adding a snakeskin belt to a silk linen skirt and assessing the effect.

'You're a natural, sweetheart,' Gerry declared, applauding her as she spun in front of him on some Louboutin killer heels. 'You have a perfect eye.'

Gerry was with her almost all the time, urging her on, making her spend the most incredible amounts of money. Sometimes, even she felt a shiver of something a bit like fright or dread when the assistant, carefully blank-faced, said something like: 'That will be eighty-five thousand pounds', and Octavia handed over her platinum card. But Gerry's exuberance and the way he implied that this was quite normal in his circles helped her to overcome her doubts and shake off her vague sense of guilt.

She might not yet have had an occasion to wear a £20,000 dress made of peacock feathers, but she undoubtedly would have, at some point.

But even though Octavia knew that her ravishing designer dress was hanging in the wardrobe at The Connaught, ready for a suitable occasion, it didn't stop her longing for something else, or hold her back when she saw another sublime gown. At this rate, she'd have enough clothes to go out to some glamorous function every week for the rest of the year . . .

She lingered outside the window of a swimwear boutique, admiring a hot-pink beach sarong and a straw beach bag.

And her social life . . . well, that was something else. Under Gerry's auspices, she was being well and truly introduced to society. He'd taken it upon himself to become her walker, escorting her to parties, launches, openings and events. The extravagant birthday party – Aunt Frances's farewell hurrah – had made people aware of her name but she'd no influential friends and certainly wasn't on any of the guest lists that counted. All that was swiftly changing thanks to Gerry. Now she was inundated with stiff cards requesting the pleasure of her company here, there and everywhere. On top of that, there were endless letters from charities requesting her patronage or asking her to join a committee, or help organise some ball or other. It sounded boring, but Gerry had helped her sift through them all and had pointed out the ones she should say yes to.

'Darling, this one is lovely Xenia Popolova's pet charity, it provides toys for Russian orphanages. You know, she had a simply tragic childhood as a penniless orphan in Moscow, and now that's she's married a gazillionaire, she's giving a little back. So sweet of her. You must join this committee, you'll meet the *best* people.'

Or: 'Has the dear duchess asked you to support her garden at Gorton House? It's going to be wonderful. You must! And then you'll be asked for one of her weekends. They're a bit tedious, to be honest, and one has to pretend a huge interest in gardening to stay on her good side – but then, she *is* a duchess!'

Octavia did whatever he said, grateful that she had a friend who could help her through this strange new world, full of so many unknown people who all knew how to behave in it. So she wrote the cheques and Gerry sent them on, once he'd ordered her some smart new stationery from Smythson, pale grey cards with her name in flowing mauve engraved script: Octavia Beaufort.

'I'm your social secretary!' he said gaily, sticking down another pale grey envelope.

'I don't know what I'd do without you, Gerry,' she said sincerely. 'I'd be completely lost.'

'Darling, it's my pleasure. It really is.' He'd given her a broad smile. 'We make a wonderful team, don't we?'

She knew he loved it: walking her into a party, her arm tucked through his. He always wore one of his signature silver-grey suits with a slender tie and knitted waistcoat, a neutral look that always complemented hers. She would totter beside him in her towering heels, showing off her latest designer purchases. It helped that she had a size eight figure: for one thing, the boutiques always had her size. For another, she knew that Gerry loathed fat women – anyone who was over a size ten was fat in his book. The slimmer the better, as far as he was concerned. 'I prefer the race horse to the plump pony,' he explained. 'The thoroughbred rather than the Shire workhorse.'

He had introduced her to some girls her own age but Octavia found them rather frightening. They seemed so worldly wise and sophisticated. Of course, they were friendly, but they'd all known each other since birth, had been to the same schools and were filled to the brim with confidence. Octavia preferred to hang out with Gerry on his own, and he didn't seem to mind too much. In fact, if Octavia hadn't known that he was gay, she would have thought that he was in love with her. He phoned her first thing in the morning, saw her at least once a day, and telephoned several more times if they were apart, not to mention the deluge of emails and texts. If he saw a pretty dress, he'd send a picture over, urging her to come at once and try it.

Octavia reached the end of Beauchamp Place and wondered where to go next. To her right was Harrods, then the Burberry store where she'd recently dropped several thousand pounds in one sitting, and then, of course, Harvey Nicks, where she could happily wander for hours, shut off from the busy Knightsbridge streets outside, in an artificially lit, calm and comfortable world where people rushed to get her whatever she wanted.

Across the road was a huge building with a domed roof.

What's that? she wondered. *A church?*

She crossed the road and saw from the sign outside that it was a Catholic church. As she looked at the large blue-painted doors beneath the great stone portico, one opened and an ordinary-looking woman in a mac came out and hurried down the front steps. Whatever the place was, it was obviously open. On impulse, Octavia walked through the iron gate and up the stone steps. Pushing open the door, she stepped cautiously inside.

Within was a stunning and enormous space, like a cathedral, with a long central aisle that led to an ornate circular altar area directly beneath the great dome. The altar-piece was a riot of gold and jewel-bright colours, with a fresco depicting Christ in glory upon a throne of clouds, beneath a blazing sun and above His beseeching saints.

Octavia walked forward. The place seemed empty. She remembered when Aunt Frances had taken them on a tour of Europe. They had been marched into so many grand churches and cathedrals that they had blurred into one for Octavia, the Duomo in Florence mixed up in her mind with St Peter's in Rome. But she recalled now how the Catholic churches always had small chapels along the side walls, each dedicated to a particular saint and decorated with more frescoes or hung with oil paintings. There would be iron stands in front of each one, flickering with candles lit to help a prayer ascend to heaven.

This place was like those French and Italian churches, she realised. It was beautiful. She walked a little way down the aisle towards the altar, which sat beneath a magnificent gold and turquoise canopy. Everywhere she looked were carvings, mosaics, gilt and colour. She stopped and stared upwards, then sidled into a row of chairs and sat down.

It was peaceful here, and the air was redolent of a rich incense. She tried to imagine praying but it seemed an odd thing to do. Churches as anything other than a tourist attraction were strange to her. Aunt Frances was not religious. While Sundays were usually spent quietly at Homerton, the girls were never taken to a service.

Sundays. Octavia shuddered. The boredom, the mind-numbing boredom of life with Aunt Frances – and Sundays were the worst of all. In the winter, they would have to spend hours in the library, reading or playing silent card games. The Brigadier would be there, rustling the papers and puffing on that awful pipe, while Aunt Frances would work at her embroidery – those nasty cushion covers that looked old and faded as soon as they were finished. God only knew where they ended up, they were never seen again once they were done.

They were not allowed to watch television, or do

anything frivolous, listen to recordings of unidentified classical music and read improving books to pass the time. Sometimes Octavia had had the urge to race about the room, screaming and pulling the untouched leather volumes from the shelves, to make something happen. But she'd never been brave enough. After all, she'd been punished before and it had not been nice. Aunt Frances had demanded complete obedience and, if she didn't get it, there had been unpleasant consequences. Octavia still remembered the time that the Brigadier had come into her room, armed with a wooden paddle like a ping-pong bat, his jumper off, his face red and his breath, musty and horrid with stale tobacco, coming fast and noisily through his nose. He had ordered her to lift her skirt and bend over the arm of the sofa. Then, to her horror, he'd reached out a bony hand and pulled down her knickers, exposing her bottom to him. The violent embarrassment had made her go hot all over, a sick feeling in her stomach – and that had been much worse than the pain of the six, stinging whacks on her buttocks.

'That hurt me much more than it hurt you,' he said in a hoarse voice when it was finished, and left her just as she was, bent half-naked over the armchair.

What a stupid lie, she'd thought contemptuously. *Miserable old bastard. Well, I'm not going to let you see me cry.*

It was that thought that had stopped the tears in their tracks, and enabled her to face them all again, with her shoulders straight and her nose in the air, though she'd refused to look at the Brigadier for days. She took plenty of beatings after that, and always made sure it was she who got them, rather than Flora. She knew that her sensitive sister would be destroyed by the experience. They had decided that they hated the Brigadier, even more than Aunt Frances. He was old and ugly with hairs in his nose and ears; he smelt strange, and was always so quiet, his bloodshot rheumy old eyes fixed on them at all times. He never contradicted Aunt Frances, just seemed to be waiting for those times when he took Octavia upstairs, pulled down her knickers and thwacked her bottom with the paddle. Each time he seemed to take just a little longer over it, and give her one more stroke. Octavia thought privately he was a dirty old man and called him the Perv-adier, but Flora seemed to have a particular horror of him and could never bear to be alone with him.

Octavia didn't mind the old man that much. She wouldn't waste her emotions on him. She was proud of her self-control and her refusal to shed a tear when he hit her. But then, there was not much else she could control in her own life. Everything was dictated: every hour of her time, everything she wore, every morsel of food that passed her lips. She was constantly examined, as though she were some kind of prize animal being bred to be best in show: the hours she'd spent in her vest and knickers with Aunt Frances and various doctors and health practitioners – half of them quacks, no doubt – all of them staring at her while she was weighed and pinched and injected and fed tablets . . . But what they hadn't realised was that Octavia had her own, very special ways of rebelling.

One Christmas they had been allowed to watch a film on the television, called *The Great Escape*, about prisoners-of-war in a German camp who used all their cunning and guile to break out. Octavia had watched it, spellbound. *That's us!* she had thought, astonished. *Flora and I are the prisoners and THEY are the guards.* She'd glanced carefully at her aunt and uncle to see if they were noting the parallels, but of course they weren't. The film inspired her. From then on, she considered herself to be engaged in a hidden and ongoing war against her captors, to win as much freedom for herself as she could. She also embarked on a campaign of quiet destruction: all around the house, pictures, sculptures and vases acquired minuscule additions – a pen scribble here or a smear of correction fluid there – somewhere could not be seen. Nearly every curtain had threads pulled out of it, or its tassels trimmed in one place. Each cushion had little scissor snips in it. Book after book had one page neatly torn out, so discreetly done it was impossible to notice unless they were read, which they never were. Wherever she went, Octavia committed miniature acts of vandalism. *I'm undermining the enemy,* she told herself. *Sapping his morale. Using up his resources.*

It gave her a sense of hidden triumph, knowing that the perfect house was in fact far from that.

Now she got up and made her way back towards the door of the church, smiling to herself as she remembered. *It's no wonder I'm relishing my liberty. It's taken a goddamned long time to get here. And now I'm going to enjoy every single minute.*

Flora stood on the terrace looking at the magnificent view of the city. A sharp breeze blew over the rooftops, ruffling her hair and making her shiver slightly. London was beautiful and terrifying at the same time. It was magnificent and imposing, with its lavish buildings and the scent of money everywhere – but it was also chaotic, frantic, and full of people, rushing about on whatever business they had. Today she'd passed a man lying on the pavement on a scrap of old filthy carpet, his face lined with dirt and holey boots on his feet. Beside him a scrawny dog had been tucked up asleep, and in front of them both was a greasy cap with some change inside it. She'd stared at him appalled. Were there still people like this in London? She'd seen beggars when they'd travelled abroad – she remembered the fright she'd had once when they'd been engulfed by a swarm of barefooted children in Rome, pulling at her clothes and chattering away in high-pitched Italian, begging for coins. The Brigadier had slapped them away with some shouts and curses – but she'd had no idea that there were beggars like that here, in this city.

We've been protected, she realised. *From everything. Everything except . . .*

She shuddered.

A memory floated into her head. She and Octavia were about ten, and they had sneaked out of their schoolroom. Miss Bailey, the latest of their governesses, had slowly but inexorably fallen asleep in the warm, fusty afternoon atmosphere, her head nodding over the book she was reading while the girls did their Latin exercises. As soon as she'd slumped over, head on shoulder, mouth hanging open, Octavia had whispered, 'Come on!'

She'd been up and out of the room in an instant. Flora had glanced at Miss Bailey, and then followed. 'Where are we going?' she'd asked, nervous, her tummy fizzing with adrenaline.

'Wherever! Come on. Aunt's out, the Brig is playing golf today. We can have an explore.'

It was dangerous but Miss Bailey did seem sound asleep. And if she woke, she was hardly like to admit to Aunt Frances that she'd nodded off and allowed the girls to go unsupervised.

'Let's find Jo,' suggested Octavia. 'She might give us something.'

In the kitchen, they found the the cook rolling out pastry for a steak-and-kidney pie.

'What are you girls doing here?' she'd demanded, but in a kindly voice. 'You're supposed to be doing lessons. I've got tea ready for you when you've finished.'

'What is it?' Flora asked.

'Don't get excited, it's not this.' Jo indicated the pastry. 'That's for your aunt and uncle. You know you're not allowed pastry. It's a red day today, so you'll be eating cold chicken and salad.'

'Pudding?' Octavia asked hopefully.

'Fruit, as usual. Plain yoghurt.'

Both the girls groaned.

Jo softened. 'Here . . . seeing as there's no one about . . . I'll give you each a biscuit, but you mustn't tell anyone or I'll be in trouble. And get yourselves back to the schoolroom. Does Miss Bailey know what you're up to?'

They'd taken a chocolate chip cookie each and wandered along the ground floor, nibbling tiny, sweet morsels off their prizes as they went. It was rare to get a biscuit. Cake was only allowed on birthdays, biscuits once a week at formal tea. They found themselves in the library.

'Look,' Octavia whispered. 'Come and see my hiding place.'

She led Flora towards the large tables at the back of the room, the ones that were hidden in the shadows beneath the gallery and covered with dark green cloths.

They don't look like tables, Flora thought. *They're not flat, for one thing.*

The girls scrambled underneath one and sat in the darkness, finishing off their biscuits.

'Oh, I wish I had another,' sighed Octavia, licking her fingers.

'Me too.' Flora savoured the last bit of chocolate chip as it melted on her tongue. Why were there so many rules? Why was everything nice forbidden? 'What are these funny tables?' she said at last. 'Why are they slopey?'

'Let's look.'

They crawled out from beneath their hiding place. There were two tables close together. They were high and the girls could only just see the tops. Octavia pushed back the dark green cloth that was covering one of them, and revealed glass beneath. Beneath the glass was a display: rows and rows of brightly coloured butterflies, each one pierced through the middle with a brass-topped pin.

'Oh!' cried Flora. 'Are they dead?'

'Of course they are, stupid. Do you think they'd be alive when they've been put on the end of a pin?' Octavia leant forward for a closer look, peering through the glass. 'Aren't they pretty?'

Flora stared down at the tiny bodies: they were start-lingly perfect, with long curling black antennae, jewel-coloured wings – blue fading into turquoise fading into green, dustings of gold and silver, velvety black spots on the feathery wings. She felt heartbroken by the sight. 'How can anyone do this? They should be out, flying around, not stuck in this horrible case!'

'It's the Brig, I expect.' Octavia stroked the glass above a beautiful yellow specimen with orange patterns on its splayed wings.

Hot tears stung Flora's eyes. Seeing all these poor dead creatures, made to be fluttering amongst meadow flowers, mummified and frozen for ever, she felt her head spin. 'It's disgusting,' she said breathlessly. 'Disgusting!'

'Let's look in the others.' Octavia went to the other table, pushed back the green cloth and gave a little scream. Flora hurried over. This cabinet was full of skeletons: a collection of tiny, fragile-looking, greyish-yellow bones, all that was left of mice, frogs, shrews, rabbits and other small creatures.

'I don't like it!' Flora cried in fright. She looked over at the other tables, her eyes fearful. What further horrors were there in those? Severed limbs? Dead babies? 'Let's go, Octavia, please!' She grabbed her sister's hand and tugged at it. 'Please.'

'All right,' Octavia said, her own nerve obviously failing her. 'All right, let's go.'

They'd run back to the schoolroom, at their desks only a few moments before Miss Bailey had snorted, woken up and composed herself, evidently hoping she hadn't been asleep for long.

Flora had been tormented for months by the thought of the dead butterflies, lying frozen in the dark, beneath the glass. They haunted her dreams. Made her feel desperately, suffocatingly frightened.

I'm free now, she thought, as she stared over the

rooftops. *Why am I still frightened?* She shivered. *I can't be alone, not right now. I need someone to help me.* Octavia had gone out and said she would not be back until after dinner. Gerry was taking her to the theatre or something, but Flora hadn't wanted to go. She couldn't face the idea of being surrounded by people. Her hand went automatically to her hair and she ran her fingers through it anxiously. Not having Octavia near was making her panic. She turned and went back inside the apartment. Picking up the telephone, she dialled a number. 'Vicky? It's me. I want you to come here. Now.'

'Now?' Her cousin's voice came down the line, full of surprise. 'But I'm at work. I haven't finished my notice yet.'

'I don't care. Leave there. I'll sort it out. I need you right now. Not just for today. For good.'

There was a pause. 'Okay. I'll be right there.' She hung up.

8

The elegant crowds promenaded about the emerald-green grass of the Stewards' Enclosure at Henley. The men wore rowing blazers in bright candy colours and straw boaters, or, if they were not rowers themselves, discreet navy blue blazers with their light flannel trousers. The ladies wore dresses and skirts, from trusty floral numbers that looked as though they had seen plenty of summer outings to high-fashion dresses – anything was acceptable so long as it covered the knee. The regatta-goers entered the enclosure via a tented gateway, where every lady's hemline was inspected by eagle-eyed officials to make sure the rules were abided by. Some of the younger girls pulled their skirts down to walk through the entrance, and then hitched them up once they'd passed muster, but it was a risky strategy: officials wandered through the enclosure keeping an eye on things and were wise to the mysteriously rising hemline. Ladies who had foolishly arrived in something thigh-skimming were turned away, no matter how hard they pleaded. Their only option was to resort to the local shops, where they could buy something more appropriate.

Amanda Radcliffe, effortlessly chic in a pale green and gold Missoni crocheted dress, would never make such an uninformed mistake. She knew very well what the dress code for Henley Royal Regatta was; she'd been coming since she was fourteen, when her brother had rowed for Harrow and got her and her friends tickets for the Stewards'. She remembered when a boyfriend of hers had been a rower, one of the fit, brawny athletes straining every muscle as they pulled down the Thames. She'd leapt up and down, screaming her encouragement, loving the tension of the intense competition, the strain on the faces of the rowers as they pumped the oars . . . and got a thrill out of knowing that, later, the tall, muscled boy sitting at six in the boat would be involved in another kind of physical exertion entirely.

The memory sent a pleasurable tingle across her smooth brown skin, tanned from the morning she had spent sunbathing on her Notting Hill roof terrace, and made her wish that she hadn't broken up with Ferdy. He might have been dim but at least he was good in bed.

She took a cigarette out of her solid silver Asprey case. She'd had it made in the exact dimensions of a Marlboro Lights box, with a hinged lid that opened just like the cardboard version and her initials engraved on the side. 'So I don't have to see that bloody death warning,' she told her friends. One of the nice things about the regatta was that smoking was permitted because the whole thing was outdoors anyway. She tapped a cigarette against the box, lit it and exhaled a plume of smoke, gazing at the people wandering by.

Her friend Claudia came up, holding two glasses of champagne. She looked glamorous in a red halter-neck sundress and Chanel sunglasses, a shiny mane of long golden-brown hair tumbling down her back.

'At last,' Amanda said, taking one of the glasses. 'I thought you must be crushing the bloody grapes.'

'You go next time,' Claudia retorted. 'The bar's packed. Some vile girls from my old school are there. Belinda Bagthorpe and her ghastly crowd.'

'Henley can be rather cheap sometimes, don't you find?' said Amanda. She dropped her half-smoked cigarette and ground it out on the grass, then took a gulp of her champagne.

'So, did you have any problems getting the day off work then?' Claudia asked sweetly.

Amanda shot her a look. 'I'm the boss's daughter, remember? I work when I want to.'

'Daddy says he'll have his arms ripped off before I have to work for a living,' Claudia remarked, sipping her drink.

'That's because he remembers only too well what working down the mine was like,' shot back Amanda.

'He runs an energy company!' said Claudia hotly. 'He's never been down a mine.' She sneered. 'At least he doesn't work in a *shop*.'

'Noble's is not just a shop,' Amanda said with dignity. 'It's an institution.'

'Like a mental hospital?'

'Ha-ha.' Amanda stuck her chin in the air. 'You know what I mean. Actually, Claudia, perhaps you haven't noticed but everybody has a job nowadays – it's not cool to sit around spending Daddy's dosh. Pansy Cooper-Stewart has opened a toy shop. Tibby Macintyre is doing things for the National Gallery – parties or something – and even Suze is running her gift-list website.'

Claudia pouted. 'I could have a job if I wanted one.'

'As it happens, Noble's is not just a job to me. I'm passionate about it and what I do there. Besides, it's my family's business. It's in my blood.'

Claudia peeped over the top of her sunglasses. 'Oh! There's Gerry.'

'Really?' Amanda gazed round swiftly. 'Where?'

'There, coming down along the grandstand.'

'Bugger.' Amanda turned away from that direction, showing a pair of well-tanned shoulders and a glossy curtain of hair, dark again since the Beaufort party. 'I'm not really on speakers with Gerry.'

'Have you two fallen out?' Claudia looked interested.

'Not exactly. Let's just say I'm rather bored with his new puppy dog routine. The way he's chasing around after that girl – it's just embarrassing.'

'Which girl?'

Amanda pursed her lips and said tightly, 'Octavia Beaufort.'

Claudia giggled and sipped her champagne.

'What?' Amanda snapped.

'Nothing . . . nothing. But he was always buzzing around you until recently, wasn't he?'

'Amanda!' called Gerry from a distance. His keen social vision had already spotted her.

'Is he with that Beaufort girl?' hissed Amanda, not turning around.

'No. He's with Molly Harradine.'

Amanda turned back with a big smile and waited

for him to approach the champagne enclosure. 'Gerry darling! How are you? And Molly, how lovely . . .'

Kisses were exchanged, and enquiries as to where everyone was lunching were swapped.

'Where's your little friend?' Amanda said brightly. 'Is she busy today?'

'Do you mean my dinky Octavia?' Gerry said sweetly. 'Well, she's moving into her new house today, so she couldn't come. Dear thing, she couldn't wait to be in it. I told her to leave it to the movers and arrive in splendour tonight but she wouldn't listen. The house is superb. Perhaps a bit modern for my tastes, but wonderful in its own way.'

'I'm surprised you're not there helping her,' Amanda said, trying not to sound too acid. 'I can just see you carrying boxes for her, like an obedient pack pony.' Claudia was chatting with Molly Harradine, a lady of certain age whose face was showing the effects of cosmetic surgery: eyes that were slightly too catlike and lips that plumped out unnaturally. The effect was disconcerting and it was hard not to stare.

'Amanda, you're not . . . jealous, are you?'

'Of course not. I hate to break it to you, Gerry, but you are not the centre of my universe. Very, very far from it. I'm delighted you've got something to occupy your spare time. I just hope you're not being diverted from your work.'

'Don't worry about that,' Gerry said with a smile. 'I have a feeling this will reap huge rewards.' He took hold of Amanda's hand, leant towards her and said confidingly, 'You know you'll always be my best girl, don't you?'

Amanda threw back her head and laughed. 'Oh, Gerry, you *whore*. You total social slut.'

80

He laughed as well, the other two turning to look enquiringly at them. 'You're right! But, Amanda, I insist you come and meet Octavia. I know you two will love each other. In fact, I'm sure of it! Will you? Are you coming to my ball? It will be the perfect opportunity.'

'Yes, I'll be there. Perhaps I'll meet your little favourite then,' Amanda said, shrugging her shoulders lightly. 'Is Harrow rowing in the next race? I must go and watch. I always do, for Harry's sake.'

'How eccentric,' declared Gerry, 'to come to Henley and watch the rowing! Come, Molly,' he put out his arm for his companion to take, 'let us go to the Pimm's bar. I never think summer's really arrived until I have a Pimm's in the Stewards'.' He cast a look at Amanda and winked almost imperceptibly. 'Don't forget, Amanda. You're coming to meet my protégée. I can't have you going any greener . . . you'll start matching that pretty dress of yours.'

Amanda watched him go, a half smile curling her lips.

'So will you . . . meet the Beauforts?' Claudia asked.

'You know what? Perhaps I will.' Amanda narrowed her eyes and took another sip of her drink. 'I can't pretend it hasn't been irritating lately. That girl is bloody everywhere.'

'You know what it's like, they'll be forgotten in no time. The new thing is always the most exciting,' Claudia said comfortingly but with a glint of enjoyment visible behind her shades.

'Mmm.' Amanda put on her own sunglasses. 'Come on. I just heard the race commentator announce that the crews have passed the Temple. Let's go and bag our spot.'

9

'Well, is it ready?' Octavia stood at the front door of her new home, her hands over her eyes. In honour of moving day she was dressed down in True Religion ripped jeans and a plain Alexander Wang jersey tee-shirt along with flat brown leather sandals, although she hadn't had to move a thing herself. The effect was effortlessly stylish.

How does she know what to wear? thought Flora, wishing she had Octavia's gift for clothes. Even though her own things were expensive – Ralph Lauren chinos and a pink sweat top – she felt frumpy next to her sister.

The apartment at The Connaught had been stripped bare, and the trunks of extra clothes and effects that the girls had accumulated during their time there brought out of storage, taken to the new house and unpacked. At the same time, new furniture and goods had been delivered, van after van pulling up to unload yet more packages and boxes.

'Yes, it's all done,' Vicky said, standing back from the front door to let Octavia in. Flora followed just behind, wide-eyed and eager to see the transformation.

Octavia had to admit that Vicky had worked miracles. She hadn't been too sure when Flora had announced that their cousin was now on the payroll and would be assisting them in every way. She hadn't thought they needed any help beyond a cleaner and a cook, but now she could see that they did. Octavia was still getting to grips with having an email account and had just about mastered how to download music on to her MP3 player – there was no way she could have co-ordinated getting the house ready to be lived in. Vicky had sorted out everything with The Connaught and settled the bill – she was now in possession of a credit card with a dizzying limit available for Beaufort spending – and arranged the movers. She had anticipated all the home purchases they needed – the things that never occurred to Octavia and Flora, like towels, linen or a vacuum cleaner – ordered and paid for them and had them delivered. Vicky had also hired the staff and arranged security. All of it was done and taken care of. The new house was now completely equipped and ready for habitation.

'Come down to the kitchen and meet your housekeeper, Molly. She'll be taking care of everything domestic,' Vicky said. 'And there are two cooks, working on rotation. There are also two maids, a cleaner, a gardener and some security, but you'll meet them as we go along. Everyone's been vetted, of course. Your driver Steve is also going to double as your bodyguard – I've got rid of that man the lawyers sent, I know you didn't like him.'

'Good job, Vicky,' Octavia said admiringly. 'Your talents were wasted as a trainee accountant.'

'You know, I think you may be right,' Vicky said with a smile. 'I'm loving my new job.'

She led them to the kitchen and introduced them to Molly, a friendly-faced woman with tied-back dark curly hair who was checking off a list of newly delivered supplies and arranging the larder. Then Vicky showed them the rest of the house, already perfectly arranged right down to Octavia's loads of new clothes, which had been sorted and stored neatly in perfect order in the large dressing room that led off her bedroom.

'This is brilliant, Vicky, thank you,' Flora said, delighted that her decision to hire their cousin had paid off.

'You're welcome.'

They all went through to the main sitting room, a softly chic room in the house's theme colours of celadon green and pebble grey. Octavia instantly threw herself on the enormous white Mongolian sheepskin rug and stretched out luxuriously.

'At last, our very own home!' she proclaimed, her soft blonde hair mingling with the white fur.

'Just a couple of things, guys, before you go off and settle into your own rooms. I'm on the third floor, as I showed you earlier, and you can reach me any time. I've got a dedicated phone line just for you to use, so you can always get hold of me. I've already programmed the numbers into your phones as well as my house email. I've told Molly not to bother you with details but to come to me in every instance, so let me know what your requirements are.'

'Oh, I think I'm going to love having you about, Vicky,' Octavia said with a grin. She got up. 'I'm going to head upstairs for a shower. All this moving is hard work. Vicks, could you see about getting someone in who can show me how to use that gym equipment?'

Vicky pulled out a tiny notebook and small gold pen, and made a note.

'Thanks!' Octavia bounced out of the room, obviously on a high to be in the new house.

'How about you, Flora?' Vicky looked over at her other cousin. 'Anything I can do for you?'

Flora went and sat on the sofa. She shook her head. 'No. You've done loads. Thank you.'

'Are you kidding? I should be thanking you. I'm living in the lap of luxury – thanks for the new car, by the way – and my job is great fun.' Vicky went over and sat beside her. 'What about you, though? I get the feeling you're not happy.'

'I know I should be. After all, I'm one of the luckiest girls in the world, aren't I? How can I complain when I have all this?' Flora looked about the room, so quietly tasteful and expensively luxurious. 'But I feel so useless. What am I going to do with my life? Octavia will be fine, she'll make friends and find something to occupy herself. But I've no idea what to do with myself.'

'I'm sure you'll find something,' Vicky said reassuringly, her eyes sympathetic. 'Don't be too hard on yourself. You've only just left home for the first time. It's a lot to come to terms with.'

'But don't you see?' Flora grabbed a cushion and held it close to her. 'I don't have any qualifications for anything. I've never sat an exam. Who would want me?'

'Lots of people,' Vicky said firmly. 'You mustn't write

yourself off. You're young and bright with masses to offer. What have you always enjoyed doing?'

'Well . . .' Flora thought for a moment. 'Painting, I suppose. I've always loved that.'

'There. That's something you can do while you work out your future. Shall I look into some art schools and see if there's a course you can enrol on?'

Flora felt the familiar nerves flutter in her stomach at the idea of going somewhere unknown and being surrounded by strangers. 'I'm not sure . . . I'll ask Octavia.'

'No harm in looking into it.' Vicky smiled. 'You can always come and talk to me, you know that, don't you?' She put a reassuring hand on Flora's arm.

Flora smiled back. 'Yes, thanks, Vicky. You're a real friend.'

'Any time. I mean it.'

Later that night, Flora went as usual to Octavia's room. This time they really were apart, she noticed. Although their bedrooms were on the same floor, they were at opposite sides of the house, Octavia's looking over the front and Flora with a view of the garden.

Flora knocked on the door and went in. Octavia was lying on her bed in her pyjamas reading a magazine. She looked up as her sister came in.

'Hi!' She grinned. 'Isn't this exciting? Our own place at last.' She sat up and held out the hairbrush. 'Come here, I'll do your hair first.'

Flora went over and sat on the bed, feeling comforted by the familiar routine. Octavia knelt behind her and started brushing out her long blonde hair, humming gently. Flora closed her eyes and let herself relax as the soothing strokes pulled rhythmically through her hair.

'Are you okay, honey?' Octavia asked gently. 'You barely ate anything at dinner.'

'I'm fine,' Flora said. 'Really.' She didn't want to admit that she had hardly any appetite, or that she was finding it hard to eat outside the regime that Aunt Frances had set down. Octavia was so happy. She clearly loved their new life. *I can't worry her. I don't want to tell her how I'm really feeling. Besides, I'll be fine in a while, I'm sure of it.*

'Good.' Octavia's hand rested gently on her sister's head as she brushed. 'There's so much to look forward to, I can hardly wait to get started.'

Flora shut her eyes and tried to banish the fear that weighed on her stomach. As long as there was this – the cosy intimacy with her sister that she needed so much – she would be all right.

10

The ball was a fabulous affair. Gerry had decreed a dress code of black tie for the men and white gowns for the ladies, and it was being held in the ballroom of Templeton House, which Gerry claimed had once been in his family but was now the headquarters of some royal society or other. The sight of the black and white figures drifting about the chequered floor gave the effect of an elegant and intricate chess game.

Octavia was with him, and had been since the very beginning.

'It's in your honour, darling,' he'd declared. 'This is my present to you, to make sure that everyone knows exactly who you are. You're simply made to be a leading light in society. You've got everything – beauty, youth and glamour. The only thing you don't have is connections, and that's what I'm terribly good at. By the time tonight is over, you'll know the whole of the *jeunesse dorée*. You'll have a million friend requests tomorrow on your Facebook page.'

'I haven't got one,' Octavia admitted. 'I've just about learnt how to turn my laptop on.'

'How chic,' breathed Gerry. 'Mysterious. Removed.' He held up a hand and looked serious. 'Never change . . . promise me *right now.* Do I have your word?'

Octavia shrugged, laughing. 'I can't promise anything of the sort! I'm changing every day, but mostly thanks to you.' She looked down at the wonderful gown she was wearing. She and Gerry had gone shopping together, and he had styled her from head to foot: the white Marchesa gown in a Greek goddess style fell in softly shimmering folds, showing off her peaches and cream skin. Her golden hair was twisted into a Grecian-style knot with long loose curls allowed to fall down her back. An antique necklace of real ancient coins, strung together on a gold chain, was twisted around the knot, and her jewels continued the classical theme: rather than diamonds, her necklace was a many-layered waterfall of aquamarines tumbling in a twisting gold fretwork.

'You look like Helen of Troy!' Gerry had cried when they'd assembled the outfit, down to the high-heeled sandals with thongs twisted about her ankles and up her calves. 'Show-stopping. I *love* it.'

Octavia had had a marvellous day. Gerry had decided that she and Flora should spend it at a spa, being pampered, massaged, buffed and polished. He had taken Octavia entirely in hand, deciding who would style her hair, who would make up her face, what scent she would wear and even what colour her nails would be painted. When finally, with her dress on and her jewels in place, she'd been allowed to stand in front of the mirror, she'd gasped. 'Is that really me?' she'd said wonderingly.

She looked so sophisticated and adult – no longer

the fairy-tale princess with platinum hair and a sparkling ball gown, but a sexy, polished young woman, shimmering with style and money.

'It's really you, my darling,' he said, coming up behind her and smiling with satisfaction. 'You are a total knockout.'

If the reactions of the other guests were anything to go by, then Gerry's hard work had indeed been a success. She'd been nervous at first but people were so flattering, complimenting her on her dress and how wonderful she looked, that her nerves subsided and she began to enjoy herself. More than one young man had given her a meaningful glance and raked his eyes appreciatively over her.

'You can take your pick,' Gerry had whispered in her ear as he noted the young and handsome heir to an earldom bow low to Octavia and kiss her hand. 'Just don't hurry into anything.'

'I won't,' she said, her stomach fizzing delightfully. Boyfriends, so far forbidden, were a territory she was very much looking forward to exploring.

She glanced over to where her sister stood. Flora was her one worry. Where Octavia was flourishing in their new life, Flora was visibly fading. Where Octavia shone and glistened, her sister seemed pale and lost. She looked beautiful in her white halter-neck Halston gown and white platform heels, her hair was long and glossy, and a fortune in diamonds by Chopard sparkled at her neck and ears and nestled in her hair. Nevertheless, there was something washed-out about her, and her shoulders looked a little bony where the halter-neck skimmed her collarbone. She stood on Gerry's other side, and was introduced by him to everyone . . . but only after Octavia had received the lion's share of the limelight.

'Here's some of the younger crowd I wanted you to meet,' he said, as a couple of sophisticated-looking girls with knowing eyes approached them. They had interpreted 'white' rather loosely. One was dressed in a yellow and ivory Moschino dress with a tutu worn underneath to create a prom-style effect. The other had several tattoos inking their way down her arms and across her breast.

'This is Jasmine Burlington,' Gerry said, indicating the girl with tattoos. 'A naughty little trouble-maker who was expelled from no fewer than three schools.'

'Shitholes, all of 'em,' Jasmine offered. She had a curious accent, drawling and posh but with an Estuary edge, and was dressed in a white lace mini-dress with spaghetti straps, a black bra showing defiantly under-neath. She leant forward and kissed Octavia on the cheek with a loud smack. 'Whoops!' she said, drawing back. 'You've got my lipstick all over you. People will talk. They'll think we've been making out in the loos or something.'

Gerry whisked out a handkerchief and wiped away at Octavia's cheek. 'Charming as ever, Jasmine. And this is her partner in crime, Rosie Gilbert.'

Rosie, the Moschino ballerina, had her dark-blonde hair backcombed on one side and shaved away almost to the skull on the other, and her make up was heavy and Gothic, eyes rimmed with layers of black kohl. 'Hiya,' she said to Octavia, looking her up and down without seeming very impressed by what she saw.

Octavia felt some of her newfound confidence melting away. She had never met girls like this before.

She had been brought up to respect the values of traditional elegance and beauty, to think of Grace Kelly as the epitome of womanhood: to her, seeing a girl who'd had her skin inked with permanent designs, or shaved her head, was remarkable. No doubt there were plenty of them in London, but not in the places where Octavia hung out. They seemed so sure of themselves, full of attitude and eager to be noticed.

'Hello,' she managed in a small voice.

Jasmine looked over Octavia's shoulder and her face brightened. 'Oh, God, look,' she cried, 'it's . . . it's . . . a friend of ours,' she finished a little lamely, shooting a glance at Gerry. 'Come on, Rosie, we've got to talk to her. Catch you 'round,' she said to Octavia. 'Are you going to an after party?'

Octavia stared at her blankly.

'Don't encourage after parties!' scolded Gerry. 'They make people leave earlier than they might have done.'

'Oh, bollocks, Gerry. We'll all be here to the bitter end, don't you worry. If you don't have anywhere to go, you can always come with us,' Jasmine said to Octavia. 'See ya.'

They were gone, skittering away across the marble floor to find their friend.

'After parties,' Gerry muttered scornfully. 'They're beginning to take over from the main parties! After all the time and effort one's put in, not to mention the expense . . .'

'Where's Flora?' Octavia asked suddenly, noticing that her sister had vanished from Gerry's side. Without waiting for his reply, she dashed off, leaving him calling after her that she must come back, the most important guests were due any moment . . .

Octavia hurried round the ballroom, holding up her skirts so she could move more easily. It was crowded now, the women sparkling in white with enormous rocks worn at their necks and ears. Wherever she went, people stared and some tried to speak to her, but she ignored them. At one point she passed Jasmine and Rosie who were now sitting in an alcove on a small red sofa either side of a dramatic-looking woman with deep auburn hair, a slash of red lipstick and a curving feather headdress, but Octavia didn't stop. She had only one thought in her head: *Where is Flora?* She didn't know why but it seemed vital to find her.

She saw Vicky picking up a glass of champagne from one of the drinks tables and rushed over, grabbing her cousin's arm.

'Have you seen Flora?' she demanded.

Vicky looked blank. 'No. Isn't she with you?'

'I've lost her. You go that way and see if you can find her. I'll go this way.'

Vicky nodded quickly, looking serious, and set off while Octavia, breathless and panicky, began to circle the ballroom for a second time, avoiding Gerry by hiding behind several broad-backed male guests. She suddenly remembered something. Where had she found Flora in the old days at Homerton? Her favourite hiding place . . . *Of course. Flora always hid in the old wardrobe in the east wing, among the coats.*

Octavia rushed back towards the entrance and pushed her way into the cloakroom, startling the coat-check girls who were taking possession of the coats and wraps of the smartly dressed people still arriving at Templeton House.

At the back of the cloakroom, she saw a white figure sitting on the floor behind a rail of coats with a puzzled attendant asking if there was anything the matter.

'It's all right,' Octavia said briskly. 'I'll take over here.'

The attendant looked relieved and went back to the busy front desk.

Octavia went forward slowly. 'Flora?' she said in a gentle voice.

Her sister was sitting bent over, her arms wrapped around her knees, rocking back and forth.

'What's wrong?' Octavia put her arms around her sister. Flora looked up at her, her eyes wide and frightened. She was deathly pale.

'These people!' she whispered. 'So many people . . . It's terrifying me . . . They're all staring at me! Watching me!'

Octavia had seen Flora like this before, overtaken by fits of fear, talking of being watched, shaking and shivering like a terrified animal. Only gentleness and her sister's presence could bring her out of it. 'It's all right,' Octavia murmured, hugging her sister tightly. Flora put her head on Octavia's arm and the trembling subsided a little. 'It's okay, Flo-flo. It's just a party, you know. Everyone here wants to be your friend. No one wants to hurt you.'

'I can't face them all,' Flora said in a small voice. 'It's too much for me. It reminds me of our birthday party . . . and you know how much I hated that.'

'It is daunting,' conceded Octavia, 'but we have to

get used to it. This is normal. It wasn't normal living the way we did, shut away from the world.'

'But it's all I know,' Flora whispered. 'I don't know if I can take this new life.'

'What's the alternative? Going back to Aunt Frances? You can't want that, can you?'

Flora said nothing and Octavia saw a brief look in her eyes that made her think that the prospect was nowhere near as insupportable to Flora as it was her sister. 'No!' she cried. 'You can't go back there! I won't let you.' She felt a wash of sadness. 'Oh, Flora, we've waited so long for our freedom. Would you really rather be back with Aunt Frances and the Brig than living with me?'

Flora stared at her for a moment and then shook her head. 'No,' she said through pale dry lips. 'Of course not.'

Relief flooded through Octavia. 'Thank goodness.' She hugged her sister again. 'Then will you be strong? For me? Will you try and cope with all of this? It's important to me, you see, I don't know why. I'm as scared as you are, in my own way, but I need to belong to this new world. I can't go back to our prison – you do see that, don't you?' Octavia stood up and helped her sister to her feet. 'Now let's go and find Vicky. I'm sure she's just as worried as I am. She can take you home any time you want, but see if you can last another hour. It's been so kind of Gerry to hold this party for us.'

Flora smiled weakly. 'All right. I'll do my best.'

Octavia hugged her, wishing she could transfer some of her own strength into her sister. 'I'm worried about you, Flo-flo.'

'Don't be,' Flora said, more firmly. 'I'll be all right. Now let's find Vicky.'

The ball was in full flow as 10.30 approached. The late arrivals had made their appearances and the reception rooms were crammed. The supper room was packed, the bar was full of people clamouring for bottles of champagne or the vanilla vodka martinis that Gerry had thoughtfully provided.

'I feel like I'm in *Clash of the Titans*,' said Amanda Radcliffe to her circle of girlfriends. 'Some of the Greek goddesses are hilarious. Have you seen Lady Frilford? She's as wide as she is tall. She looks like giant cotton-wool ball in that dress.'

They all laughed.

'Amanda, I've just seen Ferdy,' said Suze. 'He's dancing with Georgia Jagger in the boogie room.'

'Oh?' Amanda kept her composure, raising one eyebrow ever so slightly. 'He's always trying to make me jealous. It won't work. I'm not going to take him back. It's over and that's that. He can bore poor little Georgia as rigid as he likes, it's fine by me.'

Nevertheless, Amanda felt a prickle of irritation. This whole evening had been horrible. First there was someone else wearing the exact same white Temperley dress as she was. That wouldn't have been so bad, because she looked by far the better in it, but the woman in her dress was old and rather frumpy with bad hair and very bad accessories, so she'd managed to make the dress look less stylish than it was and that reflected badly on Amanda's choice.

Then there was the fact that she had no boyfriend to be her escort at the party and it was making her cross, particularly as Claudia had a new man buzzing around her, tending to her every whim, and was looking very smug about it. Amanda was beginning to wonder if she'd done the right thing breaking up with Ferdy . . . perhaps she would have to instigate a little re-warming of those particular coals . . .

But the thing that had totally ruined the night for her was Octavia Beaufort. She was so full herself, preening and posing as though she was some kind of megastar. It was annoying too that Gerry had managed to get so many people to come – important society people who would now have Octavia's name in the forefront of their minds. Amanda gritted her teeth as she thought of it.

What made the whole thing a particularly bitter pill for her to swallow was that not so long ago, *she* had been Gerry's protégée. He had fawned over her, praising her beauty, style and exquisite taste, had venerated her family money. He had taken her to exclusive parties and introduced her to the most important people and the newest stars. He had dubbed her the hottest young thing on the social scene. But all that was brutally changed. She had been dropped. Someone had come along who – Amanda's blood boiled with rage when she thought about it – was, in Gerry's eyes at least, more beautiful, more stylish and infinitely more wealthy.

He's just a star fucker! she told herself. *A vile old snob. A silly, money-grabbing, social-climbing old fool.*

Watching him squire the Beaufort girls around the room, as though he personally were responsible for them, had made Amanda sick. He'd betrayed her. She hated him, and them. Well, she didn't care much about the quiet one, it was the other sister who made her furious, with Gerry slavering all over her, and that ridiculous smug attitude of hers.

Claudia came up with her new boyfriend in tow. He seemed to like tans as much as she did; they were both a solid mahogany colour. *Like matching sideboards,* thought Amanda spitefully.

'Hello, darling.' Claudia craned her neck for air kisses. 'Mwah! Well, have you seen the belles of the ball? I have to say, they are even prettier close up, aren't they?' She looked about innocently. 'Where's Gerry, Amanda? You and he are usually thick as thieves.'

'He's doing his community service,' retorted Amanda, 'helping the socially disabled.'

There was another titter from her circle of friends. They always liked it when Amanda got all worked up and started letting the malice flow.

'I think those twins are ridiculous,' she continued, enjoying the appreciative audience. 'He may be dressing them up as though they're a couple of life-size dolls, but he can't hide the fact that they're complete retards from the Land That Time Forgot. They've absolutely no idea what the fuck's going on! And the way they look so alike is just freaky, like they're something out of a laboratory. Except that one thinks she's the most fabulous thing on earth and the other . . . well, she's a bit of a tragic case by the looks of it. Have you noticed the way she twitches and stares? I think she's got a touch of OCD – either that or she's developed a severe case of village-idiot-itis. Did you hear the way she talks? When I was introduced to her, I thought she was about to swallow her own tongue.'

Amanda imitated Flora's voice. 'H-h-h-hello, I h-h-h-hope you have a g-g-g-g-good evening.'

Suddenly she was engulfed by a horrible sense of shock as freezing water cascaded over her. She gasped and then squealed as she realised that her hair was drenched and her skin and dress soaked. '*What . . . ?*' she spluttered as an ice cube slid out of her hair and down on to her shoulder. 'What the fuck . . . !'

'How dare you talk about my sister like that!' cried an outraged voice.

Amanda blinked away drops of icy water and saw the Beaufort twin she hated most standing in front her, an empty jug clutched in one hand, her eyes sparking with fury and two angry dots of pink on her cheeks.

Everyone around was watching with barely restrained glee as they took in the extent of Amanda's drenching. Claudia had one hand clamped over her mouth while Suze's eyes were as big as saucers.

'I heard what you said,' Octavia continued in a voice of steel. 'Your nasty, spiteful remarks. Do you think Flora can help stammering? She's terrified of people like you, with your ready judgements. Do you think it's easy for her to stand there and meet hundreds of people when she's been protected from it her whole life? Well, I'd rather be sweet, innocent, kind Flora than you! You're just a mean, disgusting person, and I certainly don't want you at this party. I know Gerry would say the same. I want you to leave.'

Amanda gaped at her, still gasping and unable to take in what had just happened. It was like a bad dream, being at the centre of all these glamorous people while looking like a drowned rat.

'So get your coat and get out,' Octavia said coolly. Then she turned on her heel and sauntered away, pausing only to put the water jug back on the table as she went.

'I say, Amanda,' said one of the men, 'she's certainly showed you what for! Not quite so retarded after all.' He guffawed with laughter.

'Oh, *piss off!* All of you can go and fuck yourselves!' shrieked Amanda, anger coursing through her. Then she shook her head, spraying a shower of drops, set her shoulders and stalked off, trying to remain impervious to the stares and muttered comments as she made her way to the Ladies to find a towel.

Octavia marched away, heart racing, still full of fury. Who was that awful girl? Did Gerry know her? Well, no one was going to talk like that about Flora and get away with it!

As she headed for the staircase, a man put his hand on her arm and stopped her. She looked up at him, startled. He was a stranger, but something about his face made her feel quite odd, as though she knew him. He had dark hair cut short and a tanned face with strong, prominent features – his nose looked like it might have been broken once or twice – but it was his piercing eyes that really stood out, ice-blue against his tan. Those eyes were staring at her now with an expression that was a mixture of reproach and accusation, and he was unsmiling.

'I saw that. What the hell do you think you were playing at? Look at the state of that poor girl.'

She stared back at him. He was older than she was, his dark hair showing grey at the temples, and he wore an excellently cut dinner jacket that showed off his broad shoulders. 'She deserved it!' Octavia cried hotly. 'You don't know what she said.'

He frowned, a furrow forming between his eyes. 'Throwing water over someone is not the way adults deal with their disagreements. In fact, I would say it's the action of a spoiled child.'

She gasped angrily. Who was this man, and what gave him the right to talk to her like this? 'You don't know anything about it,' she replied fiercely. 'She asked for it. I'm glad I did it.'

For a moment he looked almost disappointed in her, then his expression turned grim. 'I see. Well, I know a hissy little tantrum when I see one. You should be ashamed of yourself. I'm going to find someone who can get a towel for that poor soaking girl.' He turned his back on her and strode away, leaving her breathless with anger, as she watched him disappear into the crowd.

'Hey, Octavia!' cried an eager voice behind her. She turned and saw Jasmine Burlington smiling broadly as she approached. 'We saw what you did. It was pretty cool.'

'Really?' The adrenaline rush was disappearing. All Octavia could think about was what the stranger had said. *Am I really a spoilt child?*

Rosie came up on Jasmine's heels. 'Yeah,' she said. 'We hate Radcliffe. She's, like, sooo lame. I loved what you did. *Everyone's* talking about it.'

'Maybe I shouldn't have done it,' Octavia said, flushing. She knew that man had been right – it was childish to chuck water over someone. *But how dare he talk to me like that?*

'Are you crazy? It was great. Like, performance art. I filmed her screaming her stupid head off on my phone and it's so going up on YouTube tomorrow.' Jasmine grinned at her. 'We're desperate for a smoke, so we're all going back to Charlie's flat. Wanna come?'

Octavia looked at them, feeling happier. They were so edgily glamorous, Rosie with her strange hair and bee-stung lips, Jasmine with the tattooed roses snaking over her icing-sugar-white skin. 'Yes, please,' she said, putting Gerry and his plans to whisk her off to Annabel's out of her mind. 'I'd love to.'

11

There was a knock at the door. Flora lifted her head. She was still lying in her bed even though she'd been awake since five o'clock in the morning, just staring into space and remembering what had happened the previous night at the party. She'd recovered from her panic attack and had clung to Vicky for the next couple of hours, trying to avoid all the people who wanted to congratulate her on the event and introduce themselves.

Then she'd begun to feel that one pair of eyes was fixed on her, as though someone were observing her closely, staring hard at her, watching her every move. She'd felt that familiar crawling sensation tingle across her back, the one that always came with the onset of nausea in her belly. Vicky had been chatting on about something while Flora had frozen. Her breath had started coming short and fast, her heart began racing and panic whirled about inside her like a small tornado, growing in size and strength. She moaned quietly, but Vicky didn't hear.

Then she saw it: a flash of red and a shimmer of

gold epaulettes. It moved through the crowd, the colour as bright as blood in all the black and white. The red flickered into view and then out again.

He's here, she thought with a dull sense of dread. *He's come here. I'll never get away.*

Possessed by cold horror, she felt herself lapse into a dream-like state. As if in a trance she turned and began walking towards the entrance. She had passed the foyer and the cloakroom and was just leaving through the great carved doors when Vicky caught up with her.

'Flora . . . Flora, where are you going?' she'd said, astonished, grabbing her cousin by the arm.

Flora had stared back at her, only half recognising her. 'Home,' she'd said blankly. 'I'm going home.'

'You can't just walk out into the street!' Vicky had cried. 'You're wearing half a million pounds worth of diamonds, for one thing! Come on, if you want to go home, we'll call Steve to collect us and I'll go with you.'

Flora had obediently let Vicky take her home, feeling as though half of her were in a nightmare that only she knew about, while the other half continued to try and function in the world where everybody else was.

Vicky, evidently worried, had given her a hot drink, helped her take off her Halston dress and made sure she got into bed.

But sleep had not come easily, and then only for an hour or two.

The knock at the door sounded again, a little louder this time. 'Flora?' Vicky said from the hall. 'Are you awake?'

Flora said nothing. She waited until her cousin had

gone away, and then laid her head back down on the pillow, staring dry-eyed into the dim light of her bedroom.

She went downstairs much later, sloppy in jeans and an outsize sweatshirt, her hair scraped back into a ponytail.

Vicky was just walking across the hall as Flora came down the stairs. She looked up and saw her, her expression instantly relieved. 'Oh, there you are! Did you sleep okay?'

Flora looked at the floor. 'Sort of,' she mumbled. 'Is Octavia around?'

'Still asleep, I'm afraid. I don't think she got in until pretty late. Come with me, and we'll get some coffee. Would you like some breakfast?'

Flora followed Vicky to the dining room where breakfast things were still laid out, even though it was almost noon. Vicky phoned downstairs for coffee and fresh toast, and when it came persuaded Flora to eat some with a good dollop of marmalade on top.

She did feel better when she'd had something to eat, and a cup of strong coffee. *I don't know what's wrong with me*, she thought. *Why do I feel so listless?*

'Have you finished?' Vicky asked. Flora noticed that her cousin's eyes were sparkling and that a smile of anticipation was playing around her lips. 'I've got something to show you.'

'What is it?'

'Surprise,' Vicky said mysteriously, and beckoned Flora as she stood up. 'Come with me.'

She got up, her curiosity pricked, and followed Vicky upstairs. They went up three flights to the storey above

Flora's room. She hardly ever came to this floor though she spent a lot of her time in the room at the top of the house, watching television or learning to use the computer Vicky had installed for her there.

Vicky led her along the corridor to a closed door, then opened it with a flourish. 'There! Go in.'

Flora walked past her into the room beyond. It was very bright with French windows leading on to a small balcony, the long windows letting in the light. In the middle of the room stood an easel, a chair, and a stand that held palettes and brushes. On a table by one wall were pads of paper in all colours, sizes and textures, as well as boxes of crayons, pastels, pencils and charcoals. A large open box revealed tubes of watercolour paints in an endless variety of shades. On the other side of the room, Flora noticed a sink and some cupboards.

'For washing brushes,' Vicky said with a grin, following Flora's gaze. 'And over there is an iPod docking station so you can listen to your music while you paint. There's a radio too.'

Flora shook her head, amazed. 'Did you arrange all this?'

Vicky nodded. 'Yes. Do you like it?'

Flora was lost for words. For the first time in a long while she felt the stirrings of something like pleasure. At last she said, 'I love it.'

'Good.' Vicky looked delighted. 'That was the idea.' She pointed at the bookshelves near the windows. 'Lots of how-to books over there. Manuals and guides to painting – just in case you'd find them useful.'

Flora smiled, her spirits lifting by the second. 'I want to get started right away!' she said, excited.

'I've got some details of art courses as well. There's an art school not far from here that offers lessons in watercolours, pastels, all sorts of things.'

Flora's smile faded. 'Oh . . . I'm not sure about that.'

'You don't have to decide now,' Vicky said gently. 'Have a play, do some painting and then see how you feel.'

Flora went to her cousin and gave her a hug. 'Thanks, Vicky, this is a wonderful surprise, it really is!'

'I'm just glad to see you happy,' her cousin said. 'Now, I brought a jam jar from the kitchen especially. Shall we fill it up with water and get you started?'

12

Octavia moaned and tried to open her eyes but they felt gummed shut and virtually dry. Her mouth was dry too, and her tongue felt as though it was stuck to the roof of her mouth. She winced as pain crashed through her head.

'Oh God, what's wrong with me?' she asked herself pitifully. From her bed she could see her reflection in the cheval glass by the window, and she was a wretched sight. Her hair was a bird's nest, her eyes were rimmed with smudged mascara and her complexion was a nasty grey colour. Last night's dress lay abandoned on the floor, her shoes scattered nearby.

She glanced over at the clock. It was 4 o'clock in the afternoon. Well, that was no surprise. It had been nearly 10 a.m. when she'd arrived back, thanks to Vicky sending the driver to collect her once someone had managed to tell Octavia the address.

Octavia groaned and collapsed back on her cool Egyptian cotton sheets. This was a hangover, she knew that. She had thought that her slightly fizzy head the day after her twenty-first had been a hangover. *It was nothing compared to this,* she thought, wondering how she would summon help. She was desperate for a drink of water and her pounding head was demanding an aspirin.

She tried to think back over the previous evening. How had she ended up feeling so grim? Oh yes, of course. The after party. She had thrown that water over Amanda Radcliffe – well, the horrible woman had deserved it for mocking Flora like that – and then Jasmine and Rosie had spirited her away. She'd left without even saying goodbye to Gerry. He'd be terribly hurt. But really, they hadn't given her any choice because within moments she'd been in a cab heading for a flat in Belgravia where a load of grungy young people were hanging out at the after party.

'These days you can't relax in public,' Jasmine confided, as the taxi whizzed smoothly round Sloane Square. 'Everyone's got camera phones. If they're not taking pics of you, they're filming you. Then they phone the papers, and the next thing you're in the gossip columns or even front-page news. I mean,' she raised her eyebrows, 'we can't so much as smoke a joint without people making a fuss. And it can get much, much worse. A friend of mine got dropped as the face of a handbag company after some waster took her picture when they were doing some speed, and sold it to a Sunday newspaper. She lost, like, hundreds of thousands. Such a bummer.'

'And they take your picture as well?' Octavia said, surprised.

Jasmine gave her a curious look. 'Haven't you heard of us?'

Octavia shook her head.

Jasmine wrinkled her nose in surprise. 'How weird. We're always being papped, aren't we, Rosie?'

'Yeah,' she drawled. 'It's a nightmare. I hope Charlie's got some Grey Goose in. I'm dying for a drink.'

'You've probably heard of my dad,' Jasmine went on, 'he's a famous record producer. That's why the newspapers are interested in what me and my brothers get up to . . . because we're famous by association. I've always had my name in the papers, I'm kind of used to it now. And Rosie's a model, for, like, really cool, edgy fashion designers, aren't you, Rosie?'

She nodded and sighed as though that was a really big drag for her.

'So that's why we need after parties. So we can do our real partying in private, with people we can trust not to grass us or film us or whatever.'

The bright young things at the Belgravia flat were welcoming to Octavia but without too much interest in her: after all, beautiful, rich young girls were the norm in their circle. The main thing, it seemed, was to have fun, and that meant drinking – huge cocktails of vodka and pomegranate juice were pressed into their hands as soon as they entered – dancing, and taking drugs. At least, that's what Octavia guessed was going on, why there were several people lying on the floor looking completely zoned out, and several more dancing manically with a crazed energy, though she didn't notice anyone actually taking anything. But then, she had no idea what taking drugs looked like: her experience was limited to paracetamol, Lemsip and cough medicine.

Her capacity for alcohol was very small; a few sips of her drink and she was light-headed. A few more and she could feel herself swaying and her tongue felt thick in her mouth. She asked for some water and managed a kind of Alice in Wonderland trick of drinking the vodka when she felt sober and water when she felt drunk, keeping herself fairly lucid until the early hours when she rather let go of her inhibitions and . . . well, she had vague recollections of wild dancing, and a group shower – everyone in their underwear – and more dancing . . .

There'd been a boy there, too, who had wanted to kiss her but she hadn't let him. She couldn't remember why she'd been so determined not to as he was rather handsome, but she'd pushed him away and given him her phone number instead.

Then the driver had come, at an hour when the rest of the world was up and breakfasting, to take her home. She couldn't even remember getting into bed – and now she felt like shit.

But it had been worth it.

Octavia managed to pick up the phone by the bedside and ask Molly to bring her aspirin, orange juice, tea and some toast as a matter of urgency. An hour or so later, she was able to make it to her bathroom and have a long hot shower. An hour after that, she made her appearance downstairs, checking her phone as she went. As predicted, there was a message from Gerry, sounding wounded and asking where she had disappeared to. There was also a call from Jasmine saying everyone had thought she was, like, cool, and maybe they could hang out together more. Nothing from that boy . . . what was his name? . . . but perhaps that was normal.

Would he call her? Would they meet again and perhaps kiss . . . perhaps more . . . she shivered with excitement. She couldn't wait to start exploring that side of her life. Octavia had more experience than anyone could have guessed, considering how sheltered she had been – and even Flora didn't know how much – but she was sure that she was light years behind everyone else.

I can't wait to catch up! I need some more experience and soon, she thought as she wandered into the main downstairs living space. One entire wall was made of smooth beach pebbles set in polished concrete and the effect was soft, warm and touchable rather than stony or cold. There was no one there, and she wondered where Flora was. Last night they'd missed their usual ritual. Octavia felt a sudden pang of worry about her sister. Flora certainly hadn't been herself at the party. *I must find her,* she thought. *Check she's okay.*

Just then, her phone sprang into life and she took it out of her pocket. Jasmine's name flashed boldly on the screen. Octavia's eyes sparkled with anticipation. Finding Flora went out of her mind.

13

When Flora put her head around the office door a few days later, Vicky started laughing.

'What?' she asked, puzzled. 'I haven't said anything yet.'

'Look in the mirror,' Vicky said. Flora went to the glass over the chimney piece and saw that she had a big streak of blue across one cheek and a green smear on her forehead. 'So I take it the studio's a success then?'

'Yes, yes,' Flora said, smiling. She went over to Vicky's desk and perched on the end of it. 'I love it – thank you so much. But . . . remember what you were saying about art courses?'

Vicky nodded, looking interested.

'Well . . .' Flora took a deep breath. 'I'd like you to book me on to a watercolour course. I love painting but I'm so ignorant. They didn't teach us anything at Mademoiselle Estelle's. Didn't you say there's an art school nearby?'

Vicky nodded. 'There are a couple I looked at.'

'Can we both go and see them?'

'Sure.' Vicky smiled. 'I'm really pleased you want to get out of the house a bit. I've been worried about you staying in so much.'

'I can't pretend the idea doesn't make me nervous,' Flora said, 'but the painting has helped me so much already.' She grinned at her cousin. 'It was a stroke of genius, Vicky.'

'Good.' Vicky turned back to her computer. 'I'll make some calls right now and let you know.'

I knew Vicky would be good at this job, but I didn't realise how good, Flora thought as they sat together in the back of the Mercedes. Vicky had arranged appointments right away to visit the schools, and now Steve was driving them to the second place, this one a little further away but with a beginner's art course that Flora could join immediately if she wanted. The first school had been very smart, with lots of ladies in pearls sitting around, learning how to make attractive little daubs. It was also booked up for another couple of months.

The second school was edgier than the first. They were shown around studios that were rough and paint-splattered compared to the immaculate rooms at the previous place. Flora glanced through a window at a life-drawing class and saw that the students were of all classes and ages, ranging from scruffy youngsters to bohemian-looking older people. The teachers looked friendly and approachable.

She liked the feeling she got in the building, and sensed that she could fit in here unnoticed.

'Do you want me to enrol you at that one?' Vicky asked as they headed home.

Flora nodded. 'Yes,' she said, 'that's the one. Definitely.'

She took a deep breath. 'It's going to be a challenge for me. But I'm determined to do it.'

'Atta girl,' Vicky said, delighted that Flora was finding the strength to spread her wings a little. 'You'll be terrific.'

Despite her brave words, though, Flora felt sick on her first morning on the watercolour course. She had signed up to six weeks of full days of tuition. *I'm going to be rubbish at it,* she thought, panicking, as she dressed in clothes that she hoped would make her as inconspicuous as possible: black trousers and a long drapey cardigan in dark blue.

Octavia had been astonished when Flora had told her what she was doing, but so pleased that Flora thought that she detected a tiny bit of relief in her sister's face. Octavia had been out even more often ever since the party, although she didn't seem to be with Gerry any more but with some of the girls she'd met at the ball. She'd begun to be out in the evenings, too, and Flora hated it when her sister wasn't there to chat with as they brushed each other's hair. She missed Octavia desperately whenever she was out of the house, and found it hard to sleep until she knew her twin was back and safely in bed. Sometimes she would wake in the night, not able to stop herself from padding quietly along the hallways and into Octavia's room. Often, after getting home late, Octavia would wake in the morning to find Flora snuggled in bed beside her.

Flora was so nervous on her way to art school she nearly had Steve turn the car round and take her home, but she managed to overcome her fear enough to scuttle into the classroom and take up a seat at the back, in the darkest corner she could find. Then, once the teacher had arrived and the class started, she found herself so absorbed that by the end of the day she had moved up two rows without even realising it. The teacher, a middle-aged man called Peter, was encouraging and kind, helping her with brush technique and paint effects in such a supportive way, she hardly noticed that he was telling her what to do, and he didn't frighten her in the least, probably because he looked at her work and not at her.

The other students didn't bother her. Flora found the classes so relaxing and refreshing that life suddenly seemed a great deal better.

Perhaps everything will be all right after all, she thought, and felt the first glimmerings of hope since leaving Homerton.

The girls sat round a table in Harvey's Diner, a big jug of iced water in front of them along with huge glasses of cold Pinot Grigio and some breadsticks. Rosie was wearing an enormous pair of Yves St Laurent square-framed sunglasses behind which her eyes looked heavy, while Jasmine's skin was even whiter than usual, if that was possible. Sometime in the previous twenty-four hours, she'd dyed her hair pink.

Octavia thought that it looked rather cool, even if it was something she would never do herself. Still, it worked on Jasmine, who was clearly in need of a cigarette if the way she was holding her breadstick was anything to go by.

'Looks like you girls have been living it up a bit,' remarked Octavia, taking a sip of her wine. She wasn't sure if she wanted it at all but drinking at any available opportunity was obviously what her new friends did, and she didn't want to appear different. No doubt she'd get used to the constant boozing in time. But how did they manage to drink so much and eat so little? Perhaps that was why they needed cigarettes . . . Octavia thought she ought to try harder with that habit too. She'd been attempting to take it up, but in the main was happy to shut her packet of Marlboro in a drawer and forget all about it. When the others said they were dying for a fag, she found it hard to understand how they could want that noxious smoke in their mouths. *But it must be nice or why would they do it?*

'Just the usual,' Jasmine said. She flicked through the pages of a magazine. 'Oh, look, we're in this one. Pics of us going into Templeton House for the party.'

They all pored over the pictures, studying the ones of themselves and reassuring one another that they looked great.

Octavia stared at the one of herself arriving at the party on Gerry's arm. She felt a pang of guilt. 'Gerry's furious with me for leaving the ball,' she said, 'he's giving me the cold shoulder. He is hardly called since, and he's usually on the phone all the time.'

'He'll get over it.' Jasmine perused the menu. 'What shall we order? How about the salad?'

'Yeah, salad,' Rosie said. 'That sounds good.'

'I'll have the burger,' Octavia said, 'and chips.' The other two looked at her. 'What?'

'Nothing,' Rosie said with a shrug.

When the food came, Octavia ate most of her burger and some of her chips. As soon as she pushed her plate away, the other two, who'd already eaten their salads, pounced on her leftovers and wolfed them down.

'Chips and mayonnaise,' Rosie murmured happily as she took a bite of a long golden-brown French fry dipped in mayo. 'God, how gorgeous.'

'If that's what you wanted, why didn't you have it?' Octavia asked.

The other two exchanged looks. 'Because we have to stay thin,' said Jasmine. 'We can't pig out on chips. We'll turn into heifers and no one will want us to advertise their stuff.'

'Oh.' Octavia frowned. This made sense, she supposed. But . . .

'Come on,' Jasmine said, consulting her Tag Heuer. 'Iseult's expecting us. We'd better hurry.'

'Who's Iseult?' asked Octavia, but in the general rush to pay and then hail a cab outside, no one replied until the taxi was roaring its way down Oxford Street and heading east.

'Iseult is like this *amazing* fashion guru. She used to be an editor of *Elegance*. Now she's a freelance fashion stylist and consultant,' Jasmine said. She leant forward to talk to the cab driver. 'Hey, can we smoke out the window?'

The driver's gaze flicked over the long legs emerging from Jasmine's tiny denim mini-skirt, and the breasts bobbing in her low-cut top. 'All right then,' he said, and the girls quickly lit their cigarettes.

'How do you know her?' Octavia asked.

Rosie looked blank. 'Everyone knows Iseult,' she said. 'We all know each other, that's the way it is.'

Octavia was starting to understand that the world she'd been offered entry to was indeed a rarefied place.

Everyone really *did* know each other in the social milieu where all that mattered was to be able to belong – through fame, through money, through family connections, through beauty. And they were all so at ease with their belonging, as though confidence had been bred into them at birth.

I want to belong too, Octavia thought. *I'm going to make it happen.* And she took another vigorous puff on her cigarette, determined to ignore the swirl of nausea in her stomach.

The taxi pulled to a halt in a dirty side street in Aldgate East. Was this still London? Octavia wondered. It wasn't like anything she'd yet seen. This part of the city was grimy and down-at-heel, there was litter everywhere, and instead of plush flats there were broken-down mansion blocks, warehouses and small factories. Every other sign advertised a wholesale garment trader and from somewhere nearby came the rattle of sewing machines.

'Sweat shop or something,' Jasmine said with a shrug as they climbed out. She pushed a twenty towards the driver with a cheery, 'Thanks, mate!'

The cab drove off, leaving them in the road.

'I hope you remember which one it is,' Rosie said, as they stared about them at the unappealing buildings.

'Course I do,' Jasmine announced bravely. 'It's over here.' She led the way through a dark alleyway to a rubbish-strewn doorstep and pressed a button on the wall. A voice said something unintelligible through the speaker, and then there was a buzzing sound. Jasmine pushed against the door with her shoulder and it opened. 'Come on,' she said, and led the way in.

Can this be right? wondered Octavia as they entered a hallway that reeked of something vile – urine, perhaps. *This doesn't seem like somewhere we should be. How could anyone let the place get into this condition? It's horrible. Why doesn't someone clean it up?* But the other two seemed perfectly at ease with the state of their surroundings so she followed them as they climbed up the five twisting staircases to the top storey.

'At last,' Jasmine said, puffing, as they came to a door on the landing. Unlike the others they had passed on their way up, this one was painted a dark, glossy purple. It was standing slightly ajar, obviously awaiting their arrival. Jasmine pushed at it, and in they went.

The outside of the flat gave no clue as to what lay behind the door. The exterior seemed to promise some mean, shabby, dirty flat, with bad furniture and nasty décor. The others in the building might well be like that, but this one wasn't. It was light, for one thing, because of the roof windows that let the rather grey sunshine outside come pouring in. For another, it was painted a pale turquoise all over: ceiling, walls and floorboards, and it was almost empty of furniture except for a large long table, six tailors' dummies standing in the middle of the room, and a white chaise-longue against one wall. The table was littered with fabrics and pairs of cutting shears, seam rippers and chalk, and on the floor were more bolts of cloth and piles of swatches. There was also a young man, pudgy and pale-faced, kneeling down on a large piece of woven pink tweed, cutting it out carefully with a pair of large shears.

But it was impossible to ignore the most colourful object in the room. Sitting on the white chaise-longue was a woman. She had fiery red hair cut into short sharp bob with a fiercely straight fringe falling almost over her eyelids. Swoops of dark liquid eyeliner batwinged her eyes, highlighting their yellowish-green colour. Her nose was large, almost too large for her face, but her strong hairstyle balanced it. Her lips were painted blood-red, as were her nails, and she was wearing a white silk forties-style cocktail dress and incredibly high lime green python-skin shoes with hidden platform soles and towering heels. Between two of her long white fingers was an antique jet and carved ivory cigarette holder, where a strong French cigarette was burning.

As the girls entered she stared at them, not saying anything until they were inside and standing in front of her. The man on the floor ignored them and continued cutting his material, his tongue sticking out of one corner of his mouth as he concentrated hard. Octavia sensed that the power in the room definitely resided with the woman who was examining them all carefully as she took a long slow suck on her cigarette and exhaled a thick plume of smoke.

What extraordinary eyes, thought Octavia, hardly able to look anywhere else. *They don't look quite human. They look like a lizard's, that strange yellow colour . . . A lizard, or a snake.*

The eyes were not interested in her for the moment, they were too busy with Jasmine and Rosie. At last she spoke, her deep voice coming out in a raspy, upper-class drawl.

'Darling,' she said to Jasmine. 'While I myself would never leave the house in a garment that even resembles a denim mini-skirt, I like what you're doing. First, you have the legs for it. Second, you're cleverly recherché. Those eighties itsy-bitsy things are going to come back, I just feel it. Do you know what I would do, though? Lose those sloppy ballet pumps. Put on a pair of men's brogues, and replace the laces with ribbons. Wear one white one with a black ribbon and one black one with a white ribbon. That would look stunning. Don't you agree, Roddy?'

She looked over at the man on the floor, but he had now moved round so that his back was to them and didn't even glance over his shoulder – simply grunted and carried on with his work.

'Sweet Roddy,' the woman said fondly. 'I shouldn't disturb him. Genius at work.' Then she turned her attention back to Jasmine. 'But – pink hair?' She sounded dramatic, outraged, and rolled her amazing yellow eyes. 'Please, darling! No! We must cling on to the few vestiges of glamour left in this world. Not pink hair.'

'Don't worry,' Jasmine said cheerfully, going forward to brush the woman's cheek with her lips. 'It's semi-permanent. It'll be gone by the end of the month.'

'Well, I'm very glad to hear it. If only that filthy mutilation you call a tattoo were as disposable. And how are you, Rosie?' She smiled at the other girl, who was slouching behind Jasmine. 'I hear you've just got the Recall jeans campaign. Well done. I always said you were destined for great things. Do you know why?' She leant forward. 'Let's face it, you're a charisma

122

vacuum in the flesh, but in front of the camera, something special happens.'

There was a pause and Rosie looked a little confused, as though she was not sure whether she had just been complimented or insulted.

'But . . . who is this?' The woman's eyebrows disappeared into her fringe as she turned her gaze on Octavia. She almost shivered under its intensity.

'Octavia,' said Jasmine, pulling her cigarettes out of her bag. 'Octavia, this is Iseult Rivers-Manners.'

Iseult ground out her cigarette in an ashtray by her side. 'Yes, but Octavia who? *Who* are you? You're rather striking, my dear. I'm sure I would have noticed you before now. Are you a new discovery? Some little model found on a train station platform in the back of beyond or spending her Saturday job money in Topshop?'

Octavia took a breath. 'I'm Octavia Beaufort.'

'Are you?' The yellow-green eyes flickered with interest. 'I know that name . . . but how?' She frowned, pouting out her red lips. Then her face cleared. 'Of course . . . Beaufort! I know all about you, darling! You're the little girl who's been shut away all her life, aren't you? Roddy, Roddy – this is the Beaufort girl! The one that you-know-who has been lionising all over town. That ball.' She looked sour for a moment. 'He didn't even invite me. I went anyway, though it meant I had to bypass the introductions.'

Roddy continued to ignore them all, and Iseult looked back at Octavia. She smiled, and her severe, quite plain face softened into something almost pretty. 'I can't fault his taste, I've never been able to do that. You're rather exquisite. Not just your face or your figure – there's something about you. Something fresh

123

and unspoiled that's increasingly rare in this knowing world of ours.' She stood up and walked towards Octavia, moving with careful elegance in her towering high heels. 'So you've been shut away from the world for years and years, like a Sleeping Beauty? What do you make of this world now that you're out in it, Sleeping Beauty?'

'Oh, I love it,' Octavia said breathlessly.

'Do you?' Iseult's face hardened and she laughed mirthlessly. 'How strange. I hate it.' She stared deeply at Octavia again and then said, 'Do you know? I don't think I'm going to let you go, if that's all right. I declare you to be a find.'

Jasmine and Rosie glanced at each other with meaningful looks and Octavia felt herself obscurely honoured, though she wasn't quite sure why.

The rest of the afternoon passed quickly. The girls, it turned out, were being fitted for outfits they were modelling in a fashion show. They were doing it as a favour to Iseult, who was Roddy's mentor and had arranged the event to showcase the designs of her protégé.

'With models like Jasmine and Rosie, the press coverage will be guaranteed!' declared Iseult as Roddy began to swathe Jasmine in the pink tweed he'd been cutting. 'And with my contacts, the people who matter most will be there to see Roddy's first major collection. The fashion editors, the heads of luxury labels, the buyers for the major stores – all the people who shape our zeitgeist. Once your name is on their lips, we've almost won the battle.' The tweed looked like nothing but a strangely cut piece of fabric when Roddy picked it up, but as he pinned it around Jasmine's shape, it became a stunning dress, like a toga with more structure. He fastened the shoulder with an oversized kilt pin.

'Fantastic,' breathed Iseult as Jasmine posed in front of a large mirror, jutting out one hip and standing on tiptoe. 'Exactly right.'

'Yeah . . . yeah . . . that's all right,' Roddy said, speaking almost for the first time. His voice was rough, with a deep Glaswegian accent. 'Okay, I'm happy with that one. Rosie.' He beckoned to her. 'You're next.'

He dressed her in a shredded baby-blue tweed mini-skirt over a tartan muslin underslip and a string vest with tiny jet spiders sewn on to the threads as if they were roaming all over Rosie's chest. He pronounced himself satisfied with the result and Iseult applauded wildly. Then she took him into the kitchen space at the side of the studio and whispered to him frantically for some minutes. After a while they emerged, Iseult looking triumphant. 'Octavia,' she cried, 'Roddy's got some wonderful news for you!'

Roddy came up to her. His head was shaved almost bald, with just a light brown fuzz covering his pale skull. A cigarette was tucked behind one ear, she noticed, and a pencil perched behind the other. 'Do ye wanna model for me?' he asked gruffly.

'I . . . I don't know,' Octavia said, her heart beating faster at the idea. 'I've never modelled before, I don't know if I could do it.'

He looked her up and down with his hazel and grey eyes. 'Yeah, ye could. I can see that already. An' I need a bride, see?'

'To close the show,' explained Iseult, her eyes glittering with excitement. 'Say you'll do it, please!'

'You've got to,' cried Jasmine. 'It's a real honour. I'm, like, so jealous.'

'You never said there was a bride,' Rosie added sulkily.

'I've persuaded him,' Iseult said. 'And I'm going to teach Octavia how to carry it off. It will be simply marvellous!'

Octavia didn't know what to say.

'Good!' cried Iseult, clutching her arm, digging her red nails into the flesh so that it was almost painful. 'I knew you would! It'll be divine, you wait and see.'

14

By the end of the second week of her art course, Flora had grown in confidence. There were only a dozen people on it, and most of them were content to keep themselves to themselves. The studio was always quiet: not in a cold, frigid way but with a sense of keen industriousness. Occasionally Peter put music on, and there were lessons on watercolour technique and practical tips, but mostly they worked away on their own, painting whatever display he had set up for them. Flora said hello and goodbye to the other students, but at lunchtime went away on her own with a book to eat the sandwiches that the cook had made for her. No one knew who she was, and she was careful to look as anonymous as possible. One of the younger students from the neighbouring gilding class asked one day if he'd seen her in the papers, but she'd shaken her head and stammered out that he was mistaken then hurried off.

It must have been Octavia, she thought, dashing into her classroom. Octavia had said that photographers were beginning to pop out at odd times and take her picture when she was hanging out with her new friends.

Once she was in the safety of the studio, Flora forgot everything else. She loved the work and could see that her technique was improving every day. Peter was encouraging and told her she had a good eye, particularly for colour, which made her feel ridiculously happy. When he saw some of her doodles and scribbles on an art pad, he gave her a book on design which he thought she might find interesting.

The season was definitely changing, Flora thought as she stood outside the art school, waiting for Steve to arrive. The summer warmth had vanished and the first chill of autumn was in the air. She pulled her jacket round her a little more tightly and looked down the road, wondering when the car would arrive.

Perhaps I'll walk, she thought. After all, she'd seen the route often enough and it didn't take so long in the car. The classes were helping her to find a bit more confidence about being outside the house. *How hard can it be to get home?*

She pulled out her phone and sent a text to Vicky. *Tell Steve no need to pick me up. I'll walk home.*

Then she set off along the street, heading in the direction she remembered him driving, and was soon lost in her thoughts, imagining how she would work on her still life the following day. She didn't know how long she'd been walking when she suddenly realised that she didn't know where she was. *I must have taken a wrong turn somewhere,* she thought, looking about her. Her surroundings looked very unfamiliar. Instead of leafy streets and gracious brick houses, she was in a rougher area. She could see tower blocks nearby and hear the rumble of heavy traffic that meant she must be near a main road or a flyover.

Don't panic, she told herself firmly. *Just look about for a road name or something.* She could see street signs, but they all told her where to find other, unfamiliar places, not where she was. A shiver of fear crept over her. *I don't know where I am,* she thought. *I must call Steve.* But she couldn't tell him where she was. How would he get to her? *I've got to find out where I am! No one will be able to find me until I know that.* She gulped, trying to control her breathing, but her heart was starting to pound and the first feelings of sick panic were uncurling in her stomach.

I'll keep walking. I'll ask someone. She carried on along the street, aware that it was getting darker. A man came striding towards her and she resolved to ask him where she was, but as he got closer, she lost her courage and couldn't speak. A taxi came past, its golden 'For Hire' light glowing like a beacon. She tried to put her arm up and summon it, but fear gripped her again. The sight of the strange driver, a hulking dark shadow behind the wheel, terrified her and she couldn't move. As soon as the cab had gone past, she let out a shuddering breath. *You idiot, don't be so stupid. You'll have to get the next one.* But no more came.

Flora kept walking, feeling more and more possessed by fear. She could tell that she was beginning to sink into an autopilot state, but there was nothing she could do to stop herself.

She came to a large interchange and found herself walking under a bridge. There was a thundering noise as a lorry rolled by overhead. Flora put her hands over her ears and squeezed her eyes shut, unable to stop herself from moaning. She felt the rumbling fade away and slowly opened her eyes.

Then she drew in a sharp frightened breath. A group of three men were blocking the way. It was as though they'd appeared from nowhere, two white boys and a black one, all with close-shaven heads, street clothes and trainers – and menace glittering in their eyes.

'What have we here?' sneered one, looking her up and down. 'It's a princess, guys. A real-life princess.'

Flora couldn't speak. Her heart was hammering away hard in her chest and her stomach was clenched with terror.

The first one, obviously the leader, began to circle her, getting closer each time. His sharp eyes picked out her jewellery and watch. 'You *must* be a princess. That's a Rolex, innit?'

The other two advanced as well. All three of them were now close to her and she could feel her breathing speed up.

The leader came nearer still and put his mouth almost against her ear. She tried not to sob. 'You must be *rich*. Where's your money, princess?'

She fumbled with her bag and pulled out a £10 note, the only cash she had. 'Here,' she said breathlessly. 'T-t-t-take it.'

'Ten quid?' said one of the others with a sneer. 'Is that it? Where's your credit card?' He reached out a hand and pulled at the glittering stud in her ear. 'Are these real diamonds?'

Flora had no idea there were any other kind so she said nothing.

The leader laughed. 'Come on, Your Highness, I think we're going to borrow your crown jewels, if you don't mind. Give us your bag. Where's your fuckin' phone?' He snatched at her bag while one of the

130

others went for her earring, tearing at her earlobe, and the third scrabbled with her wrist, trying to get the watch off.

Flora squealed with pain and fear.

'Shut the fuck up! You can spare it, you fuckin' bitch!' hissed the leader, rifling in her bag for her phone and wallet.

'*Halt!*' cried a terrible voice. All three of them stopped and turned to stare. A man stood only a few metres away, smart in a three-piece suit and carrying a dark walking stick with a bone-handled top. He was staring at them, eyes flashing. 'Stop that at once! Leave this lady alone, I command you.' His accent was German but his English was perfectly phrased.

Flora stared at him, confused. Who was he?

'You *command* us?' sneered the leader. 'You're a fuckin' wanker. Come on, boys.' He turned to face the man with a swagger. 'We can take you in about thirty seconds, you tosser.'

The man's eyes glittered. 'I don't think so,' he said. There was a flash and his cane transformed itself into a sword, its long thin rapier blade shining in the darkness. He made one or two swift thrusts and it sliced the air with a hissing noise.

'He's got a fucking blade!' cried one of the boys.

'And I will not hesitate to use it,' declared the man. He took a step forward and, with one swift movement, sliced open the front of the leader's tee-shirt from top to bottom.

'Fuck!' he snarled, furious. 'I ought to kill you for that.'

'You are welcome to try, my friend,' said the man politely.

'Come on, let's get out of here,' begged one of the others, tugging at the leader's arm. He glowered back ferociously at Flora's rescuer but a moment later allowed himself to be pulled away, and the gang of three disappeared into the darkness.

The Good Samaritan put the blade back in its sheath so that it was a walking stick again, and advanced on Flora. 'Are you all right, my dear?' he asked gently.

The adrenaline began to melt away. 'Yes, yes,' she said in a shaky voice. 'I'm f-f-fine. They didn't hurt me.'

'You were lucky I happened to be passing.' He looked at her with a half smile on his face. 'You have to be very careful, walking about these parts on your own, especially when you are wearing expensive trinkets.'

'I g-g-got lost,' Flora said. She was trembling with the aftershock. 'They've t-t-taken my bag. It's got my phone in it, my m-m-money . . .'

'Don't worry, my dear, I will make sure you get home. Now, let's get away from here just in case those men take it into their heads to come back with some friends.'

He led her out from under the bridge. A few moments later he had hailed a cab and they were sitting inside it together. Flora told him her address and soon they were heading towards Chelsea.

'You must report the thefts as soon as possible,' the man said. His accent was barely noticeable, except for a slight sibilance on 'th', and his language was a little more formal than a native speaker's. 'Especially if you had bank cards in your purse.'

Flora nodded, remembering her credit card in its pale green case. 'I w-w-will.'

'Good. And promise me you will not walk alone in

such a place again!' He smiled. He had a warm, friendly face, she noticed. His eyes were light brown with creases at the corners, and his hair was also a soft, honey brown, thick and with a wave in it. His bottom lip protruded slightly beneath a long straight nose.

'Do you always c-c-carry a sword?' she asked.

He laughed, his eyes merry for a moment. 'Of course! I know it is not strictly legal to do so, but a man must be prepared to defend himself – only if he is attacked, you understand. The world is a dangerous place, as you've just found out. Ah, here we are at your address.'

The cab stopped and he leapt out, helping Flora from the taxi. 'Will you be all right now?' he asked.

'Y-Y-Yes, thank you so much,' she said gratefully.

'You're very welcome. Goodbye, my dear, and don't forget to report the theft.'

'I won't.' She watched him climb back into the taxi and wave at her through the window, smiling broadly, as the cab pulled away.

The front door opened and Vicky came out, her face anxious. 'Flora! Thank God! Where have you been? We expected you ages ago, and you're not answering your phone. Steve is out driving the streets, looking for you.' She stared after the vanishing taxi. 'Who was that man you were with?'

'I don't know,' Flora said, staring down the street after the cab. 'I completely forgot to ask.'

15

Amanda Radcliffe was in her office on the sixth floor of Noble's, the distinguished store founded by her great-great-grandfather Sir William Noble. The huge emporium sat squarely in the middle of London's West End, a stunning building constructed in the nineteenth century in the Tudor style, its white plaster and timber-work occupying the whole corner of two streets. The beautiful interior was firmly in the Arts and Crafts tradition, with polished wooden panelling, carved staircases and even fireplaces. The oak and teak that made such a glowing, warm framework had all come from two decommissioned men-of-war, the HMS *Augustus* and the HMS *Succour*, and the great curved pieces of hull created a wonderful central atrium that extended upwards through the entire six storeys of the building as far as the glass cupola on the top of it.

The whole marvellous store was a testament to William Noble's ambition and drive. His first small shop selling fabrics had been founded on this site, and as it had prospered he'd acquired more and more property to either side. He had then decided to build something that would remain true to his design ideals of beauty and style, as well as creating an oasis of charm and tradition among the tall, classical Regency buildings that surrounded it. They all had rows of matching sash windows, marble floors, chandeliers and Neo-classical plasterwork. Noble's semed to be from an older page in history, with its leaded casements adorned with painted glass, red-tiled gables, high octagonal brick chimneys and the famous wind vane sitting on top of them, a model of the *Mayflower* in gilded copper that looked tiny from the street but was in fact over four feet tall.

Inside, the atmosphere was intimate, almost homely, but with an impressive use of expensive materials. The woodwork was hand-carved and all in keeping with the faux-Tudor design, from the fat balustrades of the atrium well to the screens between the different galleries housing the separate departments. The polished wooden floorboards were all original deck timbers taken from the old ships. In the Great Gallery were additional heraldic touches with the carved and painted arms of the Tudor monarchs and the great poets of Elizabethan times: Sidney, Jonson, Bacon, Herbert and Shakespeare.

It was quite an accomplishment for a boy originally born above a draper's shop in Wiltshire. He had told a friend once: 'If only I had my own shop, I could change the whole look of fashion and decoration,' and when he finally created the most extraordinary store in London, he was as good as his word.

Since then Noble's had become a byword for beautiful fabrics, covetable dresses, fashionable furniture and gorgeous rugs plus all manner of fitments for the best houses. Royal warrants were mounted on the white exterior of the building, though they were now, perhaps, looking a little shabby.

Amanda scrolled down on her screen, looking through the catalogue of offerings from a small fashion house. They were sending her tasters of their spring range for the following year, via an impressively crafted web campaign that led her through their accessories and clothes as though she were walking through her own, very stylish movie.

'Clever,' she said aloud. 'Very smart. And I like their stuff. But I don't think it's right for us.'

After all, 'traditional' was Noble's signature word. It was as if here style had reached its apogee in the nineteenth century, and everything since was considered vulgar, just a passing fad that couldn't hope to match the established and indisputable good taste of Noble's, whose floral prints had been bestsellers for one hundred and fifty years.

Just then her assistant knocked on the door.

'Yes?' said Amanda, turning to face her.

'You've got a visitor.'

'I'm not expecting anyone.' She frowned. 'Who is it?'

'He didn't say.'

An invisible hand pushed the door hard so that it swung open into Amanda's office and revealed Gerry Harbord standing on the threshold.

'Amanda my darling,' he cried, 'up here in your adorable little garret! So sweet.'

'Gerry,' she answered coolly, standing up. 'To what do I owe this honour? That's all right, Jenny, you can go.'

Her apologetic-looking assistant pulled the door to.

'Just coffee for me, Jenny angel, thank you,' Gerry sang out before she was quite out of the room.

'Are you staying long enough?' Amanda asked, one eyebrow raised.

'I hope so, I'm *desperate*.' Gerry came in and sat down in the carved wooden chair opposite her desk. He was wearing bright yellow trousers from Topman, an orange shirt and a white blazer with orange piping, along with white winkle-picker shoes. 'Look at this.' He held up a plastic bag in Noble's signature dark green, with the shop name picked out in coppery-gold plain font. From the bag he pulled out a magenta feather boa. 'See what I found in your haberdashery department? I had to push aside a horde of old ladies as they pored over embroidery kits and disgusting brass buttons, but there are always treasures where you least expect them, aren't there? I must come to Noble's more often. I'd quite forgotten about it.'

Amanda gritted her teeth slightly. 'What is the reason for your visit, Gerry? I am working, you know.'

'Of course I know! And it's very impressive! Everybody thinks it's simply marvellous the way you work when you really don't need to. But then, this place is so handy for the shops, isn't it? I imagine you can just pop out and get whatever you can't find here.'

Amanda took a deep breath as though she were trying to keep calm then said in a level voice, 'Please get to the point.'

'Ah, yes. Now, I haven't seen you since the ball at Templeton House, have I?' Gerry said, stuffing his boa back into its bag.

Amanda felt a flush suffuse her face. She didn't like

to be reminded of that night. It had been a horrible humiliation, the worst night of her life practically. 'No, I don't think we have seen each other,' she said, trying to sound insouciant.

'So you have no idea how fuming I am.' Gerry made a little pout with his lips and frowned.

The door opened and Jenny came in with a tray. She put down two cups of coffee and left discreetly.

'Thanks, Jenny,' Amanda said. 'Here you are, Gerry.'

'Oh, nectar, thank you.' He took up a cup and looked at it. 'Very pretty.'

'From our homeware department.'

'I guessed. It looks like something I see in my Great Aunt Susan's retirement home.'

Amanda felt a rush of annoyance. 'If you've just come here to insult me and my family's business, you can piss off!'

He held up a placatory hand. 'Sorry, sorry, you know me, I can't help teasing.'

Amanda looked at her watch. 'I'm serious, Gerry, you have two more minutes. After that, if you won't leave, I will.'

He put his cup down and leant towards her, his eyes suddenly hard. 'Do you know how much that ball cost me? All right, I won't pretend I don't get a lot of things at trade prices and discounts, but even so it was a hefty sum . . . and I did it all for that ungrateful little hoyden, that *madam*! I gave her so much . . . I gave her everything . . . my time, my advice, my very self.'

'I take it we're talking about Octavia Beaufort.'

Gerry snorted. 'Of course we are. Who else?'

'So she's no longer flavour of the month?'

'No, she's bloody not! She's turned traitor, Amanda!'

Gerry clenched his fists tightly and his knuckles turned white. 'I don't suppose it's all her fault, she's a total naïf. She's been pulled into the wrong orbit by Jasmine Burlington and that awful sullen Rosie. But even so, she must know how much it would hurt me to be dropped by her in the way I have been. She left my party before it was even over – the guest of honour! She disappeared with that louche crowd and I haven't seen her since. Oh, yes, she sent round a bunch of white roses and a rather stunning Mont Blanc pen as a thank you, but I've heard barely a whisper since. And do you know why?'

Amanda shook her head, feeling a little more cheerful than she had been.

'Because of Iseult Rivers-Manners,' hissed Gerry, eyes almost crackling with rage. 'Octavia's been turned . . . she's gone over to the dark side!'

'Oh, dear.' Amanda could barely suppress a smirk. 'Iseult! She could hardly have picked anyone worse, could she?'

Everyone knew of the long-standing feud between Gerry and Iseult. It was based on an argument whose cause had been lost in the mists of time, but ever since they'd loathed one another as only two huge, colourful personalities who were more than a little alike could loathe one another. It was well known in society that one could be friends with both only by keeping very quiet about one's divided loyalties. It was no more done to regale Gerry with tales of frolicsome week-ends spent at Iseult's Somerset house than it was to mention to Iseult the high jinks at Gerry's handsome hunting lodge in Hampshire.

'I don't need to tell you how wounded I am. Iseult

has Octavia running with her pack now. She's doing this fashion show for her young protégé Wildblood and apparently Octavia's going to be the star in it. It makes me grind my teeth down to the bone! I was there first! I found her first,' he finished petulantly.

'Well, I'm very sorry for you, but I don't really see what any of this has to do with me.'

Gerry pushed his cup further on to Amanda's desk and stood up. He walked over to the little casement window with its leaded lights and gazed out over the street below. He turned slowly back to face Amanda. Then he said in a tight voice: 'I hear that La Beaufort isn't exactly riding high in your estimation either. Didn't she throw a jug of water over you at my party, or did I hear wrong? Apparently a very pretty Temperley dress was completely spoiled.'

Amanda cocked her head awkwardly. 'No. You're right. She did drench me.' Amanda remembered very well how it had felt: the shock of that cold water, the realisation that her expensive dress and beautiful hairstyle were soaked, perhaps ruined, the sense of humiliation as everyone stared and muttered. The rage she'd felt ever since whenever she thought about it – though she tried not to – came back redoubled.

'You see,' Gerry said, coming towards her, 'that little cow doesn't have the first clue how to behave!'

'She's a bitch,' Amanda said bitterly. 'A class-A bitch. She made a fool of me in front of everyone at that party. No one's ever treated me like that before.'

'You're right. And now she's gone off with Iseult Rivers-Manners, the thing that hurts me most in the world. Dropped me like a hot potato. After everything I did for her! And,' Gerry's expression turned almost sly, 'there's one more thing. My sources tell me that Octavia has some suitors buzzing around her honeypot. And one of them is Ferdy Logan.'

Amanda tried not to react, but it was hard. Ferdy? Her ex-boyfriend? That was a little too close for comfort. 'I see,' she said.

'She's trouble,' declared Gerry. 'We'll rue the day she ever appeared! I mean it, Amanda, she's making life nasty for all of us. Well, if she wants to play with the big boys, she's going to have to get used to our methods. We can play dirty if we're forced to, right? I think we should join forces. It's time to think about bringing little Miss Beaufort down a peg or two, don't you agree?'

'Do you know what, Gerry?' Amanda said cheerfully. 'I think I do. And I'll enjoy doing it quite a lot.'

16

Preparations for the fashion show were going swimmingly. Iseult had secured a venue and was using every contact in her little black book, shamelessly pulling strings to get the big names and the acres of press that would surely follow.

Roddy was having trouble, though. According to Iseult, he was suffering from creative block.

'He's full of confidence usually, really a very self-assured and secure person,' Iseult told Octavia one night in Hurley's, a private members' club in Shepherd's Market. They sat in a dark corner on a low, velvet sofa, a single lamp glowing dimly on the table next to them. 'He's loved, you see. Such an advantage in life. Despite the fact that he's the youngest of six children or something like that, his parents utterly adore him, especially his mother. Not every working-class Catholic woman would be supportive of a bolshie, gay, dress-designing son, but Mrs Wilcox is.'

'Wilcox?' asked Octavia, puzzled. 'I thought his name was Wildblood?'

'It is now,' said Iseult with a laugh. 'But it used to

be Wilcox. Rod Wilcox. I don't know about you, but I didn't think that had quite the right ring for a fashion label. Rod Wilcox doesn't sound like a man destined for Paris and couture greatness. Roddy Wildblood on the other hand . . .' She shrugged. 'I suggested it and he agreed.'

Despite the darkness of their surroundings, Iseult was wearing sunglasses, her lips painted the usual blood red colour, and was dressed in a long vividly embroidered kimono with huge bell sleeves and a gorgeous sash. She'd teamed it with her trademark towering shoes. 'So he's lucky like that, having a mother's love to fall back on.' Iseult gave a small tight smile. 'From which you'll probably infer that I don't have any such thing. And you'd be quite right. My mother, or Mrs Rivers-Manners as I call her, left me when I was just a child. She was a very honest person, you know – there were no lies about Father Christmas or the damned tooth fairy for me – but even so she never told me the truth: that she was about to leave me and break my heart. And heartbreak when you're young . . . it's very hard to shake it off.'

Octavia blinked at her. 'My mother left me too,' she said in a small voice. Inside, she felt quite surprised. Iseult obviously felt permanently damaged by her mother's departure. *Should I feel like that too?* wondered Octavia. *Perhaps I should.* After all, her mother had vanished from her and Flora's lives when they were only four years old – Octavia remembered almost nothing about that time and had only a few, fleeting recollections of her: the scent of her perfume, the sheen of her glossy brown hair, a soft cheek and some hasty kisses. Once, in the library at Homerton,

143

she and Flora had discovered an old photo album and inside were pictures from their parents' wedding day, artistic black-and-white shots of the occasion, the guests dressed up in early-eighties splendour, the men with shaggy hair and the women with Lady Di flicks or long tresses backcombed at the top. It was obviously a lavish occasion, with the wedding in a local church and then a grand reception held in a marquee in the gardens of Homerton. It was the bride and groom who fascinated the girls the most, though. They'd spent hours staring at all the photographs they both appeared in.

'She's beautiful,' Octavia would say, stroking the photograph that showed her parents dancing together, the bridegroom bending down to hear something his bride was whispering in his ear. 'What do you think she's saying to him?'

'She's saying, "Oh, my darling, I'll be yours for ever",' Flora had guessed. 'I love her dress.'

It was a flounced ivory silk dress, mushrooming out from the net petticoats worn underneath, off the shoulder but with large puffed sleeves to the elbow. Bows and lace adorned it everywhere. The bride wore a wreath of flowers in her short curly brown hair, and the black-and-white of the photograph still showed the shimmer of her frosted lipstick, sparkly eyeshadow and dark streaks of blusher on each cheek.

'She looks like a princess,' Octavia agreed. She looked at their father then, with his dark moustache and raffish smile. 'And Daddy must have been her prince.'

Then they would put the album away and, late at night, would spin stories about Diane and Arthur and their lives together. Their father, they knew, was dead. Their mother, Aunt Frances had told them, had gone away many years earlier and never been heard of since. They both agreed that this must be standard behaviour in princesses whose princes had been killed, and neither of them ever thought to wonder if she should have stayed to look after her babies. She must have done whatever was necessary, surely. One day they went to look in the album and it was gone, and then even the photographs were only memories. As they grew older, the fairy tale began to fade away altogether, and Octavia had accepted long ago that she had no mother or father, just Aunt Frances and the Brigadier, the closest thing to parents she would ever know.

But, she thought with a creeping sense of awfulness, perhaps that was wrong. Perhaps, for all these years, she had been asleep, like the Sleeping Beauty Iseult had called her – asleep to the fact that she'd suffered something unusual and damaging when she'd grown up in never really knowing either of her parents.

But I don't want to know! she thought fiercely, pushing away the disconcerting thought as hard as she could. *I refuse to! I've just found my freedom, and I'm just discovering life. I won't have it spoilt now, just when I've broken free.*

Iseult stared at her impassively from behind her sunglasses, as though watching all these emotions scroll across Octavia's face. 'Families are pure horror,' she said almost kindly, 'and best forgotten about. They do say that a wretched childhood can make one interesting and creative. I tend to think misery breeds misery. But . . . enough of that. Let's have some more champagne. I've always found Moët a very satisfactory cure for life's ills. And I'll tell you all about my plan for us to decamp to Mabbes, so that Roddy can rediscover his muse – I want you to come too, it's absolutely vital. Will you?'

'Mabbes?'

'It's my family home, a silly old pile in the country, falling to pieces but charming. I share it with my sisters. All of us childless and unmarried, like sad spinsters from Jane Austen. Probably for the best. We'd only ruin more young lives, passing on our dreadful family streak of melancholia. So that's settled. You'll come. Good.' Iseult smiled, lowering her sunglasses for a moment so that Octavia could see her strange yellow-green eyes. 'I think you'll bring some welcome sparkle to Mabbes.'

Octavia got home to find the drawing room full of flowers, with Flora and Vicky sitting in the middle of them all, Flora hunched tightly on the sofa, and Vicky looking half amused and half angry.

'I d-d-don't want to,' Flora was saying obstinately as Octavia came in. Her stammer was worse, Octavia noticed. Usually it was better with Vicky, but it was only with Octavia that it disappeared entirely.

'What's all this?' She asked, gesturing at the roses displayed everywhere. 'Have you bought a florist's?'

Flora looked over at her, a faint expression of reproach in her eyes. 'Where were you last night, Tavy? You didn't come back till very late.'

Octavia remembered. She'd been at a party with Jasmine and Rosie, in some boy's Mayfair flat. She'd got very drunk and had a vague memory of collapsing on the hall floor when she returned, and Vicky helping her to the loo before she'd puked her guts up. She flushed and glanced at her cousin, who was looking rather stern. 'I was out . . . and today we had rehearsals for the fashion show. Why, what's happened?'

'I'm afraid that Flora was mugged yesterday,' Vicky said gravely.

Octavia gasped, her hands flying to her face in fright.

'Don't worry,' Vicky said quickly, 'she's fine, aren't you, Flora? But it could have been nasty.' She swiftly retold Flora's account of what had happened the night before. 'I'm trying to persuade her to go to the police,' she finished.

'I don't w-w-want to, it was my own fault,' Flora said sullenly. She looked tired, Octavia thought, and her eyes dull. 'And I've told you, I'm not going out.'

Octavia couldn't speak. She was still recovering from the rush of fear that had gripped her while Vicky was telling the story.

'I still think you should go to the police,' their cousin said gently. 'We ought to alert them to these people.'

Flora stayed silent, staring at the floor, her mouth in a tight line.

Vicky looked over at Octavia. 'Flora's decided she's not going back to her art course either. It's such a shame when she was enjoying it so much.' She stood up. 'I'm going to leave you two alone if that's okay. I've got some admin to deal with. I'll see you later.'

As soon as she'd gone, Octavia rushed over to her sister and hugged her, tears in her eyes. 'God, I'm so pleased you're all right!'

'I was an idiot,' Flora said, her expression suddenly frustrated. 'It was all my own fault. I knew this would happen if I tried to do anything alone.'

'It's not your fault you were attacked!' Octavia felt furious on her sister's behalf. 'They're the criminals, not you. But who was this man . . . the one who rescued you?'

'His name is Otto.' Flora smiled weakly for the first time. 'He sent all these flowers today with a very sweet note saying he hoped I'd recovered. A taxi arrived this morning, absolutely crammed with bouquets of roses. Aren't they gorgeous?'

'Beautiful.' Octavia stared around at the stunning blooms. 'Well, thank goodness for this Otto man. It sounds as though it could have been very dangerous otherwise.' She glanced anxiously at her sister. 'Are you sure you want to give up your course, though? You were loving it so much.'

Flora looked up at her with panicky eyes. 'I can't, Tavy, I can't go back. Not right now . . . maybe later . . . maybe when I've recovered.'

'All right,' she said quickly. 'Don't rush it. You've had a frightening experience. Oh, dear . . .' She felt a pang of guilt and looked away.

'What is it?'

'I have to go away in a few days. Iseult wants me to go to her country house so we can prepare for the show. I said I would . . .' Octavia bit her lip, worried. 'I'll tell her I can't go.'

'Don't be silly, you must. I'll be perfectly fine.'

'Really?' Octavia knew she ought to stay, but the longing to be with her new friends, and at Iseult's house, was overpowering.

'Of course,' Flora said. 'You go. Have fun. I'll be fine here with Vicky.'

Octavia stared into her sister's blue eyes, the mirror image of her own. She knew that in their depths she could see fear. *But I'll only be away for a few days,* she told herself, *and after that I'll devote myself to Flora and to making sure she's okay.*

'As long as you don't mind?' she said.

'I don't.' Flora took her hand and squeezed it. 'Honestly.'

17

Octavia made sure that she stayed at home with Flora for the next two days, spending as much time as she could with her twin and trying to help her recover from the ordeal. Flora was quieter than ever, she noticed, and she worried that her sister wasn't eating enough either. Octavia coaxed her with delicious meals sent up from the kitchen, but while Flora tried to eat for her sister's sake, she obviously didn't have much of an appetite.

The trouble was that only half of Octavia's mind was on Flora's problems. The other half was continually on the forthcoming visit to Mabbes, and what might lie ahead for her there. Iseult had mentioned casually that she'd invited some boys to come and stay, and Octavia was sure she must have invited Ferdy Logan who had been flirting with increasing intensity every time they met. The prospect of spending some time with him was overwhelmingly exciting; she couldn't help daydreaming about it almost constantly.

In the pool she swam endless lengths, enjoying the sensation of the warm water caressing her body while she imagined what it might be like to have Ferdy put his arms around her and kiss her. She hadn't been kissed for six years, not since the crazily passionate summer of the year she found Brandon.

They had been spending it in Connecticut, at the enormous farm Aunt Frances owned there thanks to an inheritance from a wealthy American relative. It was vast enough for them to have all the freedom they wanted and never worry about straying off their own land. It was there that she and Flora had learnt to ride, going off for hours on their horses, able to enjoy the illusion of leading a pioneering, adventurous lifestyle, while all the time remaining safely at home. Whenever they were in Connecticut, their aunt saw it as her duty to improve their physical skills and attainments: there were swimming lessons in the Olympic-sized pool, riding and dressage instruction, and, of course, tennis, the sport every elegant young woman should be able to play with grace and style.

The coach came from a local country club, a cheerful man with a leathery orange tan, a bristling grey moustache and muscles that were beginning to look a bit stringy. Every morning during their summer stays, he would arrive with his bag of rackets and tub of balls to put them through their paces and improve their strokes. The girls both enjoyed tennis and, if they weren't exactly the Williams sisters, were good enough to play a decent game. They were both at ease with Burt, enough so that Flora almost lost her stammer with him, and liked his easy-going warmth and informality.

Then, one summer when the twins were fifteen, Burt had not come to coach them. He was in hospital,

151

it transpired, having an operation that would mean some months of recuperation afterwards. His son Brandon was sent instead, an arrangement that Aunt Frances seemed happy enough with when it was explained to her.

But then, she hadn't seen Brandon. When Octavia had first laid eyes on him, she'd gasped. The sight of him was like a punch to her stomach. He was as beautiful as a Greek god, with blond hair that glowed in the summer sunshine, a tan that his tennis whites made appear even more bronzed, and a superb body that radiated all the youth and health of a nineteen-year-old athlete. He moved with a languid feline grace that transformed itself into pure power when he hit a ball or raced across the court to make a difficult volley, slamming it back with precision and tightly controlled force.

'I'm in love,' Octavia had said to Flora as they left the court after that first lesson, their cheeks flushed and hair damp with sweat.

'He *is* gorgeous,' Flora agreed.

'Don't be in love with him,' Octavia said swiftly, trying not to sound as desperate as she felt. 'Please? Let me be in love with him on my own.' Throughout their lives they had shared every passion, but Octavia wanted this time to be different.

'You can if you like,' Flora said equably, 'I don't see what difference it will make. It's not as though anything can ever happen. Anyway, who am I allowed to be in love with?'

'You can be in love with Antonio,' offered Octavia, and then they both collapsed in giggles because their riding instructor was a barrel-chested man with a huge head and torso and a very small lower half with tiny bandy legs; both Flora and Octavia found him hilarious.

But Flora was wrong – something could and did happen. Octavia did her best to communicate her attraction to the tennis coach with her eyes and movements – fluttering glances over her shoulder, coy smiles, requests for help in gripping her racket correctly that meant he had to stand behind her and put his arms around her – and as he was a healthy, heterosexual nineteen-year-old, he soon responded to the signals he was getting from the gorgeous blonde.

One day after many longing glances had passed between them, Brandon lingered after the lesson. He came up to her and said quietly to Octavia, 'Hey, any chance we could maybe have a little time on our own? Would your aunt let me take you out on a date?'

'No chance of that, I'm afraid,' Octavia had replied throatily, her heart pounding with excitement and her whole body responding to his proximity. 'She would never allow it. But I know what we could do, if you like . . .'

She already had her plans drawn up. She'd spent many night-time hours gazing wide-eyed into the darkness formulating how she could be alone with Brandon if the opportunity should ever arise. As she explained to him what they could do, he looked rather startled as his shy request for a date was transformed into a clandestine meeting, but still keen for all that.

They would have to meet early in the morning, Octavia explained. She couldn't get away in the early evening, and the alarms went on at 9 p.m. After that there was no way she could get out of the house or off the grounds. But the alarms were switched off early, at 5 a.m. when the morning staff arrived, and as breakfast wasn't until 9 a.m. while they were in Connecticut, this was her only chance to get out unobserved.

'So, can you do it?' she said, her eyes shining. 'Can you meet me at the lake house at five-thirty tomorrow morning?'

'Sure,' Brandon said, still a little taken aback but entering into the spirit of her request with a pleased expression. 'Why not? It's crazy but maybe it'll be fun.' He frowned. 'But how am I going to get down there?'

'The gateman knows you, doesn't he? Just say my aunt has requested some early-morning instruction. Her word is law round here, they won't question you. And she's well known for doing things at odd times, whenever suits her.' Octavia sounded more confident than she felt. She was sure that the gateman would just wave Brandon through but it was still a risk. She had to take it, though.

'Okay,' he said, reassured. 'I'll see you tomorrow.'

She'd been so excited it was almost impossible to sleep, and when she did it was to be tormented by delicious dreams of seeing Brandon that then turned into horrible sickening nightmares of discovery and punishment. She was wide awake at 4 a.m. and up at 4.30, showering in her bathroom and then spending half an hour rubbing scented lotions into her skin and drying her hair into a long golden curtain. The girls were only allowed a very little make-up, so she had to content herself with just some mascara on her lashes and a DIY lipstick, using a crayon from the art box and some Vaseline to give her lips some light redness and gloss. The effect was much better than she'd expected.

Then she'd slipped down to the small sitting room with French windows out on to the terrace at the back of the house. As she unlocked them she held her breath, half expecting to hear the alarms start wailing, but there was nothing. She opened them to the cool morning air, the sky a soft unclouded blue and the sunlight pure, then stepped out on to the terrace. She made her way towards the lake, staying close to the hedges when she had to pass under her aunt's window, but as soon as she was clear of the house, she began to run, her feet soon wet from the still-damp grass. She reached the lake house, panting and triumphant, but was disappointed to find that Brandon wasn't there. Octavia sat outside and waited, her knees tucked up under her chin and her arms wrapped round her legs as she stared out over the dark purply blue waters of the lake. The old rowing boat bobbed about in the reeds where it was tethered to the jetty.

'Hey, good morning,' came a laughing voice from behind her. She looked round to see Brandon striding towards her through the shaggy grass behind the lake house. 'I don't get up this early for just anyone, you know.'

'Thanks for coming,' Octavia said breathlessly. She was about to stand up, but he came and sat down next to her. He was in his tennis kit, sparkling white shorts and white polo shirt, and she could see the golden hairs on his legs. His nearness was making her dizzy. *God, he's gorgeous,* she thought, high on the realisation that her plan had worked – here they were, together, alone. *I've never been alone with a boy in my life,* she realised. This might be her only chance. She couldn't waste it.

'It's beautiful here,' Brandon said softly. 'Almost as beautiful as you.'

Her stomach flipped with pleasure. 'Thank you,' she said, flushing.

'So all this meeting at dawn stuff – I guess you don't get much freedom, right?'

She nodded, noticing his eyes wre light blue with dark rims around the iris. He was so handsome she could hardly think straight.

'Uh-huh. I've met girls like you before. Kind of over-protected, you know? Parents don't realise it achieves the opposite effect. It's always the ones who are restricted the most who turn into the wildest.' He grinned. 'But you're not quite there yet, are you? How old are you? Seventeen?'

Octavia nodded, not wanting to give the lie a voice. *I can't risk him leaving,* she told herself. *If he guesses I'm fifteen, he'll definitely go . . .*

'Sweet seventeen,' he murmured. He put out his hand and touched her hair. 'And very hot.'

She'd been meaning to play it cool but she simply couldn't help herself: she turned her body to face him full on and raised her face to his. The next moment, his lips were pressed against hers and she was opening her mouth to his probing tongue in her first kiss.

Her mind whirled; she was incapable of thinking of anything except how blissful the sensation of kissing was. It was like soaring away on a magic carpet into a night of stars as she felt herself melt into his arms, her whole being centred on the unfamiliar sensation of their two mouths pressed together.

Then she became aware that his hands were roaming all over her, but in particular straying to her chest where they were pressing down on her breasts, squeezing and rubbing them through the light cotton of her shirt. He pulled away from her kiss for a moment, panting, his eyes glassy. 'How far do you want to go?' he asked breathlessly. 'Which base?'

She had no idea what he was talking about. 'I don't care,' she said quickly, keen only to renew those hot kisses.

'You don't?' He looked half pleased, half concerned.

'Uh-uh.' She pushed her mouth back against his, impatient to taste him again and to feel that soaring pleasure.

They kissed for a very long time, lying back on the wooden deck, their hands roaming all over each other. Brandon's returned over and over to her breasts until Octavia could feel her nipples become tight and sensitive. She was aching between her legs and aware that she was wet there too: she had the overwhelming sensation that all this was building up to something, though to what she couldn't guess. She knew what the mechanics of intercourse were – Miss Bailey had taught them basic reproductive biology in a cold, formal way – but that didn't explain this curious physical yearning, a sense of being propelled towards some outcome she didn't yet understand.

All she knew was that when Brandon finally pulled away, looked at his watch and swore, saying he had to go, she felt a terrible sensation of unsatisfied longing.

'I'll see you later,' he said ruefully, standing up. For the first time, she saw the hardness in his shorts. 'God, you've driven me crazy. But I gotta go.'

'I suppose I'd better get back to the house. They'll all be up soon.' Octavia sighed.

'I'll see you on the court,' Brandon said, and with a smile was retreating across the grass.

Back at the house, Flora was anxiously looking out for her sister. 'Where have you been?' she demanded. 'Your room was empty! It's nearly time for breakfast!' Then she stared at her sister's face. 'You look different – what have you been doing?'

'I'll tell you later,' Octavia said. 'You won't believe it. Now come on, we can't keep the muesli waiting, can we?'

Flora had been appalled by the risks she'd run when Octavia told her what she'd done. 'What if you'd got caught?' she'd cried.

'I didn't. And I'm going to do it again,' Octavia said, her voice determined. 'So don't try and stop me.'

Seeing Brandon on the tennis court later that morning had been more delicious than ever. He had taken extra care over her ground strokes, wrapping his body round hers to demonstrate how to move the racket. He had said nothing in front of Flora, but at the end of the lesson had murmured, 'Same time tomorrow?' and Octavia had nodded, still bubbling inside with excitement and full of that strange languid longing that was simultaneously wonderful and frustrating.

The next week had been spent in an erotic dream. She'd almost sleepwalked through life, living only for those two hours before the rest of the world was awake when she and Brandon were together. They became more adventurous, and she had touched his hard penis, first slipping her hand down his shorts to brush its velvety soft tip with her fingers and then holding its hot weight in her palm. She had begun trying to move her hand up and down it and Brandon had responded so enthusiastically that she'd known she was doing something right. A few times he put his own hand over hers and helped her rub harder and harder until he had stiffened and made a high sobbing noise and then her hand had been covered in warm blobs of white stuff. Then he'd smiled at her, kissed her and thanked her softly.

He had begun to explore her most secret places as well, pushing his hand up under her skirt, hooking a finger under the elastic of her panties and rubbing the soft wet entrance to her pussy. He'd stroked upwards until he hit that hard little nub that was so desperately sensitive, that seemed to long for his touch at the same time as being almost unable to bear it. Despite her gasps and the way she'd twitched when he touched it, he'd go on playing with it until she felt on the brink of something huge, like being in a roller-coaster poised on the summit of its highest loop, about to plummet downwards. When he wasn't toying with that electric bud, he was pushing his fingers further and further inside her, making her want to open her thighs to him and welcome him in. He unbuttoned her shirt, lifted her bra and sucked on her nipples until they were hard, dark-pink nuggets and she thought her whole pussy was melting with liquid longing.

Then, one morning, they took off their clothes, pressing their naked flesh together. Brandon's rearing cock pushed and rubbed against her, getting closer and closer to finding its way inside her, but they stopped, breathless and gasping, just before it could press in.

Tomorrow, she thought, *we'll go all the way . . .*

But the next morning, just after Brandon had arrived and they were kissing passionately on the cushions she'd laid out on the deck, they were interrupted by a shout. They scrambled to their feet, Octavia's heart pounding with panic. It was a security guard from the gate lodge.

'Hey, you, tennis boy!' he was shouting. 'What the hell do you think you're doing?' He held his walkie talkie up like a weapon, obviously about to radio his colleagues.

'Stop!' cried Octavia.

The guard approached, his face wary. Then he saw who was with the tennis coach and his face cleared, understanding dawning. 'Oh, I see. I get it . . . a nice little get-together happening here, huh?'

'Please don't tell,' Octavia begged as the guard came up to them. 'We're not doing anything wrong . . .'

'That all depends, miss,' the guard said, giving Brandon a look. 'You're just a kid.'

'Please, please, don't tell!'

He frowned and then relented. 'Listen, I ain't going to spill the beans on you. I know what your aunt's like, we all do. But that don't mean I'm gonna let this guy back in for his early-morning visits, okay? You better stop all that right now. It's for the best,' he added, seeing Octavia's stricken expression. 'I'm a father with daughters, and I can tell you, I'm doing you a favour.' He turned back to Brandon. 'Now get out of here.'

'Yes, sir,' mumbled Brandon, and, giving Octavia an apologetic look, headed back towards the gate.

Someone must have said something because at 11 o'clock that morning it was a tracksuited lady coach who arrived to take the lesson. Brandon never came back. There were no other repercussions and nothing was ever said. It was as if he had never existed.

For months after that Octavia had been driven wild by her newly awakened desire until at last, unslaked, it had died down to a level where she was able to cope with her physical needs alone, thanks to the dream of Brandon she kept alive through the power of her imagination and her own exploration.

When she finally found the release she'd been searching for, it wasn't in Brandon's arms, the weight of his body on hers, but on her own, in the solitude of her four-poster bed at Homerton. It was pleasurable and a triumph of sorts, but she still longed for what she was sure was the ultimate climax: being driven to ecstasy in the arms of a man.

Is Ferdy that man? she wondered now, a pleasant shiver running through her. *Maybe. Maybe he is.*

18

'You can't hide it from me,' Vicky said seriously. 'I'm living here with you. I can see what's going on.'

They were in Flora's bedroom, Flora curled up under the covers of her bed, Vicky in the velvet button-back armchair opposite.

'What do you mean?' Flora said, her voice muffled by the pillow. She felt as though the only safe place in the world was here, tucked away from the world under the silk duvet in an almost stiflingly warm little cocoon.

'You were doing so well at the art school. But now . . . Flora, you *never* go out. You haven't stepped outside the front door for nearly a week.'

'What do you expect?' Irritation surged through her. 'I was attacked!' The fear had grown inside her until she could feel it crippling her. All she wanted to do was stay somewhere safe, where no one could find her and hurt her.

'I know,' Vicky said, her voice soft and compassionate. 'I think you should see a doctor or a counsellor. Someone who can help you get over it.'

Flora stayed stubbornly silent. She didn't trust doctors. Aunt Frances had paraded them in front of dozens and not one had seen to the heart of the problem. Outsiders couldn't help. They couldn't understand. Only Octavia could help her, and she was leaving in the morning for her trip away.

There was a pause and then Vicky spoke again.

'I want you to think about coming out with me. It's not right for you to be shut away, and the longer it lasts, the harder it will be to go out. Maybe tomorrow night, or the night after, we could go out together. Will you think about it?'

Flora sighed. 'Okay . . . I'll think about it.'

'Good.' Vicky got up. 'Now try and get some sleep. You still look so tired. Call me if you need anything.'

Octavia finished packing the bag she was taking to Mabbes and zipped it shut. She felt a pleasurable tingle of excitement at the prospect of the next few days. But, right now, she had to see Flora.

She jumped up and padded out into the corridor to make her way towards her sister's rooms. As she crossed the landing, Vicky appeared on the stairs.

'Hi, Octavia, where are you going?'

'To see Flora, of course,' replied Octavia. Vicky, she noticed, was wearing a plain grey tee-shirt with an excellent cut that betrayed the fact it was a designer label, and what was obviously a very expensive black cashmere cardigan along with black skinny jeans and grey Converse trainers.

She's looking much more stylish, Octavia thought. *And I'm sure her hair's different too. We must be paying her well.*

Vicky came quickly up the stairs and stood in front of Octavia, blocking the way to Flora's bedroom door. 'I really don't think you should do that,' she said, her voice low but authoritative. 'Flora's very tired. I've given her a pill to help her get off.'

Octavia blinked at her cousin in surprise. 'Are you stopping me from seeing my own sister?' she asked icily.

'I'm just saying I don't think it's a good idea. She's probably asleep by now.'

'I see.' Octavia gave her a hard stare. 'I think you should remember that you work for me, Vicky. You don't tell me what to do.'

'Actually,' Vicky said, her voice still low and measured, 'I work for Flora. My contract was issued and signed by her. It's my job to look after her, and that's what I'm doing. She's not as tough as you, Octavia, you must know that. After what's happened, she's terrified of going outside. She's still getting over it and for now she really needs to sleep. She's completely drained.' Vicky smiled, her eyes suddenly warm. 'Talk to her tomorrow, by all means, or call her from the place you're staying. I know she'd love it. All I'm saying is – leave her to sleep for now.'

Octavia hovered uncertainly, wondering what to do. She didn't want to back down, but what Vicky said sounded reasonable enough – and waking a tired Flora wouldn't be the ideal basis for a heart to heart. It could wait. 'All right,' she said. 'I'll leave her to it. But only because I don't want to wake her up if she's sleeping. Not because you say so.'

'Understood.' Vicky came a little closer. 'Listen, Octavia, I'm not here to make your life more difficult.

164

I'm here to make it easier. I'm your cousin. You can trust me, you know.'

'I know. It's all fine. It's all good. I'm going to bed – I've got a busy week coming up and I'm travelling tomorrow. Good night, Vicky.' She turned her back on her cousin and made her way along the corridor, aware all the time of Vicky's eyes on her. And somehow, though she didn't know why, Octavia felt uncomfortable.

19

The gathering at Mabbes was supposed to be for work, with Roddy designing and creating in the great solarium, the girls there to be his models and muses, and Iseult to oversee everything. But almost from the moment they arrived, driven up the long winding driveway in Iseult's shabby old Ford Mondeo – 'Such a reliable car!' she said. 'I *never* have to get it fixed and nobody ever wants to steal it!' – the whole thing quickly turned into a party. Perhaps it was because Iseult had invited some boys as well, a gaggle of handsome lads to amuse the girls, who arrived a few hours afterwards, ready to stuff away the piles of flapjacks and scones that the housekeeper had made for tea.

Octavia was enchanted at once, first by the house itself, which stood at the heart of a series of gardens that must once have been magnificent and manicured but was now a wilderness of trees, flowers and shaggy shrubs cut through with mouldering stone walls. From a distance the house looked solid and strong, a large Victorian mansion, but on closer inspection it seemed to be crumbling away into the garden, its red brick softened by over a century of Somerset rain, its roof thick with moss and missing the occasional tile, the chimneys tilted and precarious and the window frames rotting away around their glass panes. At the front door one corner of the Gothic-style brick porch was being supported by a piece of timber wedged between the roof and a pile of paving stones.

'Don't worry about that, I shouldn't think it'll fall down,' Iseult said breezily as the girls walked a trifle nervously underneath. 'It hasn't so far, and it's been there ten years or so.'

Inside the house was just as charming, but just as dilapidated. 'It's a ten-bucket job these days,' explained Iseult. 'You'll see, it's simply falling to bits. We've had to abandon the west wing altogether. We've stuck up some plastic where the worst holes are, and we've shut the door on it, just hoping it won't get any worse. No money, you see. But don't worry, we'll be perfectly comfortable.'

Octavia was reminded of a black-and-white film she'd seen once about a girls' boarding school where the pupils ran riot, treating the place like a glorious playground. That was how she felt about this place. As soon as they arrived, she was seized by high spirits and a sense of being utterly free and unrestricted. The state of the house, with its frowsy grandeur, seemed to add to the sense of grown-ups being absent. It was so unlike the buffed and polished perfection of Aunt Frances's house, the atmosphere one of anything goes.

Her room was dusty and uncared for, though at least the sheets looked clean. A large patch of ugly brown damp disfigured one corner, with the wallpaper peeling away in long dark strips, but the view from the bay window was gorgeous, the soft Somerset countryside rolling away into the distance.

They opened bottles of wine almost as soon as they arrived. Roddy took one and disappeared into the solarium, which looked to Octavia like a very large conservatory but without the mass of plants and elegant cane furniture that she remembered in Aunt Frances's version. All of Roddy's work, fabrics and equipment had been delivered earlier by a courier company and he was now ready to let his creativity come flooding back, with the help of Sauvignon Blanc and endless Marlboro Reds.

Meanwhile, the others lazed around and got slowly, comfortably drunk on the bottles of cheap supermarket plonk with which Iseult stocked her cellar.

'So . . . hi. How are things?' asked a low voice beside her as Octavia flicked through a magazine while lying on a sofa in the drawing room. 'It's great to see you again.'

She looked up, and her stomach did a pleasant forward roll of excitement at the sound of Ferdy's voice. As casually as she could manage, she said, 'Oh, yeah. Hi. I'm fine, thanks. How are you?'

She took in his good looks: a smoothly handsome face with soft, boyish features, given an almost feminine cast by full lips with a pronounced cupid's bow. His dark brown hair was carefully styled into messiness and his tall frame looked lean in a pair of baggy jeans and a vintage New York Dolls tee-shirt.

'Great.' He grinned. 'I didn't realise you were going to be here.'

'I didn't realise *you* were going to be here,' Octavia said, and smiled back. She could feel her skin tingling as her mind raced over various possibilities. They were both staying here for the weekend. Would he try to kiss her again? Surely he was bound to. Would she let him? Oh . . . She felt her lips part involuntarily at the thought of it. *Yes.*

'Then it must be fate, I guess,' he said, and grinned again. 'Listen, do you want to—'

'Ferdy!' came Iseult's insistent cry from the hallway. 'Come here at once! I need you!'

He looked at Octavia, his brown eyes a touch rueful. 'Gotta go. No one ignores Iseult, as I guess you already know. But don't move, okay? We're going out to explore the gardens later, maybe you'd like to come.'

'Yeah, sounds good,' Octavia replied casually, hoping she seemed nonchalant.

'Cool. Won't be long.' Ferdy got up and headed for the door. She watched him go, suddenly giddy with lust. *Oh, God, I hope he wants to kiss me.* She was desperate for a kiss, a real proper kiss. *Maybe tonight,* she told herself, *maybe tonight . . .*

20

I'm not quite sure how this happened, Flora thought,
bemused.

This afternoon she'd been curled up in bed, happy
to be locked away from the world in her place of security. Now here she was, drinking an elderflower and
prosecco cocktail in the bar of Claridge's, surrounded
by people.

'You're doing fine,' Vicky whispered, smiling, her
green eyes sparkling. 'Really amazing. Are you having
fun?'

'I don't know . . . sort of, I guess. It's weird to be out.'

She hadn't wanted to come. She'd protested, but
her cousin had been insistent. 'Why should Octavia
have all the fun?' she'd asked as she flung open the
doors to Flora's vast walk-in dressing room. It was
rather empty, certainly compared to Octavia's which
was overflowing with clothes, but there was still plenty
to pick from.

'This is wonderful,' Vicky had declared, scooping
up a silk jersey dress in a subtle mocha and pink print
with a tie panel at the waist. 'Ooh, it's Issa.'

'Octavia bought it and then decided she didn't want it,' Flora said, taking it from her and examining it. 'Yes, it is pretty.'

'Put it on. Now what should you wear with it?' Vicky turned to the racks of shoes. 'You're not exactly Imelda Marcos, are you? You've only got one decent pair of heels.' She picked up a pair of silver Charlotte Olympia sandals. 'Better put these on. Now, brush your hair, put on some lipstick and mascara, and we'll go out, all right? I think you need it.'

Forty minutes later they were ready. Vicky was wearing a dark green halter-neck dress with a full skirt scattered with tiny daisies, and white ballet slippers. 'Ooh, you look fantastic,' she said sincerely as Flora came down the stairs into the hall. 'That fits you so well.'

Flora grinned. 'I guess it helps having a sister who's identical to me – she can do my legwork.' She glanced at herself in the huge oak-framed mirror on the wall. Perhaps she did look all right. She'd been worried that the mocha and pink would wash her out but instead it gave her a delicate ivory look and the silk jersey glowed softly in the electric light, while her blonde hair, scooped back into a loose ponytail, glittered.

'You look wonderful. Now come on, Steve is outside ready to drive us wherever we want to go.'

Flora found the trip from the front door to the car hard enough. As soon as she was outside, she began to shake and felt a cold sweat break out on her forehead. Her breath came quickly and she could hear a tiny squeak of fear which she realised came from her. Terror streaked through her. She felt sure that someone was about to pounce on her, though from which direction she had no idea.

Vicky reassured her that everything was fine as Steve opened the door to the Mercedes. The next minute they were sitting on the slippery leather seats and the car was pulling smoothly away. Only minutes later Steve brought them to a halt in front of the hotel in Brook Street, and the doorman was stepping forward to open the door so that they could get out. Vicky took the lead and Flora followed as they walked along the red carpet that led into the hotel.

Across the road a few paparazzi were loitering with their cameras – someone famous was inside. When they saw Flora, they lifted the cameras but dropped them again, looking puzzled and muttering among themselves, obviously wondering who she was.

They went to the bar, and Vicky ordered them each a cocktail. When the drinks came they were palest green, fizzy and curiously refreshing. Flora savoured the sweetness and the gentle explosion of bubbles across her tongue.

'How are you feeling?' Vicky asked.

'Not too bad. Calmer,' Flora said. She looked about. All these people made her anxious, she couldn't help that. And she couldn't explain to Vicky her strange fear of being looked at. As soon as she felt someone's eyes on her, she wanted to shrink inside herself and disappear. It seemed ridiculous to put on a pretty dress and come to a place like this when it was what she hated most . . . but as Vicky started to chatter away, Flora's churning stomach subsided and her damp palms dried. It wasn't so bad, was it? Nothing awful had happened. Perhaps it would be all right, leaving the house . . . The cocktail went right to her head and made her feel woozy. When Vicky ordered another two, Flora insisted on having a large glass of water as well.

Vicky was running through a list of questions she had for Flora. What ideas did she have for holidays – wouldn't she like to go skiing? If so, they would need to think about the fact that they no longer had Aunt Francis's Klosters chalet, unless they asked for it. And Aunt Frances always used to charter a private plane – would Flora like to do the same?

'Excuse me,' said a quiet voice.

Flora looked up and found herself gazing into a pair of light brown eyes. She recognised them from somewhere.

The man standing beside her in a smart black lounge suit smiled warmly. 'I hope you don't mind my interrupting, but as soon as I saw you I had to come over.'

'Oh!' she said, staring at him in surprise, and then she remembered. 'You're Otto! How n-n-nice to see you again. Thank you so much for the lovely flowers.'

His eyes crinkled as he smiled again. 'You are most welcome. I received your note of thanks. I hoped they helped you recover from your nasty experience.'

'Not half as nasty as it might have been, if it hadn't been for you.' She looked at Vicky who was staring at him with great interest. 'This is my cousin. Vicky, this is Otto. He practically saved my life.'

'Hi.' Vicky grinned. 'Always a pleasure to meet a real-life knight in shining armour.'

'How do you do?' Otto said politely. 'Now, I won't disturb you ladies any longer. I'll leave you to enjoy your drink in peace.'

'I'm so p-p-pleased to see you again,' Flora said quickly. 'I never got the chance to thank you properly. Won't you join us for a drink?'

Otto glanced at his watch. 'I'm supposed to be meeting an associate. But . . . I am early and he is always late. I would much rather be with you.' He looked over at a waiter, an eyebrow raised, and instantly another chair was brought to the girls' table. Otto insisted on ordering a bottle of champagne.

'What good luck to meet you again,' he said to Flora. 'I'm leaving in a few days, and don't know when I'll be back in London.'

'Where are you going?' she asked. The waiter brought the ice-cold bottle over, along with three glasses. He poured out the champagne as they watched.

'Back to my home. Germany. I've been here on business, and always long to get back when I've been away for a time.'

'What is your business?' Vicky enquired.

'I am in consultancy,' Otto replied. 'I introduce very important people to each other and help everyone's dealings run smoothly. Modern business is all about connectivity and networks. My role is to link networks to other networks, make fresh connections from which we can all benefit.'

'Goodness, sounds very high-powered and important.'

'It certainly takes up a lot of my time. I've come to London often and yet still I know so little of it. I'm always on my way to or from a meeting.' He shrugged, looking forlorn. 'That's how it works.'

'It sounds very interesting,' Flora said. Perhaps it was because of what had happened the last time they had meet, but the moment Otto sat down with them she felt completely calm. It was as though his presence soothed her. She thought he might be anything between twenty-five and thirty-five, though from the crinkles at the corners of his eyes and the slight furrows on his brow she suspected closer to thirty-five. She liked his face: it was ordinary-looking but with a sweetness about it that appealed to her, and she knew already that beneath the gentleness there was strength.

'As it happens, perhaps I will get the chance to see more of London this time. One of my contacts has unfortunately been taken ill and cancelled our appointments. I haven't decided yet whether to go to the trouble of changing my flight home or whether to be a tourist for a few days, just for a change.' He smiled at Flora and looked hopeful. 'Perhaps, if you have nothing else to do, you might care to join me for an afternoon? I'm sure you know this city much better than I . . .'

'Oh, no, hardly at all,' she began then stopped herself when she saw Vicky shaking her head and widening her eyes.

'That sounds like a lovely idea,' her cousin said quickly. 'Why don't you get out and show Otto around, Flora?'

'Oh, I . . .' Flora stopped. Her first instinct was to refuse. The idea of roaming the city among crowds of people was nerve-racking . . . but then again, who would she be safer with than Otto, the man who had already come to her rescue?

'I would be delighted, if you think you can spare the time,' Otto said. Just then a waiter came up and said quietly, 'Baron von Schwetten, the gentleman with whom you are dining is here. I've shown him to your table in the restaurant.'

'Thank you.' He smiled at Flora. 'Regretfully, I must leave. But if you decide you would like to join me, tomorrow or the next day, then please call me.' He rose to his feet with fluid grace, reached into his pocket and took out an engraved card which he held out to her. 'You can reach me on these numbers.'

Flora took it, flushing. 'I don't know . . . if I can,' she stammered.

'Of course, I realise it is a great deal to ask,' he said, 'but it would be an honour for me. If I do not see you again, then I wish you all the best, and thank you for a charming time in your company. Now, if you'll excuse me, ladies? Good night.' He bowed his head to them and left, walking out of the crowded bar. Flora watched him go, surprised to feel disappointed that he couldn't stay longer.

'Goodness,' Vicky said. 'Let's see that card.'

Flora put it on the table and they both looked at it. It was adorned with a coat of arms in red and black held in the claws of black eagle, its wings outspread.

'Very Germanic,' remarked Vicky. 'The Baron von Schwetten, Schloss Meckensberg, Bavaria. Crumbs, he's titled!'

Flora imagined a *schloss*. How romantic. She could see it now: a grey fairy-tale castle with turrets and arched windows, high on a mountainside, surrounded by thick forests with the silver Rhine curling by.

'He seems lovely,' Vicky said. She looked solemnly at Flora. 'I really think you should consider going out with him.'

Flora blushed. 'I hardly know him,' she said, embarrassed.

'I don't mean a romantic date! I just think it would be fun for you to get out and do something. Otto seems like the perfect escort. After all, he's already proved that he can look after you, hasn't he?' Vicky picked up the card and looked at it again. 'Promise me you'll give it some thought, won't you? I don't see what harm it could do, and you might actually enjoy yourself.'

Flora thought about Otto again. There was a slight air of melancholy about him that appealed to her. And she couldn't deny that she liked his company.

'I'll think about it,' she said. 'I really will.'

'Good.' Vicky grinned. She tucked Otto's card into her handbag. 'Now, let's have some more of that delicious champagne.'

21

The candlelight in the dining room made it hard to make out what Iseult was holding up but her enthusiasm was unmistakable. 'Look at these, just look at them!' she cried. 'I adore these pictures.'

Octavia could make out elegant swirls, long pencilled lines, the turn of an arm or leg. Roddy sat at the opposite end of the long dining table, smoking away on a cigarette, a large glass of red wine in front of him. He smiled when Iseult held one of his drawings aloft for them all to admire.

'Aye, I like that one,' he remarked.

'It's stunning,' declared Iseult. 'Pure theatre, pure art – but incredibly wearable. I can see exactly how this will look.'

'It's inspired by this place,' he said. 'It's changed the whole direction I was going in.'

'Good. Good! Dear old Mabbes.' Iseult held up her glass. 'Come on, everyone, a toast! To Mabbes and to Roddy, a perfect combination.'

Octavia seized her glass, a delicate flute engraved with vines and flowers. None of the champagne glasses matched but the table looked all the more charming for that. She held it up and said, 'To Mabbes and Roddy!' before gulping back a mouthful. Roddy downed his in one. Across the table, Ferdy smiled at her as he put his own glass back down, his eyes sparkling in the candlelight.

The meal had been quite something, a chaotic series of odd-tasting dishes, from the instant soup they'd started with to the watery roast lamb and the pavlova that tasted of dust. Everything appeared after very long intervals and was almost stone cold by the time it got to the table. As the housekeeper had left early that day, Iseult had done the cooking herself, but the quality of the food didn't matter when they were all having so much fun. It didn't make any difference to them if the pudding didn't arrive until 2 a.m. – what did they have to get up for in the morning except more amusement?

Octavia looked down the table at Roddy Wildblood. He seemed more cheerful and talkative than she'd ever seen him, talking loudly to the boy next to him – Piers, she thought his name was – and laughing his odd ratcheting laugh when he was amused. He scared her a little, with his brooding personality and the aura of discontent that surrounded him, but Iseult had told her that was simply a result of his being so driven and wanting success so desperately.

'He's a pussy cat underneath!' she declared. 'A sweet, darling little bundle of loveliness. You'll see.'

Octavia could not quite see that, but she was prepared to be converted to Roddy's charms. She knew that the next day she was supposed to be with him in the solarium as he created the wedding dress for the finale of the show, now only a few weeks away, and she was nervous about it.

'Come on,' cried Iseult, pushing away her coffee cup and lighting a long slim cigar. 'Games! Who wants to play games?'

There was a general cheer, and she ordered the table to be cleared. Everyone picked up plates, dishes and cutlery and hurried through to the kitchen, dumping them all on the large scrubbed pine table in the middle of the room. Back in the dining room, Iseult had turned off the lamps, leaving only the flickering candelabra on the table to provide any light.

'First, secrets,' she said. 'And then . . .'

They went round the table and each person had to tell something about themselves that they'd never told before, or that they thought the others could never guess. Jasmine's secret was that she had had drug-fuelled sex with a man engaged to a minor member of a European royal family. Everyone shrieked and then spent ages trying to guess the royal's identity but Jasmine refused to say. Ferdy said that he had once spent £5,000 on his father's credit card, hiring hookers for a stag party, and his father had never noticed. Octavia wondered what on earth she could say. When they got to her, she said, 'I don't have any secrets. I was never allowed any.'

'Don't be silly,' Iseult barked. 'Everyone's got secrets. Come on, you must have something.'

She racked her brain, trying to think of something. Brandon? No, too adolescent and silly. Besides, she didn't want them all laughing at it. *My whole life is a ridiculous secret*, she thought.

'I know a secret you can tell us,' Roddy said suddenly.

He leant forward. His face looked rather frightening in the candlelight. 'Why don't you tell us how much money you've got?'

'Oh . . .' She felt herself flush, her face getting hotter and redder.

'That's a good one, Roddy,' Iseult said, staring at Octavia. 'That's the kind of secret people least want to share, isn't it? Sex, drugs, nudity, puking . . . no problem. My current account? I don't think so. Will you tell us, Octavia?'

'My . . . my inheritance is . . .' She faltered over the words, though she hardly knew why. 'I don't think I can say . . .'

'Don't pretend you don't know,' Roddy said sharply.

'Perhaps she doesn't,' Iseult countered. 'I'm sure I never know how much I've got. I only know it's not much. So, Octavia . . . less than twenty million or more?'

Octavia opened her mouth but said nothing.

'All right, more.' Iseult laughed. 'Oh, dear, this is terribly vulgar after all. I'm feeling very uncomfortable, so goodness knows how Octavia is feeling! Come on, let's leave it at more than twenty mill, and let the poor girl be. Now – Rosie. It's your turn. You can tell us anything as long as it doesn't include the words "heroin" or "cocaine". Or, in fact, anything drugs-related because it's just too dull.'

More bottles of champagne were opened, and then Roddy called for whisky, and the meal ended with the girls stripping down to their knickers and being wrapped in tartan rugs by him so that they seemed to be wearing couture dresses, then they did a fashion show down the dining table, strutting their stuff as they stepped over pepper pots and salt dishes.

'Move the candles!' squealed Iseult, laughing wildly. 'Or you'll set light to yourselves!'

The candelabra were whisked away and the boys applauded as the girls pouted and posed, Ferdy clapping extra loud and whistling when he caught Octavia's eye.

'Now, hide and seek!' cried Iseult. 'Off you all go, darlings, into the darkness, and I shall hunt you down.'

As soon as they were out in the garden, Octavia felt herself clasped around the waist. She turned to see Ferdy, his face close to hers.

'Alone at last,' he said. 'I haven't been able to take my eyes off you all evening.'

She giggled. 'I've noticed.'

'You're gorgeous. I fancy you like mad. Kiss me.' He pushed his face towards her.

At last, she thought, a little delirious with alcohol, the dissipated atmosphere in the house and the lust that had been churning inside her since that afternoon. She didn't need another invitation. The next moment his lips were devouring hers, his tongue pressing urgently into her mouth.

They stumbled about together, kissing passionately, then he pulled away, grinned at her and took her by the hand. 'Come with me,' he whispered naughtily. She went with him, giggling, and he led her into a small sitting room, lit only by the moonlight that came pouring through the large windows. He pulled her over to the sofa and they fell down on it, kissing, his hands going up under her top and rubbing at her breasts.

'We can't stay here,' she panted. 'They might come in!'

He groaned and then said, 'They'll never come in here.'

'They might, it's hide and seek.'

'All right.' He jumped up and pushed the sofa away from the wall, then slung some cushions down behind it. 'There!' he said proudly, and they slid over the back of the sofa and on to their newly made bed. There was very little room, so as soon as they lay down they were pressed up against each other. Ferdy's hands were pushing up Octavia's skirt now and fumbling around her knickers, which were already damp with her arousal.

She unbuttoned his jeans, wanting only to feel at last what it would be like to have a man inside her. She remembered how it was with Brandon, this hot, stomach-melting lust and the fierce desire to be joined to someone, and she knew she wanted to have Ferdy right now, and to hell with the consequences. She pushed his jeans down and then his boxers, revealing his cock standing up and pressed hard against his stomach, already pulsing with desire. It wasn't like Brandon's, she noticed with surprise. Were they all different then? Somehow she'd thought they'd all look the same, but Brandon's had had a smooth dome-like top while Ferdy had loose skin around the tip, skin she could pull back and forth. He moaned when she did that and scrabbled to pull her knickers down.

The alcohol in her bloodstream made her fearless and she pushed them down herself, wriggling until they slipped off entirely. Now she was naked from the waist down, her tee-shirt pushed up under her arms. She hooked one leg over Ferdy's hips and he grasped his cock in one hand, directing it to the mouth of her pussy. Their open mouths joined together in another wild kiss as he found her entrance and pushed in with a strong thrust. She gasped as she felt herself open to let him in. It was tight, but deliciously so, a strange sensation of being expanded and filled with warmth as Ferdy's hard penis moved further up her passage. She expected it to hurt, but no pain followed. Perhaps Brandon's busy fingers had prepared her well. Instead she felt the delightful sense of completion that she'd been hoping for all those summers ago, and as Ferdy was engulfed in her to the root of his cock, she felt his pubic bone press against her bud, sending marvellous tingles all over her. He began to thrust into her. The tight space they were wedged into meant that his body continually exerted pressure on her clitoris as they fucked, and the combination of the hot cock in her pussy and the pressure on her bud was almost overwhelming. She began to gasp.

'Ooooh, fuuuuck,' murmured Ferdy, panting hard in her ear, his thrusting getting stronger.

'Ohhh,' she gasped. 'Yes . . . that's right, Ferdy . . . please don't stop . . .'

He pushed in faster and faster and she threw back her head as the pleasure mounted in her, rolling out from her groin and building in intensity until suddenly, almost to her astonishment, she was possessed by a fierce tidal wave of sensation, the culmination of all the wonderful things she had experienced so far. She felt as though she were turning inside the tidal wave over and over, lost in a roar of lovely noise.

'Oh! Oh,' cried Octavia. She squeezed her eyes shut and a long moan came from deep within her.

'Crackerjack!' cried Ferdy, and he came too.

22

'Hello, Otto, it's . . . it's Flora,' she said into the phone, trying not to sound as nervous as she felt. 'We met up in the bar at Claridge's yesterday.'

'Of course. The beautiful Flora. Does this mean that you've decided to join me today?'

She could hear the hope in his voice.

'Y-y-yes,' she said as firmly as she could.

'That's marvellous,' he said, obviously delighted. 'Why don't we meet somewhere central after lunch, and go on from there?'

'That's a good idea,' she said, and they arranged a place to rendezvous.

'Well done,' Vicky said approvingly when Flora came to report her success. 'Steve will take you when you're ready.'

After a light lunch, Flora went upstairs and dressed. She wore a denim button-through skirt and flat boots, with a slim-line cashmere jumper and a blazer, which she thought would be right for walking in the autumn sunshine. Vicky pronounced the outfit perfect, and very soon it was time to go.

Otto was waiting for her near Trafalgar Square, looking quite different out of his formal business suit. He wore jeans, a dark jacket, Timberland boots, and a red cotton shirt over a tee-shirt. He was also carrying a camera and a guidebook.

'My tourist credentials,' he said with a grin as she approached.

'I think we're going to need those,' Flora laughed. 'I haven't the foggiest idea where anything is. Where do you want to start?'

Otto looked about. 'We seem to be in the heart of things, don't we? What's that building there?' He started flicking through his guidebook.

'That's the National Gallery,' Flora said. 'I know that much. Shall we go and have a look?'

They went first to the Sainsbury Wing, and walked through galleries of religious art, admiring the medieval paintings that were thick with gold and bright colours.

'These baby Jesuses are all so funny,' whispered Otto, his eyes bright. 'Most of them are not babies at all, just fat little men. That one over there is also rather green.'

He was right, and Flora giggled as she looked at the serene-faced Madonnas holding their naked 'babies'.

'But some are wonderful,' she murmured as she saw a stunningly beautiful Mary holding a heartbreakingly innocent-looking child.

'The real masters,' Otto said, nodding. 'Come, let's see something else.'

They wandered through the galleries and into the main building, stopping to look at whatever took their fancy, eventually arriving in front of Holbein's

186

The Ambassadors. Otto showed her how to stand at the side of the painting so that the optical illusion painted so skilfully at the front fell into place and she could see the skull that appeared, at the feet of the Tudor nobleman.

'How brilliant!' she declared.

Otto nodded. 'The anamorphic perspective. A Renaissance invention.'

'But why did he put a skull there?' Flora wondered.

'A memento mori, perhaps. You know, a reminder that we are all mortal. Or just to show he could.' Otto smiled at her. 'Let's go and get some tea. It's four o'clock. Don't you English drink tea at four?'

They went to the gallery café and had tea and scones. Afterwards, they walked across Trafalgar Square and down Whitehall until they came to Parliament Square, dominated by Big Ben and the Houses of Parliament on one side, and Westminster Abbey in all its magnificence on the other.

'Shall we go inside and have a look?' Flora asked, looking at the great church. 'Lots of famous people are buried here.'

Otto looked at his watch. 'It's already too late, I fear. The Abbey will be closed to visitors by now. It's after six o'clock.'

'Is it?' she said, surprised. The afternoon felt as though it had just begun for her.

'And I must leave you now. I have a business dinner tonight.' Otto smiled at her, his brown eyes soft. 'You have been charming company.'

'So have you,' Flora said. She felt happy for the first time since she had stopped painting.

'Then, perhaps tomorrow?' he suggested tentatively.

187

'I have one more day before I return to Germany. I have so enjoyed myself.'

'Yes, yes.' Flora smiled back at him. 'I'd love to.'

The following day they set out earlier. The weather was fine and bright, perfect for sightseeing. They went to the Abbey first thing and then walked across Westminster Bridge and wandered along the South Bank towards Tower Bridge, passing Tate Modern and the Globe Theatre as they went. Flora didn't mind the crowds or feel lost while she was with Otto.

At lunchtime, Otto insisted that they go to Fortnum's in a taxi, where he bought them some picnic food. They went to Hyde Park to eat it. In the afternoon they went in a boat on the Serpentine, Otto rowing them, and then to the Mandarin Oriental on the Knightsbridge side of the park for tea.

'I've had a marvellous time,' Flora said, her eyes sparkling, as they sat in the hotel lounge sipping Earl Grey.

'So have I,' Otto replied. 'I don't think I've ever enjoyed a trip to London more.' They looked at each other, smiling, and she felt a flush creeping into her cheeks.

'I have to leave tomorrow but I'll be coming back to London next week,' he said softly. 'I wonder, would you allow me to take you out for dinner?'

She felt her insides flip. She knew what he was really asking. They had spent two pleasant days together as friends, laughing and enjoying one another's company. She had never been friends with a man before; had been frightened at the idea. But Otto was so comfortable to be with, she found it very easy to talk to him about anything inconsequential that crossed her mind. They had not exchanged life histories but had talked about the things around them, both of them finding everything equally new and exciting.

But dinner out together . . . That was a date. That meant romance, didn't it?

Otto was looking worried. 'Have I spoiled things, Flora? I hope not.'

'No, of course you haven't.' She thought for just an instant longer then said decisively, 'Yes, I'd love to come out for dinner with you. I really would.'

'Oh, my goodness!' Vicky laughed as she looked at Flora, who had come waltzing into the sitting room and thrown herself down on one of the sofas. 'Look at you.'

'Look at me . . . what?' Flora asked, grinning.

'Well.' Vicky gave her a knowing sideways glance. 'I'm getting romance vibes. *Huge* romance vibes. Don't tell me that the Baron has stolen your heart away . . .'

Flora blushed scarlet. 'Don't be so silly,' she said quickly.

'That's a shame.' Vicky idly turned the page of the newspaper she was reading. 'I thought he was excellent romantic material.'

'Mmm.' There was a pause and then Flora sat up straight. 'Vicky, can we go shopping tomorrow? You're right, I really don't have anything in my wardrobe. I think I need to sort it out.'

'Do you now?' Vicky laughed again, then saw Flora's expression. She held up one hand. 'Sorry, sorry . . . I'm not really laughing at you, I'm just happy that you seem so much better than you were. Spending time with Otto has obviously worked wonders. Yes, let's go shopping. I'd love it.'

Flora sat back again, thinking about her happy days spent wandering about town with Otto. *I wish Octavia were here to share it,* she thought forlornly. But her sister was still away, due back the next day. *I'm dying to tell her everything* . . . Flora hugged her secret to herself. *Am I in love? Could this be the beginning of something?*

It was just too exciting. As soon as her sister returned, it would be time for a proper bedtime chat.

23

I wish I had a helicopter, thought Octavia. *Perhaps I'll get one. How much are they?*

But she needed one now, because she was bone tired and all she wanted was to be at home, sleeping in her own bed, recovering from the madness at Mabbes. A helicopter would get her back in minutes.

It had been exciting, that was for sure. She'd achieved one of her goals, which was to become well and truly experienced at sex. There was a long way to go, no doubt about that, but she'd made a good start. *An orgasm with a man,* she thought, pleased with herself, feeling a tingle of arousal at the memory. *And not just one.*

Steve had driven the Mercedes all the way to Mabbes to pick her up, and now they were gliding back along the M3, effortlessly overtaking every other car on the road. She was curled up on the back seat, watching the vehicles as they disappeared in the wake of the powerful Merc, wondering about the lives of their occupants, where they were going and why. In the darkness, on the soft leather, she hovered between being awake and asleep, replaying the most vivid moments of the weekend.

Was it only this morning she had woken up in bed with Ferdy? He'd been zonked out beside her, his breathing sonorous and his arm thrown out so that it lay heavily across her back. She'd turned over to escape it and he'd woken up, yawning. He'd kissed her and his kisses had tasted sour at first and then sweeter and sweeter, and then they were unable to resist the desire for each other that possessed them. A moment later, she was on her back, opening her thighs to him and he was plunging inside her again. The effect of their hangovers seemed to make the sex even more intense than the night before and they raced to a fast and vigorous climax. With their initial desire slaked, they were able to spend a lazy hour in bed, playing with each other, kissing and fondling and licking each other, until they each came again, this time under the influence of tongues and fingers.

Sex is gorgeous, Octavia thought, happily. *Ferdy and I must have something special between us for it to be like this.*

After a shower and breakfast, she'd been summoned to see Roddy for her fitting. The dress had been lying on the floor of the solarium as she entered and he was cross-legged with its neckline in his lap, sewing away.

'There you are,' he said, looking up with a grin. 'Did you have a good time last night?'

'Yeah. Brilliant.'

'I thought you did. All this is new to you, isn't it? Still loads of fun.' He pored over his needlework again. 'The charm wears off after a while, I can promise you that. Now . . .' He tied and cut the thread, then shook out the dress. 'Here we are! The theme is, the Virgin Queen. What do you think?'

The dress was pure white – not the off-white, cream or ivory beloved of most brides, but an icy, almost futuristic white. It fell in a full silk skirt, and over that panels of white paper embroidered with silken thread in curling, Renaissance-style designs. The bodice was a mixture of silk and embroidered paper and a grand ruffled collar stood stiffly around the wide neckline, made of what Octavia could now see was white card intricately cut to resemble fine lace.

'Wow, it's amazing.'

'Come and try it on,' Roddy ordered.

Octavia slipped off her jeans, feeling self-conscious. 'Don't be embarrassed. I've seen more minge than Peter Stringfellow. Models drop their clothes all the time and don't even think about it. It's like a nudist colony backstage at a fashion show. Come on, down to your bra and knickers, chop chop.'

She obeyed, and when she was in her underwear, he helped her into the dress, easing it over her head and cautioning her to be very careful in case it ripped.

'It's not terribly practical,' he said, pulling it down centimetre by centimetre, 'but that's the point, isn't it? It's supposed to be noticed. And no one wears a wedding dress twice. Not the same one anyway.'

It fitted her perfectly. Roddy stood back to examine it, his hand on his chin, frowning critically. 'Hmm, let's see. That skirt's off a bit.' He knelt down beside her and began to make tiny alterations. 'This suits you. And you've got a just-fucked look that I find rather appealing, though it's more like the morning after the

193

wedding than the day itself. Or maybe you've just been in the vestry with the best man, getting your brains shagged out one last time before you're chained for life, eh? I know that's what I'd do.' He pushed a hand up under her skirt and cupped one of her buttocks in his palm, squeezing gently. 'What do you think? Shall we fuck? The thought of all your money makes me horny.'

Octavia looked down into his upturned face, confused. Did he really have her bottom in his hand? Had he really just said what she thought he'd said?

Roddy laughed, showing his surprisingly straight teeth. 'I've shocked you, I can tell. You may have been initiated into our crowd, but you're nowhere near jaded enough are you? I expect you're thinking: *He's as queer as a coot, what's he talking about?* Well, I *am* queer, but that doesn't mean I can't get it up for cunt occasionally.'

She blushed a violent red, too embarrassed to speak. She'd never heard the word 'cunt' spoken aloud.

'Maybe another time,' Roddy said carelessly. 'You've obviously been well serviced today already. I can smell Ferdy all over you, darlin'.'

He went back to pinning the dress, humming softly to himself.

They had all been too hungover for much partying on the Sunday so it had been a restful day, though that didn't mean there wasn't plenty more drinking done as they lazed outside in the autumn sunshine. Ferdy stayed close to Octavia, not too clingy but with a definite air of possessiveness. Iseult hardly spoke, but wrapped herself in a long black robe and retreated behind a huge pair of sunglasses, lying on a rusty old sun lounger for most of the afternoon.

Octavia had called Vicky that morning and asked her to send Steve, not able to face the train. The others were going on to another party in Scotland, and though they said she could come along if she wanted, she had suddenly longed for home. Ferdy had kissed her goodbye and said he would call her.

Octavia was beginning to understand how her new tribe lived: for them life was really just a long series of parties with brief recovery periods in between. Because their jobs were so nebulous – if they had any jobs at all – it was possible to pursue this nomadic existence of constantly moving about, socialising all over the world. It was Scotland this week, but there was talk of meeting up in France or Italy, and getting together in New York, or going to So-and-so's big bash in LA.

In the car she eventually fell fast asleep, only waking up when Steve pulled to a halt and announced that they'd arrived. The house was in darkness, the others were asleep. It was all Octavia could do to take the lift to her floor before collapsing into bed and sleeping far into the next day.

24

At Vicky's suggestion they went to the private suite at the top of Harvey Nichols where Flora met Talitha, her personal shopper, whose mission was to bring the girls all manner of sumptuous things while they relaxed in luxurious surroundings, decorated with soft camel colours and a wall of mirrors that made observing the clothes as easy as possible. Soon the long banquette seat was littered with discarded garments from Chloé, Moschino, Donna Karan, Missoni, Stella McCartney and many others.

Vicky picked up a Vivienne Westwood asymmetric jacket in blue and white stripes, and tried it on. 'Ooh, I like this,' she said. She admired her own reflection, pushing her hair up on her head with one hand so that it made a big messy pile on top. 'I look a bit like Vivienne Westwood like this.'

'Do you?' Flora had no idea what the designer looked like. 'Oh, here's Talitha.'

A tall, slim, stunning black girl came into the suite, her arms full of clothes. She was grinning happily, obviously pleased with her latest haul. 'I think you're going to love some of these,' she announced. 'I've got some amazing occasion dresses here.' She gave Flora an anxious look. 'That was what you wanted, wasn't it? It's a special occasion?'

Flora nodded. 'Dinner out.'

'Somewhere smart,' added Vicky, with a smile.

'How romantic.' Talitha laid her finds carefully on the sofa. 'You'll adore this – it's a chain-mail mesh dress by Balmain.' She held up a black long-sleeved mini-dress with bandage panels and chain-mail mesh inserts at the hip and sides. 'It's incredibly now. All you have to do is team it with some chunky high gladiator sandals and a metallic clutch, and it will be perfect for dinner somewhere glam.'

'But it's so *short*,' said Flora, her eyes wide. 'I can't imagine ever wearing such a thing.'

'Go on, try it,' urged Talitha, but Flora shook her head, laughing.

'I'd feel too self-conscious,' she declared. 'Definitely not.'

Talitha looked surprised. 'But you've got the figure for it – and why wouldn't you want people to notice how wonderful and stylish you are?'

Flora's smile faded and her eyes lost their sparkle. 'I said n-n-no.'

'Let's see something else, Talitha,' Vicky said softly. She obediently put down the Balmain and picked up a demure coral shantung Chloé frock with a modest hem at the mid-calf. 'This is a gorgeous tea dress. Not strictly for dinner, but you could easily dress it up with some accessories . . .'

'Or how about this?' Vicky said, picking up a knee-length dress of soft peach georgette and silk. 'This looks like your kind of thing, Flora.'

'That's Donna Karan,' Talitha said. 'It's beautiful, isn't it? Very soft, very feminine. It's a wrap dress, and ties at the waist with a bow.'

'I do like that,' Flora said, brightening.

'Good. Then let's try it on.'

The hours passed very quickly as Talitha styled Flora and Vicky too, who couldn't resist the wonderful clothes the personal shopper brought in by the armful.

'Oooh, this is a bit tight for me,' she said, squeezing herself into a white quilted Alberta Ferretti skirt with frayed black edging. 'You're slimmer than me, Flora!'

'I can get you a bigger size,' offered Talitha immediately.

Vicky looked over at Flora, who said, 'Of course, you must get whatever you like, Vicky.' It felt very odd only to buy things for herself – and, besides, Vicky deserved it. She'd worked so hard for them over the last few months.

'Oh, God, can I?' gasped Vicky. 'Wow . . . I could just *never* afford anything like this myself. How much is it?'

'That's part of a suit,' Talitha said. 'It's four thousand altogether.'

'Have it, if you want it,' Flora said. 'Really, please – I want you to. Today is a special day, we're going to buy anything we like.'

Talitha's expression didn't change. She was obviously used to women spending vast amounts of money, charging it to their black Amexes or platinum private bank cards.

'Have you secretly been swapped with Octavia?'

Vicky said with a grin. 'I think she's got a rival in the shopping championship stakes.'

'Don't get too used to it,' Flora said, smiling back. 'I don't intend to do this every week! Twice a year should sort me out. Now, I need some jeans . . .'

By the time they left, there was far too much for them to carry or to fit into the car, so Talitha arranged for it to be sent on: boxes and boxes of shoes, accessories, clothes and make-up. Flora had put the whole lot, totalling nearly £100,000, on her card, a replacement for the stolen one in an identical mint green leather case.

When they got back to the house Octavia was there, looking exhausted with deep dark shadows under her eyes. She was eating chicken noodle soup from a tray in front of the television in the small den off the drawing room, but came out when she heard the other girls return.

'Hi, where have you been?'

'Shopping!' said Vicky with a big smile. 'We've had so much fun, haven't we, Flora? You should see what's coming in a Harvey Nichols van later!'

Octavia looked hurt, casting a quick glance at Flora. 'You went shopping without me?'

'You were asleep,' she said quietly. 'We seem to be keeping completely different hours these days.'

Octavia frowned, then sighed. 'If you'd said, I would have got up. I'd have loved to come.'

'Next time for sure,' said Vicky gaily. 'Come on, Flora, I expect Molly's got something for us in the kitchen, and I don't know about you but I'm *starving*.'

* * *

'Did you have a good time?' Flora asked. She knelt behind Octavia on the bed, brushing out her sister's hair.

'Oh, yes,' Octavia replied. 'It was wonderful.' She wanted to tell Flora everything – talking was one of the things they did best, after all. They'd only had each other to talk to their entire lives. And yet . . . for some reason, Octavia didn't want to tell her about the sex she'd had with Ferdy, not in detail anyway. And she didn't really want to describe some of the antics of her new crowd – she had the feeling that the things she found charming, sophisticated and impressive wouldn't come across as well when she tried to explain them. Something was holding her back. It was a strange emotion in relation to her sister, something she had never felt before.

I think it's Vicky, she thought. *She's coming between Flora and me. It should have been me shopping with her.*

Octavia glanced at her sister in the mirror opposite, where she could see Flora kneeling behind her, brushing out her hair. 'You seem much happier.'

'What?' Flora looked up and grinned. 'Oh, yes, I am. Actually . . . I've met someone.'

Octavia noticed suddenly that her sister looked better than she had in a long time. Her eyes were bright and her skin was glowing. 'You met someone?' she said, amazed. 'Last week you couldn't leave the house! Who have you met?'

'Do you remember the man who rescued me from the muggers? I met him again by chance in Claridge's. And he's lovely, Tavy, he really is.'

Octavia blinked at her, lost for words. Then she said, 'You went to Claridge's?'

Flora nodded happily. 'It was Vicky's idea.'

Vicky again, thought Octavia coldly.

'I've been spending time with Otto, and he's so kind and sweet. He's taking me out for dinner next week. A proper date! That's why we went shopping.'

'I see.'

Flora stopped brushing and looked at her sister in the mirror opposite. Octavia could see that her expression had become worried. 'What is it? What's wrong?'

'Nothing. It's just . . .' Octavia gazed at their reflection, each of them a copy of the other. 'I can't believe you're doing all this without me, that's all. You're seeing someone and I didn't even have the first idea.'

There was a pause. Then Flora resumed brushing her sister's hair as she said quietly, 'But you're the one who isn't here, Tavy.'

'I'm doing this fashion show,' burst out Octavia, feeling indignant though she knew she shouldn't. 'And . . . and . . .'

'And you're living your life,' finished Flora. 'So am I. It doesn't change us, does it? Nothing will come between us, remember?'

Octavia said nothing, but inside she was thinking, *Only if you let it, Flora. Only if you let it.*

'Now tell me about Mabbes and this fashion show,' Flora said. 'I want to hear all about it.'

25

At the far end of Le Café Anglais, under the curved Art Deco window that looked out over the concrete jungle of Queensway and Westbourne Grove, a party of two was enjoying Parmesan custard with anchovy toast. The woman, who had taken the banquette seat, was a tall, elegant dark-haired figure, dressed in a Giambattista Valli bouclé tweed pencil skirt and a crisp white Jil Sander shirt, along with high square-heeled, peep-toe patent Lanvin shoes. Opposite her was a white-haired man wearing a lilac jumper over a Prada shirt, tight white Calvin Klein jeans, and highly polished Gucci loafers.

'This is absolutely my favourite, favourite morsel in London,' Gerry said happily, dipping his strip of toast into the small pot of custard and stirring it round. 'I don't want it to end. I may order it again. Or perhaps I'll just have more toast . . .'

'I can't be too long, Gerry, I have to get back to work,' Amanda reminded him. 'What have you got?'

Gerry put down his toast and picked up a jade green leather document wallet. 'Plenty,' he said with satisfaction. 'An enjoyable few hours at the computer doing some research and I managed to amass quite a lot. It's funny, I thought I remembered all about the Beaufort custody case – but it's incredible how much I'd forgotten. This has brought it all back. Honestly, we couldn't get enough of it at the time. It was in all the papers, even the smart ones.'

'I don't know much about the detail,' Amanda said, taking a sip of her fizzy water. 'I was only a child myself at the time. The twins' father was killed in an air crash, wasn't he?'

Gerry nodded. 'One of those senseless accidents. He was piloting his own plane and misread the conditions. At least, that's what people thought . . . but there was no way of knowing exactly how he came to crash into the sea. He was fairly experienced, apparently, but even so – anyone can make a mistake, and sometimes it's okay and sometimes it isn't. Whatever, he was killed. He'd been on his way to collect his wife and children, so everyone was grateful that he'd crashed on the outward journey and only killed himself, rather than taken them all with him on the return. The girls were only babies.'

Despite herself, Amanda felt some sympathy. 'Poor things. It can't have been easy, losing their father like that.'

Gerry raised his eyebrows and pulled a face. 'That was just the start of it. The wife, Diane, was a raving beauty. Funny how all multi-millionaires fall in love with raving beauties. Perhaps it's something in the brand of water they drink. Anyway, by the terms of Arthur Beaufort's will, his whole fortune went into trust for the girls. There was a payment to Diane, but nothing like as much as you'd expect for the widow of someone as rich as him. But, as guardian of the girls, she was entitled to a vast house and enough cash to keep them as little Lady Fauntleroys would expect: ponies coming out of their ears, velvet knickers, diamond-studded crayons – whatever it is pampered little rich girls need.'

Amanda frowned. 'So what happened to the mother? How come they ended up living with their aunt?'

'Well, that's where it all starts to get really spicy.' Gerry sat back and gave her a sly smile. 'It was only a few months after Arthur Beaufort's death that the paternal aunt, Frances Staunton, sued for custody of her nieces, alleging Diane Beaufort's unsuitability to be their guardian. I've got some of the cuttings here . . .' Gerry opened the leather wallet and pulled out some sheets of paper. 'There isn't all that much on the net, because the court case was in the early nineties before the papers went online. I had to go to the London Library, would you believe, to find some old clippings. But it was fascinating, I must say. Look at this.'

Gerry passed a sheet over to Amanda, who looked at it with interest. The photocopied article had a black-and-white photograph that showed two girls of about four years old walking either side of their mother, holding her hands tightly. Diane Beaufort had short dark hair and a fine-boned face. Her expression was strained, her eyes wide with tension as she passed through the glare of the press taking their pictures, but nevertheless she still looked dignified and beautiful, elegant in a long dark coat and high heels. The small girls who accompanied her had white-blonde hair pinned neatly back with ribboned clips. They were wearing matching pale coats with velvet collars, and smart white leather shoes.

Amanda stared at the children. 'It doesn't say which is which.'

'No one could tell the difference, I expect.'

'But one of them is smiling.' She put a long slim finger on the photograph next to one of the girls who seemed to be giving a broad smile that showed all her teeth. The other twin wore an expression similar to her mother's: tense, stricken, and with more than a hint of fear.

'Yes, it's the same in all the pictures,' Gerry said, cocking his head to see what Amanda was pointing at. 'One of them always seems to be giving it her best film-star smile, which seems odd in the circumstances. After all, they're in court to find out if they're going to be taken away from their mother. Not exactly a smiling matter, is it? But then I found this photo, taken from a different angle, where you can see the face a bit better . . .' he pulled another sheet from the sheaf before him and pushed it towards Amanda '. . . and I realised that this little one isn't smiling at all. She's baring her teeth in an awful grimace of pain. Like an animal.'

'Oh.' Amanda stared. 'Yes, you're right. It's not a smile. More like a scream.' There was a pause while she looked at the photograph. 'I wonder which one it is.' Then she looked up at Gerry, fixing him with her green gaze. 'So what happened? Why did the court find against the mother?'

'Well, it never did. Frances Staunton played every card she had during the case, alleging some pretty fruity behaviour by Diane – all kinds of sexual shenanigans, drug-taking, alcoholism, you name it – and claimed that the marriage between Arthur and his wife had been on its last legs, virtually over when he died, but it still looked as though Diane would keep the children. She was their mother, after all. Then, on the day of the judgment, she arrived at court with the children and asked for an interview with the judge. They were closeted in his chambers briefing and then Diane emerged and it was all over. She'd surrendered her rights to the girls and requested that their aunt be made their legal guardian. Then she walked out of the courtroom, leaving them behind. As far as I know, no one ever saw her again.'

'Fascinating. Intriguing.' Amanda stared at Gerry. 'I wonder how much they know about all this?'

'I'd be willing to bet almost nothing,' he declared. 'And the rest of the world has forgotten all about it too, I expect. There's been very little about them since but for a few column inches in the society pages. My ball got some nice mentions, and there were some glam pics in a few of the glossies, but no one's picked up on the old case.'

Amanda looked at her watch. 'Damn. I really am going to have to get back to Noble's. There's a board meeting this afternoon.'

'What a bore . . .' Gerry turned down the corners of his mouth. 'I was enjoying our chat.'

'Yes, but I can't miss it. It's an emergency meeting to discuss—' Amanda stopped herself, as though remembering that she was talking to the biggest gossip not just in London but perhaps the entire northern hemisphere. 'Well, just to discuss things.'

'Problems at the shop?' enquired Gerry sweetly.

'Yes . . . No . . . nothing serious, nothing we can't handle. A bit of a retail downturn, that's all.'

'Nothing Noble's hasn't seen and survived before, I'm sure. Such a venerable old institution. I must say, Amanda, you've changed a bit since you've started taking your job there so seriously.'

'Have I?'

'Yes. Perhaps you're not spending quite so much time with that dreadfully bitchy circle of yours – that Claudia girl really is the end, I've never understood why you hang around with her.'

'I have seen a bit less of that lot lately, if I'm honest,' Amanda said slowly. 'And with things the way they are at work . . . well, I haven't had any choice but to knuckle down. Listen, can I take these articles with me? I'd love to read them through.'

'Certainly. I've got more copies at home. Let's get together again after you've read them.' Gerry picked up another strip of toast. 'By the way, have you had an invitation to Iseult's fashion show?'

Amanda nodded. 'Of course.'

He looked disgruntled. 'Hmm. Well, I haven't. Not that I'm surprised. Sometimes this feud of ours is *very boring*. Now, off you go, sweetheart. I'm going to stay and order the crab salad.'

26

I don't know why I'm so nervous, Flora thought, watching the sparkle of the West End pass by the darkened windows of the car. *It's Otto, after all. Not some terrifying stranger.*

After he had left London, she'd received several lovely emails from him: sweet, supportive messages recalling the days they'd spent together and telling her small details about his life. The most exciting had been the one where he'd written to say he was coming to London very soon, and was she free for dinner at Le Caprice?

Of course she was. And, thanks to her shopping expedition, she had the perfect outfit to wear too.

'Do I look all right?' Flora had asked Octavia, her stomach percolating with nerves.

Octavia had smiled at her proudly. 'You look absolutely stunning. Any man would consider himself lucky to spend an evening with you. You'll bowl him over.'

A hairdresser and make-up artist had called at the house earlier. Flora's pale gold hair had been dried into loose waves, and her face simply and naturally made up, with touches of shimmer on her lids and cheekbones and a wash of gloss on her lips.

'That dress was the perfect choice,' added Octavia. 'I couldn't have picked anything better.'

From the front, Flora appeared to be wearing a classic little black dress, modest with its high neck and long sleeves but still sexy with its clinging, form-fitting jersey. The back, though, was dramatic and attention-grabbing: it was cut low, almost to the waist and black ribbons criss-crossed Flora's naked back, standing out vividly against her ivory skin and tying at the nape of her neck in a soft bow. The effect was stylish and very sophisticated, with a dash of pizzazz helped along by her black spike-heel Jimmy Choos and the sparkling Judith Leiber crystal clutch purse that she carried.

Octavia had hugged her, careful not to rumple the dress or disturb her hair. 'Now, go get him, girl. And tell him he has to come and meet me as soon as possible!'

It took all Flora's courage to get out of the car and walk through the door of Le Caprice alone. Her heart was thumping so hard it made her breathless, but she knew she had to rise to the challenge.

The maître d' showed her to the table where Otto was already waiting. He looked serious and sombre in dark suit and plum-coloured silk tie but his expression was transformed the moment he saw her. He jumped to his feet, smiling, his brown eyes sparkling. 'Flora. You look beautiful,' he said as she arrived at the table. 'I'm so happy you could come.'

He leant towards her and kissed her cheek, his lips smooth and dry against her skin. She felt her flesh tingle where he touched it and was full of happiness to be with him again. The maître d' held out the chair for her and she sat down. For the first few minutes, she was still nervous, stuttering over almost all her words until she flushed with frustration, but Otto's soothing presence and the restorative glass of champagne he had ready for her helped her to calm down. By the time they'd ordered their food, her stutter had gone back to manageable levels and she was able to talk quite naturally.

Their starters came – seared scallops for Flora and pea and prosciutto tortellini for Otto – and she relaxed enough to be able to enjoy the atmosphere of the restaurant. The other diners seemed worldly and quietly elegant, the staff discreet and observant. There was nothing loud or frightening about this place. She was sure Otto had chosen it for just that reason.

When they'd chatted for a while, she said, 'Tell me about your home in Germany.'

Otto brightened. 'I love it there, more than I can say. My family have always lived in Bavaria,' he explained in his soft accent, 'for as far back as we can trace. Our fortune came from our land – the wonderful pine forests that stretch over the estate, our vineyards, our farms. And later generations used their skills to enlarge the family coffers through canny trading and land purchases. At one time we owned estates all over Germany but circumstances changed and most of those are gone now. Only the last and greatest of them, Schloss Meckensberg, survived the wars and upheaval that followed. The castle –' his face lit up '– oh, Flora, you should see it. Perhaps one day you will. It's so beautiful. Originally it was medieval but few parts of

210

the original remain. Instead it was rebuilt by one of the wealthiest of my ancestors in the eighteenth century, and it is now a Rococo delight. I would spend every day of my life there if I possibly could – the peace and beauty are astounding.'

'It sounds amazing,' Flora said, as the waiter cleared away their plates from the starter. 'Do you live there alone?'

'Oh, no, my mother also lives there. She watches over it for me when I'm forced to be away. I have no brothers and sisters – I am the last von Schwetten. Last in the direct line, anyway. There are distant cousins. But no one else who, like me, was brought up at the castle, has a love for its stones running through their veins. I would die to protect it.' Otto's eyes flashed with emotion.

'Goodness.' Flora was impressed by this revelation. 'What is your mother like?' she asked shyly.

'Ah, she is a saint. A wonderful woman. I love her because she is my dear mother, but I also respect and admire her. You two are very alike, in the best way – you share the qualities of strength, patience and goodness.'

Flora laughed. 'Oh, dear, I don't feel very strong! Quite the opposite most of the time.'

'You are wrong, my dear,' Otto said softly. 'I can sense your strength. You have more than you realise perhaps. I would love you to meet my mother, I am sure you would get on very well.'

'Perhaps one day,' she replied, blushing lightly at the suggestion that this might happen, with all its connotations. 'Oh, look, here are the main courses.'

Over dinner, Otto talked a little about his work,

explaining that he was helping a large company break into the Chinese market. He had many contacts there and in Hong Kong, he said, and there was good business to be done. China, he predicted, would emerge strongly from the current economic downturn, with its large, low-paid workforce and the government's ability to impose any austery measures it chose on the people.

'I'm afraid I don't know anything about the world at all,' she said, impressed by his grasp of international affairs. 'I'm very ignorant. I've never even been to school.'

Otto looked surprised. He took a sip of the excellent Bordeaux he had ordered to go with his beef, and then said, 'That is unusual. Tell me about your life. I know so little about you. I know you live with your twin sister and that you love to paint. Apart from that, you have said hardly anything about your home circumstances.'

'I don't like talking about myself,' Flora said hastily. 'I'd prefer not to. For family reasons, my sister and I were educated at home. But there are limits to a governess education, and we never went to university.'

Otto smiled. 'But that is part of what is so wonderful about you. You are so unspoiled, dear Flora. You are unlike any woman I have met before.' His expression became intense for a moment. 'That is something I like so much.'

Flora stared down at the tablecloth, happy and flattered that Otto seemed to think so highly of her but also painfully self-conscious. *Why can't I relax and enjoy it?* she asked herself, feeling her cheeks warm again. *A normal woman would. This is normal, for goodness' sake!*

Going out for dinner with a man is a perfectly ordinary thing to do.

Otto seemed to sense that he had embarrassed her a little and instantly changed the subject. They talked about food and he told funny stories about some of the more outlandish meals he'd eaten, and spoke again of his home in Germany and how he loved to have a traditional meal whenever he arrived home: 'Sauerkraut, *Kartoffeln* – that is, potatoes – and *Wurst.* Wonderful! If I'm away from home for too long, I begin to dream about it.'

Over pudding she talked about Octavia. Otto looked interested. 'Octavia? Her name means the same as mine – eight. That is a coincidence.' He smiled at Flora, his stare intense again, and she felt a strange fluttering inside her. She started to talk quickly about something else but the sense of something portentous hung in the air.

The evening was over far too quickly. Flora was surprised when Otto looked at his watch and said regretfully that it was time to go.

'My driver is just around the corner,' she said. 'I can send him a message and he'll be outside almost at once.'

Otto leant forward and took one of her hands in his. He held it close to him, wrapping it in his long fingers. 'Flora, Flora,' he murmured, gazing into her eyes. She felt herself tremble. 'If you were a different woman and I a different man, perhaps I would be suggesting that we go somewhere – to a bar or a club – to sit and drink and continue talking. Perhaps I would suggest that we return to my hotel to have coffee and listen to music. Perhaps we would allow ourselves

213

to follow our natural instincts. But we are not that kind of man and woman, are we? No. We are different from other people.'

He looked down at the tablecloth for a moment, and when he looked up his expression was grave. 'You must guess that I have feelings for you. Ever since I met you, I've been unable to think of anything else. When we're together, I cannot take my eyes off you. It is not just your beautiful face but also the beauty of your spirit. You are so sweet and pure and good.' He smiled at her, a gentle smile with that hint of melancholy that always surrounded him. She couldn't speak, her heart was beating so hard. She could only listen. 'I dare to hope, to dream, that you might one day return these feelings. Please don't say anything now – I don't want to rush you. I only wanted to tell you how I felt.'

She was lost for words. Otto spoke so movingly, she hardly knew how to answer him without sounding clumsy and stupid. Her face flamed again and she could feel her hands trembling. The things he was saying made her very happy. They made sense. And he didn't want to kiss her or force himself on her. He knew that she needed to take things one step at a time. *He understands me,* she thought happily.

Otto watched her patiently, still holding her hand.

At last Flora said, 'I-I-I feel as though we know each other so well already. We are friends, I know that. And I would like to see you again. I love spending time with you.'

'Good!' he said vehemently. 'Good.' He dropped one small, quick kiss on her fingertips. 'I ask for no more.'

* * *

Flora came into the house, dreamy and happy.

'So it went well?' Vicky asked. She had waited up for her cousin, appearing in the hallway as soon as she heard a key in the door.

Flora nodded with a sigh. 'Is Octavia in?' Suddenly, more than anything, she wanted to talk to her sister. They'd shared important moments all their lives, and she felt she was on the brink of something huge. All she wanted to do was curl up with her twin and talk and talk and talk.

Vicky shook her head. 'I'm afraid not. She's out at rehearsals for this fashion show.'

'Oh.' Flora felt a stab of disappointment.

'But you can tell me all about it, I'm dying to hear!'

'All right. Let's get some tea and I'll tell you every-thing.'

27

Backstage at the fashion show, someone was passing around a tray of cocaine along with tiny straws to snort it through. The models were all keen to partake but it was Roddy himself who took the most, coming back for line after line.

'He's nervous,' Iseult said to Octavia, watching as Roddy, high and energetic and outwardly full of smiles, dived for the tray and laid out another thick sausage of white powder. 'In fact, he's terrified. I can't blame him. It's a make-or-break moment as far as he's concerned. But he doesn't need to worry, he's got talent. Anyone can see that.'

Iseult herself looked stunning in a black suit nipped in tightly at the waist. She was wearing her green python platforms again, with a lime green satin blouse peeping out from under her jacket. Her face was half obscured by a veil that fell from a high black comb set in her auburn hair, her blood-red lips visible below it. She turned towards Octavia, eyes sparkling behind the black mesh. 'Look at Jasmine and Rosie squabbling over that tray of powder. Are you going to have any, Octavia?'

She shook her head. 'I don't think so. Not really my style.' She didn't want to betray her absolute inexperience of drugs, and was shocked to find other people were so open about taking illegal substances. So far she hadn't been tempted, but that was more from fear than any desire to be good. What on earth was that stuff everyone was merrily taking up their noses? It could be anything. It could do anything to her . . . Besides, life was exciting enough as it was. She couldn't imagine what it might be like if it were heightened any further.

'Very wise,' Iseult said. 'It does get so tiring when everyone is high all the time. They like to talk and talk for so long. And what does it always culminate in? Sex, of course. *That's* what it's all in aid of.'

'Then you don't do drugs, Iseult?'

'Oh, yes, tons and tons. But not the kind everyone else takes. Mine are dinky little pills that my doctor gives me. Now, shouldn't you be getting your make-up done?'

The clothes were waiting on their rails for the models to put on at the very last minute. All around them people were crammed into the small backstage area. Some of the models lounged about half-naked, drinking champagne, while others were having their make-up done in front of the bank of brightly lit mirrors or else having their hair styled into the look Roddy had decreed for the show. Helpers in plain black clothes were hurrying about, doing sound and lighting checks, finalising the running order, organising the clothes and accessories so that they were easily located once the show was under way.

Iseult had hired the magnificent Holland Park

house that had once belonged to the Victorian artist Lord Leighton and had since been restored as a museum. It was a grand residence, even by the standards of the time, and had been painstakingly brought back to the condition of its glory days. The show was going to take place on the ground floor, with the girls getting ready in the library before marching out into the tiled hallway, called – perhaps appropriately – the Narcissus Hall thanks to the statue of the Greek god that stood on a marble plinth in the centre. The models would walk across this hallway, where some of the less important spectators would sit, then cross into the grand drawing room, circuiting the room where the majority of the audience would be. Then they would return to the hall before ending up in the stunning Arab Hall, a showpiece room that Lord Leighton had added to his house to display his incredible collection of antique tiles from Syria, Turkey and Iran. The mosaics that covered the walls were in rich blues and turquoises, whites, creams and jade greens, in intricate patterns, some spelling out verses from the Qu'ran, others showing lush flowers, exotic birds, animals and creatures of legend. Here the most important guests would sit, waiting for the models to give them a close-up view of Roddy's creations.

It was not the easiest venue for a fashion show and technicians had been grumbling all day to Iseult about the difficulties of setting up the sound and light, while the museum staff had been fluttering about anxiously, concerned about the priceless surroundings and all the electricians stomping around with wires, hot lights and gaffer tape. Iseult had refused to be worried.

All problems could and would be solved. Everything would be perfect. She wouldn't contemplate it being any other way.

Octavia found it all interesting and exciting and could tell the other girls were buzzing as well, though it was hard to distinguish between a drug-induced high and genuine excitement. Roddy and the clothes had arrived very late indeed – even Iseult had started to look a fraction less cool than usual – but when they did, it was obvious that they were sensational. The house was exactly the right frame for them as they were based around a theme of nineteenth-century boudoir influenced by Turkish and Gothic fashions: intricately embroidered slouchy velvet gowns worn like robes, bound at the waist with golden tasselled sashes; high heels made to resemble Turkish slippers with curling toes; harem pants in gauzy chiffon or embellished with tiny metallic mosaics, shimmering gold and bronze, teamed with ruffled sheer blouses or silk cowl-necked sleeveless tops; evening dresses in rich dark oranges and greens in floating many-layered chiffon, cowl-necked and sleeve-less, again worn with long, loose fabric belts or sashes in silk embroidered in gold thread; tops and jackets in jewel-coloured silks and velvets. The collection was wildly sensuous, opulent and lavish, a riot of colour and texture.

'They're all amazing,' Octavia breathed, reaching out a hand to stroke one of the velvet gowns. 'I love these. I want to wear one right now. It's like the most gorgeous dressing gown in the world. I like this one in midnight blue with the silver stars all over it and the oyster satin lining . . .'

Iseult lifted her veil for a moment, showing her yellow-green eyes. 'Every single one is a masterpiece, hand-finished by Roddy. Buy whatever you can, darling. One day every museum in the world will be begging to purchase it from you. I mean it. I should know, I've bought just about everything else he's made.'

Octavia's make-up had been done. It wasn't exactly what she herself would have chosen: it seemed far too dramatic even for party wear, with the shimmering peacock eyes, vast blue false eyelashes that glittered in the lights, and golden metallic lipstick – but she could see why this look had been designed. It emphasised the Byzantine richness of the collection, and brought out its themes of Eastern opulence and Victorian adoration of pattern and deep colour. With their hair put into long, loosely combed ringlets, all the girls resembled a Brontë heroine who had just unpinned her bun in order to go to bed. Octavia stared at herself in the mirror, noticing that her eyes were even more violet with the iridescent blues and greens around them. She looked quite unlike herself, though.

For the first time in my life, I look different from Flora, she realised. That felt very strange. Nerves fluttered in her belly. *I'm going to walk out in front of hundreds of people soon – important people, clever people – and they're all going to be looking at me.*

It was terrifying. But it was exciting too. She blinked at her reflection, seeing the blue eyelashes flutter like fans. *My new life. I'm the muse to a fashion designer on the brink of fame. Ferdy will be waiting after the show. It's all wonderful . . . I'm having a fabulous time.*

*   *   *

220

The show was a triumph. Roddy walked out to massive acclaim when it was all over, his models thronging after him in their gorgeous outfits. Octavia was among them, feeling a high like no other she had experienced. She'd been nervous as she'd stalked out to do her walk, but Iseult had trained her well, teaching her how to thrust out her hips and advance with that swinging strut, gazing impassively ahead. She'd done two circuits, one in harem pants and jewelled corset, and the other as the finale to the show in her amazing wedding dress.

As she'd walked through the sumptuous rooms, she'd seen Otto and Flora in their seats a few rows back, craning to watch as she strode past, smiling their admiration and encouragement.

'Wonderful, wonderful!' declared Iseult when they were all back in the library, buzzing with excitement and full of pleasure at the show's obvious triumph. 'You were all fantastic.' She came up to Jasmine, Rosie and Octavia, who were busy getting out of their clothes and scrabbling about for their own gear. 'Thank you, darlings. You looked exquisite. Everyone's gathering in Hurley's after this. I'm buying champagne, so don't be late because I can only afford three bottles. After that, it's every girl for herself!'

Octavia changed quickly and hurried out to find Flora and Otto who were lingering in the Narcissus Hall, hoping to see her.

'Tavy, you were stunning!' cried Flora. 'I had no idea you could look so different.'

'The most beautiful girl in the show by far,' Otto said, kissing her cheek in congratulation.

'Thank you. As I'm your girlfriend's identical twin,

you can say that with impunity,' Octavia replied with a laugh. She liked Otto. Flora had invited him to meet her the day after their romantic meal at Le Caprice. Octavia had been expecting some kind of tough guy with a moustache and a square jaw, her ideas of a German baron coming from the movies, so she'd been surprised by this quiet, unassuming-looking man with the kind face and the gentle manner. But he was rather funny, and very charming, and she could see exactly why he would appeal to Flora. What was strange was seeing her sister so . . . well, gooey was the only word she could think of. Flora was obviously in the full fervour of romance and Otto seemed just as smitten in return. It was sweet, and it made Octavia think a little wistfully of herself and Ferdy, and how different their relationship was. Romantic was not exactly the word to describe it.

'We're going to a club that Iseult belongs to,' Octavia said. 'Would you like to come?'

'Oh.' Flora exchanged a quick glance with Otto. 'We were planning to go out together. Otto has tickets for a late show at a jazz club.'

'Of course you must go and enjoy yourselves,' Octavia said quickly. 'I'll be fine. It's a fashion thing anyway, so don't worry.'

They said their farewells and she watched her sister and Otto hurry off together, obviously eager to be alone, then went to find the others so they could share a taxi to the club.

Hurley's was packed with fashionistas all vying to outdo each other with the up-the-minute trends they were sporting. Iseult and Roddy held court from her favourite sofa, so large that it was almost a bed and entirely filled the small room she'd dubbed 'The Fuck and Buggery Chamber'. The two of them reclined on cushions like dissolute monarchs receiving their court while people thronged in, eager to congratulate the designer and pay homage to his talent. Bottles of champagne in ice buckets were propped everywhere, gifts from Roddy's new fans.

'God, I'm having a brilliant time,' Jasmine said, sniffing hard, her pupils fully dilated, jaw moving furiously.

She was very high on coke, Octavia realised. There'd been so much available at the show, and Jasmine had obviously dived right in. The other girl's expression changed and she suddenly looked scornful.

'Christ,' Jasmine said bitingly. 'There's Radcliffe. Who the hell invited *her*?'

Octavia followed her gaze and saw Amanda Radcliffe standing at the edge of the room, looking about.

'No one's seen much of her lately,' Jasmine said, 'ever since you doused her at that party. Perhaps it was because I got thousands of hits on YouTube when I posted the footage.' She giggled. 'Very effective. She's a laughing stock.'

Octavia glanced over at the other woman, who stood looking tall and rather elegant as she observed the raucous crowd. *Have I really made her a pariah?* she wondered. *Well, she deserved it – those awful things she said about Flora.* At that moment, Amanda looked directly at her and their eyes met. They stared at one other for what seemed like a long while and then, to Octavia's surprise, Amanda's expression became almost triumphant and she smiled a strange half smile before turning on her heel and marching out.

What was that for? Octavia wondered, feeling apprehensive. She noticed that Rosie was sitting among a crowd of people, staring into space and seemingly completely out of it. 'Is Rosie all right?' she asked Jasmine, who looked over at her friend.

'Fuck, she's out of it on K again! I'll check she's okay . . . you get some water.'

Octavia made her way through the crowd, trying to get to the bar. There were so many people, it was hard to see exactly where the bar was but she kept pushing until she found herself not by the bar as she'd expected but by the door. She stood there for a moment, puzzled, when a man arrived in the doorway, frowning at the sight of the heaving throng.

He looked down at Octavia and said, 'What's going on? Is there some kind of private party happening here?'

She stared up into his piercing blue eyes and gasped. She recognised him. He was the man who had reprimanded her at the Templeton House ball, after she'd chucked the water over Amanda Radcliffe. He was well dressed in a dark suit and a navy silk shirt, but she noticed again that he wasn't good-looking, with his heavy brows, large nose and strong-looking face. He seemed harsh and rough around the edges compared to the polished beauties and male models everywhere. But once again she had the curious sensation of connecting with him; he had a powerful physical magnetism about him that she couldn't help responding to. 'It's . . . it's an after party,' she said a little lamely. 'We've just had a fashion show.'

224

He smiled at her, and immediately his face transformed into something quite different, going from craggy to almost handsome in an instant. Octavia was disconcerted by the attraction to him that buzzed over her. She quelled it immediately. *Ferdy's here*, she told herself sternly. *He's my type. Not this guy. He's old and ugly and he was damn rude to me as well.*

'I'm assuming you're one of the models,' he said, looking down at her appreciatively. 'Unless you wear that kind of get-up all the time.'

Octavia realised she was still wearing the iridescent peacock-coloured make-up on her eyes, although she had changed into one of Roddy's shredded tweed miniskirts and a silk top, which she wore with long boots. She put a hand on her hip and cocked her head at him.

'Actually,' she said, summoning all the attitude she could, 'I'm the girl you were so vile to at the Templeton House Ball. Remember? You told me I was a spoilt child.'

He stared at her uncomprehendingly for a moment, then recognition dawned in his eyes and a look of amusement crossed his face. 'Of course. How could I forget? You're the little Aquarian.' He raised an eyebrow at her. 'I'm glad to see you've come without your jug.'

'*I* certainly haven't forgotten,' replied Octavia tartly.

'Well, if I upset you, I apologise. But you've got to admit, it wasn't exactly a constructive way to settle an argument. I've been in a lot of dicey situations myself, and I've generally found chucking water around to be the least effective way of sorting them out.' He smiled at her again, and she laughed despite herself.

225

'So, this is a fashion party,' he said almost to himself, glancing around the room. He noticed a pair of outrageously dressed men who were screaming and laughing with one another, and then looked at a girl who was ostentatiously wiping white powder away from her nostrils. He frowned at Octavia, studying her face intently. Then he said, 'You shouldn't be with this crowd, you know. I've seen these kinds of people at play and it isn't pretty. They're drug-takers and drunkards. I'm surprised the management here are closing their eyes to it.'

'These are my friends, actually,' Octavia said defensively. 'And they're just having fun.' *Who the hell are you to judge us anyway?* she thought crossly.

He seemed almost sad. 'Fun? I don't need to remind you, do I, that Class A drugs are illegal? This stuff is serious. I've seen it in Colombia and I know what I'm talking about: organised crime, trafficking, murder and whole countries suffering so that a load of over-privileged idiots can get high. If they knew what misery their habit causes, maybe they'd think again.'

Octavia opened her mouth but didn't know what to say. She had never thought of it like that before, and was suddenly gladder than ever that she didn't take drugs. She wanted to tell him that she wasn't part of that scene, but at that moment Jasmine came staggering up, supporting Rosie around her waist. She looked as manic as Rosie seemed blank and withdrawn.

'Where's that water, Octavia?' Jasmine demanded. 'What are you doing here? Ferdy's been looking everywhere for you. Come and join the party. Rosie will be over the worst in a bit and then we'll kick some ass. One of Roddy's friends has some fantastic coke, apparently.'

The man at the door looked at the girls, taking in their state. Then his gaze moved to Octavia, something like disappointment in his eyes. 'I see,' he said quietly. 'You'd better go and have your fun. Who cares about anyone else, huh?'

'Wait, you don't understand . . .' Suddenly she wanted more than anything to convince him that she wasn't like that.

But his eyes had become icy and his face hardened again into craggy harshness. 'I should have realised. All spoilt little rich girls together, snorting Daddy's money, risking your own lives and other people's.' He shrugged, a look of distaste on his face. 'Well, I'll leave you to it, if that's all right. This isn't my sort of party.'

'You're not being fair! You don't know anything,' Octavia began hotly, but he had already turned on his heel and headed out of the club.

'Who was that?' asked Jasmine, struggling to hold Rosie up. 'Kind of dishy for an old guy.'

'I think he's ugly. And arrogant.' Octavia tossed her head, wishing she could have convinced him of the truth, or else responded with a witty killer putdown. *Why should I care what he thinks anyway?* 'Come on, let's get that water.'

28

Otto and Flora had seen one another every day since the night at Le Caprice. He had taken over her life, but in a marvellous way.

Two months ago, I was a shivering wreck, she told herself. *I'm not like that any more.* She was standing in his suite at a Mayfair hotel, a simple but stylish room in a discreet brick building off Berkeley Square. She looked out of the tall windows at the grand old house opposite. In one hand she held a glass of chilled Sancerre, the other played with the string of pearls at her neck as she thought about the way her life had been transformed over the last eight weeks. Otto had not only helped her to overcome her irrational fear, he had opened up a new world to her, a world she had never been allowed to see when Aunt Frances had shut her away behind the great doors of Homerton. Otto had taken her to atmospheric little clubs where grizzled men played mournful jazz into the early hours. He'd shown her how to eat sushi, bought tickets for all kinds of theatre, from Shakespeare plays to brittle society comedies, and taught her how to enjoy life.

This evening he had taken her to the opera and Flora had utterly adored it. They had seen a production of *The Marriage of Figaro*, staged in period costume with a lavish set and such beautiful music she had frequently been moved to tears. She'd been so carried away that she'd laughed through her sobs as she clapped furiously during the curtain calls. She hadn't wanted it to end – Otto had had to coax her out of her seat so that they could make their table at The Ivy. Something that evening had been subtly different though she couldn't say what. The whole atmosphere had been more loaded, more heavy with significance.

For the first time Otto had suggested that they come back here to his hotel. Until now, apart from kisses to her cheeks and hands, he'd not attempted any physical contact. Flora had wondered why not. She was sure she had fallen in love now. She woke every morning with a warm sensation of happiness all through her, wondering how long it would be before she would see Otto again. She fell asleep every night with his image in her mind. She knew that she wanted him to kiss her and hold her. Beyond that, she wasn't sure. One step at a time, she told herself.

Perhaps tonight is the night, she thought, and shivered with delicious anticipation. She'd asked her sister for advice. Just open your mouth and do what comes naturally, Octavia had said with a grin. *Great advice*, Flora thought wryly. *I could have worked that much out myself.*

'Flora . . .'

She turned. Otto stood in the doorway, smiling at her. He advanced towards her. He had changed, taking off his suit jacket and putting on a soft cashmere jumper. As he neared her, she felt her insides quiver with excitement. His face was solemn but there was the light of happiness glinting in his light brown eyes. He stopped, standing very close to her. Then he lifted one hand and pushed back a strand of golden hair that was hanging loosely over Flora's shoulder.

He searched her face with his eyes, smiled and said in a low voice, 'My darling . . .'

Her breath started to come quickly. She had the sudden desire to press her fingers to his mouth and tell him not to say anything, but she couldn't move and in the next instant he had grasped her hand, lifted it to his lips and pressed them to it.

Something's about to happen, she thought, her heart racing.

'My darling, it has been forty-five days since I met you. You have possessed me utterly. I've fallen madly in love with you.' He gazed into her eyes, smiling. 'I know I'm not worthy of you – you're so pure and beautiful – and I know that many would consider this madness. But, Flora, I simply cannot live without you. I offer you all I have: my noble title and my family lineage, my home and all I own. You would make my existence paradise on earth if you would agree to share these things with me. Could you . . . would you . . . do me the honour of giving me your hand in marriage?'

Flora gasped. She felt dizzy and strange, almost sick, but happy as well. 'Oh! Oh . . . my goodness . . .' This was far more than she'd expected. She'd thought they would kiss, perhaps even go further, admit their feelings. *But a proposal?* He was right, it was crazy, it was beyond whirlwind, but . . .

'I know it is very fast, my love. We've known each other a comparatively short time. But ever since we met, when you were at the mercy of those ruffians, I've felt that our destinies are meant to be united.' He bowed his head over her hand again.

She remembered that day: the terrible fear, the menace – and then Otto's bravery, coming to her rescue. 'Yes . . .' she breathed, thinking of it.

He looked up, his eyes sparkling with pleasure. 'Yes?'

Flora stared at him. She had said yes. *She'd said yes.*

'You've made me the happiest man in the world, my darling!' He threw his arms around her, hugging her tightly, laughing with delight. Then he pulled back, gazed her at tenderly, and she saw his eyes glisten with tears. 'Am I dreaming? Have you really said that you will be my wife?'

She felt as though she were standing at an open door, and at this very moment she had to decide whether to step through it or not.

Otto looked at her beseechingly. 'We would be so happy,' he said.

She saw at once this delightful way of life she had enjoyed with him going on for ever: they would travel together, he would show her everything there was to see. And he would protect her. He would keep her safe, just as he had that very first night.

She smiled at him. She was ready. What other life was there? What other life could she possibly want? But Otto was right. It was amazingly fast. 'Otto,' she said quietly, her voice trembling with emotion, 'I love you. I think I want to marry you. But . . . please give me time to think about it? Just a day or two.'

'Of course, my darling. If you think there is the slightest chance for me, I will wait for ever.' He pressed his lips to hers, tenderly at first and then more passionately.

His tongue flicked out and licked her lips lightly. She opened her mouth and felt it dart inside, probing her softly and tentatively. It was a warm, pleasant sensation, if strange at first.

My first kiss.

'My beauty,' murmured Otto, his lips moving against hers. 'My love. My destiny.'

Yes . . . yes . . . Whenever he spoke that, she felt his words chime with her. It was the truth. He *was* her destiny. She was sure of it.

29

The Mysterious Heiresses From the Past!
Beautiful twins grow up to inherit a dazzling fortune . . .
Last seen during the bitter custody battle of the nineties, the
gorgeous girls re-emerge in society . . . but what is the truth
about their doomed family?

Octavia picked up the paper with a trembling hand. Molly had brought in the breakfast tray and said that she thought Octavia ought to see the morning papers. Not that it was really the morning any more – it was well after lunch, in fact. But she was stunned to see on the front pages of the tabloids huge pictures of her wearing Roddy's amazing wedding gown, and next to them the screaming headlines. And there were other pictures: of two small girls, identical in looks and dress, walking beside their mother, one smiling broadly, the other looking white-faced and wide-eyed.

Octavia stared at them. Did this really happen? She had no memory of it at all. She could barely remember her mother, but here she herself was aged about four. Didn't most four-year-olds have proper memories?

Her heart pounded as she looked at her younger self and the glamorous woman whose hand she was holding. They were connected. There was a relationship. That small hand was tucked inside the larger one with absolute trust.

Aunt Frances had rarely spoken of their mother and the girls had learnt not to ask, for what they invariably received instead of an answer to their question was a lecture on the merits of their father. It wasn't that they weren't interested in their father – they loved looking at the wedding pictures they'd secretly discovered – but Aunt Frances had managed to dilute the romance around him by making him sound so terribly dull. It was hard to feel anything for someone so perfect, like a saint in a Bible story, although they dutifully sniffed and looked sad whenever Aunt Frances described his death in the plane crash, with tears flooding her own cheeks.

Their mother was never allowed to become deified into oblivion because she was never mentioned except when a direct question was asked, and even then Aunt Frances would become so icy and rigid it was not at all conducive to a conversation.

'Your mother,' she would spit, her eyes hard, 'was not a proper person. She should never have married Arthur and she certainly should never have had babies. She was damaged, girls, and that is why she went away.'

Damaged, they assumed, meant sick and unwell, and therefore they reasoned that their mother must have died, just as their father had. It was fitting that she should waste away and expire, it was how a true love affair ought to end, beautifully tragic like *Romeo and Juliet*.

So what is this? Octavia wondered. *What the hell is this?*

She read the article. When she had finished, she was shaking from head to foot. Throwing the paper down, she buried her head in her pillow and wept.

Flora raced to her sister's room, elated and fizzing with happiness. She knocked on the door and then flung it open.

'Tavy? Tavy? Are you awake? I can't wait any longer, you've been asleep for ages and Vicky isn't here so . . .' She came to an abrupt halt as she realised her sister was twisted in the covers of her bed, a satin duvet wrapped round her. 'Tavy, are you all right?'

Octavia lifted her head, showing her tear-stained face and reddened eyes. 'No . . . no, I'm not.'

'What's wrong?' Flora advanced and sat on the bed, looking anxiously at her sister.

Octavia picked up the newspaper and pushed it towards Flora, who took it and scanned it. As soon as she saw the headlines, she gasped. She went paler and paler as she read. Her fists clenched and she shuddered as she reached certain revelations. When she'd finished, she looked up at her sister, her own eyes burning. 'But . . . I don't understand! We've never been told any of this!'

'I know,' replied Octavia. She sat up. 'Aunt Frances never said anything. Did she think we wouldn't find out? And how come we can't remember anything about it?'

Flora stared at the article, her face strained. 'This is incredible,' she muttered. 'Just incredible. We've been such idiots. Why haven't we asked more, demanded to be told?'

'Because we've been controlled,' declared Octavia. 'We've been kept back like stupid children, and taught never to ask questions. Well . . . I'm damn well going to ask them now, I can tell you that.'

'It says here that after the custody battle, our mother simply vanished. Disappeared.' Flora pushed the paper aside and fixed her sister with a look. 'It doesn't say anything about what happened next.'

'But what about all the things Aunt Frances said about her and why she was unfit to look after us . . . She was a drunk, a drug-user, lived like some kind of prostitute from the sounds of it.'

'Our mother's lawyer argued against all that, if this report is right,' Flora said softly. 'It sounds like she lived a bohemian life, all right, and maybe she did do some of the things they said . . .'

'Why would they make it up?' Octavia asked. 'Why? And after everything that happened in court, she still left. She didn't have to leave, but she did. She gave us up . . . left with us with Frances. Why would she do that if the things Aunt Frances said about her weren't true?'

Flora looked thoughtful. 'This is a hell of a lot to take in. I just can't absorb it. But something is telling me that there's stuff here that's wrong. And look what it says at the end . . .' She picked up the paper and read aloud: '"Diane Beaufort is believed to have left the country and moved abroad, but nothing has been heard of her in over fifteen years."'

Octavia blinked at her sister. 'How can they hear anything of her if she's dead?'

'It doesn't *say* she's dead,' Flora pointed out. 'And if no one knows she's dead, then is she?'

'Of course she is!' blurted Octavia, her eyes filling with tears again. 'How could she be alive? She would have come to find us years ago if she was, wouldn't she? She *must* be dead.'

Flora said nothing, putting the paper aside. 'Yes,' she said at last. 'You're right.'

'I just hate this – our private lives, our pasts, all over the papers, and we've never known anything about it! This is horrible!' Octavia rubbed hard at her eyes and sniffed. 'But what did you want to tell me? You looked so happy when you came in.'

'Something rather exciting happened last night.' Flora smiled at her sister. 'Otto proposed to me!' Then she laughed at the sight of Octavia's astonished face.

'What did you say?' Octavia demanded, her eyes revealing a flash of panic.

'I said I'd think about it.' She grabbed her sister's arm. 'Come on, get up and I'll tell you all about it.'

While they were having breakfast and Flora was telling Octavia the events of the previous night, the first taxi arrived. It was full to the brim with the same dark red roses he had sent last time. They'd used up almost every vase in the house by the time the second taxi arrived, this one full of lilies.

'I don't know what we'll do with all these!' cried Vicky, as the twins helped unload the flowers, laughing.

'There must be a hospital or a nursing home nearby that would like some flowers,' Flora said, taking out another huge bouquet.

'I wonder how they would feel about balloons?' wondered Octavia as a third taxi arrived, silver and pink heart-shaped balloons bobbing against its back windows.

'And here's another one, full of peonies!' Vicky looked at the sisters, and they all burst out laughing. 'Otto's really going for it!'

They were still finding homes for bunches of flowers when the doorbell sounded. Vicky answered it, wondering aloud what on earth they could expect now. 'A parade of baby elephants?' she quipped. 'A partridge in a pear tree, perhaps?'

She came back with a package addressed to Flora. 'Ooh, what can this be?'

'How exciting,' cried Octavia. 'Good things come in small packages! Open it, open it.'

Flora obediently pulled off the tape and opened the packet. Inside she saw a green velvet box stamped with a gold coat of arms and accompanied by a tiny engraved card that read *With the compliments of the Baron von Schwetten.* She pulled it out.

'Looks promising,' Octavia said, peering over her sister's shoulder.

Flora, who had gone pink with pleasure, opened the box to reveal an antique ring of white gold with a cluster of diamonds in the centre, arranged to look like a flower. She gasped.

'Oh my God,' Octavia said, grasping her sister's arm. 'Is that what I think it is?'

Flora lifted the ring from its green velvet cushion and held it up. 'It's beautiful,' she said in a small voice.

'Flora,' said Vicky in astonishment, 'that's not an engagement ring, is it?'

'Call me an old romantic,' remarked Octavia, 'but

isn't the man supposed to put the ring on the girl's finger himself? Rather than have it delivered by a man on a motorcycle and let her slip it on without him?'

'He showed it to me last night,' Flora said dreamily. 'He said it wasn't an engagement ring. It's his grandmother's dress ring. It's a gift, to remind me not to forget his proposal – as if I could. I tried it on last night, but it was too big so he's had it altered to fit me . . . how amazing.' She slid it on to the middle finger of her left hand and held it out so that she could admire it.

'Otto's proposed?' Vicky looked bewildered. 'That was quick work.'

'The ring is gorgeous.' Octavia took her sister's hand, her eyes anxious. 'But you won't rush into anything, will you, Flo-flo? I don't want you to get married and leave me.'

Flora gazed into her sister's eyes, her expression candid. 'I'll never leave you, Tavy. But we have our own lives to live, haven't we?'

Octavia stared back at her and then dropped her eyes, almost as if she were embarrassed to acknowledge that she had been the one who'd been absent most of the time, away with her new and exciting circle of friends. When she looked up again, Flora saw that Octavia's eyes were full of tears.

'Don't cry!' she said, throwing her arms around her sister. 'Please . . .'

'I'm sorry. It's just been such a strange day. First finding out about our mother, and now this . . .' Octavia sniffed, and gave her a woebegone smile. 'I'm pleased for you, I really am – I like Otto and it's obvious he makes you happy. But please don't do anything rash. You've got your whole life ahead of you.'

'I won't, don't worry.'

The twins hugged as Vicky looked on silently.

30

Octavia tried to forget the emotional upheaval produced by the press revelations the best way she knew how – by partying. The usual call came from Jasmine, with arrangements for another riotous night. This time the excuse for it was to thank Iseult and Roddy for throwing a wonderful fashion show and sizzling after party, and the venue was to be Jasmine's Camden flat, an area where the journalists and paparazzi roamed free, hoping to catch bright young things and up-and-coming stars out socialising. The big prize would be to find one drunk, perhaps stumbling and half-dressed, doing a drugs deal or wiping white powder from a nostril.

The young ones – Jasmine, Rosie, Ferdy and the rest – met in a Camden pub first and lounged in a private upstairs seating area, alternating pints with tequila shots, talking and laughing and pulling out the press coverage of the fashion show to giggle over. It had been featured in all the papers, and in the weekly magazines too – photographs of the girls and detailed analyses of what they were wearing. But the coverage was dominated by Octavia's involvement: her sudden appearance on the social scene, at the heart of the glamorous young crowd led by Jasmine and Rosie, had piqued the interest of the press. There were many articles about her, and wherever there was an article, there was that vintage photograph of the twins and their mother going into the courtroom.

The gang seemed unimpressed by the revelations, however, which were almost pointedly ignored. 'We've all been there, sweetie,' Rosie mumbled. She was dressed entirely in black today – torn leggings, a tight black dress, ballet pumps and a black leather jacket. Her make-up was Goth as well, more of her favourite heavy kohl pencil outlining her eyes, this time worn with white lipstick as well for a touch of eighties retro. 'It'll blow over, it always does.'

Octavia was relieved that she didn't have to talk about it. She'd been dreading questions, but her crowd were not interested in the past, only in the pleasure to be had here and now.

When they left the pub at 11, a couple of shabbily dressed men emerged from the darkness and snapped shots of Octavia with large telephoto-lens cameras, so that the flashes popped in her face. As she walked, they ran backwards down the pavement in front of her, clicking away. They were taking photographs of the others as well, but Octavia seemed to be their main target. Despite Jasmine shouting at them to fuck off and giving them the finger, they followed the group all the way back to the flat, only letting up when the door was shut on them.

'Arseholes,' commented Rosie.

'Yeah,' agreed Jasmine, lighting up a cigarette.

'Fucking paps! Glad they got this outfit though, I kind of like it.' She was wearing a vintage fifties prom dress in lemon yellow with polka-dot netting over the top, which she'd teamed with a denim jacket and gladiator sandals. 'Maybe they'll put me in *heat*.'

Jasmine and Rosie were always vying with each other to appear in the best-dressed sections of the gossip magazines, and Rosie was currently winning by a nose after *heat* magazine had breathlessly dissected her latest look.

Inside the flat a crowd had already gathered, a bottle of Grey Goose open on the oriental dark-wood coffee table, along with cranberry and grapefruit juices for mixers and a silver bucket of ice cubes. A small bonbon dish held a collection of pills for anyone who wanted one. Iseult, resplendent as usual in a cheong-sam of violet and silver silk, wedge-heeled violet metallic shoes and an orchid in her hair, was holding court in Jasmine's kitchen, wielding her cigarette holder like a conductor's baton as she talked.

Octavia came in, wondering if she should be wearing vintage rather than a gorgeous shimmering red Lanvin silk dress which she'd dressed down with a grey boyfriend blazer, the sleeves rolled up to show the pale striped lining, and grey mules.

'There you are,' said a rough Scottish voice and Roddy appeared out of the murky back corridor of the flat, his eyes somewhat glazed. 'Thank you very fuckin' much, Octavia. I ought to deck you, you wee bitch!'

'Hi, Roddy,' Octavia said hesitantly, looking at his dilated pupils and the red flush across his cheekbones.

She was used to his casual swearing but tonight he looked as though he might mean it. 'Are you okay?'

The last time she'd seen him he'd been off his head, being carried out of the fashion show after party by a couple of young men who'd been circling him all evening – new friends from the fashion world, no doubt. They'd put him in a taxi, climbed in with him and gone off to God only knew where – perhaps back to that flat in the grotty part of London they'd visited that first day. But Roddy had been in fine form then: ecstatic that the show was over, and that the VIPs had turned up and even stayed behind afterwards to congratulate him and assure him that he had definitely made it. Iseult had declared that tonight a new star had joined the constellations and Roddy had looked as though he believed it. He'd certainly celebrated, pouring gallons of champagne down his throat and hoovering up a plateful of cocaine.

'I'm fine, darlin',' he drawled. 'Just wanted to say thank you, that's all. Thank you for totally stealing my limelight! The biggest night of my life and what do the papers say the next day?' He struck a dramatic attitude, rolled his eyes and put on a fake English accent. '"Who is this mysterious beauty arrived from nowhere? Let us tell you about her intriguing past, the scandals, the court cases . . ."'

'Oh, I hadn't thought of it that way. I'm sorry, Roddy. It hasn't really spoilt your big moment, has it?' Octavia felt a terrible pang of guilt even though there was nothing she could have done about the press coverage. 'If it's any consolation, I absolutely hate it. It's been awful . . .'

'Has it, darlin'?' he cooed. 'My heart fuckin' bleeds!'

'That's enough, Roddy.' Iseult appeared in the corridor. 'Octavia isn't to blame. If anything, she got you even more attention than you could have expected. You were front-page, my sweet, front-bloody-page. Every time they mentioned Octavia, they mentioned you too.' She leant forward and kissed Octavia's cheek. 'We should be thanking you. Come and have a drink.'

'I don't want a fuckin' drink,' said Roddy grumpily. 'I want a bloody blow job. Where's that boy who was talking to me earlier? He'll do.' He stumbled off down the corridor.

Octavia turned and saw Iseult's stricken expression, but when Iseult noticed that Octavia was staring at her, she instantly recovered herself. 'You mustn't mind him. I've said it before – he's a genius and you have to make allowances for that. Now come with me, let's have a drink together.'

Octavia and Iseult sat in the tiny and, from the looks of it, largely unused kitchen, making themselves vodka cocktails. Iseult smoked while they talked. From the sounds coming out of the sitting room the party was taking off – there was loud music, singing, shouting and whoops of laughter. The strong sweet smell of cannabis came wafting into the kitchen.

'They live in total madness, these children,' Iseult said, knotting a piece of lemon peel and dropping it into her glass. 'Just you be careful, Octavia. Don't get too caught up in this way of life. Never forget that to live authentically we must be artists – we must work to express ourselves. Constant chemical highs deaden the ability to feel properly, and after that . . . well, the work won't come.'

'Don't you worry about Roddy then?' asked Octavia, intrigued. 'He seems to be very keen on narcotics.'

Iseult looked sad as she shook her head, her sharp auburn bob shaking with it. 'He's deadening the pain. We all do that differently. He takes drugs to survive, to give himself a reason to go on, and he cuts himself as well when it all gets too much. You can't compare Roddy to anyone else, I'm afraid. Except, perhaps, me.'

'But you said you don't take drugs?' Octavia said. She was awed by the older woman's sophistication and the sense both of her glee in life and the tragic sensitivity that surrounded her.

'Just the pills to keep my brain chemistry on track. If I don't take those, I'm liable to be very stupid indeed. Driving cars into walls . . . that kind of thing.'

'Really?'

'Oh, yes! I took out my last car that way. I survived the whole thing, to everyone's astonishment, though I took a while to heal. Broken hip, cracked spine, lots of bumps and bruises. Still, it helps. Hurting banishes the demons for while.'

Octavia couldn't believe it. Life to her seemed constantly entrancing and fascinating. How was it possible to feel so bleak and miserable that one wanted to die? Particularly when someone was as talented and unusual and fascinating as Iseult.

She threw back her head and laughed. 'Oh, darling, your face! Don't worry, I'm not about to go and jump off Jasmine's roof! I've found Roddy, you see, and he needs me. Together we're going to conquer the world and stop each other from falling off it. Now, sweetheart, that's enough of cloistering yourself in here with me. I've just seen that scamp Ferdy and he's clearly got you on his mind . . .'

In the sitting room the party was getting raunchy, with some of the girls dancing stripped down to their underwear. Two or three were sitting zoned out on the sofa, obviously in a private, drug-induced place. Some boys were playing a drinking game with coins and a bottle of vodka, though one had already passed out nearby. A small group was sitting around the coffee table, cutting out lines of cocaine.

'Hi, gorgeous.' Ferdy came up to Octavia and put his arms round her, pressing his body against hers. She felt strange and spacy, though she'd had nothing more powerful than vodka, but even so, the feel of his body against hers aroused her. Just the warmth of his skin coming through his shirt made her feel that unmistakable buzz as lust stirred again. All at once she only wanted his mouth on hers and those big, golden-skinned hands all over her body, and then to be able to marvel again at his cock and where it could take her.

But this isn't love, is it? she asked herself as they hurried down the corridor to one of Jasmine's spare rooms. *This overwhelming desire to have him touch me and lick me and fuck me . . . that's something else. It's not what Flora feels for Otto. Is that true love?*

In the darkness of the bedroom, they began to devour each other, Ferdy's open lips locking on to hers and his tongue thrust deep in her mouth while he scrabbled to find the zip on her dress.

'It's at the side!' Octavia gasped, as he fumbled at the back, and then he found it and she wriggled out of it.

'God, your tits,' he groaned, pulling down her black lace bra and revealing them, pale and pointed with rosy tips. 'They're gorgeous.' He latched on to one of her nipples, grazing it with his teeth and sucking hard until she was erect in his mouth, while he tweaked the other with his fingers. It was an almost unbearable sensation, something between pain and pleasure, but it did its work: Octavia was breathless and desperate to feel him inside her.

'Are you on the pill yet?' he murmured as she undid his jeans and pushed them downwards, then grasped the solid column of his cock. It was thick and hot in her hands, smooth and dry and twitching as though it longed to find a home inside her warm, wet pussy.

'No,' she said, 'not yet . . .'

He reached for his jeans and pulled a condom packet from his pocket. 'We'll need this then. Can't risk it too often, can we?'

They were too impatient to be fucking to bother with much foreplay: Ferdy put the condom on with a practised hand, and a moment later she was lying on her back, opening herself to him, and he was between her parted knees, pushing himself inside her.

'Fuck, yes,' he said as he drove down on her, making her tight passage expand around the girth of his cock.

Octavia moaned as the pleasurable feelings overcame her, and a moment later he was thrusting hard, pushing against her bud with each movement inside her. Every nerve in her responded to it as though she were already primed, ready, almost there . . .

'Oh, God, I don't think I can . . . I don't think I can hold it . . .' she gasped, astonished at the speed with which everything was happening.

'Just go with it,' whispered Ferdy, and covered her mouth with a kiss. She pushed her tongue up into his mouth, wrapped her arms tightly around his back, and gave herself over to the extraordinary, tickling pleasure that radiated from her core. She began to moan again, and then she felt that delightful wave begin to build deep within and an instant later was riding it, unable to resist as the judder of her climax gripped her. As soon as she began to come, she triggered Ferdy who started to buck on top of her as his own orgasm took hold. It seemed to go on for ages, as they pressed together, riding out the peak until the sensations subsided.

'That's what I'm talkin' about!' he declared as he rolled off her. 'You were born for fucking, Octavia. I've never made any girl come so fast.'

Octavia smiled luxuriously and wriggled with pleasure. *Even if it isn't love . . . I like it.*

31

In the boardroom of Noble's, the atmosphere was strained and difficult.

At the far end of the polished walnut table, Amanda stared at the results page in front of her. She could follow a basic balance sheet but this one was a bit beyond her, considering she'd never been to business school or done an accounting course. It was a comprehensive overview of Noble's financial structure, and Amanda knew enough to recognise that it didn't look at all good. Figures in brackets meant they were losses – and there were brackets everywhere. The final, overall figure was a big fat one, surrounded by those two little marks that meant this was money that was going out, not coming in.

'I really don't know how I'm going to present this in any kind of positive way to the markets,' the chairman was saying bleakly. 'Our operating loss is almost six million pounds.'

The finance director looked grim-faced. 'We are certain to see our share price drop even further. We're going to have to look immediately at what we can do to cut overheads, save money and capitalise. To put it frankly, Graham, we need a cash injection – and fast.'

'What I don't understand is how it's come to this,' said the chairman. 'Noble's has such a fine pedigree, such a wonderful brand. Why aren't we able to make a profit?'

The chief executive sighed impatiently. 'Graham, I've been telling you for months this was bound to happen. Look at our costs – they're immense. The payroll alone is huge. The capital expenditure eats into our entire turnover. Then there's the debt. We're paying three million a year in interest, just servicing the money we owe the bank! Soon they're going to want to discuss repayment of that debt, and we're in no position to pay back anything – we're not even in a position to restructure the debt. Once they see the state of our figures, we'll be lucky if they don't want to call it in immediately and start forcing the sale of our assets.'

Graham Radcliffe looked frightened. 'We *can't* sell anything. Our whole security is based on our assets – the factories, warehouses and this building. Without those, we can't operate at all.'

Amanda stared down the table at her father and felt sorry for him. He'd never wanted to take on the business, not in this capacity. He'd always been happiest on the shop floor, talking to customers, discussing fabrics and beautiful objects with them. He hadn't wanted to move into management but his father had forced him into it. Now here he was, presiding over the decline of Noble's and likely to be the man whose legacy was the final destruction of the grand old place. But they were all desperately trying to save it:

after all, the last chief executive and finance director had been given their marching orders only six months earlier, walking away with enormous payoffs that Noble's could barely afford. Graham Radcliffe had then hired Robert Young to stop the rot and reinvigorate the place.

But while Young might have been a whizz kid in some businesses, he didn't understand Noble's at all. He was eager to bring in cash and so was keen to start disposing of copyrights in their famous prints, selling chunks of their business, shutting down their British manufacturing arm and moving the entire operation abroad . . . perhaps even selling the wholesale fabric business altogether. Each one of these suggestions caused Graham Radcliffe great anguish. Not only did it mean destroying the heart of the business, it meant squandering the only way left to them to restore it: the fabric, the copyright prints, the English spirit of Noble's, were its truly priceless assets. Once gone, those things could never be regained.

'We need to look at a ten percent reduction in staff immediately,' Robert Young was saying. 'And I mean right away. We've got to slash our buying budgets too. There must be a way to stock cheaper goods and still keep our retail prices high.'

Amanda felt anger stirring in her stomach. So this was how it was going to be, was it? *I might not be Donald Trump, but I can still see that this is the wrong way for the business to be going. We can't just turn ourselves into some kind of bargain-basement outfit. We're in a prime location in London's luxury centre. It's madness to cheapen ourselves!*

She studied her father's miserable expression as

252

Robert Young started rapping out orders about how the interim results statement was to be worded, and decided she could bear it no longer. She got to her feet. 'Would you excuse me, please, Robert?' she said crisply. 'If we're done here, I've got an appointment.'

'What? Oh . . . yes.' He gave her a condescending glance. Amanda's area – women's fashions and accessories – meant nothing to him. In fact, none of it did. *He ought to be in a steel-and-glass building in the city shouting 'Buy, buy!' or 'Sell, sell!' or whatever the hell they did – those sharks in the banks. Not walking around this building, surrounded by art and beauty and not seeing any of it.* Amanda walked out of the boardroom, giving her father a sympathetic look and a smile as she left him to his mauling from Young. Outside she stood still in the blue-carpeted corridor and let out a long sigh.

'Christ,' she muttered to herself. 'What a nightmare.'

She'd taken up her position at Noble's two years before, and only then because her father had asked her to. Up until that time she was far too interested in pursuing her social life, being lionised by Gerry Harbord and his crowd, and hanging out with the gang of girls she'd met at secretarial college. They weren't the nicest collection of people, she'd known that, but they'd wanted her to be a part of their group and she was flattered – she'd always been rather a loner before that, but Claudia, Suze and the rest seemed to want her to belong to their rich, Sloaney gang who spent weekends at each other's country houses or skiing in Verbier. They liked her sharp tongue and amusingly malicious wit, and she'd played up to it. That had got her into trouble more than once – not least at the Templeton House Ball.

She'd been stupid, talking like that about the Beaufort twin. It wasn't meant seriously, it was just part of the bitchy humour they all used. Except that since she'd been humiliated by Octavia Beaufort, her so-called friends had melted away. Only Suze was still calling her and wanting to meet up at Daphne's or the Bluebird Café for those endless, inane talks over cappuccinos. Suze could make a discussion about which skiing jacket to buy last three hours and still not came to a decision.

As a result, Amanda had been spending more time at her job and to her surprise, had begun to enjoy it and find in it a refuge from the outside world. Ever since she was a girl, she'd adored the magnificent old shop with its beautiful dark-wood interior and atmosphere redolent of a gracious past. It had been like a second home to her. She used to love coming to work with her father in the school holidays: as a small child, she'd roamed about, having adventures and exploring, making dens in the rug department or seeing how quickly she could climb from the ground floor to the sixth, cross the width of the building and get back down again via the magnificent main staircase. As she grew older, she became bewitched by the beauty of the goods for sale in the shop. Her focus changed to the clothes, sold on the first floor in hushed luxury, by gorgeous sales girls, and to the make-up and fragrance department, taking up a sweetly scented quarter of the ground floor, where she could spend happy hours making up her face, rubbing unguents and creams into her skin or discussing the merits of floral scents against musky ambers with the lady on the perfume counter. She often thought that, if she had to, she could happily live her whole life inside Noble's, eating in the delightful second-floor tea room, dressing from the clothes department, and sleeping in the great carved four-poster bed on the fifth, which took centre stage in a show bedroom swathed entirely in Noble's fabric.

Christmas had always been the best time of year here. The days when the holiday windows and their opulent displays were unveiled were the most magical in her memory. She would be taken to the fifth floor, where part of the furniture department was transformed into a sparkling Christmas shop, stuffed with every type of decoration, from plain-coloured baubles to wonderful delicate crystal stars. Sweets and gifts spilled from jars and lined shelves; festive cards and ribbons were piled on tables, and miniature Christmas trees glimmered everywhere. Best of all was the grotto festooned with glittering pretend snow where Father Christmas himself could be found, along with his elf helper and a sackful of presents plus one rather bored photographer.

Even as she grew up, the Christmas shop and the grotto never quite lost their magic for Amanda, although she began to prefer the sparkles to be found in the jewellery room, the candy-cane colours on offer in the make-up department, and the glossy boxes containing the latest Mulberry or Chloé bag, designer dress or beautiful pair of shoes from the third floor.

It was because she'd always loved the gorgeous things on sale here that her father had thought she'd be the perfect person to run the women's clothing and accessories department. She had almost no experience but he'd been so keen for her to take on a role in the family business that Amanda had agreed. She'd learnt a lot very fast . . . not least what a hell of a hole the company was in. It was a great worry, she couldn't deny that.

The problem was that her buying budget now looked to be under threat while her sales figures were not good, and getting worse. Young had bawled her out only last month, telling her that she was stocking the wrong things, that no one wanted to buy them. When she'd yelled back that it wasn't the stock that was wrong, it was the customers, he'd stared at her as though he couldn't believe his ears.

It was a ridiculous argument in retail, she knew that. The customer was, after all, always right. But she was sure that if Noble's continued to attract only the older market, eventually demand for their goods would die out altogether. She could spend her time stocking safe florals and two-pieces for country weddings and nice smart shoes that were more comfortable than beautiful . . . but there was precious little creativity and excitement in that, and they would definitely never attract a younger market to the shop.

Amanda marched towards the lift, smoothing down her Preen black crêpe ripple-pleated pencil skirt as she went. It was exactly the kind of thing she wanted to stock on the first floor – if Young would ever let her invest in smaller luxury labels. That was unlikely now, she had to admit. At moments of stress, she liked to wander around the shop, seeing how everything looked, watching the way customers reacted to the wares on offer and checking out who was coming in.

A huge majority of the people wandering round were tourists, wanting to see the famous emporium for themselves and usually leaving with nothing more than a Noble's teddy from the gift and souvenir section on the ground floor.

Amanda rode down in the lift, admiring the carved wooden panels adorned with Arts and Crafts motifs of flowers and vines as she went. The doors opened smoothly and she stepped out on to the ground floor. The central atrium was devoted to Noble's print scarves, ties, notebooks, toilet bags and other bits and pieces. It was all very nicely laid out, but it wasn't exactly exciting. The usual gaggle of tourists were wandering around, picking things up and looking at them but usually putting them back.

This is our problem, Amanda thought grimly. *Everyone's looking and no one's buying.* She wandered through the ground floor, into the handbag department and over to the staircase that led up to the first floor. She began to climb it slowly, her heart heavy. The company was in dire straits. It was hard to imagine life without Noble's in it, let alone to think of what else she might do with her future . . . It was simply too depressing.

Emerging on the first floor, she looked about the almost deserted womenswear department. As she moved towards the racks of clothes, an elderly lady came up to her and said, 'I need an outfit for my grandson's wedding – do you have anything I could see, dear?'

'Of course. I'll get a sales assistant to show you some of our beautiful skirts and jackets,' Amanda said brightly. 'I'm sure we'll be able to find you something perfect.' She signalled to one of the sales girls to come over and help the customer. Then she walked on, feeling even lower.

Then she heard a laugh, high and girlish, and turned to see where it had come from. Over in the next gallery she could see a woman, young and obviously fashionable in her nude-silk shorts and high tan sandals with criss-cross leather straps across the foot – Miu Miu, Amanda noted – and a loose peach silk shirt worn over a cream vest. She had long blonde hair and was wandering through the store, chatting on her phone as she went.

Amanda felt a flicker of interest – this was more like the profile of the customer she was hoping to attract. And then, as she got closer, a feeling of dread began to form in the pit of her stomach. The girl seemed familiar – that build, the hair, the way she moved . . .

Oh my God . . . it's Octavia Beaufort! It was only a week ago that Gerry's careful planting of the Beaufort story had made the front page of all the tabloids. Amanda had imagined that Octavia was hidden away somewhere, licking her wounds, having had that smug pride of hers well and truly dented.

Just as she thought this, she heard Octavia say, 'Oh, Ferdy, you are mad. But I forgive you when I think of all the lovely things you do to me . . .'

Furious, Amanda flew across the polished floor, reached out and grabbed the girl by the shoulder. She spun round, her expression startled. It was indeed Octavia Beaufort. The last time she'd seen Amanda, she was drenched in icy water and gasping in shock. For a moment she didn't realise who was confronting her.

'*You!*' hissed Amanda. 'What the hell are you doing here?'

258

'What?' Octavia's violet-blue eyes looked wide and frightened as she took in who had grabbed her. 'Oh! It's you. What are *you* doing here?'

Amanda gained control of herself somehow, despite the fury racing through her and making her head buzz. She drew herself up and took a deep breath. 'This is *my* goddamn shop. You can get the hell out!'

Octavia's expression was confused for a moment, then she said slowly, 'Oh, I see. This is payback because I emptied a water jug over your head after you insulted my sister.'

'Did you hear me?' Amanda put one hand on her hip. 'You'd better get off these premises right now or I'm having you thrown off!'

'What is your *problem*?' demanded Octavia, cross. 'Why are you being like this? I'm shopping – or trying to – not that there's much here to buy anyway.'

Amanda's eyes flashed and she felt her temper rising. It didn't take much to set her off usually, and this girl was making her see red in double-quick time. 'You have ten seconds to get yourself out of this place or I'm calling Security!'

Octavia looked incredulous. 'Is this how you treat your customers? No wonder this place is so empty.'

'It's how I treat spoilt little bitches.'

'It's not my fault if you're pissed off because your ex prefers me to you,' retorted Octavia.

Amanda pulled a phone from her jacket pocket and pressed a speed-dial number. 'Hi, it's Amanda here. I want Security on the first floor, by the lifts, *now*.'

'I can't believe you'd be so crazy,' Octavia said, shaking her head. 'Listen, I'm going. Believe me, I don't want to stay here another moment. You and your shop can drop off a cliff for all I care. I'd heard this place was famous but it makes me think of a church hall jumble sale.' With a shrug of her delicate shoulders, she walked elegantly to the lift and pressed the button. The doors slid open immediately, and as she stepped inside, Octavia turned, gave Amanda a ravishing smile and said, 'You're going to be sorry you got on my bad side. I'm so looking forward to seeing what I'm capable of in the revenge stakes.'

With that, the lift doors closed and she disappeared.

32

Otto had been obliged to return to Germany to work, but was calling Flora every day. The taxis full of gifts had stopped arriving, at her insistence.

'The flowers are gorgeous but we haven't got so much as a jar to put them in!' she'd said, laughing. 'And I really don't need any more balloons, or *anything*. I just want you back.'

'I'm desperate to see you,' he'd said down the phone. 'I'll return as soon as I can.'

Flora, seized with romantic longing, had said she would be on the first flight over, that she could charter a plane if necessary, but Otto had explained that the house was having some work done on it and he wanted it to be perfect for her when she had her first glimpse of it. 'Not yet, my darling. When you come to Schloss Meckensberg, I want it to be absolutely right. Besides, I'll be back in a few days, as soon as my business here is sorted.' His voice dropped. 'Will you have an answer for me then, my love? I don't know how long I can bear the tension of waiting . . .'

'I will have an answer, I promise. I can't say what it is yet, but I will.'

When Flora had put the phone down she stared at it for a while, thinking. She hadn't told Otto about the newspaper revelations and he hadn't seen them as far as she knew. It seemed a strange coincidence that her past should come to the surface just as a new future opened up before her. It was that which had made her realise what she had to do before she could give Otto the answer he wanted.

Octavia was swimming her lengths in the pool, cutting through the water with ease, lost in the calming repetition of each stroke. As she came up for air and went to make her turn at the deep end, she noticed that Flora had come down to the pool and was standing at the side, watching her glide through the lucid blue water.

Octavia stopped her lengths and swam over her, breathless from the exertion. 'Morning,' she said, brushing drops of water from her eyelashes with one hand. 'What are you doing here? Coming for a swim?'

Flora shook her head. She looked serious.

'What's up?' Octavia asked. She held on to the side of the pool, kicking her legs in the warm water.

'Tavy, I've come to a decision. I'm not sure what you're going to think about it but . . . I'm going to see Aunt Frances.'

'What?' Octavia frowned. Both she and Flora had vowed that they would never go back to Homerton. If their aunt wanted to see them, she would have to come to them. And so far she hadn't even contacted them to see how they were. 'Why?'

Flora took a deep breath. 'I want to ask her about our mother.'

Octavia stared at her sister, feeling confused and panicked. 'What are you going to ask her?'

'What happened, of course. I want to know. Don't you?'

Octavia could see that her usually quiet twin was full of determination. It wasn't like her. Octavia got the feeling that Flora was going to do whatever she wanted regardless of what her sister thought. 'I don't understand what you think she can tell us.'

'I'm pretty sure she can tell us a hell of a lot actually.'

'But . . .' Octavia felt a surge of painful emotion take her in its grip. 'For God's sake, Flora, I think we should leave it be. If our mother is dead, then it changes nothing. If she's not, then I don't think I want to know her, if I'm honest. She's dead to us, at any rate. I don't think you should rake it all up. It's bad enough that we've got all this shit in the papers as it is. I'm finding it hard to cope with all of that. I don't need anything else to handle right now.'

'I can't let it lie,' Flora said, setting her shoulders and fixing her sister with a steady gaze. 'My life is changing. I might be going to get married. But I need to understand the past before I can move on. I hope that makes sense to you, Tavy, because I have to do it. Do you want to come with me?'

'No!' Octavia burst out, feeling herself buckling under the strength of her emotions. 'Why would I want to see that horrible old cow? She hasn't been in touch with us once, to see how we're getting on or to ask to come and visit. Don't you see? She never loved us, not really. She was only obsessed with our bloody father. I don't want to see her!' She blinked hard, not sure if the stinging in her eyes was from the chlorine or the tears she knew were there.

Flora sat down on one of the cane loungers by the poolside. 'I don't want to see her either – and you're right, it's hurtful that she hasn't called to find out how we are. But she's the only one who can tell us the truth behind those stories in the newspaper. She's the only one who knows.'

'The truth? We know the truth. Our parents are dead.' Octavia splashed water as she said it, her face hard.

'We never knew anything about that court case,' Flora said. 'And that's kind of weird, don't you think? We were always too afraid to ask Aunt Frances to tell us what she knew. But I'm an adult now. Before I can even think about getting married, I need to know everything she can tell us about our past.'

'She won't say anything,' Octavia warned. 'And who knows if we can believe what she says anyway?' Then she cried out, 'I don't want to go back there, and I can't believe you can bear it either. Every day I spend out of Aunt Frances's control makes me realise how awful our lives were with her. I never want to see her again! Oh, go if you want. I don't care.' She turned and dived under the surface of the water, kicking herself off and then gliding away through the depths, her outline shimmering in the turquoise blue.

33

Flora and Vicky set off, Vicky at the wheel of her Audi, heading out of London and back to Northampton, to the place Flora had thought she would never see again.

They arrived within two hours, pulling into the familiar driveway and passing between the high iron gates. Flora knew that her aunt would be there – she had phoned the house and spoken to Maggie – but she hadn't wanted to warn Frances herself, in case she tried to avoid the interview with her niece.

Maggie had arranged with the gatehouse that Vicky's car would be allowed in. As it was, the gatekeeper brightened up when he recognised Flora in the passenger seat, and waved them through without question.

'Here we are,' Vicky said, as she turned off the engine. They both looked up at the forbidding grey exterior of the house. The windows were dark and dead. There didn't seem to be any trace of life behind them. *Was it always like this?* Flora wondered. She had lived here almost her entire life, and yet it seemed odd and almost frightening to her now.

She'd at first found her existence outside these walls so daunting that she'd come to think of Homerton as a place of safety and refuge. Looking at it now, she remembered all the confusion and fear she had actually felt here.

'Y-Y-Yes, h-h-here we are,' stuttered Flora, faltering over the words. She looked at Vicky, who stared back with sympathetic eyes. The stutter always grew worse when Flora was suffering from stress. This visit was clearly going to be harder than she'd expected.

Maggie answered the door to their knock, gasped with delight and gave Flora a huge hug. 'It's lovely to see you again! Look at you! You look so much more grown up. Come in, come in.'

Maggie chattered away as she led them inside and it was only by promising that she would visit the housekeeper before she left that Flora managed to get her to stop talking and take them to Aunt Frances.

'She's changed since you left,' confided the housekeeper, leading them through the house towards the conservatory. 'It's as though her main reason for existing has gone with you. She hardly does anything now . . . she and the Brigadier almost never go out. She spends half the morning dozing in the conservatory. That's where we'll find her now, I expect.'

Flora's mouth was dry and her heart pounding as they approached it. They stopped in the doorway, feeling the humid warmth from within. The whole room was full of plants, a jungle of lush, tropical greenery with white cast-iron garden furniture hidden among it.

'I'll leave you to it,' whispered Vicky. 'I'm going down to the kitchen with Maggie. We'll wait for you there.'

Flora nodded.

'Madam is probably on the sofa near the back. She likes to be able to look out over the garden,' murmured Maggie. She smiled at Flora. 'Now don't you be frightened. She's just an old woman. Don't let her make you feel like a small girl again. You've got your own life now, haven't you? Can I bring you anything?'

Flora shook her head, a little comforted by Maggie's words. She rubbed her palms on her jeans. She was most certainly nervous. *Maggie's right, she's just an old woman. What can she do to me?* she told herself. And advanced into the fetid atmosphere.

Her footsteps sounded unnaturally loud against the stone floor. She advanced through the conservatory, avoiding the encroaching foliage as she went. The whole place seemed to buzz from the sheer amount of vegetation crammed inside it. Towards the back, Flora came into a clearing. Instead of the white cast-iron furniture that stood everywhere else, there was a long rattan sofa covered in comfortable cushions. Lying on it was an old woman, her feet crossed at the ankle, a book on her lap, open and standing like a tent, one hand fallen next to it as though she had dozed off while reading.

Flora approached, a sick feeling making her giddy. She stared down at her aunt for a moment: Maggie was right, she did seem older, her hair almost white and her face lined and tired-looking. Her mouth hung open and her breath came in loud semi-snores as she slept.

'Aunt F-F-Frances?' Flora's voice came out reedy and hesitant.

The woman started, her eyes flicking open as she

jerked awake. She looked confused for a moment, and then caught sight of her niece. 'Flora?' she said querulously. 'What on earth are you doing here?'

That vulnerable old woman had vanished, noted Flora, to be replaced by the strict and frightening guardian she remembered so well; the woman who had forbidden her young charges to have anything to do with the outside world. She felt fear rising inside her and gathered all her strength to quell it.

'Well?' snapped Frances. 'Why didn't you tell me you were coming?' She eyed her niece critically, staring at her jeans. 'What on earth are you wearing? Surely I taught you better than to wear denim when making a formal visit?'

'I'm very well, thank you, Aunt,' Flora said as haughtily as she could, ignoring the comment on her clothes and only stammering a little over her words. 'So k-k-kind of you to ask.'

Frances blinked at her in surprise. She wasn't used to any kind of retort from the biddable Flora. Octavia, yes, but Flora . . . always the quiet one, the malleable one. The one who didn't answer back.

'Sit down.' The old woman gestured to one of the hard iron chairs, and Flora took it. 'So? Your new life . . . You'd better tell me about it. And what that firebrand of a sister of yours is up to. No doubt she's getting into plenty of trouble. I've seen her flaunting herself in the papers.'

'We're both f-f-fine, thanks,' Flora said sitting down. 'Neither of us is in any t-t-trouble.'

Her aunt looked cross. 'So you still haven't managed to fix that stutter. It's terribly irritating, Flora. Can't you stop it?'

She remembered how her aunt had tried to force her to control her speech in the past: making her stand in corners, hold ice cubes in her mouth, wear a special brace like a bridle over her tongue, having her hands slapped with canes when she couldn't get a word out. All of it had simply made the problem worse and increased her terror of opening her mouth at all. And her aunt had never bothered to find out about what was really making Flora stutter and tremble and shrink under the gaze of others . . .

'No, I can't,' Flora said, the words coming out quite crisply now. 'This isn't really a social visit, Aunt. I've c-c-come to ask you some things. I want you to tell me about the court case. About our mother.'

The old woman's expression hardened. There was a long pause and then she said, 'I see. I've been expecting this, but I assumed it would be Octavia who turned up on my doorstep. Ever since those articles appeared all over the press, raking up things that are best forgotten.'

'We were never able to remember it afterwards,' Flora said. 'Neither Octavia nor I can remember going to court with our mother, or anything about it.'

'Children often don't,' retorted her aunt, shrugging. 'I can hardly be blamed for that.'

'But why didn't you tell us?' As she said it, Flora realised that question lay at the heart of everything. Why hadn't the girls been allowed to know anything about their own past? Didn't they have a right to be told?

Aunt Frances frowned and pushed the book off her lap, sitting up straighter. 'It was not in your interests to know,' she stated. 'What good could it have done?' She sighed and then looked up at Flora, staring at her hard, suddenly invigorated. 'Don't you understand? Your blessing was to be fathered by my brother – but your curse was that mother of yours. Believe me, your lives would have been infinitely more difficult and utterly miserable if you had been left to grow up with that degenerate. It was my clear duty to my brother and to you to take you from her. There was no way she could be allowed to look after vulnerable children, not with her tendencies. The morals of an alley cat on heat!' Frances sniffed and made a sour face. 'I warned Arthur against her from the start. Told him she was too beautiful, too sensual. Women like that are enslaved by their own bodies. They are natural pleasure-seekers. And your mother was certainly one of *those*.'

'So – the stories in the paper were true? The things that were said about her in court?'

'About her hedonistic lifestyle? Of course they were! She dragged Arthur into her sordid world and made him just like her. The drinking, the drugs, the sex parties . . .' Frances shuddered. 'But he had already seen the error of their ways. The marriage was as good as over and he was about to escape her clutches when that accident happened. Believe me, the timing of it broke my heart. Just when he was going to get away from that evil harridan . . .'

Flora felt herself wince inside every time her aunt described her mother in such terms. 'But he was on his way to see her and us, wasn't he? When his plane crashed?'

'Yes.' Frances's face was full of bitterness. 'She demanded it. Treating him like some kind of glorified taxi! And he could never say no to her, even when he knew her for what she really was. And look what the kindness of his heart did . . . it killed him.' The faded old eyes filled with tears.

'But . . .' Flora felt she must press on while her aunt was answering her questions, saying more than could ever have been expected after a lifetime of silence. The physical distance between them for the last few months had obviously broken down some kind of barrier. Flora trembled as she phrased the next question. It was the one that had been haunting her day and night, ever since she had read those pieces in the paper and seen those photographs. Its resonance had increased as she had fallen deeper in love. She had begun to wonder who she was, and how a mother could leave her children . . . She hesitated and then spoke. 'What happened to our mother? Why did she leave us, and where did she go?'

Frances looked away, staring out over the lush leaves of her exotic palms and shrubs. Bright purple flowers with long yellow-tipped stamens shone against dark green leaves, providing a strange backdrop to the withered old woman. Her face hardened again and she said in a low voice, 'Your mother left of her own accord. She recognised, at last, her own degeneracy. And when she understood that she could no longer protect her children, she surrendered you to me, as she should have done from the start.' A look almost of glee came over her harrowed face. 'What you don't know, Flora, is that your mother was granted access by court order. She was permitted to visit you once a month . . . and she never did. Not once.'

It was as though she'd been punched in the stomach. 'Wh-wh-what?' Flora said breathlessly.

'You heard me. Your mother could have come here

if she'd wanted. But she never did.' Frances smiled a nasty, tight smile.

Flora shook her head and covered her face with her hands. 'I can't believe it,' she murmured. Then she looked at her aunt. 'But she's dead now, isn't she? Our mother?' She rose shakily to her feet. 'I need you to tell me where I can find her grave. Do you know? I want to visit it before I get married.'

'Married?' Her aunt looked astonished, then she laughed – a short, sharp, mirthless sound. 'I see. You girls are very fast workers. You little fool!'

'Where is the grave?' demanded Flora. Her aunt's attitude had made up her mind for her. She would accept Otto's proposal the minute he returned.

Frances looked her straight in the eye, one eyebrow raised and her mouth set in a smirk. Then she said, 'Your mother isn't dead, Flora. Or not as far as I know. She has always been paid a small stipend by the family trust. According to my sources, she is still drawing it, even after all this time. But I know nothing else. Don't try to pester me with more of your questions, there is nothing left to tell you. Now, if you don't mind, Flora, I have things I must be doing . . .'

34

'I can't believe that cow did that to you,' proclaimed Jasmine, sipping her glass of champagne.

'Totally,' agreed Rosie. She looked strange, somewhat pie-eyed, but seemed to be following the conversation all right. 'Amanda Radcliffe deserves what's coming to her.'

'I've never been so humiliated in my life,' Octavia declared. This girly get-together had been just what she needed after the awful incident in Noble's. She really had never experienced anything like it: she was used to going through life feeling important and treasured. Whenever she went into a shop, she was treated like royalty or a film star, cooed over and given the best of everything. The power of her credit cards and her growing profile in the press – they were still hanging about at every social occasion she went to – meant that she received VIP treatment everywhere. And she'd grown used to it exceedingly quickly, first with Gerry and now with her racy set of rich kids.

The sensation of being thrown out of a shop had been nasty, to say the least. She'd been consumed with rage as she'd called for Steve to come and collect her, and then had put out a hasty call to the girls. In a rush of sisterly solidarity, they'd hurried round to the house to support her.

'Amanda is just jealous,' Jasmine said. 'She needs to realise that her day is done. She used to be top of the heap, what with Gerry taking her round to everything and presenting her as if she was some kind of star. But she's a loser. It's all over for her now.' She looked over at Octavia. 'She hasn't got a single ounce of your star power. You need to grind her into the dust, once and for all.'

'But how?' Octavia frowned. Her blood was up as far as Amanda Radcliffe was concerned. She had spent her younger years plotting and scheming how to win her freedom from her captors. This was a new kind of challenge but it felt weirdly familiar too. *Don't mess with me, I will take you on and I will bloody well beat you . . .* It was how she'd coped with the restrictions placed on her as she'd grown up and she was prepared to carry on thinking that way if someone made her feel persecuted – and Amanda had made her feel exactly that.

Jasmine laughed as she pulled out a cigarette and lit it. 'I know! I've got it. That rackety old shop . . . It's what she cares about most, isn't it? If you want to hurt her, you should take it away from her.'

Octavia was puzzled. 'Take it away? How?'

Jasmine shrugged as she relaxed back on the sofa, stretching her long legs out in front of her. 'I dunno. But you've got money, haven't you? What you need to do is buy it.'

'Is it for sale?'

'With your kind of dosh, everything's for sale.' Jasmine grinned at her and puffed out a stream of cool menthol smoke. 'You should meet my brother Giles. He works in venture capital, knows all about this stuff, and he's got friends who might be able to help.'

Octavia felt a tremor of excitement and then shook her head. 'No, it's a ridiculous idea. I can't buy a shop! What on earth would I do with it? I don't know the first thing about shops.'

'Maybe not. But wouldn't it be worth it, just to see Radcliffe's face? Why don't you talk to Giles about it? It couldn't hurt.' Jasmine toyed with her leather bangles. 'I'll give him your number.'

'Hey,' Rosie interjected, 'can we go down to your pool? You've got a sauna and steam room, haven't you? Can we try them?'

'Of course.' Octavia smiled. 'We can do whatever you like. As long as it doesn't involve Amanda Radcliffe.' She got up and led the way down to the basement pool, wondering if it were really possible simply to buy a shop like Noble's. *Could I? But more to the point, would I?* Then she remembered the snarl on Amanda Radcliffe's face as she'd ordered her off the premises. *You bloody bet I would.*

Flora sobbed all the way back to London.

Vicky kept a diplomatic silence, as though she understood that, right now, Flora needed to feel the pain that her aunt's announcement had caused.

Our mother's alive! And all this time we thought she was dead . . . but why hasn't she ever seen us . . . why?

The thoughts circled round in her head, each orbit causing her a fresh flood of despair and a new wave of tears. *I have to see Octavia. She's the only one who can understand this.*

As they pulled to a halt in front of the house, Flora leapt out of the car and raced inside. Running into the hall, she shouted, 'Octavia? Where are you?'

There was no answer. But then, her sister might not even be in the house. In fact, if her recent movements were anything to go by, she was probably in some exclusive designer boutique, or in the arms of her boyfriend, or getting trashed in a trendy bar. Flora pulled out her phone and fired off a quick text: *Where are you? I need to see you right now. Important news.*

Vicky came in behind her, having parked the car. 'Are you okay?' she asked gently, coming up and hugging her cousin. 'Let's have a cup of tea and talk about this.'

Flora looked agonised. 'I have to talk to Octavia, I have to tell her . . .'

'Tell her what?'

Just then there was a babble of laughter coming up the back staircase, the one that led directly to the swimming pool on the lower-ground floor. A moment later Octavia appeared in her bathing suit and a towel, with a couple of other girls next to her. They were all laughing and buzzing with excitement.

Flora dashed forward. 'Tavy, there you are! I have to talk to you right now!'

'Oh, yes, how was our dear Aunt Frances?' Octavia asked sardonically, sashaying forward as she retucked her towel around her. 'Still the same boot-faced old battleaxe?'

Flora gazed at her, stricken. 'I have to talk to you alone,' she whispered.

'Why?' Octavia put a hand on her hip and struck an attitude, as though conscious of the eyes of the other girls on her. 'Whatever you've got to say, just say it.'

Flora wrestled with herself for a moment then said in a low voice, 'Come with me *right now.*' She grabbed her sister's arm and pulled her through another doorway into the barely used dining room, staring at her in amazement. 'Why are you acting that way, Tavy? Don't you know how important this is? Are you so obsessed with your friends that you don't even care about us any more?'

Octavia narrowed her eyes. 'You're the one who's obsessed! I don't want to know about the past, why can't you understand that? I want to let it go. There are no answers out there for us. We've got everything we need – all the money, everything. Let's live for now.'

'No, you're wrong!' cried Flora. 'We don't have everything we need – and there *is* an answer. Aunt Frances told me today that our mother is still alive!'

Octavia froze, her eyes suddenly frightened. Then she pulled the towel more tightly around her, shivering. 'What?'

'Yes – but no one knows where she is and Aunt Frances refused to say any more.' Flora clutched both of Octavia's arms. 'Don't you understand? Our mother is out there! We can find her!'

'I don't want to find her.' Octavia's face had turned stony. 'Why would I? She may as well be dead. I told you, I don't want to know! Just leave it, for Christ's sake, Flora. Now, I'm going back to my friends, if you don't mind. I don't want any part of this morbid delving into the past. I look forward, not back.'

And she pushed past her sister and stormed out of the room.

35

Octavia pounded along the pavement, her earphones delivering a suitably upbeat hip-hop song to keep her moving as she followed the path of the Thames. She ran, lost in her own world, scarcely aware of the long lines of traffic passing her in both directions, or of the other runners and pedestrians sharing the foot-path with her. The river, wide and grey and lined on the other side by flashy glass and steel blocks of flats, reflected her mood: sombre and low.

Last night Flora hadn't come to her room to brush her hair and it was hurting Octavia more than she could ever have guessed. She knew that she shouldn't have spoken the way she did or walked out on her sister, but everything was so confusing and horrible lately. It was just too much for her to cope with.

Why had Flora done it? Why had she gone back to open that can of worms? What good did it do to know that their mother was still alive? Octavia wiped away a trickle of sweat from her temple as she increased her pace and overtook some slow joggers taking their time in the centre of the pavement. Maybe Diane wasn't alive anyway. It was quite possible their aunt didn't know the truth herself. Vicky had told her what Flora had said in the car about a trust fund still paying out. Well, money could easily float away into a bank account somewhere and accumulate there, untouched.

It made no difference. Their mother was dead to them. They were orphans who only had each other. It was Flora who wanted to change all that, Flora who had broken their vow not to go back to Homerton, and had insisted on finding out about their mother despite Octavia's feelings. And it was Flora who wanted to get married and go away. She was considering marrying a man who lived in Germany, for God's sake!

It was painful to think about. Contemplating the loss of Flora, her adoring twin, her soul-mate, was like feeling a limb being torn off.

But what can I do? wondered Octavia. *She doesn't seem to need me any more. She talks to Vicky more than she talks to me.*

She'd heard the buzz of voices the night before coming from behind the closed doors of Flora's room when her friends had left and had known that Vicky was in there, deep in conversation with Flora. It had made Octavia feel sick and shaky, as though she'd been kicked out and replaced.

She realised she'd run a long way: she'd already passed Vauxhall Bridge and Tate Britain and she could see the spires of the Palace of Westminster growing clearer and more pronounced against the sky with every step she took. If she carried on like this, she'd find herself heading out to Greenwich. She turned round and started running back towards Chelsea.

Perhaps Octavia could persuade her sister to try and forget what Aunt Frances had said about their mother. *There's no point. No bloody point at all. I don't believe she's alive.*

She was nearly back at the house when the music playing through her iPhone was interrupted by the ringing tone. She took it out from the case strapped to her arm and examined it. The number was not one she knew. She hesitated. Then, on impulse, she pressed it to her ear. 'Hello?'

'Hi, Octavia Beaufort? My name is Giles Burlington . . . Jasmine's brother.' The voice was very deep and grown up. 'Jasmine tells me you're interested in a business opportunity.'

Octavia remembered Jasmine mentioning her brother. She'd been as good as her word. 'Yes, that's right. She said you might have some advice.'

'I could give you some advice, I suppose, but it might be more worth your while talking to a friend of mine. He's a hotshot Aussie who's been working in the States. He made a pile over there and now he's here, looking for new opportunities. Why don't I put you in touch with him?'

'Mmm, all right,' Octavia said. 'What's his name?'

'It's Ethan Brody. Listen, I'll give him your number and he'll give you a call, okay?'

'Okay, fine. I'll look forward to it.'

Flora sat at her window, staring out over the garden. She could hardly believe the way her world had transformed itself in just twenty-four hours. Their mother was not, as they had thought, dead. But where was she? And why had she never tried to contact her daughters?

And as for Octavia's behaviour . . . who had her sister become? The Octavia who had shared every moment of their odd, enclosed childhood would never have reacted like this. What had changed her? Hadn't they both always longed to know the end of the story – what had happened to the princess after her fairy-tale wedding?

Now they knew a lot more: about the tragic court case, the custody battle. But the fact that their mother was out there somewhere . . . that was the most extraordinary thing of all.

'You could have rescued us!' whispered Flora to herself, staring out at the trees that were leafless and bare against the sky. 'You could have found us. Why didn't you? Why didn't you love us?'

Just then there was a knock on the door. It opened. 'Flora?' It was Vicky. 'Flora – you've got a visitor . . .'

'I don't want to see anybody!'

'But you might want to see this one.' Vicky came further into the room. 'It's Otto.'

Flora lifted her head, amazed. 'Otto?'

Vicky nodded. 'He's just arrived out of the blue. Were you expecting him?'

'No!' Her misery vanished. She rushed to the mirror to examine her face. She picked up a brush and pulled it through her long fair hair. 'I was waiting for him to call. I can't believe it! How wonderful. Give me a moment to change and fix my face. Tell him I'll be right down.'

Vicky disappeared to look after Otto as Flora rushed to her dressing room and looked for something to change into. Her spirits soared. *He must have sensed that I needed him! Oh, God, I'm so lucky to have him . . .*

I can tell him about my mother, discuss it all with him. He'll know what to do. But first she would tell him that she'd decided to accept his proposal. They would be engaged.

Ten minutes later she was ready, refreshed and feeling pretty in a floral silk tea dress and teal-coloured peep-toe slingbacks. She went quickly down the stairs, wondering if Octavia was back from her run. Flora went to the drawing-room door and opened it, smiling brightly. Otto was standing with his back to her, looking out of the window.

'Hello, my darling,' she said happily. 'What a wonderful surprise!'

Otto turned. His face was sad. He didn't make any move to approach her or even to smile. 'Flora,' he said, and his voice sounded mournful.

'W-w-w-what is it?' She felt horribly frightened all of a sudden. What was wrong with Otto – *her* Otto who was always so kind, so supportive, so loving, so adoring . . . She approached him, but instead of holding out his arms to her he stiffened. She stopped. 'Otto – what's wrong?'

'My dear Flora,' he said sadly, 'I've come to tell you that, with great regret, I must end our relationship.'

She gasped. Horror filled her with a cold, sick feeling and the ends of her fingers prickled. '*What? Wh-wh-why?*'

'Why?' Otto drew himself up to his full height and squared his shoulders. 'Because I am a proud man, Flora. I thought we had told each other everything, that we had no secrets.'

Flora opened her mouth but no sound came out. Of course there were secrets. There were things she'd never told anyone.

'I do not think we can continue. I love you but I fear that no true love story can begin with deceit.'

She felt as though she might faint. What was he talking about? 'But, Otto, what do you mean? How I have deceived you?' she pleaded.

'You never said a word.' He walked over to the carved marble fireplace and turned his back to it, so that he faced her. 'You never explained yourself – that you are a great heiress. A woman of enormous wealth.' He threw out his arms, gesturing at their surroundings. 'This – this is all yours! Not a father's, not a mother's – yours and your sister's alone. Do you realise what people will say? That I am a fortune-hunter! A gigolo! That I wish to marry you for your money!' He shook his head, his brown eyes sad. 'I say again, I am a proud man, Flora. I am the last of the noble Barons von Schwetten. I cannot allow my family name to be besmirched by accusations of this sort. You should have told me who you are, that you have inherited the fortune of your family. Then I would have understood the situation . . . we could have made the world understand that we were in love and nothing more.'

'It could still be like that, Otto! No one knows we're together yet.'

His mouth turned down at the corners and he looked grim. 'But that is only part of it. You did not tell me everything, you were not open with me . . .'

'I didn't think it mattered!' she said, grasping the back of the sofa for support. She felt her heart racing and her breath coming quickly. 'P-p-please, Otto, please understand . . . I never m-m-meant to lie to you . . .'

I'm sorry, Flora. I love you, but I fear this has destroyed us. If our relationship begins this way, what does that say for us?' He shook his head again. 'No. We must part.' He walked towards her, took her hand and stared at her, looking deep into her eyes. 'Goodbye, my love.'

Then he left, pulling the drawing-room door to behind him.

Flora fell to the floor in a dead faint.

36

Octavia dropped a kiss on her sister's forehead. Flora seemed to be calm now. She was almost asleep, Octavia could see that. The sleeping pill that Vicky had supplied, the hot drink and the fact that she had cried herself out, had all combined to help her relax and slip into a doze. Soon, no doubt, she would be asleep.

Octavia turned and tiptoed out. Vicky was waiting for her in the corridor, looking anxious.

'Is Flora okay?' she whispered as Octavia shut the door quietly behind her.

Octavia nodded. 'But let's go and talk.'

They went to Vicky's sitting room on the next floor. Octavia sat down on the green sofa, pulling her grey wool cardigan tightly about her. She was wearing leggings with long, pink cashmere socks over the top.

'I just find it so hard to believe,' she began as Vicky went over to an armchair and flopped into it. 'Why on earth would Otto break up with Flora? He seemed absolutely mad about her.'

'Well, he certainly chose his moment,' Vicky muttered. 'It's the last thing she needs right now. You didn't see her coming back from Homerton. She was heartbroken. She told me everything last night about . . .' She looked uncomfortable. 'About your mother.'

'Then you probably know how I feel about that.' Octavia couldn't help sounding curt. 'I think she's wrong. I want her to leave it be.'

'Flora thinks she needs to know,' Vicky said softly.

'I don't see that anything good can come of it. What we learn can only hurt us.' Octavia was adamant. She sighed. 'But who knows what she'll want to do now? It's so cruel. Every time Flora builds up her confidence, something happens to knock her down.' She frowned. 'I thought Otto was a nice guy. I still can't understand why he did it.'

Vicky shook her head, her chestnut hair glinting as the light caught it. 'Flora wouldn't tell me. Did she tell you?'

'Nope. I couldn't get anything out of her. Poor Flora.' Octavia stood up. 'Vicky, have you ever checked this guy out?'

'Well, no . . . I can't say I have.' She looked worried. 'We've got no reason to doubt him, have we?'

'Of course not. But . . .' Octavia glanced around her. 'Where's your computer?'

'It's next door, in my office.'

'Let's go and have a look.'

They went to the office. Vicky sat down and booted up the computer, pulling up an internet search engine. She typed in Otto's name and instantly a large number of results were listed. She began to scroll through them. 'Looks like it's mostly business stuff. He's mentioned in business journals, quoted in trade papers. This is his company website.'

'Let's take a look,' said Octavia, leaning on the desk and peering at the screen.

Vicky clicked on it and pulled it up. It was only a few pages, stylishly and tastefully presented, explaining the concept of networks and creativity, and what he could offer his clients.

Vicky put on her glasses and read the content quickly. 'The usual corporate guff. Nothing mysterious there. He's a bit like a dating service but for businesses, as far as I can make out.'

'Anything about him personally?'

Vicky pulled up the page about Otto. There was a photograph of him, smiling, above a short biographical piece. 'Baron von Schwetten has extensive experience in his field. He studied Business at Heidelberg University . . .' and it went to give Otto's credentials.

'Just as he said,' Vicky said, with a shrug.

'Go back to the search results,' Octavia directed, and once they were back, saw that Otto had a Wikipedia entry. 'Try that.'

The page was short, giving his date of birth and a few facts about him. He was the only son of the previous Baron von Schwetten. He lived at Schloss Meckensberg. He ran his own business. A link directed anyone interested back to the company website.

'Shall we keep looking?' Vicky said.

Octavia sighed and stood back. 'No. We're probably wasting our time. Besides, if he and Flora are finished, then it doesn't make any difference anyway.'

'I always liked him,' Vicky offered. She clicked her

computer into hibernation. 'I'm a little bit less enamoured right now, though.'

'Yeah. What an arsehole, treating Flora like that.' Octavia remembered the awful sight of her sister lying dead white and unconscious on the floor of the drawing room. She had come round only a few minutes later, but seeing her twin like that had terrified Octavia.

'She loves him, though,' Vicky said almost sadly. 'She really does.'

'I know.' Octavia shook her head. 'That's what breaks my heart.'

Octavia stood under the stream of hot water, letting the force of the shower pound her skin. The tension seemed to leave her body as she bent her neck to the water. She felt better as she climbed out, ready to face the world again and to support Flora.

So long as she understands that we need to leave the past where it is.

She got out, dried herself and wrapped her soft white bathrobe around her body. Back in her bedroom, she found that a text message had arrived.

Hi. I understand you're interested in a business venture. Why don't we meet to talk about it? Tomorrow night, 8p.m., Paramount Club okay for you? E. Brody

He's a cool customer, she thought. *Not even a call first.* But something about the message intrigued her. Ethan Brody. An Aussie hotshot. *I'd like to meet him.*

She texted quickly back.

Yes. See you there. Octavia.

* * *

Flora lay in the darkness. She'd slept a few hours and then woken in the night. She'd alternated between waking and dozing, and whenever she was awake, tears had spilled from her eyes even though she sometimes wasn't even aware that she was crying. All she could wonder was why, why on earth, Otto had left her. The sense of abandonment was overwhelming.

Molly brought in a breakfast tray for her, to see if she could be tempted to eat. Octavia came tiptoeing in during the morning to ask if Flora was all right and if she could do anything. Flora muttered that there was nothing, she only wanted to be left alone. When Octavia ventured in a small voice that perhaps it was for the best that the relationship was over, Flora had snarled at her twin to go away – and, shocked, Octavia had scuttled out. Later, Flora had heard the internal phone sound and was sure that Steve had been summoned to take her sister somewhere.

Lucky Octavia, Flora thought bleakly. *She never suffers the way I do.*

It was early afternoon when the door opened again and there were soft footsteps over the carpet. Someone sat down in the armchair by the fireplace and stayed there quietly, watching and waiting. Eventually, Flora looked up. It was Vicky, gazing at her with clear, sympathetic eyes.

'I feel like my life is over,' Flora said despairingly, putting her head back on her pillow.

'Well, you can't stay here for the rest of it. There's an awful lot of it to go, you know,' Vicky said with a half laugh.

'I just don't know what the point is, that's all.'

Vicky leant forward, looking serious. 'You've got to

stop this, Flora. I mean it. You have to take control of your life and what happens to you. Do you want Otto back? If you do, then go and get him.'

Flora gaped at her, then said, 'But how?'

'You conquer your fears, you go and tell him the truth, and you see what happens. Maybe it's not meant to be – but if it is, then you shouldn't let it slip away.'

'I don't understand.' Flora sat up, interested despite herself.

'It's not too late to grasp what you want. You have to be prepared to take risks, that's all. It takes courage to put yourself on the line – but sometimes it's the only way to get results.'

'But . . . but . . .' Flora frowned. 'What should I do?'

Vicky smiled. 'Well, why don't we make some plans? I have an idea that just might work.'

37

The lift doors opened to reveal the interior of a glamorous bar. While it was lushly impressive, it was nothing compared to the view of London that spread out below for miles in every direction: the whole city glittered beneath them, pinpoints of light moving everywhere as traffic flowed through it.

A woman in a smart dark suit came up to Octavia as she waited at the entrance. In one swift glance she took in her Prada dress, Pringle cashmere wrap, Louboutins and the Hermès Kelly bag slung over one arm, and gave her a welcoming smile. 'May I help you?'

'Yes, I'm meeting Ethan Brody . . .' Octavia peered past her into the bar area, trying to see if she could spot the man she was meeting.

There was the faintest lift of one eyebrow. 'Of course. This way, please.'

Octavia followed the woman as she led her over to a table. As they approached the people in the bar, she tried to guess which one of them was Ethan Brody. As soon as she saw him, she knew that this was the man she was meeting. He was staring at his iPhone, messaging someone from the looks of it, but charisma almost shimmered off him. Even though he was sitting down, he looked to be tall, well over six foot probably, and his broad shoulders were encased in a sharply cut Gieves & Hawkes suit in navy blue with a faint pinstripe. He was frowning as he typed, a furrow in his otherwise unlined brow that brought together bold dark eyebrows above blue eyes speckled with hazel. His hair was short and dark blond, and he had almost cartoonishly handsome jutting features – a prominent nose and a square chin – but the effect was strong and masculine.

The moment she saw him, Octavia felt the power of his attractiveness. It made her a little dizzy and weak, then a small tornado of excitement began to whirl inside her.

I've always been a pushover for blonds, she thought, *but this is ridiculous.* She felt as though she wanted to walk right up to him, climb on the table, put her hand on the back of his head and pull his mouth to hers.

He looked up as they reached the table.

'Your guest, sir,' said the woman.

He smiled, one corner of his mouth raised higher than the other in a charmingly lopsided effect. 'Hi.' His Australian accent coloured a warm, attractive drawl.

'Hello. I'm Octavia Beaufort,' she said, sounding like a nervous child.

'I guessed.' He got to his feet, and she felt breathless as he towered over her. His masculine presence was quite overwhelming, almost frightening. Ferdy was a boy, rangy and slender, while this man was . . . well, most definitely a man. He held out an enormous hand. She took it and they shook hands. 'Good to meet you. I'm Ethan. Can I get you a drink?'

Octavia nodded, her mouth dry. 'I'll have a vodka and tonic, please.'

'Two of those, please,' he said to the greeter, who nodded and left. Ethan stepped from behind the table and pulled out a chair for his guest. 'Would you like to sit down?'

Octavia slipped into the chair.

'So,' he said, with another of those lopsided smiles she was already finding fascinating, 'let's talk business.'

Flora knocked on the door of the hotel room, her heart racing at double speed. She had an almost over-whelming urge to run away as fast as she could, but it was too late to go back now. She'd done it. She pushed her hands deeper into the pockets of her trench coat.

'*Ja?*' said a man from behind the door. She knew that voice.

'Room service,' she said in a low tone, hoping that it disguised her identity effectively.

There was a pause and then the voice said curtly, 'One moment.'

She waited. *Don't be frightened, remember what Vicky said. Sometimes you have to reach out and grab your destiny. It's the only way.*

Now she was here and it was actually happening, Flora could feel her courage mounting. She was going to see Otto and it was important that everything about her was positive, strong, attractive. She breathed in deeply and shook out her hair.

A second later the door opened and Otto stood there. For a moment he stared at her, his expression blank. Then he blinked, his soft brown eyes looking astonished. 'Flora?' he said.

She swallowed, then dropped her chin so that she was gazing up at him through her lashes. 'Otto,' she purred. 'How wonderful to see you.'

'But . . . what are you doing here?' He frowned.

Flora put a hand on his chest and pushed him gently backwards, advancing on him as she went. 'I had to see you. I couldn't let it end the way you wanted it to. I couldn't stand the idea that the last memory you would have of me would a miserable one . . . not after all the happy times we've had. Don't you agree?'

He looked bemused. 'Flora?' he said again, as though he suspected she was actually someone else.

'That's right. Flora.' She reached for his tie and pulled his face close to hers. 'Just one night. That's all I'm asking for.' She pressed her lips to his in a kiss. At first he resisted and she felt a gentle pull away from her. Then, as if he couldn't help himself, he made a noise like a low growl deep in his throat and surrendered to her. His lips met hers and he began to kiss her, pushing his tongue into her mouth. *Yes . . . this is what I want . . . just relax.* She opened her mouth wide and touched his tongue tentatively with her own. The feel of it made her stomach twist with excitement and she felt a twitch of arousal between her legs. She had never been touched there by anyone but herself; perhaps now, for the first time, she would know what it was like.

She pulled away, unbuttoned her coat and opened it, revealing that she was wearing only underwear: a black bra, suspender belt and stockings, and knickers of black, wispy lace that showed her pale blonde bush beneath. 'I want to make love to you, Otto,' she said in a low voice.

He stared at her, obviously affected by the sight of her. His breathing quickened. 'Oh my God,' he said. 'Flora . . .' He moved in to kiss her again, wrapping his arms around her and holding her head with one hand, the other stroking her back. He moaned gently as he touched her bra strap and the band of her suspender belt.

'Will you take me to bed, Otto?' she murmured against his mouth, and then he led her through the apartment and into his bedroom. They lay down on the bed together and began to kiss again. Flora wondered if she was supposed to do something or whether she should wait for him. *I'll make the first move . . . after all, I'm being passionate and bold tonight.* She reached her hand down to the waistband of his trousers and began to fumble with the clasp. Men liked to be touched, she knew that, so surely Otto would like her to . . .

She felt his fingers around her wrist, gently pulling her hand away from his trousers. He kissed her face delicately, speaking softly between each kiss. 'My darling, I want us to move very slowly.'

'Of course,' she whispered, 'there's no hurry, is there?'

'No . . .' He smiled down at her. 'No hurry.'

'Then . . we're not finished?' She rubbed a hand over his chest. 'Can the pride of the von Schwettens put up with me?'

He laughed. 'I've never seen this side of you, Flora! Do you know . . .' he turned to her, his eyes warm, his lips smiling, '. . . I like it. Very much.'

She rubbed up against him, her soft breasts pressed to his shirt, the nylon of her stockings scratching against his trousers. He put his hand down to her panties and rubbed his fingers across the lace, pressing down where her clitoris was and sending a tickling sensation rippling out from her groin. He slipped his fingers inside and rubbed lightly at her thatch, then stroked her outer lips, which she could tell were full and swollen with excitement.

'Has anyone ever had you before, darling?' he whispered in her ear.

'No,' her reply was barely audible.

He seemed to like this, and pressed his fingers harder against her pussy, rolling one of them around her entrance, pushing the tip in just a tiny way and then taking it out. His breathing was hard and fast now. He moved his fingertip, slippery with the moisture of her pussy, up to her clitoris and began to massage it with soft, circular movements, delicate at first but increasing in pressure as she responded.

She was startled by the pleasure she began to feel from the insistent pressure of his fingertip on her bud. She was powerless to resist and couldn't stop herself moving in rhythm to his circling finger. The feeling grew in intensity until she couldn't think of anything else but the deliciousness of it. Then her back stiffened and she clutched at Otto, panting out with the rush of pleasure that gripped her.

'Oh . . .' she sighed, smiling as she opened her eyes. 'Oh . . .' Everything she wanted to say seemed to be expressed by that one word. He put his arm around her and kissed her.

'You do not mind if I wait?' he asked tenderly.

'No, of course not! So . . . are we back together . . . ?'

'Perhaps.' He closed his eyes for a moment, then opened them, laughing. 'How can I resist you? Yes, then, we are back together – but on one condition.'

'What's that?' she asked, a tiny flutter of fear in her chest.

'We get married as soon as possible.' He ran a hand over her hair. 'Now I have had you like this, I do not think I can be without you for long.'

She wrapped her arms round him tightly. 'It's what I want too.'

You were right, Vicky, she thought. *I went out, and I got it. I made it happen. It's the right thing, I just know it.*

38

The block of flats was as unpleasant as Octavia remembered, and this time she had to climb the stairs alone as the others were already in the top-floor flat. She'd been summoned that morning by an urgent text from Iseult and had left before Flora was up.

As she reached the landing, she came face to face with the occupant of the flat opposite Roddy's. He was a mean-faced man in a tracksuit, baseball cap and trainers, and stared at her furtively, standing close to his front door, which he had obviously just closed. There was a fetid stench in the air that seemed to come from within his flat.

'Hello,' Octavia said uncertainly.

He grunted at her, shrugged and muttered something that sounded like 'fuckin' faggot', looking in the direction of Roddy's door.

Charming, Octavia thought. *Why doesn't Roddy move? This place is grim.*

Her knock was answered by Jasmine who said with a grin, 'Radcliffe's *really* fucked up this time.'

Inside, there was a council of war going on, with everyone sitting around Roddy's vast cutting table that had been cleared of its usual debris for once. Iseult was smoking furiously and looking very military in a utility shirt dress, given a little sparkle by a huge diamond brooch pinned to the breast. She sported a tiny pill-box hat on one side of her red bob, and chunky platform Mary Janes on her feet.

'Hiya,' Roddy said with a smile, pushing a bottle of wine towards Octavia. 'Have a drink, sweetie.'

'What's going on?' she asked, wide-eyed. The tone of the group was usually upbeat, if tinged with bitchiness at times because of the constant point-scoming and teasing. But Iseult looked really, properly angry today.

'Octavia!' she pronounced. 'You were right all along. Amanda Radcliffe is rotten to her bloody core.'

Octavia sat down and poured a glassful of Chablis. 'I've said so all along. What's she done now?'

'She has rejected Roddy!' declaimed Iseult. 'Can you imagine? Her shitty little shop thinks it's too good for his designs. I went to her with a brilliant idea – we would create a boutique within Noble's devoted exclusively to Roddy. He would also theme the whole shop along his own lines using Noble's furniture and fabrics. Together we would create a wonderful fashion news item, bringing life-giving publicity to all of us. It was beautiful – Noble's is exactly the right space, especially for the last collection.'

'Won't one of the other big stores give Roddy a boutique? After all, he's such a success since the fashion show . . .' ventured Octavia. She took a sip of the crisp, dry white wine.

Iseult looked disgruntled. She took a long drag on her cigarette and as she breathed out a cloud of smoke, said, 'Of course someone would. But it wouldn't be news – not really. What's so new about Harvey Nicks or Selfridges stocking a designer? They already have the best brands in the world, it's so hard to stand out there. But at Noble's, Roddy could be news. There's no one else to outshine him. And the space is so wonderfully unique. But . . .' She looked sour. 'Radcliffe was having none of it.'

'She's got a grudge against us,' piped up Jasmine. 'That's why.'

'I had to *crawl* on my *belly* to her,' snarled Iseult.

'She did, I was there,' Roddy said with a smile. He seemed more amused than anything else, as though he was enjoying seeing Iseult in full tigress mode.

'She let me go through the whole spiel. She listened to all of it. I flattered, I fawned, I grovelled. I told her how marvellous she is, how much I love her fucking miserable shop is, what we could do for each other. And after all that, she simply said no. How lovely but no. And that was that. We had to leave with our tails between our legs.' Iseult's eyes flashed at the memory. 'So humiliating.'

'But she's crazy,' Octavia said, puzzled by Amanda's behaviour. 'It's a brilliant idea, anyone can see that.'

'Hmm. It is, isn't it?' Iseult looked a little mollified. 'But we haven't an earthly . . .'

'Unless . . .' Jasmine leant forward and stared at Octavia. 'Unless you're serious about buying Noble's.'

Iseult was instantly attentive. 'What's that?'

Octavia laughed almost nervously. 'Oh, it was a bit

of a joke. Jaz suggested that I should buy Noble's after Amanda threw me off the premises.'

'Threw you out? You see!' Iseult looked even more indignant. 'She's a menace!'

'But buying the place and throwing her out is perhaps a bit of an extreme reaction.' Octavia took another sip of her wine.

'I don't think so at all,' said Iseult, her tone cool as she tapped her ash into a marble ashtray.

'It's kind of classy,' Roddy said admiringly.

Jasmine fixed Octavia with a stare. 'My brother said he'd introduced you to his friend. Apparently it's quite interesting as a business idea – Giles says Noble's is ripe for a takeover and fresh investment.'

Iseult was excited. She looked about, the little pill-box hat bobbing on her head. 'What fun! Our own shop. Think what we could do with Noble's, how we could reinvent it. We could showcase Roddy, but we could also make it a wonderful haven for British design – and new talent from all over the world. It has so much potential!'

'I suppose it does,' Octavia said, trying to sound casual. The meeting with Ethan Brody had, if she was honest, passed in a cloud of lust. She hadn't really seriously entertained the idea that she might buy Noble's, it had just seemed like a fun idea, and then she'd hardly heard a word he'd said, she'd been so enraptured by the sight of his broad shoulders and hazel-flecked eyes. She'd been stupidly disappointed when he'd looked at his watch and said that he had to go. Was it her imagination or had he seemed a little regretful? They'd left it that he would be in touch when he'd done some more research into Noble's.

'Call this man at once!' cried Iseult. She was very animated, her eyes bright and her cheeks lightly flushed. 'This is perfect, Octavia! A wonderful use for your frankly immorally huge resources.'

Roddy fixed her with a gimlet gaze. He was wearing a stunning tartan shirt with mother-of-pearl buttons sewn all over it. 'Are you serious about this, Octavia? Or is it just little rich girl talk – you want to take Amanda's toys out of her pram?'

All eyes were fixed on Octavia while they waited for her answer. She was disconcerted. It had been a throwaway idea and yet it was gathering a momentum she simply hadn't expected. Everyone was taking it seriously . . . very seriously from the looks of things.

Do I really want to buy a shop? What on earth would I do with it when I had it? Octavia stared down at the table and traced a groove, probably made by a pair of Roddy's cutting shears, with the tip of her finger. *And yet . . . Iseult's ideas really do sound exciting. And there's nothing in the world I love more than shopping. What better than to have my own place to play in?* And then there was the simple question of what she was going to do with her life. Could she really spend the next sixty years buying things? Was that all she was ever going to do?

She'd vaguely imagined how she would spend her time once the initial excitement of her new life was over: she had thought of charity work – though what exactly she didn't know – or perhaps investing in things that interested her: films, shows, art – those nice, glamorous activities that involved plenty of parties . . .

So what could be better than taking on one of the most famous shops in the world and breathing new life into it? She smiled as another thought crossed her mind. *And*

302

I can't pretend it wouldn't feel very nice indeed to rub Amanda's nose in it. Exquisite, in fact...

Octavia looked up. 'You know what? I'm very serious. I'll call Ethan today. I'll need you all to help me. But why the hell shouldn't we take it on, and make a success of it?'

Jasmine clapped her hands with glee, while Iseult cheered and called for wine. Roddy stared at Octavia, his grey eyes inscrutable, a small smile playing about his lips.

And now I've got the perfect excuse to spend a great deal more time with Ethan Brody, she thought, and a ripple of pleasurable lust ran through her.

39

The bus journey had not been as terrifying as Flora had feared, though it had still been stressful. She was so ignorant of the city, and found the sheer number of people everywhere daunting. But the bus had been preferable to the underground, which she was still too frightened to venture into. She could have asked Steve to bring her, she trusted in his discretion, but something had made her want to keep this visit completely secret. She had not even told Otto, even though they were now engaged. She wanted to confide in him, but not yet.

Perhaps it was crazy, but she was acting on complete impulse. The thought of doing this had crossed her mind before, but it was only after her relationship with Otto was re-established that she had decided to do it. Now. At once. *What did Vicky say? I've got to make things happen. She was right. I've won Otto back. Now I'm going to start finding out what I need to know.*

She walked along the Soho backstreet. Heavily made-up girls stood in front of doorways with glittering curtains obscuring the interior, and there were seedy-looking bookshops, underwear and rubber goods shops, and others displaying blacked-out windows and printed warnings that only adults should pass beyond the entrance.

'How much, love?' a man called to her, and laughed as she walked past. Flora ignored him but she felt painfully self-conscious in her Chloé wide-legged wool trousers, long camel overcoat and Tod's loafers. She looked as though she should be strolling down New Bond Street, not walking past prostitutes and sex shops in a red light district.

God, I hope I'm doing the right thing. The address had meant nothing to her when she had found it on the internet. If she'd known what kind of area this was, she doubted she would ever have considered keeping this appointment.

At last she found the address she was looking for. To her relief, it was at the more salubrious end of the street, between an inoffensive-looking movie memorabilia shop and a colourful Italian deli. Flora looked for the name: there it was. A small label next to the buzzer read *Falcon*. She pressed it, and a moment later there was an answering buzz and a click as the door lock released.

She pushed it open. Inside a narrow hallway, a steep flight of stairs led upwards. Flora climbed them, trying to suppress the fear that lay just below the surface. Keeping calm was an effort, but she knew she had to. If she started to panic, God alone knew what would happen . . .

I've got to get control, she told herself sternly as she neared the top. *Just like Vicky said. After all, I'm going to be a married woman soon. I'm an adult now. I can't be like a frightened child all my life.*

Not that she was frightened by the idea of the wedding. Otto had been adamant that he wanted a small, quiet occasion, with only immediate family there. No fuss, no frills, nothing to draw attention to them. They had even decided against a formal announcement of the engagement, fearing it would only bring unwelcome press attention and more delving into the twins' lives and pasts. Otto had been very sympathetic when Flora had told him what had recently happened. 'Then we will make sure these vultures have nothing else to get their nasty beaks into!' he had declared. 'Why should our private affairs be made public? We will keep ourselves to ourselves.' She'd been grateful for his under-standing. But she hadn't even told Otto about what she was doing now.

The door at the top of the stairs had a modest brass plate screwed to it, also reading *Falcon* in engraved letters. Flora knocked on the door. A moment later it opened to reveal a man with a slightly anxious expres-sion. 'Yeah?' he said. His accent was American and he was wearing a shabby dark suit with a black jumper underneath it. His eyes were dark and his thick black hair rather messy. His face, though tired and shad-owed with stubble around chin and jaw, was startlingly handsome, with a strong straight nose and full sensual lips.

'F-F-Flora,' she stuttered, 'B-Beaufort . . .'

'Huh?' He frowned.

'I h-h-have an ap . . . an ap . . .'

'Appointment?' he suggested. Then his face cleared. 'Oh, yeah. Lily said. I thought you might be the guy come about the air conditioning. It's kaput again. The goddamn thing eats money. Three times I've had it fixed, this summer alone. Come in. Come in.'

She followed him into a shabby office lined with filing cabinets. There was a Formica wood-effect desk with a computer on it and a telephone. He consulted a book lying open on the desk. 'Oh, yeah, here you are. Please, come into my room.'

He went to another door, opened it and showed her into an even shabbier, messier room, with yet more filing cabinets and a much bigger desk, though still cheaply veneered. A grubby window with a vent in an upper pane looked down on to the street below. He went behind the desk and sat down, gesturing to Flora to take the chair in front of it. He spent a few minutes looking at his computer screen and moving the mouse, then sat back, stared at her and said, 'So. How can I help?'

'You're Nick Falcon, aren't you?' she said shyly.

He laughed. 'Yeah, I forgot my side of the introductions.' He stood up and held out his hand. 'Nick Falcon at your service. How do you do? Would you like coffee or something? Lily will be back in a moment with milk and cookies.'

'No, thanks.' Flora smiled back. She couldn't help warming to him, even though she'd only known him a few moments. Perhaps it was his easy American style but she could feel her nerves melting away and she relaxed. 'I think I spoke to Lily on the telephone? I told her a little about what I want.'

'Oh, yeah. She left me a note here.' He picked up a scrap of a paper and looked at it, his dark eyes scanning the handwriting. 'Okay, so it's a missing person, is it? It says you're searching for your mother.' He looked up at her, fixing her with a steady gaze. 'So you were adopted or something? Want to find out who your birth mother is?'

'Not exactly. I know who she is. But until very recently I thought she was dead. My aunt – who brought me and my sister up – has just told me that she believes my mother is still alive. If she is, I want to find her.'

Nick nodded, an understanding expression on his face. 'Sure. Sure you do.' He put down the paper, pushed his chair back from the desk and put his feet up on it, crossing them at the ankle. Then he pressed the tips of his fingers together and stared at the ceiling. 'Okay, so you maybe want to trace your mother. That should be straightforward enough, if you can give me the necessary information. But first I have to ask you to think through whether you *really* want to find her . . . I gotta tell you that there are plenty of people I've worked with who end up wishing like hell that they'd never started looking for a long-lost parent. They have a wonderful dream of this person who's going to welcome them with open arms, cry all over them, then listen to and solve all their problems.' Nick shook his head. 'I've never seen that happen. Not even once. I've seen some tears and some hugs – but I've never seen anyone find what they really want, which is perfection. So before I tell you that I can make your dreams come true, you ought to know that.'

Flora stared at him, biting her lip. 'M-m-maybe you're right,' she said, suddenly unsure.

'Let me guess.' Nick put his feet down and leant towards her. His eyes, she noticed, were extraordinarily intense, almost black in colour. Was he Italian?

Spanish? 'Your aunt was like a mother to you, but she didn't always understand you, maybe didn't give you much attention. But when you find your mom, she's gonna be all over you and make everything better, right? Maybe, just maybe, that will happen. But why did she go away in the first place? Now, I'm not making judgments. I'm just saying – ask yourself the question first before you start all this.'

There was a pause. Flora stared down at her hands. *I need to think about this. He's right. What am I going to gain? Is it right to dig it all up? Maybe I need to be like Octavia and forget all about it. Maybe I need to move on . . .*

'Hey, it's okay,' Nick said kindly. He smiled at her. 'I don't mean you shouldn't do it. Just that you should go into it with your eyes open.'

Flora smiled back weakly. 'You're right. But . . . I'm getting married. I feel like I want to know the truth about my past before I can move on with my future. Maybe that's just stupid . . . My sister and I were involved in a big court case, you see, because our family has a lot of money. My mother mysteriously gave up custody of us, and I just want to know why . . . why she left us. Why she's never been in contact . . . Why she won't be at my wedding day . . .' She stopped, feeling her eyes filling with tears.

'Hey, I understand. It's only natural. Hell, I love my mother to bits, can't imagine life without her in it. Why should you have to live without yours? And I guarantee I can find her for you, that's not the issue.' Nick smiled again. 'Listen, did you bring any information with you today?'

Flora pulled a file out of her bag. 'I printed off

309

everything I could find on the internet, and I wrote down everything I could remember about my parents and what my aunt said.'

He reached for the file. 'That's great. You leave this with me, go away and think about it. If you want to proceed, just give me the word. Meanwhile, I'll send you details of my fees and the likely costs of the operation once I've had time to assess it. Does that sound okay?'

She smiled and nodded, feeling comforted.

He stared at her again, as if seeing her for the first time. 'So you're getting married, huh? If you come from as much money as you look like you do, then you'd better be sure you're getting a pre-nup.'

'Oh, I am,' Flora said earnestly. 'Otto insists on it.'

'Otto? Your husband-to-be a Brit?'

She shook her head. 'He's German.'

Nick smiled at her. 'That's lucky. Make sure you get your pre-nup done in Germany, okay? It'll hold weight there. A British pre-nup is about as effective as writing to Santa Claus. Means nothing.'

Flora laughed. 'Thanks for the advice.'

'You're very welcome.' He put the file down on his desk and patted it. 'Leave this with me. And I'll be in touch.'

40

Octavia put down the phone and sighed, shivering delightedly. That sexy Australian voice . . . she only had to hear Ethan's low drawl and she started to turn to jelly. *He's delicious*, she thought.

And keen to see her, from the sounds of it. He'd arranged to come round to the house the following evening, to talk through the Noble's scheme.

Octavia heard the front door slam and went out into the hallway. Flora was there, taking off her coat, her face flushed from the cold outside.

'Hi,' Octavia said, grinning, 'I'm glad to see you're up and about. Vicky said she'd had a talk with you and you're feeling much better.'

'Yes . . . yes . . .' Flora's flush deepened. 'I've been meaning to talk to you about that. We've been missing each other.'

'Come and talk to me now then,' Octavia said. 'I'm all yours.' They sat down in the drawing room. It was already almost dark outside and the streetlights were beginning to glow orange against the inky sky.

Flora sat down opposite her. Something in her eyes

made Octavia apprehensive. 'What is it?' she said, trying not to sound worried.

Her sister ran her hands through her hair and took a deep breath. 'I'm . . . I'm back with Otto.'

Octavia frowned, absorbing the news. 'Right . . .'

'And we're engaged. Properly engaged. He wants us to get married as soon as possible.'

Octavia opened her mouth to say something but she was speechless. She could only blink dumbly at her sister, trying to come to terms with this surprise.

Flora rushed in to fill the gap. 'I know what you're going to say, honestly I do.'

'I was going to say – that was fast work. You've only just broken up with him,' Octavia said, trying to sound jokey. She couldn't maintain it. Her smile faded. 'But Flora – why would you get back with him when he dumped you like that?'

'It was a misunderstanding,' she said firmly. 'We've sorted it out.'

Octavia summoned an image of Otto to mind. He was nice enough, but was he really the man Flora should spend the rest of her life with? There was something so ordinary about him. He didn't have the pin-up pretty-boy looks of Ferdy, or the crackling charisma of Ethan Brody. But Flora must see something in him. Octavia said tentatively, 'Have you . . . have you slept together?'

Flora's face went crimson. She gazed at the floor and then said quietly, 'No – but almost. Otto wants us to take things slowly.'

'Jesus, Flora! He wants to take sex slowly, but he thinks you should get married right away! That sounds completely arse about face to me. How can you even consider marrying someone you haven't slept with? You're still a virgin! You haven't had any experience of the world.'

'We're engaged, we've got all the time we need to discover each other.' Flora's expression changed and she looked sad. 'Oh, Tavy . . . I thought you'd be happy for me.'

'I am, I am . . . but . . . oh, it's all so sudden, so fast!' Seeing her sister's expression, Octavia tried to make a joke. 'You weren't supposed to get married before me!' Then her smile faltered and she buried her face in her hands.

Flora rushed over to her twin, kneeling at her feet and reaching up to clasp her hands, pulling them away from her sister's face. Octavia found herself looking into those dear, familiar violet-blue eyes that were now so desperate and pleading.

'What are you worried about, Tavy?' she asked. 'I'm so sure, and so is Otto. He says he's my destiny, and I believe him.'

'But this is the guy who wanted to dump you! Break your heart and dump you. How can you marry him now?'

'Because I love him,' Flora said simply.

Octavia gazed at her sister, stricken. 'But, Flora . . .' She looked imploringly at her. 'You're going to leave me. I can't bear it. Why do you need to get married?'

'What else do you do when you fall in love?' asked Flora. The happiness in her eyes was so great that Octavia couldn't bring herself to keep arguing against her obvious bliss. 'I'll always be here for you, nothing will change that, even if we live apart sometimes. Please be happy for me, Octavia,' she said quietly.

'Well . . .' Octavia managed to summon a smile. She could see how much it meant to Flora. *She loves Otto. I can't make her choose between us. And I can't risk losing her completely.* 'I'll try, sis. And . . . if I do . . . will you promise me something?'

'You know I will – what?'

'Promise me you'll leave all this stuff about our mother alone?'

Flora went very still for a moment and then she said in a small voice, 'All right.'

Octavia smiled. 'Then I'll be behind you all the way.'

'Thank you, thank you!' Flora smiled broadly and gave her a hug. 'And you'll be my bridesmaid, won't you? I couldn't dream of asking anyone else . . .'

'I'm glad to hear it! Of course I will, darling!' Octavia hugged her sister back hard, hoping Flora would think that the tears pouring down her face were ones of joy.

When Flora told Vicky about the engagement, her cousin seemed delighted though there was a slight shadow of reserve in her eyes, and she added the caveat 'As long as you're sure' after her congratulations.

'I am sure,' Flora said with determination. She had come into Vicky's office, from where she ran everything to do with the twins' lives, and now sat down on the chair opposite her cousin's desk.

Vicky spun round in her swivel seat so that she faced Flora, and smiled. 'Good for you. I know it's what you wanted. So when is the wedding?'

'I don't know. We've not even discussed dates yet, it's all been so fast. Otto's left again today to go the States but he'll be back in a few days. I know he wants it to be soon, and so do I. But there'll be plenty to organise. I'm going to rely on you a bit there, Vicky.'

A shadow passed over Vicky's face.

'What is it? Is something bothering you?' asked Flora, concerned.

'It's nothing, nothing . . . I've just been so happy here, working for you and Octavia, I've loved the last few months. I didn't want anything to change, I suppose. And now your hero has arrived to carry you off.' Vicky played self-consciously with her fountain pen and stared at the floor.

'You mustn't worry about that,' Flora said earnestly. 'We're still going to need you – probably more than ever. We'll have this home to run no matter what, and I'm going to suggest to Otto that we keep our main base here. After all, this house is so enormous, I'm sure with a bit of jiggling about, we can more than accommodate us all. And he's already spoken about expanding his property portfolio and buying a place in New York and perhaps in Hong Kong as well. There's no question about it, Vicky, you'll always have a place here. I'd never be able to cope without you, if I'm honest.'

Vicky's face cleared. 'That's a relief. I can't pretend you haven't set my mind at rest. I was selfishly thinking of myself.'

'Don't be silly. I understand.' Flora smiled.

'There's one more thing,' Vicky said, and looked worried again. 'I don't want you to think I'm prying but . . . you are going to get a pre-nup, aren't you?'

Flora laughed. 'You think he might be after my money? Please, you don't have to worry about that. Believe me, we're going to have a pre-nup. And do you know why? Because Otto wants one! He says he loves me, but he has to guard the von Schwetten inheritance against any possibility of divorce.'

Vicky couldn't prevent a look of disbelief from crossing her face. 'He wants to stop *you* getting any of *his* money?'

'Yes! You see – he's not after my fortune. He has his own.'

There was a pause while Vicky absorbed this. 'Well ... that's good then. I'm glad you're being sensible,' she said at last.

'And we'd better start planning the wedding right away,' Flora added, 'because if I know Otto, he's going to want to do it the day after tomorrow. You will help me, won't you?'

'You don't have to ask,' said Vicky, looking instantly alert and ready for business. 'Whatever happens, you can count on me.'

41

Octavia picked what she was going to wear for her next meeting with Ethan Brody very carefully. She wanted to look drop-dead sexy, so she rifled through her extensive wardrobe, looking for exactly the right thing. *I shouldn't be doing this,* she told herself, as she scoured the packed rails of her dressing room. *I have a boyfriend after all.*

But she'd always known that what she had with Ferdy wasn't love. It was, she realised, nothing like it. It wasn't even physical infatuation, she could see that now. It was a sweet, fulfilling liaison that had been exactly what she had needed: Ferdy had given her the beginning steps, taught her the first things about sex, but she wanted to move on now, get to the next level. Her initiation had been just right, helping her to explore the sensual world without fear or pain, and she was grateful for that, but she sensed something more earth-shattering waiting out there and she was hungry for it.

If her physical reaction to Ethan Brody were anything to go by, she might have found the man who could take her to the next stage. Being with him was

317

like being mesmerised; she could hardly take her eyes off him and it took all her strength to fight the impulse to reach out and touch him. The sound of his voice, deep and gravelly, sent shivers down her spine and aroused her all on its own.

Octavia selected a scarlet Giorgio Armani dress and studded black stilettos that had a slight air of bondage about them. If this didn't say sexy then she had no idea what did. She gazed into the mirror. The dewy look that she'd had all her life was perhaps a tiny bit faded . . . a legacy of her recent late nights and the fact that she was learning how to tolerate her drink better. She had begun to notice that the whites of her eyes were often bloodshot, and that her skin was dry and flaky in places as a consequence of dehydration. *I must book myself in for some decent treatments,* she thought, a little aghast to see the effects of her partying lifestyle. But, as she stroked mascara on to her long lashes, she knew that she was still a knockout. Nothing could diminish the magnetic quality of her violet-blue eyes, or the shimmering curtain of golden hair, or the delicate cheekbones that she highlighted with a light dusting of glittering bronzing powder.

She stood back and assessed herself: *Not too bad.* She spun on her toes so that she could inspect her back view – the neat bottom and long slim legs. *I only hope Ethan notices, that's all . . .*

The house telephone went: it was Molly, announcing Ethan's arrival. She had put him the library, as Octavia had instructed. It was intimate and cosy in there, a panelled room with bookshelves, pictures, sofas and an open fire, and much less formal than the drawing room.

He's here, Octavia thought, excited. Her eyes sparkled. *Go get him, girl.*

Ethan was standing by the bookcase examining the volumes, a crystal glass of fine single malt whisky in his hand which Molly had obviously supplied.

Octavia wanted to gasp at the sight of him: he was even more broad-shouldered than she remembered, with a rugby player's physique. Instead she stood in the doorway, dropped one shoulder seductively and said in a low voice, 'Well, hello.'

Ethan turned round, and smiled at the sight of her, obviously impressed by what he saw. 'Hello. I'm just admiring your collection of books.'

'Thank you.'

He came towards her and Octavia's heart raced with excitement. Leaning forward, he kissed her on each cheek and she smelt the warm vanilla scent of his cologne. She hoped he didn't notice that she was shaking slightly, and that her knees were decidedly weak when he came close to her.

'Do you live here with your parents?' he asked, as they walked round to the sofas. Octavia had asked Vicky to redesign this room not long after they'd moved in. It contrasted with the cool modernism of the rest of the house with its snug air. The sofas were covered in a muted tartan with big soft cushions all over them, and a thick pale grey sheepskin rug covered the floor.

She shook her head as she sat down, her very short skirt riding up even higher. 'No. With my sister. So what did Giles Burlington tell you about me?'

Ethan sat down on the sofa opposite her. 'He said

319

you're a friend of his sister's and you've got some money you want to invest. I assumed it was a birthday present or a legacy or something. Maybe fifty grand, maybe less . . . and you're interested in buying a stake in your favourite shop.'

Octavia laughed. 'It's not quite like that.' She got up, went to the drinks table and poured herself a measure of vodka, added a shot of fresh lime juice and topped it up with soda water and ice. Then she looked Ethan right in the face. 'I don't have fifty grand to invest. I've got more like . . . fifty million.'

His mouth dropped open and he gaped at her. She couldn't help laughing again at the astonishment written all over his face.

'Fifty . . . *million*?' he spluttered.

'Yes. My sister and I are orphans, and we've inherited our father's fortune.'

'Hang on. Octavia . . . ?'

'Beaufort,' she supplied helpfully.

'*Those* Beauforts? The steel dynasty?'

She nodded. Surprise transformed his face, making him look adorably boyish.

'But . . .' He swallowed, and took a quick sip of his drink. 'That means you've got . . .'

'As I said, millions.'

He gazed at her. 'You could buy the whole thing, lock, stock and barrel,' he said frankly.

'Could I?'

'Well, I'm exaggerating a little. The premises are worth a pretty penny as you can imagine. And I wouldn't advise it anyway . . . But . . .' He shook his head, trying to take it in.

'As you can probably guess, I'm completely ignorant

about business. I'll need you to explain everything,' Octavia said, sitting down again and crossing her legs. 'If I wanted to buy Noble's, what would I do?'

Ethan looked at her smooth, bronzed limbs and took another mouthful of his drink. 'Well, it's lucky for you that the structure of Noble's is fairly simple. It's been in the Radcliffe family for years, and they haven't ever streamlined their affairs – which is probably why they're in the trouble that they are.' He looked happier now he was back on familiar territory and seemed to have absorbed Octavia's bombshell. 'They're a public company, they have shareholders, but to be honest they haven't paid out a dividend for a long time. In fact, they're more likely to make a rights issue, the way they're going.'

'Rights issue?'

'Ask their shareholders for money to prop up the company. They are in debt big time and haven't made an operating profit for years. Sooner or later they're going to have to do something drastic.' Ethan rolled his glass so that the amber liquid swirled around the crystal. 'If you're serious about buying in, then I would suggest that you form a company and set about buying a managing stake in Noble's. You'd be surprised how little you need to own into order to have control. But the family and shareholders will have to let you do that.'

'Form a company?' Octavia frowned. 'That all sounds very businesslike. Are you sure?'

'If you want to get into business, then you are going to have to be businesslike.' Ethan grinned at her. 'But you don't have to do it alone. I'm happy to take on all the boring aspects and look after them for you.'

'You mean . . .' Octavia leant forward, aware that she was giving him a seductive view of her breasts as they emerged from her dress, '. . . we could start a company together?'

He raised an eyebrow at her. 'I'd say that's a very good idea. I know how all this works but I don't have the kind of capital at your disposal. You've got the capital but you're lost in the corporate world. I think we'd make an excellent partnership.'

'Practically perfect,' murmured Octavia. She took a sip of her vodka and soda. It prickled pleasingly across her tongue. She stood up and went to the fireplace, looking at her reflection in the mirror above it. She put down her glass, then ran her fingers through her hair, piling it up on top of her head before letting it fall down in a golden waterfall. She heard Ethan get up and the next moment he appeared behind her in the mirror.

'You are a very sexy girl,' he said, looking at her appreciatively.

'Did you always think so? Or is it since you learnt about my money?' she said.

'I thought you were gorgeous the moment I laid eyes on you. How could I not?' he said, and the devastatingly attractive lopsided smile curved his lips. 'But you know what they say about money being an aphrodisiac . . . Maybe it makes you even more high-octane. If that's possible.'

Octavia licked her lips and looked up at his reflection from under her lashes. Her belly was burning with desire and she could feel dampness between her legs. No one had ever had an effect like this on her. 'Is it wise, us going into business together?'

He stood closer to her, so that their bodies were almost touching. 'I don't think we're going to be able to stop ourselves,' he replied. She felt his hand touch her waist, very lightly. The next moment she'd spun round and was lost in a hot, passionate kiss as he pulled her tightly into his arms.

'Oh, Ferdy darling, it's so sweet of you to call me, but I don't think I can come with you today.' Octavia lay in bed, naked, enjoying the sensation of the sheets against her skin. Her body seemed to have come alive in an electric way since Ethan had kissed her the previous night. *Imagine how I'm going to feel when he makes love to me,* she thought with a kind of wonderment.

'Really?' Ferdy sounded disappointed. 'I thought you were on for it.'

'I was, but . . .' Octavia took a deep breath and said, 'Actually, I think we should just be friends from now on. Not boyfriend and girlfriend any more. Okay?'

There was a pause and then Ferdy said in a surprised voice, 'We're breaking up?'

Octavia rolled on to her stomach, making an agonised face and wishing this conversation was over. 'Well, in a way. I mean, we can still be friends. But I don't think we should see each other like *that* any more.'

'But why?'

'Just because . . . oh, please, Ferdy, don't make it difficult for me. You're a lovely bloke but . . . I don't think it's meant to be forever that's all. We had great fun together, but now . . . I have to move on. I'll see you soon, darling. 'Bye!'

She clicked the phone off, feeling guilty on the one hand but relieved on the other. Just one kiss with Ethan had been more unbearably erotic than her whole adventure with Ferdy. Why should that be? After all, Ferdy was attractive, good in bed, well endowed . . . why should there be this burning magic with Ethan when there was so little with Ferdy? It was a mystery, but Octavia had no interest in finding out the answer. All she felt was an extraordinary sense of excitement: the whole world, her future, seemed bright and thrilling, now that she was going to be sharing them with Ethan. She rubbed a hand luxuriously over her naked skin, wishing that he were there to kiss her, touch her, suck on her breasts and delve with those long, cool fingers . . . She shivered.

There wasn't long to wait.

42

It was Octavia's idea to get Roddy to design Flora's wedding dress.

'He's absolutely amazing,' she said breathlessly, bouncing on her sister's bed with enthusiasm. 'And no one else will be able to make something in the time.'

'We haven't got a firm date yet,' Flora said, massaging Crème de la Mer into her face. She was fresh from the shower in a white cotton bathrobe with her damp hair up in a towel turban. 'Otto's back the day after tomorrow. Then we'll settle the actual day.'

'Yes, but you want to do it as soon as possible. A designer dress takes months and months usually! If you don't go with Roddy, you'll never get anything.'

'Oh, I'd be happy with something off the peg. It doesn't have to be fancy. Won't Harrods have something?'

'Well, I expect they will, but it won't have half the cachet of a properly designed dress! And we can get some publicity for Roddy too.' Octavia seemed very pleased with herself.

Flora put down her pot of face cream, looking dubious.

'I'm not sure about that . . . Otto doesn't want any fuss around the wedding. He'd be cross if he thought we'd turned it into some kind of publicity circus.'

'Don't be silly, of course we won't. We'll just release some pictures after the event, for the odd paper or fashion magazine that will be interested, that's all.' Octavia gave her sister a pleading look. 'Won't you consider it? For me?'

Flora thought for a moment and then said, 'He can show me some designs if he wants, but I have to like it, and he has to be able to make it in the time left. I can't be without a dress.'

'Yay! Thanks, Flo-flo!' Octavia jumped up and danced around. 'I can't wait to tell him! And if it goes pear-shaped, we'll just get something else. How hard can it be to find a wedding dress?'

Octavia arranged a meeting for the very next day. They gathered in the Blue Bar at the Berkeley, with Iseult along for general style advice. Both Iseult and Roddy were noticeably struck upon seeing the sisters together.

'You really are identical!' said Iseult, her eyebrows disappearing into her red fringe. 'How extraordinary. You're like something from classical mythology – beautiful stars turned into women or something like that.'

Flora looked a little embarrassed but Octavia was used to Iseult's hyperbole and simply laughed.

'The next show, I want you both to model for me,' Roddy said, grinning. 'I can think of a few surprises we could pull off. It'd be fun.'

'I don't think we'd be up for that,' Octavia said swiftly, seeing Flora's horrified face. 'But do you think you could make a wedding dress in double-quick time?'

'How soon?' he asked.

'Let's say . . . three weeks.'

Roddy sat back in his chair, fiddling like mad with a pencil although it was hard to tell if he was desperate to draw with it or yearning for a cigarette. At last he said, 'It's utterly crazy. We'd have to sew day and night. You'd have to be prepared to come in for fittings whenever I call for you – no matter what you're doing.'

Flora nodded.

Octavia took a sip of her coffee and then said, 'What about the time it takes to design something?'

Roddy shrugged. 'That's not the problem. I could do that now, if you liked. I can design an entire collection in an afternoon if I feel like it.'

Iseult leant forward and patted his arm. She was looking as stunning as usual in an acid-green wrap dress with strings of huge purple beads round her neck. The black high heels she wore seemed to have small pairs of wings attached to the back of them. 'Roddy's only problem is not getting bored. He'll do you something amazing, I'm sure of it.'

'I can do it right now.' He picked up a linen napkin and looked over at Flora. 'What kind of dress do you want?'

'Oh!' she gasped, hunching her shoulders and pushing her hands together, frightened at being put on the spot. 'I don't really know . . . I was just going to look in the shops and see what there was . . .'

'Don't worry, dear,' Iseult said kindly. 'Do you have a colour scheme? A theme?'

'We should have brought Vicky,' Flora said helplessly to Octavia.

'Don't be silly, we can manage perfectly well without her.' She turned to the others. 'There's no particular theme. Flora wants white or cream, don't you? And we're thinking of having the reception at the Savile Club.'

'They have a very pretty ballroom,' murmured Iseult to Roddy. 'Think the ball scene in *My Fair Lady.*'

He nodded, instantly understanding. 'All right . . . then we could go for a Cecil Beaton look, if you like.' With a few quick lines of his pencil, he created a gauzy fifties-style gown, with a tight pleated bodice and layers of netting for the crinoline skirt. '*À la* Princess Margaret in those pastel portraits Beaton took . . .'

'It's b-b-beautiful,' Flora said, not wanting to criticise something so lovely, 'but . . .'

'Not quite you?' He turned the napkin round so that he had another blank canvas. 'Okay, something straighter, maybe? A column dress . . .' He sketched out an empire-line dress, cut low across the shoulders and with long sleeves. It flared out a little at the bottom into a small train.

'Oooh, that's nice,' Octavia said, leaning forward so that she could see.

'Um . . .' Flora said. She felt bewildered. There were so many possibilities. How was she supposed to choose? Surely it would be easier if she could just look at some actual dresses.

'You don't have to decide right now, don't worry,' Roddy said. 'I'll draw up a whole load of ideas and bring them round.' He looked over at Flora as though seeing her properly for the first time, and frowned as he studied her. 'Wait a minute . . . You know what? Iseult was right. I'm going to think about you as a classical goddess, a star made into a woman. Let's see . . .' He began to sketch again, a little more slowly this time. The dress started to take shape under his pencil point, a few long lines creating a fluid form. 'But we don't want you to look like you're straight out of a movie about the fall of Troy,' he muttered to himself. 'Nothing faux-Grecian for you.' He cocked his head to one side as he drew. The others waited and then he put down the napkin with a satisfied, 'There.'

They all looked. The dress, as far as they could see from the hurried sketch, was stunning – form-fitting but elegant, tight at the waist and belted with twisted chiffon before flowing down into a long skirt. There were sleeves but they seemed to be of gauze or chiffon, long ribbons of it that wrapped around each arm and ended in a trailing piece of veil.

'Wow!' breathed Octavia.

'Another masterpiece,' Iseult said proudly, and beamed at Roddy.

'S-s-s-stunning,' said Flora in a small voice. As soon as she saw it, she knew it was perfect for her. The dress of her dreams. 'Could you really make me this?'

'I think so,' he said, pleased by their reactions. 'It is quite bloody good, isn't it? We'll have to begin this afternoon. Come back to my studio and I'll start measuring you. Then I'll have to go hunting for fabric. Lucky for you I've got lots of contacts and a few favours to call in.'

They had called for champagne after that, and toasted the new design, which they called, of course, 'Flora'.

It's really happening, she thought with delight. *I'm*

*really going to be married! And tomorrow Otto's coming back.
I can't wait.*

Octavia went round to see Iseult at her flat, a crazily
eccentric space in a house in a rather down-at-heel
area of Bayswater, so that they could arrange between
them what Roddy would be paid for the dress. It wasn't
simply a question of the fabric or labour or even his
talent, but of the superhuman effort of making a
designer dress, with all attention to detail and perfection that entailed, within such a short space of time.
The price agreed was more than generous, and would
give Roddy's business a much-needed financial boost.
Even though the fashion show had brought a lot of
interest in him and his designs, that had yet to be trans-
lated into real money.

'We'll get publicity for this dress,' Iseult said to
Octavia. She was wearing one of Roddy's Turkish
dressing-gown robes, and lying on a sofa covered in
an antique tigerskin. 'That sort of exposure is invalu-
able.'

Octavia was puzzled. 'Why hasn't he got a shop?'

'Well, my dear . . . in a word, money. He needs
money for premises and kitting it out. A designer like
he is has to have a prime retail spot, or his market
won't value him. I'm talking about New Bond Street
or Sloane Street. Anywhere else is hardly worth the
candle. He'll need half a million at least to fit a shop
out. Then there's the cost of production – translating
a pencil sketch into a real piece of clothing takes
incredible skill, if you want atelier-style quality. You
can't charge designer prices for high-street production values. It's not possible.' Iseult shook her head,

and reached for her packet of cigarettes. The whole flat was drenched in the smell of stale tobacco. 'Open the French window for me, there's a love.'

Octavia opened the window on to a minuscule terrace that overlooked a busy road. Buses crawled past, the upper-deck passengers gazing almost into Iseult's sitting room. The panes of glass were grimy with the accumulation of exhaust smoke and dirt.

'No point in cleaning them,' Iseult said cheerfully when she saw where Octavia was looking. 'They get filthy again in moments.' There was a spark as she lit her cigarette and then, exhaling, said, 'Roddy would never accept second-rate anyway. He's got to be the best. And he will be, I just know it. This dress will help. I'll get little featurettes in *Vogue* and the society mags. My pal has just taken over a magazine, she's desperate for features. Perhaps you and Flora could do an interview . . .'

'But, Iseult.' Octavia came back into the room and sat down on a green velvet chaise-longue opposite her friend. 'If it's just money, well . . .' She smiled. 'Why don't *I* invest in Roddy?'

Iseult stared at her for a while, her yellow-green eyes blinking thoughtfully. Then she took another drag, pursed her lips and expelled a long thin stream of smoke. 'I can't say that the idea hasn't crossed my mind. But Roddy's frightfully proud, sweetheart. He'd rather go to the bank than let anyone think he's just the plaything of a rich girl – but the banks won't touch him, not yet, not for the money he needs. I know, I know,' she said quickly, seeing Octavia's expression. 'Of course he wouldn't be your plaything. It would be a sound business investment. But it's a question of perception, isn't it?' Iseult ground out her cigarette and said, 'Let's have a White Lady. It's nearly noon, after all.'

She collected a silver cocktail shaker from an Art Deco drinks cabinet in the corner and started assembling the drinks. She looked over her shoulder at Octavia while she worked. 'How did it go with that financier you've been meeting? Did you tell him our scheme?'

Octavia flushed scarlet. 'Yes,' she said, as coolly as she could manage.

'Oh. So that's the way the wind blows, is it?' Iseult said as she shook the cocktail shaker. 'I wondered why we hadn't seen Ferdy lately. Nursing a broken heart, I suppose. Is he very gorgeous?'

'Nothing's happened. Well, just a kiss . . .'

'A kiss is bliss. And sex is next.' Iseult poured the pale liquid into martini glasses. 'There. Get that down you, darling, and we'll talk some more about how you might be able to make Roddy's dreams come true – without bruising that pride of his. And about Noble's.'

Octavia nodded. 'I'm meeting Ethan tomorrow, as it happens. I'll speak to him about it.'

Iseult laughed. 'I'm sure you will. Just be careful, young lady. He's very likely to be a grown-up, you know. Not like us. So watch out.'

43

Flora flew down the stairs and into Otto's arms. She covered him with kisses, thrilled to see him again.

'Hello, my love,' he said tenderly, embracing her.

'I'm so happy you're here.' She looked at him with shining eyes. 'This is so exciting. You're going to stay with us, here in the house for the first time!'

'Yes.' He gazed around him at the hallway. 'Already I prefer it to my usual hotel.'

She laughed and led him through to the drawing room. 'Would you like a drink? Something to eat? I'll order whatever you like.'

He wandered about the room, looking at books and photographs. 'No, no. I will wait. How are you?'

'I'm fine, fine. We've been very busy, organising the wedding. All we need now is to decide the date.'

'Do you know . . .' Otto looked up at her with a smile '. . . Christmas is only a few weeks away. I thought – what could be more romantic than Christmas Eve?'

Flora clasped her hands together in delight. 'Yes, what a wonderful idea! I'll have to ask Vicky if she can investigate for us. And there'll be some red tape to sort out.'

'It can be done,' Otto said, with a sweep of his hand, 'if only we wish it!'

They all dined together that night, Otto listening as the girls talked excitedly of dresses and colours and ideas for a Christmas wedding. Flora described the fittings she had already had at Roddy's flat in the East End.

'Such a strange place,' she said. 'Not what I expected at all.'

'Horrible, isn't it?' Octavia said, wrinkling her nose as she speared some broccoli. 'Pongs too. Really nasty.'

'Pongs?' Otto looked puzzled.

'Smells,' she explained. 'Rather whiffy.'

'And this where your wedding dress comes from?' he said, surprised. 'A smelly, nasty place?'

Flora laughed. 'The dress is not at all nasty, I can promise you that. Just wait and see.'

When they went to bed, she was full of joy to have Otto close to her, in her own room. She went into the bathroom to clean her teeth and undress and came out again, trying not to feel self-conscious in her bra and knickers, carefully chosen to appeal to her fiancé. Otto was already in bed, his pale shoulders visible above the covers.

'Come here, my darling,' he said softly, and she went over. 'You are very lovely.'

'Thank you,' she whispered. She climbed into bed next to him and he pulled her to him, pressed his lips against hers and began to push his tongue into her mouth in soft small stabbing movements, sometimes twirling it round a little. She opened her mouth to him, wondering if she was kissing him back correctly. It didn't feel quite right.

He took his mouth away from hers then ran a hand over her breasts, cupping them in his hands for a moment and murmuring softly as he touched them. *'Schön. Sehr schön.'*

He had left on his boxer shorts and she could see that they tented where his erection pressed out at the front. She tried to put her hand down and touch it, but he pushed her gently away.

'Not yet,' he whispered. 'Soon. Not yet.'

He returned to her mouth, kissing her in the same way, as his fingers trailed lightly down her belly and then busied themselves in the wetness between her legs, stroking and rubbing as he had before. He pushed his fingertip into her entrance, but only fleetingly, pulling away to return to her most sensitive place, tickling her delightfully until she shuddered in his arms, gripped by her climax.

'And the best we will save for when we are married,' he said, kissing her hair, as she relaxed. 'Tomorrow we must go on a visit together. Is that all right?'

'Of course, Otto. Where are we going?'

'You shall see tomorrow.'

The first visit was to Hatton Gardens where a jeweller spread an array of dazzling stones before them, and Flora and Otto selected the one they wanted. Flora chose a solitaire diamond baguette in a platinum setting. The jeweller measured her finger and said it would take a week to make the ring. Otto paid the deposit and they came out of the shop, Flora laughing and excited.

'Our next visit is not quite so romantic, I'm afraid,' he said, with a touch of melancholy, 'but at least it is close by.'

They walked through the biting winter wind, weaving their way through Christmas shoppers and office workers.

'Where are we going?' Flora asked.

'To the lawyers.' He gazed down at her tenderly. 'My darling, I hate all that this stands for, but I'm sure you understand – I must protect my inheritance for those who come after me, even though I am certain that we will see our children and grandchildren in Schloss Meckensberg one day. My mother, though, would never forgive me if I did not take proper steps to ensure it remains in the von Schwetten family.'

'I understand,' Flora said, smiling. The words of Nick Falcon, the private detective, came back to her. *He said I should get my agreement done in Germany. But I don't see what difference it makes. It's Otto who wants it after all.* She had had an email from Nick with his company's terms and conditions and an estimate of what her request to trace her mother would cost to carry out. Did she want him to continue? Flora hadn't replied. She almost wished she had never gone to visit him at all, and she had promised Octavia that she wouldn't pursue the matter any further. *I'll do nothing for now. I'll wait until after the wedding and then decide.*

They went to an office in Chancery Lane, up some winding stairs in an old Tudor-style building to where a stressed-looking solicitor was waiting behind a desk. He talked quickly throughout the meeting, pushing long and complicated documents in front of them both and giving them very little time to read anything.

'It's all quite standard, and straightforward,' he kept saying. 'No nasty surprises here.'

'It's all right,' Otto said quietly to Flora, as she stared at the masses of printed words that seemed to be blurring in front of her eyes. 'I've had everything checked by my people. It's all fine.'

'Should I have it checked as well?' she asked, wondering if she should send the papers to Mr Challon, the family lawyer.

'That is what Mr Landray here is for. He's acting in your interests,' Otto explained.

'Oh. I see.'

When she was passed a slightly leaky ballpoint pen, Flora signed obediently what felt like a dozen times, on various dotted lines placed all over the document. Otto signed too. Mr Landray and his secretary, called in from the outer office, witnessed it.

'All done,' Landray said with a smile, and a moment later Flora and Otto were emerging into the daylight outside.

'There,' Otto said, taking her hand. 'Now there is no obstacle to our marriage. Soon you shall be my wife, and I will take you to our home in Germany.' He pressed his lips to her cheek. 'I can't wait.'

'Nor can I!' Flora said with all her heart. *Then, at last, real life will begin.*

44

Ethan took Octavia to The Wolseley for dinner, and then to The Ivy Club. During dinner they made small talk – he told her about his flat in the city, his boyhood in Australia and his family back in Sydney – but their glances said a lot more than they could about the attraction burning between them. When the coffee came, Ethan said, 'The traditional time for business,' and brought out a file of papers.

'The good news is that if you want to buy into Noble's, you can,' he said. 'And as a seasoned venture capitalist, I have to tell you that I think they're a good opportunity. I'd advise any client to consider them. But you're in a special position. You've got a lot of money to spend, and Noble's is crying out for cash, oodles of it. They've got a great big debt to service and it's crippling them. Any sensible shareholder would want you on board. But . . .'

'But what?' Octavia crossed her legs, admiring her gold python Louboutins as she did. She'd really pushed the boat out tonight, and was wearing a shimmering gold mini-dress covered in hundreds of square sequins.

It was sleeveless, showing off her smooth golden skin. She shook out her hair and balanced her chin on her hands, displaying her slender wrists to Ethan, who was looking even more handsome than she remembered. She could hardly take her eyes off his mouth, she was so eager to kiss it again.

'Well, to be honest, your lack of experience is going to play against you. You're so young and have never worked in the industry – or any industry. That's not going to help your cause. So here's my idea . . .' Ethan leant forward, his dark blue eyes intense. 'I suggest we form a new company. It will be your company, and I'll be on the board as your business advisor. And we'll also recruit some other people who know this industry, to be the voices of experience and reassure the shareholders. I know a few likely people and I'm sure you will too.'

'That's a brilliant idea,' Octavia breathed. 'I'll ask Iseult if she'll join us. She's so incredibly talented.'

'I know a guy who's worked in some of the major luxury brands, and I'm sure he'll know some other key names too.' Ethan gave her a sideways look. 'You'll have to be prepared to invest quite a lot in this. You'll need to pay people well if you want them to join us. Talent doesn't come cheap.'

'Money is no object,' she said swiftly.

Ethan raised his eyebrows at her. 'I have to admit, I've done a bit of research on you. You really are staggeringly rich, aren't you?' He took one of her hands. 'I wish you weren't quite so loaded. Because it means that when I take you to bed, you might think it's your filthy lucre I'm after instead of you.'

Her insides somersaulted in a deliciously exciting way.

'Are you going to take me to bed?' she purred, hoping that she sounded sophisticated and knowing. She ran a fingertip along the length of his index finger.

'Once we leave here,' he said, looking around the dimly lit club where actors, supermodels, businessmen and glamorous girls were talking, laughing and sipping drinks, 'I'm going to take you back to my place, and when we get there I'm going to do my best to seduce you.' He grinned at her. 'I thought I should lay my cards on the table.'

'So there's no one else in your life right now?' Octavia said carelessly.

'No one who matters,' he replied, and touched his lips to her hand.

Oh, God, I wouldn't care if he had six wives, Octavia thought, shivering inside, *he's so gorgeous, I would let him have me right here if he wanted.*

But that wasn't necessary. They finished their cocktails with almost undignified haste, now that they both knew what awaited them. In the taxi back across London, it was all they could do to keep their lips from touching. They were both breathing hard, Ethan's warm hand on Octavia's smooth thigh and the tell-tale bulge in his trousers showing that he was more than ready for her. He paid the driver with a couple of twenties, not even bothering to look at the meter or wait for change. Instead, he and Octavia hurried through the door of his apartment building and into the lift. In the mirror inside it she saw their reflections: they were both hot-eyed and flushed with the force of their lust for each other. The moment the doors closed, his lips were on her, his arms pulling her tightly to him. By the time the doors opened on the fifth floor, his shirt was open and her dress had already slipped down to the ground where it lay in a sparkling golden puddle around her shoes, leaving her in just a pair of turquoise satin panties and hold-up stockings.

'Thank God there's no one here to see me like this,' she gasped, bending to scoop up the dress.

'I can't think of a nicer sight,' said Ethan, taking her hand and leading her across the corridor to his front door. A moment later they were inside. As the door slammed shut, passion gripped them again. They kissed hard, hungry for each other, and Ethan slipped off his shirt, revealing a body that both excited and scared her. It was a proper man's body: his shoulders were broad, his arms and pecs heavy with muscle. Dark blond hair curled all over his chest up to the base of his neck, with a thick trail curling round his navel and down below the waistband of his trousers. Octavia's pulse raced. His masculinity was overwhelming. Beside him she felt soft and small and intensely feminine.

He swung her up into his arms and carried her through the flat, pushing open a door with his shoulder and taking her into his bedroom, where he laid her on the bed. She lay, writhing a little with pleasure as he quickly stripped off, his white briefs revealing an almost terrifyingly massive bulge above rugby-player thighs covered in more dark blond hair. As he took off the briefs she was scared to look at what was beneath, and then she did: a huge, upstanding cock met her gaze, its domed head smooth and purple, its great veined shaft rearing up out of a thick nest of hair. Below it his balls hung dark and heavy. She felt her mouth go dry: this was something different from holding Brandon's erection or feeling Ferdy's sweet but slender penis inside her. This thing looked like it could split her in two. But she wanted it more than anything she could imagine . . .

Then he was lying next to her on the bed, sucking at her nipples and kissing her, biting her neck and running his hands through her hair and over her skin. It was electrifying: her body felt as though it had come alive in a way she had never known before. This was sex, real proper sex, and it seemed as though everything else had been mere adolescent fumbling by comparison. He moved down, kissing and licking her with a mixture of hot lust and pure reverence, muttering in between times how beautiful she was, how hot and sexy. It was revving her up, and she could feel her pussy swelling and gushing with soft slipperiness. Then she realised what he was going to do, and pulled in a sharp breath. *Oh, God, he's going to kiss me there* . . . For a second, she didn't think she would be able to stand it, she was already on fire, but then he pulled down her wet panties and discarded them, opened her thighs gently, and bent his head to her swollen lips. The sensation was glorious as his tongue slipped gently into her pussy and then up over her clitoris, moving around it and nipping it gently so that it buzzed and sparked almost unbearably. And yet, with all that incredible sensation, there was something amazingly soft and gentle about it as his tongue lapped and lapped at her.

She threw her head back, her arms over her head and holding on to the rails of the bedstead. 'Oh God,' she cried, wanting to open to him as far she could.

Her voice was high and breathless. 'Oh my God, Ethan!'

'Don't come yet, baby,' he said, glancing up from her pussy, his face shiny with her moisture. She could see the great ramrod between his legs, stiffer and more powerful-looking than ever. She wanted to kiss it, slide it between her lips, lick it and touch it. But not yet. Now Ethan was on his knees between her open legs and she knew what he was going to do.

'Yes,' she begged. 'Please . . .'

He didn't need a further invitation, putting the great purple head at the entrance of her pussy, looking for the spot where he would be able to get inside her. An instant later, he was pushing the huge rod into her with exquisitely small movements, tantalising and teasing her until she was dry-lipped and desperate for him to fill her up completely. When, finally, he was engulfed in her, his balls heavy against her bottom, she felt utterly replete, as though he was filling her belly as well. Then he began to move, slowly at first and building up. She wrapped her legs around his back, and the next moment the fucking overtook them entirely so that they were rolling over in the bed, changing their positions every few minutes, unable to get enough of one another.

He pulled out of her, turned her round on to all fours and pushed into her from behind, thrusting so hard that her whole body jerked and she gasped out with the force of his hips pushing his cock deep inside her, while he reached down with one hand and tickled her swollen clitoris with his fingertips. Eventually, she pulled away and sank down on his body, taking as much of his cock as she could manage into her mouth, licking her own juice off his shaft, playing the end of her tongue over the head of his penis, rubbing it over the hole on the tip. She never wanted this luscious voluptuousness to end; her whole body felt alive and made for pleasure as they pressed their hot skin together, revelling in their desire for each other.

Then, at last, he rolled her on to her back, and began the endgame: they were both so hot and ready it took little time to ride the last great stretch; as she rushed up the wave of her climax, she realised that she was crying out loudly, begging him not to stop before she was lost inside the whirl of pleasure, flying through the blissful spasms as Ethan drove her onwards, exploding in his own fierce climax as she began to end. Finally, they collapsed, panting and sweating in one another's arms, utterly and happily spent.

'This is damn near perfect,' Ethan said lazily. They had recovered from their exertions and he had collected cool drinks from the kitchen for them and brought them back to bed, where they lazed in the lamplight.

'It is, isn't it?' Octavia said, propping herself up on one elbow to look at him. He really was beautiful. Her stomach flipped every time she looked at him.

'You know, I think we're pretty good together.' He grinned at her. 'I don't just mean the sex, though that is fantastic.'

'My thoughts exactly.' Octavia put a hand on his chest, idly stroking the hair that curled there between his nipples.

'You know . . .' Ethan rolled over towards her and gazed into her eyes '. . . I want to see you properly. I

344

want us to have a relationship. I really like you, Octavia, and I think you like me.'

Her insides turned to liquid. 'Oh, yes,' she breathed, 'I *do* like you.'

'And I can help you. I can help with business, money . . . your whole life. If you want me to?'

'Of course I do,' she said, delighted. 'I need someone to guide me.' The more time she could spend with Ethan, doing the delicious things they'd just done to one another, the better.

'So you're agreed we should work together? As well as . . . play?' He picked up her hand and interlaced her fingers through his.

'Yes,' she said firmly.

'Then I'll get started forming our company right away.' He kissed her fingers and smiled.

45

The wedding day was set for Christmas Eve, and Vicky was doing everything she could to make sure things ran smoothly. Otto was sometimes there to help direct things, and sometimes not. His business called him away every few days. He would vanish on a plane to some far-flung spot, reappearing a day or two later, a little travel-worn.

Octavia found herself more and more bemused by him. She liked him well enough and yet it seemed odd to her that the quiet family wedding he had decreed was growing by the day, with all the names he was adding to the guest list. Vicky showed them to Octavia, most of them were foreign, reflecting his business interests perhaps, along with grand-sounding titles – Dowager Lady thises and thats, Barons, Baronesses, Counts and Princes with von and zu before a string of odd place names.

'And his mother . . . he simply calls her "*meine Mutter*". Am I supposed to address an invitation to "*meine Mutter*"?' Vicky asked, laughing. 'No one else on the list appears to be related to him at all. What with

Flora's lack of family as well, this is going to be a very odd wedding.'

Octavia cast her eyes over the list. 'Has she said anything about their honeymoon?'

Vicky shook her head. 'Apparently Otto's taken care of the arrangements. All she knows is that they're heading to the *schloss* right after the ceremony.'

As Vicky said those words, Octavia felt a heavy sense of doom fall on her. This man was taking her sister away from her, far away, to Germany. They had never been parted before. Not even Aunt Frances had attempted that. But soon Flora was going off with this person they barely knew. Panic twisted inside Octavia. She looked up at Vicky but her cousin seemed quite calm, chatting away about the difficulties of booking the venue and finding caterers, not just at short notice but at Christmas too.

'Honestly,' she said, rolling her eyes, 'I won't tell you how much cash I'm flashing to get what we want.'

Octavia barely heard her. *I can't let this happen*, she thought. *Not without being sure*. She thought hard, a plan already forming in her mind.

Octavia gave a false name when she rang for an appointment, although she wasn't exactly sure why. It seemed the kind of thing one did when trying to investigate someone secretly.

It was easy enough to find the office. Ethan had brought her to Soho a couple of times, to dark, sexy clubs where couples lounged in corners, drinking and talking. She buzzed at the door and the receptionist let her in. A few moments and a short climb later, she was on the upper floor, standing in front of the receptionist's desk.

'Oh, yes, Miss Brown,' the receptionist said, looking as though she knew full well that this was a pseudonym. 'Please go through. You're expected.'

Octavia walked across the small office and knocked at the door the receptionist had indicated. A voice inside called, 'Come in!'

The room she entered was messy, and a man with striking dark looks sat behind a singularly untidy desk. 'Mr Falcon?'

He glanced up and his expression changed. His mouth dropped open for an instant, then he got hold of himself. He looked very pleased to see her, almost avuncular in his eagerness to stand up and shake her hand. 'Hey, you've come back! I wondered if you'd show. I never heard from you after I sent my initial report and costings. Didn't you get the email? Thought you must have changed your mind. What's with the fake name anyhow? Now come on in, sit down. Let's take a look at the stuff I sent you.'

He beckoned her over to a chair as he started to rifle through papers and files on his desk. He continued in his strong American accent, 'If you'd let me know you were coming, I'd have been more prepared, you know? But I've got it here somewhere.'

Octavia hadn't moved. 'You know me?' she said, when she'd found her voice.

He glanced up at her with a smile, his eyes full of charm. 'Course I do. Flora Beaufort. I'm not likely to forget a girl like you, if you don't mind me saying. You want me to find your mother for you.' His expression changed as he took in her stricken face. 'Wait . . . you *are* Flora Beaufort, aren't you?'

'No. No, I'm not,' Octavia said in a cold voice. 'But I take it my sister has been here and asked you to look for our mother?'

'Ah.' The man looked confused, staring down at his desk with a furrowed brow. 'Um . . . this is a strange one. I really can't say. I wouldn't have said a thing if I hadn't thought you were the . . . er . . . other Miss Beaufort.' He shook his head. 'Wow. I've never seen two people look so similar.' He looked up at her hopefully. 'Is there something I can help you with?'

'No,' said Octavia, her mind racing and her stomach churning. 'Not today.'

She turned and ran back through the outer office and down the stairs. On the street, she hailed the first taxi she saw and ordered it home.

Flora was poring over a list of possible canapé combinations. She hadn't realised that there was so much to decide when planning a wedding. Vicky was doing most of the legwork, but still there were bouquets to be chosen, orders of service to have printed, shoes to select . . . it went on and on, and it was all happening at breakneck speed so that they could have the perfect, romantic Christmas wedding.

She was just ticking the sushi selection when Octavia came bursting into the room, her eyes bright with anger and her cheeks flushed.

'You promised!' she shouted. 'You promised you weren't going to look for her!'

'What are you talking about?' Flora said, looking up,

bewildered. 'What's wrong?' She had never seen her sister look so furious. Was that anger directed at her?

Octavia marched up and jabbed a finger at her. '*You!* You have commissioned a private detective to find our mother!'

Flora was taken aback. She gasped but couldn't speak.

'Don't try and deny it, I know you did,' spat Octavia. 'You promised me you'd leave it . . . and all the time you were going behind my back.'

'No . . . no!' Flora said, holding up her hands, desperate to stem the flood of Octavia's rage. 'I *have* let it go.'

'Your private detective doesn't seem to think so! He's under the impression you're still interested in finding her.'

'Wait.' Flora went very still, her mind whirling as she considered what her sister had just said. 'How do you know about my private detective? I haven't told anyone . . . not Otto, not Vicky, no one. Did you look at my email account?'

'Don't be stupid, of course I didn't,' snapped Octavia. 'I found him by chance.'

Flora went very white. A cold feeling of horror swirled in her belly. 'I know,' she whispered. Suddenly she saw it very clearly. 'I know why you went to him. You were going to have Otto investigated, weren't you?'

Guilt flashed across Octavia's face and Flora knew she was right. Fury raced through her. 'How *dare* you?' she said through gritted teeth. Then she screamed: 'How DARE YOU, Octavia?'

Octavia looked frightened. She'd never seen her sister in anything like this state before.

'Don't you think I've had enough?' Flora yelled, rising

350

to her feet, her eyes flashing. 'I've been spied on all my life! Watched! Monitored! I didn't think I would ever, ever find that *you* had turned against me too.'

Tears filled Octavia's eyes. Her own anger had vanished completely. 'I haven't turned against you . . .' she said, her voice trembling.

'Ever since we left Homerton, you've left me alone. You've deserted me for your new friends and your new life. You let me suffer all the time and you didn't care. And now that I've found a little bit of happiness without you, you want to spoil that too!'

Octavia was sobbing now. 'No . . . no, that's not true.'

'Well, for your information, I've signed a pre-nuptial agreement with Otto and I'm completely protected. I don't need you spying on me, so you can forget about that right now! I never looked for our mother again once I'd promised you I wouldn't – not that you have any right to stop me! And for as my marriage . . .' Flora narrowed her eyes and glowered at her twin, her face still tight with rage. 'You can count yourself lucky that Otto and I even want you to be there after this! Do you understand?'

Feeling that she couldn't be near Octavia a moment longer without breaking down entirely, Flora swept past her sister, leaving her weeping desolately.

46

The day of the wedding dawned clear and bright. It was a beautiful Christmas Eve. London sparkled with glitter and lights, and buzzed with the excitement of the holidays.

Octavia's reflection showed that she was pale and nervous. Flora, on the other hand, looked serene and happy. *I thought it was always the other way round*, thought Octavia. *The bride is supposed to be the one with the nerves. Not the bridesmaid.*

In Flora's room, the dress was hanging under its protective cover. Roddy had brought it over late the night before, having done the final, final fitting the previous morning. He'd also brought Octavia's bridesmaid's dress, adapted from one of the evening gowns from the last show.

The shoes and jewellery, chosen with Iseult's help, were in their boxes, waiting for her to don them.

The sisters were quiet as the make-up artist and hairdresser arrived to do their work. When Flora finally slipped on the dress, a vision of loveliness made from Irish ivory silk and chiffon, Octavia started to cry.

'Please . . .' Flora went to her sister. 'Don't cry, Tavy. Please be happy for me. I'm very happy myself.'

'I don't want you to go away,' Octavia whispered, sniffing a little and wiping away her tears with a tissue before her mascara could run. 'I don't want you to leave me.'

'I'll be back in no time, you'll see. A few weeks at the *schloss*, and then I'll come home. You can visit me there.' Flora reached out and took her sister's hand. 'Come as soon as you want. We'll both want to see you.'

Octavia stared at Flora, who looked so incredibly beautiful, and felt sadness wash over her heart. There was a chasm between them, she knew that, and she didn't seem able to bridge it. Ever since that awful scene a fortnight ago, when Flora had screamed at her as she never had before, there had been a rift between them that couldn't seem to be mended. From that moment, she'd felt Flora go away from her, and it was hurting Octavia more than she could ever have dreamed. Even though she'd begged forgiveness and Flora had granted it, the strange coolness between them had persisted and Octavia was at a loss how to end it.

Now she had to swallow any lingering apprehension she had about the wedding. She had to trust that Flora knew what she was doing and hope that, in time, the gulf would be closed and they could go back to where they once were.

Flora smiled at her. 'Come on, Tavy. We have a wedding to get to.'

* * *

Steve, wearing his full chauffeur's uniform and peaked cap, drove them to the ceremony in a huge cream Daimler.

Vicky met them at the Savile Club, looking fantastic in a silk Armani dress in dark green. She seemed calm and in control as she helped Flora out of the car. 'You look exquisite, darling. Everyone's here, they're all waiting for you.'

A gaggle of photographers dashed forward as the girls stood on the pavement. The club doormen and Steve held them back as the flashes exploded. Flora grimaced.

'What are they doing here?' she cried, trying to shield her face with her bouquet of white peonies and ivory roses.

'I've no idea,' Vicky said grimly. Octavia kept quiet. 'Come on.' She led them along the red carpet and into the club.

Once they were inside, the doors were firmly shut in the faces of the press. But another man stepped forward.

'This is Gil, the official photographer,' Vicky explained. 'He's going to take some pictures now before we go in.'

While Flora was posing at the foot of the imposing staircase, beneath a glittering crystal chandelier, Vicky said to Octavia, 'Something's happened . . . Otto's mother isn't here. She's ill apparently. Had to stay home in Germany at the last moment.'

Octavia made a face. 'It could be worse, I suppose. She could have died or something.'

'Octavia!' said Vicky reprovingly, but they both giggled.

'Let's hope,' Octavia said, tightening her grip around

her own posy of peonies, 'that's the worst thing that's going to happen today.'

The harpist began the entrance music and Flora, unaccompanied except by her sister walking behind her, began her stately progress through the rows of gilt chairs to where Otto was waiting for her, dapper in his morning coat, an ivory rosebud in his buttonhole. She gave him an exquisite smile as she reached him and the congregation sighed almost as one at the sight of the gorgeous bride.

The ceremony was over in a moment, or so it seemed to Octavia. There was no singing by the congregation, but an alto and a soprano sang a heart-soaring aria from *Così Fan Tutte*; there were readings, too, one by Vicky and one by a friend of Otto. The wedding vows were short and to the point, and would have seemed quite prosaic it had not been for the obvious happiness of the bride. Octavia looked over the assembled congregation, recognising very few of them. Aunt Frances and the Brigadier were in the front row, their aunt looking very boot-faced considering she was at her niece's wedding. Behind them were the other Stauntons, Vicky sitting next to her brother Laurence and their parents. There were a couple of faces Octavia recognised from finishing school, and some of their American relatives. She remembered that Vicky had chartered a plane and booked the best hotels in order to get them all over here at such short notice. She didn't know anyone else.

Is this how it's supposed to be? she wondered. *A roomful of strangers? Who are they all anyway?*

It was not even a roomful, come to that. The congregation filled about five rows.

With the formalities at an end, the new husband and wife turned to smile at everyone and then processed out to the Wedding March, played again on the harp.

So that's it, Octavia thought. *Now they're married.* It seemed strange that they had walked into that room as separate people and were now walking out bound together for ever. Even if they were divorced, they would always have been married. There was no erasing it now.

Please God she's done the right thing, thought Octavia. As much as she wanted to be happy for her sister, she couldn't help a terrible feeling of depression from descending upon her. Flora was gone from her now, perhaps for ever. If only she hadn't found out about the visit to the detective there might not be this awful distance, this coldness, between them.

Octavia longed for comfort and affection. She glanced at her watch and wondered if there would be time, after the reception, to call Ethan and arrange to see him. She needed to feel his strong arms around her.

The reception was held downstairs, waiters circulating with trays of canapés and glasses of champagne. It was a curiously muted affair, perhaps because so few people knew one another.

It couldn't be avoided, Octavia realised. She would have to speak to her aunt, standing at the side of the room, stiff and po-faced in her lavender suit, her husband beside her clearly longing for his pipe.

'Aunt Frances,' she said, going up to them and kissing them dutifully. 'Uncle.'

'Octavia,' Aunt Frances said with an edge to her

voice. 'Well, I'm surprised you let this happen. What does the girl think she's doing? She's far too young for marriage.'

'Flora's old enough to make up her own mind, I think,' Octavia replied coldly.

'She'll regret it,' sighed her aunt, and shook her head. 'They always do. Look at your beloved father.'

'Can't we get through two minutes without your mentioning my father?' Octavia replied furiously. 'For Christ's sake, we've had this our entire lives! Can't you see that *you're* the one who brought us up? If we're fucked up, there's only one person to blame and that's you!' She threw a scornful look at the Brigadier. 'You and that hopeless blockhead of a husband of yours. You should never have been allowed within two feet of any children, ever!'

Her aunt gasped, her face looking pale and horrified. 'Octavia! How dare you? I did my best for you two girls.'

'Yeah, right. By turning us into freaks. *And* you lied to us about our mother. I know all about it. So what do we have to thank you for? Precisely nothing. The day we left you was the happiest day of our lives. And if Flora is rushing into this marriage – well, it had everything to do with you and the fact that she was never loved!' Octavia's eyes stung with tears. She had barely realised she felt so strongly before this.

'Well,' said Aunt Frances indignantly, 'It's clear we're not wanted. We shall leave as soon as the speeches are done.'

'No, you're not wanted. I can't understand why you came in the first place.' Octavia turned on her heel, tossed her head and stalked off without even saying goodbye, hoping she would never have to speak to them again.

It was, she realised, a relief to have spoken her mind for the first time in her life without fear of punishment. It was a small triumph but a meaningful one, and she smiled with satisfaction. Maybe she was grown up after all.

Soon they were lost in introductions, then toasts and speeches. There was no speech made for Flora, though, as no one had walked her down the aisle and she was far too shy to make one herself. Otto gave a short, formal address in which he thanked everybody for coming, and then, with a bow, thanked his new wife for marrying him before asking the room to toast Octavia, the bridesmaid.

The best man, who had read a poem at the ceremony, made his speech in a strong accent and then asked everyone to toast the happy couple, which they did with great aplomb. Then, to all intents and purposes, it was over.

Flora was glad it finished so soon. She didn't want to linger there, among so many people she didn't know. She longed to be alone with Otto, beginning their life together. She knew that a plane was waiting for them at City airport with their luggage already aboard, and that they were on their way to his ancestral home. All she wanted was to get there. Then they could start to recover from the wedding, and she could begin to take stock of everything that had happened recently. She needed time and space to think about Octavia's underhand behaviour and to confront the painful distance that now lay between them.

As soon as they were alone, she said to Otto, 'I'm so sorry your mother couldn't be here.'

'She was heartbroken, but she could not travel.' He looked searchingly into her eyes, then said quietly, 'My wife. My dear wife.'

He kissed her. *My husband,* she thought, a great sense of calm coming over her.

Upstairs, Flora changed into her going away outfit: a classic Chanel suit in pale green, woven with metallic thread, and a pair of ballet pumps. Then she and Otto made their way to the waiting car, Octavia throwing confetti at them, the official photographer snapping away, and everyone cheering and calling goodbye. It was done. She was married.

Octavia watched her sister go, tears in her eyes. It felt as if a chapter in her life was closing. *But it's what she wants,* she told herself, *and if she wants to leave me, what can I do about it?*

47

In the car, Flora cuddled up to Otto and he put his arm around her, but they were both too tired to talk much. They were taken through the VIP channels at the airport, and quickly boarded the small, twelve-seater private jet.

'I thought we might buy our own plane,' Otto said idly as they settled themselves.

'Do we need one?' Flora asked, surprised.

'Of course. I travel a good deal. I will look into it as soon as we get home. I shouldn't have to slum it, should I?' He smiled at her. 'I'm sure you want me to travel in comfort.'

'Yes,' she said, 'I suppose so.'

They took off a few minutes later, soaring out across London, and were over the sea within moments. The afternoon had turned grey and chilly, dark clouds falling low over the city, and the plane's air conditioning made Flora feel cold. She shivered. Otto pulled out a business book and started to read, so she got one of the blankets from the overhead locker and wrapped it about herself. She thought back over her wedding day: it had been beautiful, all in all. Before long, she fell asleep.

They landed at Munich airport and were met by a Range-Rover that drove them out of the city and into the countryside, heading for the Bavarian hills. It was dark now, and Flora snuggled into the back seat, another cashmere blanket wrapped round her, feeling both excited and calm at the same time. *And it's Christmas!* she thought, remembering the gifts she had brought for Otto in her luggage. When would they open their presents? Tonight? Tomorrow morning? He sat in the front with the driver, talking in rapid German and laughing, seeming more animated than she had ever heard him.

My husband, she thought, trying out the words again. Was that man in the front seat really her husband? He sounded like a stranger. *But that's exciting, amazing . . . we've got all our lives to get to know each other.*

She was asleep again when they finally pulled to a halt in front of Schloss Meckensberg.

'Flora! We're here,' called Otto, jumping down from the car. He strode off to the front door, leaving her to blink sleepily, yawn, unwrap herself from the blanket and stumble out, while the driver unloaded their luggage from the back. She walked across the driveway to the open front door. Gravel crunched under her feet. She could see very little in the darkness, just a great black shape lit with yellow rectangles. A moment later she was walking through the enormous oak front door and into a stone hall with hammer beams in the ceiling. Otto was standing there, near an empty fire-place that was big enough to fit six grown men standing upright. All around the room hung shields, swords, daggers and other weapons. Apart from that it was remarkably bare, without even a rug on the stone floor. *Where are the Christmas decorations?* she wondered. She would have expected a Christmas tree in this great room, and a Yule log in the fireplace.

Otto was talking to a middle-aged, plain-looking woman, his voice sharp and businesslike.

'Ah, Flora,' he said, seeing her. 'We shall have some supper first. It is waiting in our room.'

'Good,' she said. 'That sounds lovely.' She smiled at the woman, who was observing her with interest. This must be the housekeeper, she decided. Flora wanted to seem as friendly and approachable as she could, so she made a small bow in the housekeeper's direction. The woman returned the gesture with a nod of her head.

'Come,' said Otto curtly. He turned and marched from the room, calling over his shoulder, 'They will bring the bags. Follow me.'

They walked down a long stone-floored corridor lit only by the occasional wall lamp until they reached a winding staircase, still of the same dark grey stone without any floor covering. The air here was bitterly cold, as though it had never felt so much as a beam of sunlight. Up they went, footsteps tapping on the stone, round, and round until they reached a small, arched wooden door. Otto opened it, and led her along another corridor, carpeted this time but still dimly lit. It was hard to get much of an impression of the place as a whole.

Except that it's a real Gothic castle! Flora thought. She felt excited still, as though she were on some kind of adventure.

'Our quarters,' Otto said, opening another door with an old-fashioned iron latch on it. He entered and then stood to one side to allow her to pass. 'Ah, they've made it ready for us.'

Heavy brocade curtains were shut against the night outside, and a supper table laid for two glowed in the light of a pair of candles. A large dark-wood four-poster bed hung with more brocade curtains dominated the rest of the room.

'Sit down, let's eat,' he said. 'I'm sure we're both hungry.'

They sat down to the simple meal: black bread, rye bread, a selection of cold meats and cheeses and pickles. Otto poured them both a glass of red wine.

Flora stared at it all a little anxiously. She wasn't very hungry but he urged her to help herself so, in the interests of a harmonious end to her wedding day, she loaded her plate. She took a small biteful of the black bread. It was dry and nutty and took a very long time to chew. Eventually she swallowed it and looked down at the rest of it on her plate. *How will I finish all that?* she thought. She picked up a piece of salami. *I'll just eat the meat for now.*

Otto didn't appear to notice. Instead he began to talk triumphantly of the people who had attended the wedding. 'This will do me a lot of good,' he said happily. 'Did you see the chairman of DeWalle Bank? I'm sure he'll have appreciated the invitation. I've done business with him. He's a good man, an excellent man.'

It seemed that most of the guests at the wedding had been business associates.

Well, business is important to him. And he has no brothers and sisters.

'Now.' Otto got up, wiping his mouth on his napkin. 'I think we are both ready for bed, are we not?'

Flora stood as well, tired despite her naps on the plane and in the car. But first, surely, there was the small matter of their wedding night . . . She smiled at Otto, aware suddenly of the silk underwear she was wearing, the ivory lace suspender belt and the silky stockings that rasped on her thighs when they rubbed together. She was ready for a night of love – or, at least, an hour or two – before a long sleep and a lazy morning together.

Otto moved towards her, a tender light in his eyes. 'My wife,' he said in a gentle voice.

She smiled at him as he approached her, expecting his embrace. Then, as he neared, his expression changed. His lips curled and his eyes darkened. She saw him pull back his right arm. Just as she was wondering what on earth he was doing, she realised he was swinging it rapidly back towards her. In the next instant, she saw his fist come flying towards her face and then a vicious punch sent her flying backwards on to the four-poster bed. The shock and pain stunned her. Wetness and a metallic taste filled her mouth.

Speechless and reeling, she put her hand to her mouth and pulled it away to see her fingertips were dark with blood.

What happened? she thought dully, unable to process what had just occurred. Then Otto swam into view, a huge dark shape looming over her, his eyes hard and his mouth twisted.

'You can forget your romantic dreams, my dear,' he said in a harsh voice. 'This is what your life is going to be like from now on.'

Part Two

48

Eight months later

The sun burned so brightly on the blue of the Mediterranean that it was hard to look at the surface of the water, which glittered like diamonds. Everything was hot to the touch. The only place to be was in the shade.

Octavia, protected from the glare behind her Balenciaga metal-framed sunglasses, was reclining comfortably on a well-cushioned sun lounger, beneath the shade of a striped deck umbrella. She was wearing her new yellow Gucci bikini, the one that set off her deep tan beautifully, and her hair was tied up in a loose knot so that her neck stayed cool. She was lazily reading a fashion magazine and wondering if she had the energy to lean over and buzz one of the stewards so that she could be brought a long drink and a bowl of chilled melon.

Life on board Ethan's yacht, *The Great Bear*, was always relaxed and utterly luxurious.

Just then Ethan came up on deck, a phone pressed

to his ear. He looked suitably nautical in white shorts, a blue polo shirt and white deck shoes, a pair of black Raybans shielding his eyes from the glare. 'Yeah, great. That's brilliant. Thanks, Robert. You've done the right thing. You won't regret it.'

He clicked the phone off and came towards Octavia, grinning.

'What's up?' she said lazily.

He sat down on the lounger and ran a hand along her smooth leg that glistened with the sun oil she'd massaged into it. 'We've got something to celebrate,' he murmured.

'Really?' She dropped her magazine and sat up straighter.

Ethan nodded. 'Uh-huh. The deal has gone through. We're about to own the majority stake in Noble's – or, at least, Butterfly Limited is.'

'He went for it?'

'He certainly did. Like a child for a lollipop. And you also own the freehold of the property, via BC Investments. And everything's controlled via OctCo Holdings, our company based in Bermuda.'

Octavia laughed, taking off her sunglasses so she could see him clearly. 'It all sounds amazingly complicated!'

'It *is* quite complicated,' Ethan said frankly, 'but it all makes sense in the long run, you'll see.'

Octavia threw her arms around him. 'All I know is that it's incredible! Thank you, my darling! I can't wait to tell Iseult.' Then she remembered. 'But of course . . . I'll see her tonight at Roddy's party. We can celebrate our success then.'

Life for Octavia had been transformed over the last

few months, ever since she and Ethan had got together. He had urged her to spend big money, or, as he put it, to *live rich*. 'You've got to impress people,' he'd said. 'It isn't enough to have money. You've got to show it off as well. You need to have all the toys. Believe me, honey, I've seen how the big spenders live and you should be up there with those guys, on the A-list moneybags scene where you belong.'

At first, Octavia had found it an odd concept. Yes, she'd always been surrounded by every luxury money could buy. Anyone looking at Homerton, the Connecticut farm and the other properties, would have known in an instant that only really substantial wealth could maintain all this: the kind of wealth that didn't just own properties but also employed huge staffs to run them. But there was nothing ostentatious about the way Aunt Frances lived. It was done in quiet good taste and resolute privacy. Aunt Frances had no desire for the outside world to know anything about her; for her, a private jet had been a functional necessity, in order to keep her clear of the irritating world of crowded waiting areas, shared seating and other more uncongenial aspects of public travel. Ethan said that had to change: if Octavia wanted people to take her seriously as a businesswoman, she was going to have to start using her spending power.

This sumptuous yacht was part of his living rich plan: he had persuaded her to come in with him on buying it so it was really half hers, though they pretended it was Ethan's. She had put up ten million and he had found the other ten million, and then he had bought this beautiful 120-foot floating luxury home, with its own tennis court and pool, lavish reception rooms, library, spa and cinema. They had already spent several weeks on her, cruising the warm blue seas of the Med and the Caribbean. On Ethan's advice, Octavia had bought a penthouse flat in New York, a smart apartment in Paris (which she'd never seen as it was being redesigned by a top team of interior decorators) and a house near Bondi Beach in Australia. Now he was showing her brochures for a beach-front estate in Thailand and telling her what an excellent investment it was.

She'd learnt a lot over the past few months, and it was all thanks to Ethan, she knew that. He was an astute businessman, entirely self-made, and was clearly excellent at what he did. When they weren't cruising on *The Great Bear*, eating out at the most fabulous restaurants or shopping as though it was going out fashion, Ethan was hard at work on her behalf. He'd set about creating the network of companies that would allow her to buy into Noble's and gain overall control, while remaining as tax-efficient as possible. He'd asked Octavia how much cash she'd be able to put into the business. When she'd said airily as much as she wanted, he'd been surprised.

'Isn't your money controlled by trusts?' he'd asked, frowning.

She'd shaken her head. 'No. It's just sitting there, available to me.'

'That's pretty unusual.'

'Is it?' Octavia had shrugged. 'That's just the way it is. I know I should start investing or whatever it is you're supposed to do with it. The lawyers tried to make me but I ignored them. That's why I'm so glad I've met you.'

Ethan had enveloped her in a hug then. 'Don't you worry, I'm here to look after you. It's all going to be fine. You just tell me what you want, and I'll make sure it happens.'

Ethan was in charge of everything, her trusted partner, and that was fine with her. He was smart and educated and she respected that. She knew that he was on the boards of all the companies they'd created and that he'd arranged to be paid a handsome salary, but that was quite fair. He was earning it, as far as she was concerned. He'd already shown her spreadsheets and documents that projected excellent returns on the money he was investing for her. The properties, artworks, wine – everything he bought on her behalf – would all appreciate into even more valuable assets. And Noble's, once they'd reinvigorated it, would begin to reward them handsomely.

Meanwhile Ethan was making a few investments for himself. His old flat wasn't quite the thing any more; it didn't match the lifestyle that he was enjoying with Octavia, with the bespoke suits and shirts and hand-made shoes. He found himself a smart four-storey townhouse in Notting Hill instead and had it completely overhauled with the help of a designer responsible for several other eye-wateringly expensive but very impressive houses.

'I must be paying you well!' joked Octavia when he'd shown her round.

'You *are* paying me well,' Ethan said, looking serious, 'but it's just the market rate for this kind of business.' He grabbed her round the waist and stared deep into her eyes, so that she could study every fleck of hazel in his. 'You trust me, don't you?'

'Of course I do.' She knew he was more than capable of making her ventures a success. After all, he was a prosperous businessman before he'd met her. But more than that, life with Ethan was a constant whirl of excitement, and Octavia was continually carried away by his enthusiasm and passion. She loved being able to say 'yes' when he came to her with a new idea or a suggestion for something he thought they should own. Besides, he always rewarded her in the best way possible: when he was happy, he took her to bed and made love to her, driving her to ecstasy with his magnificent body. She was addicted to the gorgeous feeling. He only had to look at her in a certain way and she'd be hot and ready for him, desperate to possess him all over again.

Was there anything more seductive than sex and business? she wondered. Sometimes, as they lay in bed, Ethan would explain the whole thing to her. Her money might be behind all the companies he'd created, he said, but most of her personal fortune would remain untouched. He'd designed BC Investments to limit her risk; she put in five million and Ethan went out to find other people willing to put in similar amounts, with a minimum initial stake of five million, until they had a big enough fund to invest in Noble's.

'BC Investments is going to buy the freehold of the store,' Ethan explained to her. 'Then Noble's will lease it back at the cost of two million a year while also repaying a big chunk of their bank debt. Think of it as a two-pronged attack. Buying the property is one way in. Securing shares is another.'

Octavia had nodded, trying to follow what it was

about but finding, in the end, that she preferred to leave it to him. She had a say in who was appointed to the board of Butterfly Ltd, the company that would set about acquiring shares in Noble's, and had insisted that Iseult be brought on to it. Ethan agreed, and recruited a further four board members. They were identikit men in suits as far as Octavia was concerned, though he told her they all had impressive business backgrounds and experience in luxury retail.

Now, as they sat on the deck of *The Great Bear,* Ethan nuzzled at Octavia's neck where she smelt of warm skin and suntan lotion. 'This is making me horny,' he murmured. 'Spending fucking obscene amounts of cash always does.'

She giggled, her body tingling in response to his. 'Then what are we waiting for?' she asked.

Three minutes later they were on the bed in Ethan's cabin. He'd stripped off quickly so that he could devote himself to her smooth brown body, pulling down the bikini briefs to reveal the strip of blonde hair above her already swollen sex.

'God, you're ready for me,' he breathed, sinking his face into her pussy and pressing his tongue inside so that he could lick out her sweet juices.

Octavia was ready to come the moment his tongue touched her; she gasped and writhed, tossing her head on the pillow with abandon. She grabbed for his shoulders and pulled him up towards her.

'Fuck me, please,' she begged, feeling a wild yearning for the sensation of his girth filling her up. 'Right now.'

He grinned, eyes burning with desire. 'You want it, baby . . . you got it.'

She opened her thighs and he entered her, pressing his tongue into her mouth at the same instant as his cock rammed into her hot, waiting pussy. The intensity of it was almost overwhelming as they began to thrust together, her hips coming up to meet his. She felt as though she couldn't get enough of him: the musky smell, the taste of his sweat on his skin, the sensation of his prick pounding her to that sweet resolve.

They rode it fast and hard, both eager to reach their peaks, and a few moments later Octavia felt the great surge overcome her and cried out with the strength of the blissful feelings possessing her.

Ethan grunted as he rolled over, his prick dripping with their combined juices. 'That was amazing,' he said. He looked over at her and grinned. 'Always is when we've just won.'

'So Noble's is ours,' breathed Octavia, relishing the languor of her post-orgasmic release.

'Thanks to me.' Ethan stretched out luxuriously. 'And Robert Young, I suppose.'

'So he sorted it all out for you?'

'Yep. Old man Radcliffe was totally against us buying in, not surprisingly. Threatened to resign. He didn't, of course. Young pointed out that it was ludicrous to reject an offer that would help the company to escape from some of its debt burden. If they didn't accept, they would have to find fifteen million to repay another instalment on their loan, with the shop still operating at a loss and without paying a dividend for years. He brought the rest of the board over to his side, and that was that.'

'And Radcliffe gave in and signed.'

Ethan shrugged. 'He didn't have a choice, really.

374

And now we've revealed that Butterfly Limited has been buying shares on the quiet. We kept it a secret right up to the point where we had to declare that we own an eight percent stake in the shop. Yesterday Butterfly announced that we intend to acquire more until we have a controlling stake and can complete a takeover.'

Octavia shivered with excitement. 'You know what?' she said, caressing Ethan's chest and moving her hand slowly downwards. 'All this talk of takeovers and stakes is giving me an appetite all over again . . .'

49

Amanda pulled her chin up under knees and watched an insect crawling slowly over the wooden floorboards of the tree house. She hadn't been up in it since she was a teenager, when she used to escape the family by coming out here with a rug, some apples, a thermos of sweet tea and a pile of books. It was reassuringly the same, if a bit tattier and more weather-worn than before. One day, she supposed, it would fall down, but it still seemed secure and sturdy enough. The ladder up to the platform had taken her weight without any trouble.

If only everything could remain so comfortingly constant.

She looked out over the lawns, soft and velvety in contrasting green stripes, to the well-tended flower beds teeming with pale pinks and lavenders, and over to the sixteenth-century manor house where she'd lived all her life until she'd moved to London.

No matter what happens, Fa and Ma will always be here, she told herself. *It doesn't matter if the shop goes, if it all goes. We'll still have this, and we'll still have each other.*

The announcement of the sale of Noble's premises

had been a dark day for the Radcliffe family, her father in particular. Young had tried to persuade them that it was for the best, and that the agreement was water-tight – the shop could never be ousted from its premises, the old building could never be sold to anyone else. At least this way they had the money they needed to keep the whole thing afloat.

Amanda could see it made sense, but that didn't stop her from mourning the loss of the grand old place. It was horrible, going into her office, knowing that the magnificent building now belonged to some faceless corporation, a collector of assets to whom the history of Noble's meant nothing at all. They didn't care that Victorian ladies had bought their paisley shawls there, or that the beau monde had once flocked to Noble's see the latest Art Deco furniture and fitments. They didn't care that twenties flappers had sought out tassels and boas from its haberdashery department, or that the fifth floor had seen wartime lectures on how to make do and mend. It was just a figure on a balance sheet to them. An asset. A piece of property that meant no more than any soulless supermarket hangar on a piece of scrubland. It broke Amanda's heart.

And that, she had thought, was the end of it. With the cash injection, surely a new era had begun. She'd been hopeful that Robert Young would let her increase her budget and perhaps implement some of the changes she'd been begging to make. But he'd been quite adamant: the company had to concentrate on getting back in the black, and that meant spending less, not more.

Stupid prick, she thought, tracing a knothole in the floorboards with her finger. Amanda knew her father bitterly regretted appointing Young but now that he was there, it was extremely hard to get rid of him. *Too late now anyway. The damage has all been done.*

They had only just learnt of the fresh danger facing them. Young had called them in to an emergency board meeting on Friday to tell them that a new company had shown its hand: Butterfly Ltd had already accumulated 8 percent of the shares in Noble's, enough to give them sizeable voting power. They were on the way to rivalling the 12 percent owned by the Radcliffe family and once that happened, would have control of the company. It was obvious that this was a hostile takeover bid, and that soon the shareholders would be consulted on the prospect of this unknown company buying the majority holding. Butterfly was going to show its hand at a shareholder meeting later the following week, and explain its motives.

I'm looking forward to it, Amanda thought grimly. *I'm damn well going to fight against this. I don't know who these Butterfly people are, but I'm going to tell them what they can do with their eight per cent.*

Just then, she heard a commotion coming from the house. Her mother was shrieking, and then she saw the back door open and her father come stumbling out.

'Amanda!' he roared, his face red. 'Amanda!'

'Yes!' she cried, leaping to her feet and scrambling down the tree-house ladder. When she reached the bottom, she raced across the grass towards her father who was standing at the edge of the lawn.

'It's Young!' Graham said in a broken voice. 'That bastard . . . He's sold us out.'

'What? What do you mean?' she gasped.

'He's joined Butterfly Limited. He's taken his five

percent and sold it to them. They've got overall control. The company's been taken away from us.'

'Oh, Fa, no!' She clutched at his hand, hardly able to believe it.

He nodded, too choked to speak.

'Damn Robert Young! How could he?' Hot tears sprang to her eyes. 'He owes everything to you, to the company. And he's sold us out. They must have made him some pretty exciting promises. Oh, God!'

Graham's eyes had turned glassy. 'Noble's . . . our company . . . gone . . . after a hundred and fifty years. . . . What would Father say? Grandfather? How could I lose their creation like this?'

'It's not your fault,' cried Amanda fiercely. 'You mustn't think that!'

But Graham didn't appear to hear her: his face was flushing even harder, growing more and more scarlet, and his breath was coming ever louder, with a strange grating sound to it.

'Fa – are you all right?'

Graham turned his head towards her but his eyes had a far-off expression, a faint light of panic in their depths. He was fighting for breath, she realised, pulling air into his chest with heavy, rattling gasps.

'Fa? Fa! Fa – what's happening?' Amanda felt paralysed. All she could do was watch as his face began to set into a rigid expression and his eyes opened wide, with his mouth a black hole in the middle of his face. Then he stiffened and fell slowly to the ground, eyes still staring.

'Fa!' Amanda screamed. Then she turned and ran for the house, shouting to her mother to call 999.

*   *   *

The ambulance seemed to take an age, though it was perhaps only ten minutes or so, speeding through the Kentish country roads to find them. The green-uniformed paramedics raced over to Graham, carrying resuscitation equipment, oxygen masks and canisters. They bent over his body, using all their resources to revive him. They shouted incomprehensible things to each other – numbers and statistics. They used their defibrillator, pressing the pads to his pathetically white bare chest, making his body jerk horribly as they applied the electric shock that they hoped would bring him back. After twenty minutes of ceaseless effort with no change, they loaded Graham on to a stretcher and into the ambulance, still working at resuscitation.

Amanda stood to one side, her arms around her shaking, weeping mother. As the ambulance pulled away, leaving only the detritus of abandoned sterile wrappings on the lawn, she said that she would drive them both to the hospital.

'We'll see how Fa's doing when we get there,' she said gently, but in her heart she knew that it was useless. She had seen him die right there on the lawn. Nothing they had done had been any good at all. He would be dead on arrival, she was certain of it, but it was easier for them to record the death at the hospital than here, on Graham's own beloved lawn by the house he'd lived in all his life.

'Come on, Ma. Let's go,' she said, stroking her mother's hair. Deep inside, Amanda's heart had turned to stone. *They did this. Young. Butterfly – whoever the fuck they are. They killed him.*

50

Roddy's party was at the Hôtel du Cap, a glamorous white-walled place perched high above the brilliant blue Mediterranean Sea, surrounded by lush pine forests. It had been a favourite of high society since the 1920s. The Duke and Duchess of Windsor had honeymooned there, Somerset Maugham had drunk himself stupid there, and any number of film stars and tycoons had made their way from fabulous yachts to its jetty, and from there into its luxurious interior.

The wind ruffled Octavia's hair softly as the launch bumped over the sea towards the hotel. It was going to be a wonderful evening. Roddy's parties were amazing. He loved theatre, adored creating show-pieces. There was always something to draw a gasp from even the most jaded of party-goers. The small boy from the rough side of Glasgow was able to show them all how it should be done.

Ethan turned to her, eyes invisible behind his sunglasses but a wide smile revealing his amusement. 'It's funny to think that the whole Noble's thing started in order to help Roddy get into the big time. He doesn't exactly need it now.'

'No.' Octavia smiled back. 'We need him much more than he needs us.'

'Well, that's thanks to you,' Ethan said, turning to look back at the approaching coast line with its rocky cliffs and pine trees. 'If you hadn't given him the initial investment he needed, he never would have exploded on to the fashion scene the way he has.'

'True.' Octavia slipped her sunglasses on. 'But the person he owes it all to is Iseult. She had faith in him right from the start. She's the one who really made him.'

After Flora's wedding, photographs of the bride had been in all the papers and the accompanying editorials had sighed over her dress – so beautiful, so stylish, so amazingly well designed . . . by Roddy Wildblood, the hot new designer whose debut fashion show had caused such a stir recently. One of the papers, though, had printed a picture that showed the bride staring into the lens of a camera with lips pulled back in a grimace that looked like a cross between a snarl and a strange, bitter smile. *Wedding day nerves?* asked the caption. *Flora Beaufort, sister of socialite Octavia, on her way to marry businessman Baron Otto von Schwetten.*

But it was the dress people talked about most. Iseult, as good as her word, had pulled every string and had Roddy featured in *Vogue,* his photograph taken by Bailey. In *Go!* magazine there was a reportage on Roddy, a series of black-and-white photographs taken in his East End studio, showing him hard at work and deep in the creative process: designing, cutting and stitching. The last photograph was of Octavia, hair loose, high-cheekboned, hand on hip, staring provocatively into the camera as she modelled the outfit he had been creating in the previous pictures. It was fantastic publicity. Roddy Wildblood became the name on everyone's lips.

The day those pictures were taken was also the day Octavia had told Roddy she was going to become his backer. Butterfly Ltd was going to invest a million pounds in his business, in return for a 20 percent stake. Ethan had told her that she could have got far more of the business – after all, where were the other backers? They weren't exactly lining up, and if they had, they would have driven a much harder bargain. Ethan thought 50 percent at least was what she should push for, but Octavia had refused.

'I can't take Roddy's identity away from him. He is the business, the business is him.'

'You've left him eighty percent,' Ethan protested. 'That's far more than he needs.'

'I'm not in this for money. I want to help Roddy.'

Ethan had been exasperated by that, telling her she would never succeed in business if that was how she thought, but Octavia would not back down.

Then, fate intervened. Just when she, Iseult and Roddy had picked out a shop on New Bond Street, a good position opposite Cartier, and the lease was about to be signed, everything changed. Sy Hoffstein, managing director of Celadon, a company that owned many prestigious luxury brands and fashion houses, rang Roddy up and offered him the job of chief designer at the House of Delphine.

It was an extraordinary coup. Delphine was a wonderful fashion house, created by Delphine Rouchard in the 1970s in order to realise her vision of playful, wearable, modish clothes for young women. She had been the inspiration behind city shorts, those crisp, sharply creased sexy little numbers, worn with platform heels or knee-length boots and floaty lace blouses. Her signature look was sophisticated yet girlish: the Delphine woman didn't wear formal two-pieces or pearls or carry stiff handbags. She wore high-waisted flares, long-collared, slim-fitting shirts, owl-eyed sunglasses with white frames, low-cut tee-shirts with pocketed mini-skirts, or dungaree-dresses cut high across the thigh. She carried slouchy leather bags, or slung fringed purses on long slim handles over her shoulder. She was unutterably cool.

But the House of Delphine had lost its way over the years, especially after Madame Rouchard retired in the early nineties, and had subsequently gone through several renaissances, with top-name designers brought in to reinvigorate and refresh the brand. Some had succeeded better than others. The last big name, Sally Sands, had done brilliantly, sparking off new trends for sailor-girl dresses; huge white leather handbags and platform espadrilles, but then she had gone off to raise a family and Delphine had slumped again in the care of more mediocre talents.

Now Roddy was being offered the most incredible opportunity to revitalise the house. He would be based in Paris, designing six collections a year, heading up a hand-picked team and earning himself a small fortune in the process.

'You'll take it, of course!' Iseult had screamed when he had told them the news.

He'd grinned. 'I'd be fifty kinds of fool not to, wouldn't I?'

And they'd all celebrated together: the Bond Street shop could wait while Roddy found fame and fortune in Paris.

The time had felt absolutely right for him. In fact, he'd been trembling on the brink of something big for ages, and this was just what he needed to break through. The workload had seemed impossible at first. As soon as he started, he had to prepare a collection to show in only two months' time. But Roddy being Roddy – an untamed genius, as Iseult put it – he not only designed his main collection but a full accessories line as well, and the new Delphine look stormed the Paris fashion shows, to be received with rapture by the cognoscenti and buyers alike. The most obvious sign of success, though, was that the High Street shops all had copies on their racks within weeks: tiger-striped leather mini-skirts, denim tee-shirts and high wedge-heeled clogs were everywhere. The couture customers were crazy about his delicious evening gowns, inspired by Boucher and Fragonard: mad, floral-printed shepherdess dresses, with wild netting, cheeky corsets and silken bustles.

'But these,' sighed Iseult, holding a pair of shoes from the evening-wear line, 'these are the ones I'd like to be buried in!'

They were a towering stiletto with a five-inch heel and a small platform under the sole, in lavender satin, embroidered with crystals in the pattern of flowers and edged in lace.

'They are gorgeous,' Octavia said admiringly. She'd wanted to buy them herself but it was clear that Iseult had claimed ownership, so instead she bought a pair of lime green satin heels embroidered with jet beads and edged in violet tulle. They were £2000 a pair and sold out in minutes – a sign that Roddy really had arrived.

He took to the high life like a duck to water: he abandoned London in the flash of an eye, though he kept his funny, tatty old studio there, and made his home in the glamorous St Germain area of Paris in a flat bought for him by Celadon. He acquired a French boyfriend called Didier and began to party as though his life depended on it.

And now here they were, about to celebrate the success of his latest collection and the return to prominence of the House of Delphine.

Ethan helped Octavia out of the launch and she walked carefully along the jetty. Tonight she was wearing a long silk Maria Grachvogel dress in suitably oceanic swirling blues and turquoises. It was a halter-neck with a low cowl back that showed off her tanned shoulders and an expanse of smooth brown back. She'd teamed it with a pair of Louboutins called 'Poseidon' because they looked as though they were made from silver mermaids' tails, with glittering scales overlapping one another. The heels were twelve centimetres high. Roddy would love them, she knew, though he would also be a little jealous that he hadn't designed them himself.

The ballroom had been given over to his party. Immediately she entered the room, Octavia clocked the familiar faces of A-list actresses, supermodels, heart-throb film stars and sports heroes. A famous footballer and his pop-star wife were chatting to their movie-star pals. One of American's sweethearts was flashing a toned brown thigh while telling her latest leading man a funny story about how her earring fell off and plummeted down the front of her dress while she was on the red carpet. A short and rather tired-looking supermodel was asking if anyone wanted to go outside with her for a fag, while another was imperiously ordering her coterie about, sending them running round to satisfy her every wish. Roddy had pulling power now – anyone who was anyone wanted to be part of his glittering crowd.

The theme of the party was Bacchanalia, and the ballroom had been decorated in vines heavy with lush purple grapes. Gilded Horns of Plenty and lyres peeped through the vine leaves. Everywhere were youths dressed as fauns – bare-chested above, and in hairy goat-skin breeches below, small goatee beards on their handsome chins and pert little horns nestling in their curly hair. The fauns carried pitchers of wine and champagne, moving around the guests and constantly topping up their goblets. Others carried platters of mezze: stuffed vine leaves, goat's cheese rolled in fresh herbs, miniature skewers of prawns, stuffed olives, pieces of lamb marinaded in honey and spices – a feast fit for Olympian deities. On another table was more conventional food for those who couldn't live without Beluga caviar, smoked salmon, or quails' eggs with truffle oil.

Around the edges of the room were beautiful living statues of the gods and goddesses, all semi-naked. There was an exquisite Athena, a tiny stuffed owl perched on her wrist and a shield in her other hand, her full breasts revealed under her draped white robes; a wing-heeled Hermes displayed perfect buttocks and a ribbon of fair hair leading from his navel to his groin.

Zeus, Hera, Aphrodite (particularly lovely, with only her flowing dark hair to cover her nakedness) and many others stood about the edges of the room on their marble plinths, tall, proud and unashamed.

'Hands off Apollo,' Roddy said, as he kissed Octavia on the cheek. 'He's mine! I've already bagged him, okay?' He grinned over at a handsome man on a nearby plinth, with a laurel wreath in his hair and a lyre in his hand. His thick firm thighs were covered in soft brown hair and his groin area bulged promisingly under its tiny loincloth. 'Don't tell Didier.'

'I won't,' laughed Octavia. 'This is amazing!'

'What else did you expect?' Roddy's eyes were already a little lazy with drink. 'How are you, honey?'

'I'm fine, fine. I got some good news today. It looks like I'm the new owner of Noble's.'

'Hey, fantastic!' Roddy squeezed her hand, though his eyes were scanning the room. 'I'm so pleased for you.'

Just then, Didier came up. He gave Octavia a look that could have been a friendly hello but appeared to be chillier. 'Roddy, you wanna come to the toilet?'

'Huh? Oh, yeah.' He smiled at Octavia. 'Just time for a little pick-me-up. You want some?'

'No. I'd like some of that champagne, I think.'

'Okay. Just hail a passing faun.' Roddy giggled as Didier pulled him away by the hand. 'See ya later!'

Ethan brought her a goblet of sparkling vintage Cristal. 'No expense spared,' he murmured as he gave it to her. 'Have you seen the naked ice statues?'

Octavia shook her head.

'Worth a look. One is a little winged Cupid pissing vodka. His mate Psyche has breasts spurting—'

'Tonic?' suggested Octavia.

Ethan laughed. 'Nothing so innocuous. She's got fuckin' Napoleon brandy coming out of there!'

'Painful on the nipples, surely?'

'Nah. Anaesthetic.' He looked into her eyes. 'Makes me want to suck on you though. Maybe later . . .'

Octavia shivered with pleasure.

They were soon lost in a crowd of people, greeting friends and swapping gossip, exchanging yacht details and making plans for more get-togethers, lunches, parties. Occasionally Octavia caught sight of Roddy, who seemed to become more and more manic as the evening progressed. People started dancing on a raised stage at the back of the ballroom – beautiful girls striking poses and writhing while looking pretty wasted, men staring into space and making the odd robotic move.

Roddy stopped by Octavia just long enough to point out an A-list all-action movie star, busy mingling with his wife, and say, 'See him? Begged me for a blow job. I sucked him off in his limo. Queer as a two-bob note, darling. Don't tell, though. He sues quicker than you can say "litigious closet gay".'

It was a little after midnight when Octavia found Iseult. She was wearing a magnificent vintage Schiaparelli ballgown with a floral headpiece of great silken purple flowers, and standing on the balcony puffing away at her cigarette while she chatted to another partygoer. Beyond her was the velvety midnight sea where the lights of yachts twinkled golden in the darkness.

'Iseult, there you are!' Octavia went up and kissed her. 'How are you?'

'Fine, my sweet, fine!' She returned the kisses and then said to her friend, 'Would you excuse us, darling? Private moment needed.'

The friend nodded and went off, leaving Octavia and Iseult alone on the balcony. Iseult gave a great sigh. 'It's a success, isn't it? A huge success. *He's* a success.'

'Yes. Aren't you proud?'

'Of course. And yet . . .' Iseult sighed again, even more heavily, and shook her head, her eyes sad.

'What is it?' Octavia had never seen Iseult outwardly depressed. She had always put on a show of high spirits for other people. But there was an unmistakable air of melancholy around her now. Octavia wanted to give her friend a hug, but she had never felt able to be so intimate with Iseult.

There was a pause while the older woman looked thoughtful, then she said, 'You know I've devoted my life to Roddy ever since I discovered him. I don't think it's unfair to say that he owes his success to me. Of course it's his talent that counts, but he would still be slaving away in that Savile Row tailors if I hadn't spurred him on and put my own reputation on the line to back him. I thought that when he fulfilled his potential, he wouldn't forget me. When the call came to go to Paris and be the Delphine designer, he would surely take me with him.' She stopped and took a furious drag on her cigarette, then said in a sharp voice, 'I don't have much money, you know that. What I have had, I've given to Roddy, and gladly. He could have used his influence to repay me with a job at Delphine. Some kind of position. But he hasn't. There has been nothing.'

'Oh, Iseult.' Octavia took hold of her hand. 'Have you said anything to him?'

'Of course not. I'm far too proud. And I don't want you to say a word either, you must promise me that. I'm not a charity case. It's the fact that it wasn't offered that has hurt me so much.'

Octavia felt sorry for her as she wrestled with her pride and an obviously wounded heart. 'If it's just money . . . you know you have a position on the Butterfly board, and I'll pay you well for that. It's not charity – I need your expertise.'

Iseult managed a small smile. 'I know, darling. I treasure you for it. I can't wait to help you with Noble's, we're going to have so much fun.'

There was a raucous shout from inside the ballroom and they looked round to see Roddy prancing wildly on the dance stage, obviously completely wired on drugs.

'He's on a roll,' Iseult remarked. 'It will be back upstairs to his suite later, and then tomorrow they're going to fly to Spain to continue the party at some rich kid's villa.'

'I know, he invited Ethan and me along, but we've got a house party back home.' Octavia looked anxiously at her friend. 'You know, you should speak to Roddy if you feel this way. He ought to know.'

'Perhaps. We shall see. If he ever comes back down to earth, I'll consider it.'

It was a searingly bright morning. Octavia poured a glass of orange juice and drank it gratefully. She needed the liquid and the vitamins to combat last night's excess.

She and Ethan had left the hotel just after three to return to the yacht. The party in the ballroom had ended at two, but at least a hundred people had gone up to Roddy's vast suite to carry on, drinking, taking drugs and – in one of the bedrooms – enjoying an impromptu orgy. It was decadent beyond anything Octavia felt comfortable with – although Ethan had popped into the orgy room just to have a look at what was going on, emerging with a broad smile on his face – so they'd decided to head back.

The yacht was a haven of peace after the wildness of the hotel suite and Octavia had fallen with great relief into bed, far too knackered to think about any sex action although Ethan, turned on by what he'd witnessed in the orgy room, had kissed her neck and pushed himself against her buttocks for a few moments before he fell into a deep sleep as well. Now it was another beautiful, bright day and the stewards had laid the usual sumptuous breakfast on the main deck. Ethan was still snoring below deck. She reached for the bowl of natural yoghurt which she poured over her fruit and then added a sprinkle of toasted oats and a drizzle of maple syrup.

Just then one of the stewards came up, holding one of the ship's telephones.

'A call for you, madame,' he said politely.

'Oh, thank you. I left my phone in the cabin,' she said, putting down her spoon and taking the handset. 'Hello?'

'Hi, Octavia, it's Vicky. I couldn't get hold of you on your phone.'

'Sorry, it's downstairs. How are you?' She was used to receiving a daily call from Vicky, who did much more work for her now that Flora had gone. They were always co-ordinating dates and times, making sure that all of Octavia's hair and beauty appointments were in the on-line diary and confirming arrangements for travel. No doubt Vicky wanted to know if they would be requiring the plane that was on stand-by at Nice airport.

'I'm fine . . . I just wondered, have you spoken to Flora lately?'

Octavia stood up and went over to the rail of the yacht, looking out over the sparkling sea. It was easier to cope here, far from the familiar surroundings of home, not having to see the closed door to Flora's empty room. 'I spoke to her a few weeks ago. It was the usual thing.' The calls were almost more painful than not hearing from her sister at all. She sounded so strange and cold that it was though the old Flora had died and been replaced by this other person, who wanted to keep Octavia at a distance. This was so painful to contemplate she tried to close her mind and her heart to it, though inside she was utterly bereft.

'It's weird,' Vicky said, sounding puzzled. 'She's just cancelled my trip out to see her. Again. That's the sixth time in a row. This is getting beyond a joke. Has she said anything to you?'

'No.' Octavia laughed mirthlessly. 'Hardly! She doesn't confide in me any more. I guess that's what marriage does. What do you think the problem is?'

'I don't know,' Vicky said. 'But it's not like her . . . I know you two fell out before the wedding and you're both still smarting from it, but this doesn't feel right.'

Octavia stared into the blue, faintly misty horizon. 'Okay. Listen, I'm coming back to London the day after tomorrow. We'll talk about it then and sort something out.'

'Okay.' Vicky sounded relieved. 'I'll make sure all the arrangements are in place.'

51

Sitting in her office in the London house, Vicky put the phone down and stared at the computer screen.

It was a comfort to talk to Octavia, but she still felt very uneasy. She re-read the email from Flora's new address: floravonschwetten@schwetten.com. Something wasn't right, she knew that. She had spoken to her cousin a few times, and each time had thought that Flora wasn't herself. She didn't sound ill or unhappy, just . . . different. Octavia had said something similar, describing it as though Flora wasn't quite there.

At first, they weren't surprised not to hear from her. No doubt she was caught up in the excitement of her new home, the bliss of being married, and the fatigue that would undoubtedly set in after the wedding. A day or two went past, and then there were a few emails, telling them how happy she was and that she'd be in touch soon. Then, after a week or so, the phone calls began. The strange thing was that they always came from Flora. They could never reach her directly themselves. Her phone, she said, got no reception in the castle. The only person to answer the landline there was Otto.

Sometimes he fetched Flora to the phone, and sometimes he said she was too busy, or asleep, or out.

Vicky knew what Octavia thought. She believed that her sister was still punishing her for their falling out just before the wedding. Vicky didn't know what it had been about and Octavia hadn't said, but it must have been serious to come between the sisters like this. Why else would Octavia go all this time without seeing her twin, the other half of herself?

Vicky stood up and stretched. *I need fresh air,* she thought. When she needed a walk, she would usually go to the Chelsea Physic Garden and stroll among the botanical specimens, soaking up their quiet calm. Today, though, she needed the buzz of other people, so she pulled on a silk cardigan and headed out towards the King's Road.

It wasn't just Flora who'd changed, Vicky thought, digging her hands into her pockets as she sauntered along the road. It was a hot August day and the smell of frying tarmac was in the air. Octavia had been transformed in the months since Flora had gone. Now that she was in a relationship with the undeniably sexy Ethan, she'd become a pampered rich girl, living a life that seemed to come straight from the glossy magazines. She was hardly ever at the Chelsea house any more but spent most of her time at Ethan's in Notting Hill where she had accumulated a whole wardrobe of clothes and everything else she needed. Vicky knew she was avoiding the old house because it felt so empty and lonely without Flora.

When Octavia gets back, we'll sort this out. I'm prepared to get on a plane and just turn up at that damn castle if I have to.

Vicky walked down the busy street, glancing in shop windows and avoiding the buggies and shopping bags that were in danger of bashing her ankles. Then she saw him.

She stopped dead, her mouth open, staring hard. Was it him? He was standing a few metres away from her on the pavement outside a restaurant, shaking hands with someone, and then he was turning so that she could see him face on. Yes, yes . . . he was unmistakable.

'Otto!' she shouted, and began to move forward.

Had he heard her? She could have sworn he had. His eyes seemed to fix on her for a fraction of a second and Vicky was sure she saw recognition in them. But then he continued turning towards the road and put up his arm to hail a passing taxi.

'Otto, it's me!' Vicky tried to rush towards him but a pushchair was suddenly in her way and she had to step to one side to avoid it, only to find herself in the path of a little old lady with a shopping trolley.

He didn't appear to hear. The taxi stopped beside him and in a few seconds he was inside it. Just as Vicky got free and came dashing up calling his name, the taxi accelerated away, taking the man inside with it.

She stood on the pavement, panting. Had that really been Otto? It had certainly looked like him, but then . . . brown-haired businessmen in suits could look rather similar to each other. If it was, though, what the hell was he doing here? Was Flora with him too?

Vicky frowned and turned back to retrace her steps home. There was a mystery here, and she was determined to get to the bottom of it.

52

Flora sat in her bedroom, in the window seat. It was her favourite place. From here, she could look out to the forests beyond, and the hazy blue mountain tops on the other side of the river. She couldn't see the castle itself, with its ramshackle exterior and broken windows, although she knew that was beginning to change. There was scaffolding all over the west side of it, and workmen were beavering away, restoring and replacing the outer stonework and repointing the ancient mortar. The roof on that side was also being meticulously repaired and retiled – apparently water had destroyed several fine pieces of furniture being stored in attics there and it was a matter of urgency for the leaks to be stopped. It was all a matter of urgency. The whole place was falling to pieces.

Flora had known that her own fairy tale was as insubstantial as air the moment Otto had swung his fist into her face on their wedding night, splitting her lip and bruising her face.

'You arranged those photographers!' he had hissed at her. 'You had them there, taking photographs. What were you thinking of?'

'I didn't! Otto, please, you have to believe me!' she'd cried, holding a blood-soaked tissue to her mouth.

But he'd refused to listen to her, and her storm of tears had irritated him so much that eventually he'd marched out, slamming the great oak door behind him. Flora had wept in shock and horror until she'd fallen asleep at last on the four-poster bed. When she'd woken in the morning, it had been a relief to find Otto snoring beside her. It had been the stress of the wedding, she told herself. A blip. Now peace would be restored, and this awful episode would be forgotten, she was sure of it.

She'd got up and found the bathroom down the corridor, a rusting, clanking old room with a giant cast-iron bath and a lavatory with a high cistern and a dangling chain. The water had come out tepid and faintly brown. Flora had never known anything like it.

When she got back to the bedroom Otto had vanished, so she dressed and made her way downstairs. The kindly looking housekeeper from the night before was in the great hall, standing on a chair and dusting one of the arrangements of daggers that hung on the wall.

'Ach, there you are. Hello, my child. Would you like some *Frühstück?*' She climbed off her chair and put down her duster.

'Yes, please. Is there any coffee?'

'But of course. Follow me.' She led Flora out of the great hall and along dark corridors to the kitchen, a large vaulted room at the back of the castle. On a wooden table there were some breakfast dishes and an abandoned plate and cup.

'Otto's,' explained the housekeeper. 'He has gone out early this morning, hunting. He is mad for hunting. He likes hunting the wild boar best of all, though he also catches foxes, rabbits, game. He has a pack of hounds nearby, a mile or so. On a clear day, with the breeze in the right direction, you will hear them barking.'

Flora sat down at the table and the housekeeper brought her a pot of strong coffee, hot milk and a plate of bread and cold meats – just the same as she had eaten for supper the night before. *It's Christmas Day*, she remembered. There was not a sign of any festivities. What kind of place was this?

'Ach, your face!' the housekeeper said, looking at Flora's cheek. It was bruised and swollen. 'Let me get you some arnica. Good for bruises.' She didn't ask how Flora had hurt herself but simply brought a tube of cream for her to apply to her face.

It was only later when Flora stood up to leave, wondering what she should do with herself now, that she said, 'Wh-wh-where is Otto's m-m-mother? I must introduce myself to her. Is she still s-s-sick in bed?'

'Sick in bed?' The woman had looked amused at this. 'No, no.' She had given Flora a look of sympathy. '*I* am Otto's mother.'

'Oh.' Flora had been painfully confused. 'But . . . I don't understand.'

Her mother-in-law had shrugged. 'What is so hard to understand? All will become clear in time.'

After breakfast Flora had returned to her room and

unpacked her clothes. Her handbag, she noticed, was missing. Perhaps she had left it in the car the previous night. She put the gifts she had brought for Otto on the table by the bed and wondered if perhaps Christmas was going to happen later, or if it was all done differently in Germany. With nothing else to do, she wandered off to explore the castle on her own. It was far from the romantic place of her imagination – dilapidated in the extreme. There was almost no furniture in the place – empty, dusty, cold rooms followed one upon the other. Where there was plaster, it was peeling and damp, stonework was crumbling and bare bulbs flickered unreliably in the depths of dark corridors. Outside it was even worse: the roof was falling to pieces and window frames were rotting. The outbuildings were no more than hovels and the driveway was covered in ugly, cracked concrete.

Flora could not believe it. Otto had said it had been restored to a Rococo delight, which was manifestly not the case. Could this really be the noble ancestral home of the von Schwettens? Was this the place that he had been determined to protect, in case of an expensive divorce? It couldn't be worth much, not in this state . . .

After a morning spent looking about the place, Flora went to find Otto's mother again. She was still in the kitchen, this time swathed in a large apron and stirring something in a saucepan.

'Madam Baroness,' she began awkwardly. She'd been worrying about how to address Otto's mother all morning, now that she'd realised that this very ordinary-looking woman must in fact be a titled aristocrat. 'Madam Baroness, may I ask you something?'

The woman had looked at her with eyes full of pity. 'I'm sure there are many things you wish to know,' she said in her softly accented voice.

'Why is the castle like this?' Flora asked. It was the first question that came into her head from the many she wanted to ask.

'Why?' The woman shrugged and turned back to the potato soup she was making. 'It was like this when we arrived four years ago. Goodness knows how he could afford it in the first place.'

Four years ago? But Otto told me this place had been in his family for generations! Flora didn't know what to ask next. Had she misunderstood him? Was she remembering clearly? She knew she was, but the awful emotions threatening to engulf her meant that she could hardly speak.

She ate her potato soup almost in silence, her brain still teeming with questions, while Otto's mother sat beside her, talking cheerfully about the weather and asking about the wedding although Flora could scarcely answer her.

Otto returned late that night, tired, dirty and ravenous but obviously in a good mood. Flora and his mother, who had eaten earlier, sat and watched as he devoured a hearty meal of stew and noodles. Between mouthfuls, he described the thrill of that day's hunt and the wild boar they had finally brought to ground. There had been, he said, a merry Christmas lunch in the middle of the day, with *Glühwein*, venison and rich slices of *Stollen*. The two women had said little, apart from Otto's mother congratulating him on his successful hunting. Then it had been time for bed.

'Otto,' Flora had said tentatively. She was sitting on the edge of the mattress in her nightie, feeling sick and nervous.

'Mmm?' He was stripping off, a musky, sweaty smell wafting across the room towards her.

'Don't you have anything to say to me?' Flora said pleadingly. She had hoped that he would apologise for hitting her the night before, or begin to explain the difference between the stories he had spun and the reality she found herself living in.

He turned around then, a half smile on his face. 'Not at all, my dear. Should I?'

She stared at him, confused. 'I-I-I have a present for you,' she said, gesturing at the bedside table as though the gift might restore the old Otto to her. 'For Christmas.'

'How kind. I will open it later. For now, I have a present for you too.' He pushed down his boxer shorts, revealing his short thick penis which was already standing in semi-erection. It was the first time she had seen it. He took it in one hand and began to massage the shaft so that it soon stood firm and erect, a fat little barrel with a dark top. 'Your life is going to be quite different from what you expected, and I can't pretend that it doesn't give me pleasure to know that I've accomplished exactly what I set out to achieve. In fact, I find it somewhat exciting.' He moved towards the bed and, when he reached her, pushed her down on the floor and directed the tip of his penis towards her face. 'Come, you know what to do, I'm sure . . . Take it in your mouth.'

Flora felt horror seize her, but she was also afraid. He was pressing the musky tip of his penis, its purple head exposed, against her lips. She could smell urine and the dark sweat of his pubic hair. Obediently she opened her mouth and he pushed his penis hard inside. She wanted to gag but instead tried to keep calm and relax. She closed her eyes. *This is what wives do for their husbands,* she told herself. *This is normal.*

She sucked cautiously. Otto moaned and began to thrust harder into her mouth. She moved her mouth up and down the shaft, and a moment later it was flooded with hot, salty, thick liquid. He pulled his penis out, already limp and reduced to just a few centimetres in length. Flora coughed and retched then, with a monumental effort, swallowed. It left a strange, burning, hollow feeling in the back of her throat.

'Oh,' said Otto, disappointed. 'Has it gone? You've taken it down? Ah, well, you'll learn next time, I'm sure.'

There was no further discussion. A few minutes later he was in bed beside her and the light was turned out.

The next few days followed the same pattern: Flora would wake alone, find Otto's mother in the kitchen and then pass the day by herself. On the second day, her handbag appeared in their room but the mobile phone inside it had gone. She looked about the castle for a telephone but, when she asked Otto's mother, was told in an apologetic tone that there was only one telephone and it was locked inside Otto's study where no one else was allowed.

'We are a little remote here,' said her mother-in-law. 'It is a simple life. Secluded but happy. I'm sure you will grow to like it.' Her eyes had shown some level of understanding but Flora was still unable to express herself properly. She was too confused and ashamed.

When she'd asked Otto where her phone was, he'd said brusquely, 'Not yet. You will simply tell stupid stories to your family. When all this is sorted out and we understand each other perfectly – then you will get your telephone back. The newlyweds are not to be disturbed right now, huh? But that reminds me . . .'

He'd taken her up yet another staircase to a small room at the top of one of the turrets, set behind a red wooden door with a large lock on it. Inside was the most modern part of the castle Flora had yet seen: a large desk held a computer, printer, fax machine and telephone. Otto went to the desk, sat down and logged into his computer. 'We must reassure your sister,' he told her. 'Come here. Call up your email account.'

She'd gone round and obediently opened her email. He'd watched carefully as she signed in. There were several messages waiting for her, mostly from Octavia and Vicky.

'We shall reply.' When he'd read and dictated replies to the messages, Otto seemed satisfied, although she wondered what the others would think when they received the slightly stilted messages that surely didn't sound like something Flora herself would write. 'That will keep them happy for now,' he'd said. 'But there is something else . . .' He'd closed her account and opened a new one. 'This is your email address from now on – in your married name. Let us write a message to your sister and Vicky telling them that this is now where they should contact you.'

Flora had been unable to protest, too frightened to

405

speak up. What exactly was Otto capable of? He'd already hit her. He was already forcing her to give him oral sex every night.

'There. Now we shall be able to control what comes in and what goes out.' He'd smiled up at her, a kind of warmth and approval in his brown eyes. 'Very good, my dear. Very good.'

Since then, she'd not been allowed back into the office, or anywhere near the computer or telephone. She had no idea if Octavia or Vicky had replied, or what they'd thought of her strange emails.

Each morning, she woke up feeling dazed, still wondering if she was in some kind of dream and if today was the day that Otto would turn to her, laugh, and tell her he'd been playing a silly trick on her. She wasn't really a virtual prisoner here in his wreck of a home. They could go back to London now, to the comfort of the Chelsea house. But she pushed those images out of her mind. She couldn't bring herself to think of home. It was too painful.

What have I done? Flora asked herself in the night, as she lay next to Otto, shrouded by those suffocating heavy curtains. *Oh, Octavia . . . I'm so sorry. I need you now. More than I ever have before.*

53

Ethan stayed on for some business meetings – the enjoyable kind held on the decks of superyachts, with oligarchs in shorts and sunglasses making deals over frozen margaritas – while Octavia returned to London. She was glad to be home, even if the Chelsea house held a mournful air for her ever since Flora had left.

Steve brought her bags in while Octavia took off her white blazer and shook out her hair in front of the hall mirror. She heard footsteps and looked up to see Vicky coming down the stairs, her face streaked with tears.

'Thank goodness you're back, Octavia,' she said, hugging her.

'What's wrong? Why are you crying?' Octavia stepped back to look at her cousin's face.

'Come and see this.'

They went quickly up to Vicky's office, Octavia wondering what this was all about. Vicky led her over to her desk and showed her an email open on the screen. She gestured for Octavia to read it. 'I've been sacked. Flora's sacked me.'

Octavia gasped, and scanned it quickly. It was a brief notice, informing Vicky in formal terms of her immediate dismissal. 'But . . . why?' she breathed, stunned.

'I've no idea.' Vicky sniffed and wiped her eyes. 'All I know is that I sent her an email asking if Otto had been in London. And I got this in reply.'

'Why would he be in London without telling us?' Octavia frowned.

'I can't even be sure it was him,' Vicky said, 'but I thought I saw him, and wondered if he'd popped over on one of his flying visits, though I thought it was odd he wouldn't bring Flora with him. And now this.'

Octavia sank down in the chair by the desk. 'Well, the first thing is, you're not sacked. I don't know the legal standpoint but if this is what Flora wants – I'll just hire you again. So don't worry about that.' She smiled ruefully. 'If you still want to work for a couple of crazies like us, that is?'

'You know I do,' cried Vicky. 'Thanks, Octavia. But why would she want to sack me?'

Octavia looked again at the message. 'It's very odd.'

Vicky nodded. 'I agree. This doesn't sound like Flora at all, does it?'

'Look at the way it ends. "With the compliments of the Baroness von Schwetten".'

'Perhaps it's just a standard email sign-off,' Vicky suggested. 'An automatic signature.'

'Mmm. Maybe. I'm not sure. It's just – not like her.'

'What shall we do?'

'I'll call her,' Octavia said decisively. 'It's time we stopped all this nonsense and got to the bottom of what she's playing at. This time I won't take no for an answer.'

It was easier said than done. Flora's mobile went to voicemail, and the castle landline rang unanswered for long minutes.

Octavia sighed in frustration and rubbed her eyes. How the hell could it be so hard to talk to someone? She rattled off an email to her sister, asking what she was playing at by sacking Vicky, and requesting her to call at once. Otherwise Octavia was going to get on the first plane out there and sort this out face to face.

She pushed Send and watched the message appear at the bottom of the column. There. That was all she could do for now.

'We'll just have to wait for her to get back to us. I'll give it twenty-four hours,' she said to Vicky. 'Then we'll have to think of something else.'

Ethan flew in early the next morning and arranged to meet Octavia for breakfast at a French café in Piccadilly. He looked a little jaded when she saw him, and she guessed he'd been partying hard with the latest Russian billionaire to cross his path.

'Good time, darling?' she cooed. 'Did you work hard?'

'Yes, thanks,' he said in his Aussie drawl. 'You know me. Always hard at it.'

'Mmm. I hope so.' She gave him a flirtatious look over the top of her sunglasses. The waitress brought steaming cups of caffe latte and set them on the table while Octavia contemplated being able to forget her anxiety about Flora for a little while in Ethan's arms. 'Why were you so eager to see me?' she asked.

'I've got a bit of news, actually. I wanted to tell you myself.'

409

'Oh, yes?' She tried to quell the anxiety rising inside her.

'There's good news and bad news. Good news is that the deal for Noble's has been done and dusted. I've arranged for us to go there tomorrow and take a tour of our new possession.'

'That's fantastic!' she said happily. At least this was going right.

'But . . . something's happened that's cast a bit of a downer over proceedings. Old man Radcliffe has only gone and had a heart attack. He's dead.'

'Oh.' Octavia blinked as she took the news in. 'But, Ethan, that's dreadful.'

'I'll say. It puts us in a sticky PR position.'

'Yes, but . . . it's not just that, is it?' She remembered Amanda Radcliffe, the flashing-eyed brunette with the malicious curl to her mouth. That night Octavia had thrown water over her seemed so far away, as though it had happened to two other people. She felt she'd been a silly child back then. She remembered too how furious she'd been when Amanda had ordered her out of Noble's. That all seemed so petty now. Especially in the face of death. 'Poor girl,' she whispered. Suddenly the idea of taking Noble's from her rival, which had once seemed so funny and clever, appeared distinctly less attractive.

'Huh?' Ethan picked up a croissant, ripped a piece off and dipped it in his coffee. 'What poor girl? The point is, it's not going to ease the takeover in terms of staff morale, and so on. So we'll need to bear that in mind when we go there.'

Octavia looked over at him. He was just as handsome as ever, his short dark-blond hair delightfully ruffled over those sharp blue-hazel eyes. She wanted him just as much as she ever had. All he had to do was give her the cold shoulder and withhold that fabulous body from her and she'd always surrender and do whatever he liked. But somewhere at the heart of their relationship she had the sense that something was missing. Why couldn't she confide in him about Flora? Her true feelings of loss and hurt and abandonment? She could only forget them when Ethan was making love to her, taking her to the place where all that mattered was sensual pleasure. But that didn't seem right.

He looked up and saw her worried frown.

'Hey, don't sweat it, honey,' he said, putting a hand on hers and rubbing it gently. 'They'll all forget the old man in no time. It won't be a problem, I promise.'

54

Flora had been in the castle almost a week when, at breakfast with Otto's mother, she said, 'Madam Baroness, does Otto go hunting every day?'

'It is unusual for him to go as often as this. Castle business often keeps him here. But he loves it.' The woman looked embarrassed. 'I wish you would not call me Baroness, my dear.'

'Oh . . . but . . .' Flora was puzzled. She had assumed that Otto's mother must be a baroness. Or else how had he inherited the title?

Otto's mother got up and picked up their breakfast dishes to take to the sink. 'I am Frau Gestenholtz, that is all. But you may call me Marthe if you wish.'

The Germanic pronunciation of Marthe sounded like 'martyr'.

'Then – how can Otto be a baron?' ventured Flora.

'Best not to ask,' Marthe replied brusquely, walking to the sink. 'Otto does what he wishes. You will learn. There is no point in challenging him. Just accept.'

* * *

412

But Flora would not just accept. When she was alone, she spent long hours searching the castle, certain she would eventually find some way of contacting Octavia or Vicky. Perhaps there was a hidden key to Otto's study. Perhaps there was another way into it. All the time, she was constantly watching and planning, noting everything that happened and everything she saw. One day Otto might be careless and leave his mobile where she could find it. All she needed was that one slip-up and she would be free.

She knew, instinctively, that she must not be defiant. Whatever happened, he must believe that she was beginning to accept the situation, even to enjoy her new life. He must start to trust her, and she had to do all she could to make that happen.

As their first week together came to an end, Otto finally allowed her to speak to Octavia. It was obvious he could no longer keep the sisters apart without arousing suspicion. But, he explained in a harsh voice, there were limits to what Flora was allowed to say – and he handed her a printed sheet with sentences on it that she should use as a prompt:

It's amazing here! I'm so happy!
I'm in love – Otto and I only want to be together at the moment. I'm sure you understand.
The castle is beautiful. Soon you must visit it, but we are building right now, it's not the right time.
Please don't worry if I don't call you. Life here is so wonderful, I forget the outside world.

The ridiculous sentences went on and on. Would anyone believe them? Surely, Octavia would hear their forced quality and become suspicious.

'H-h-hello? Octavia?' she'd said, when the phone was answered.

'Flora! Oh my God! How are you? What are you doing? Why haven't you called? Tell me all about it! It's almost New Year's Eve, are you going to a party?'

Flora had felt Otto's steely eyes boring into her. 'It's wonderful here. I'm s-s-so happy.'

There'd been a tiny pause then. She could picture her sister frowning. 'So . . . it's good then?'

'Y-y-yes,' Flora said, trying to inject a note of desperation in to her voice without Otto noticing. 'The c-castle is so beautiful. I f-f-forget everything when I'm here.'

'That must be why you haven't called. I've missed you, Flo-flo,' Octavia said tenderly. 'We've never been apart for so long.'

Flora felt tears in her eyes. She wanted to cry out to her sister, beg her to come and get her, tell her that she'd been right to be worried – but she dared not. 'I know. I miss you too. I w-w-w-want to see you again,' she said simply. Then she sensed a movement. Otto was staring at her malevolently, his lip curled and fist clenched. She glanced quickly at her piece of paper. 'O-O-Otto and I only want to be together at the moment. I'm sure you understand.'

There was another silence down the phone. 'Well . . . all right. I was going to come and visit. I'm dying to see you and this famous castle of yours.'

Otto clenched his other fist.

'Soon, very soon,' said Flora quickly.

414

'Okay. Well, when are you coming back? I want to see you!'

'S-s-s-soon. I have to go now. I love you, Tavy.'

'I love you too, you silly thing.' Octavia sounded surprised at the sudden declaration.

'Goodbye.' Flora put down the phone, unable to bear talking to her sister a moment longer. She bit back the tears that threatened to overwhelm her.

'Well done,' Otto said softly. 'You sailed close to the wind there. But you did well.'

On Sunday it was New Year's Eve. Otto did not go hunting and they spent their first day together. Flora wondered if he'd been hunting so often in order to avoid her as he seemed tense during the morning, but he relaxed when he realised that she wasn't going to scream or shout or throw a tantrum. He became positively warm towards the afternoon, after they'd all shared a large meal cooked by Frau Gestenholtz and Otto had swigged down several large glasses of red wine.

Later, in the great hall, he had taken his seat in one of the large wooden armchairs padded with tapestry cushions and said to her, 'Soon work will begin on this place. It will be vastly expensive, I can't deny it, but you must be able to see how badly it needs renovation and you'll be as delighted as I am when it is finally restored to its original glory.' He looked around, smiling to himself. 'We shall enjoy ourselves then, my dear, touring the showrooms and auction houses of the world, finding treasures to house here. Great paintings, magnificent furniture, antique rugs . . . it will be quite splendid, I promise you. But that will be after the renovation, and my builders tell me it will take quite some time.'

'And . . . I will pay for it?' Flora asked quietly, not wanted to antagonise him but unable to resist asking the question.

Otto's eyes turned icy. '*I* will pay for it. It's true that the money was once yours, but when we married you signed everything over to me.'

'I did?' she asked, amazed.

He nodded. 'Oh, yes. In our pre-nuptial agreement. You know what they say about reading the small print, my dear. You will find that it was not quite what you thought. I apologise for that. But, you see, it's important I should have full control. A husband cannot come begging his wife for money, you understand.'

Flora had been unable to reply, her hands shaking. She concentrated on keeping outwardly calm, breathing deeply and nodding as though Otto's actions were perfectly reasonable, not fraudulently criminal.

'Yes,' she'd said, her heart breaking as she realised the magnitude of the trap she had fallen into. 'I understand.'

55

Steve pulled the car to a stop and Octavia looked out. It was hard to believe that this whole glorious place was hers. But it was. All right, strictly speaking, the grand old building belonged to BC Investments, in which Octavia was merely an investor. But BC Investments was owned by OctCo Holdings, and she was the owner of that. And she might only own 13 percent of the store, via Butterfly Ltd, but that was enough to make her the *de facto* owner, the person whose word was law.

Steve opened the door for her and she stepped out, one high heel and slender ankle followed by the rest of her elegant figure. She'd chosen a businesslike look for her debut as a shop owner: a scarlet silk dress with strong, well-padded shoulders, a wide black leather belt and her black Rupert Sanderson heels.

Robert Young was standing on the pavement waiting to welcome her, a large man with a big paunch concealed under his Ede & Ravenscroft shirt. He looked nervous and sweaty. The old board had gone, all dismissed with massive payouts, and the only remnant of it was Young. The new board was the Butterfly one, carefully composed by Ethan and Octavia, and the members were all already inside. First the Noble's staff were lined up ready to meet their new boss. Robert Young conducted Octavia along the line of employees, introducing them and explaining which department they worked in.

There was a distinctly hostile air as she shook hands, smiled and tried to be as charming as she could. No one was anything but polite but very few of them returned her smiles.

They resent us, just as Ethan warned. She wanted to say something respectful to them, to pass on her condolences on the death of their previous chairman, but she had no idea how to start.

When the introductions were over, Young took Octavia on a tour of her new domain, leading her over all five floors of the treasure trove before finally taking her into the sixth-floor boardroom. There the other board members were waiting, sipping glasses of vintage Krug that he had laid on to celebrate the dawn of a new era.

'Octavia darling!' It was Iseult, dashing forward to hug her, a smile on her scarlet lips. 'Isn't this fun? Aren't we going to have an absolute ball?'

'Yes . . . yes, we are.' Octavia hugged her back. She was relieved to be among friends again, away from the accusatory stares of the staff downstairs.

Ethan conducted the rest of the introductions: she met the new finance director, the new operations manager, and a handful of non-executive directors.

'We're all new kids here,' Octavia said happily, shaking hands and smiling.

'And this is Shalagi Golanmi,' Ethan said, bringing forward an exquisitely turned out, slender dark-haired beauty.

'Just call me Shagi, everyone does!' she chirruped brightly. Her coffee-coloured skin was flawless and her deep brown eyes perfectly made up.

'Shagi?' Octavia smiled at her and shook her hand. 'Okay then.'

'I love this shop! It's just super-classy!' She gave Octavia a dazzling smile.

'Shagi is a very highly qualified businesswoman,' Ethan said, 'who'll make an excellent addition to our board. She runs her own mining and excavation business, don't you, Shagi?'

'Oh, yes! I love business. Adore it. I can't wait to be a part of your venture!'

'Are we all ready?' asked Ethan, putting down his champagne glass. 'Time for a little business, I think.'

They had a long meeting around the boardroom table, and there were various presentations on the screen on the far wall, but it was all quite meaningless to Octavia. She sat back and tried to pay attention, but there were so many other things on her mind. There had still been no call from Flora. Her deadline had passed and tonight she would see about taking a flight to Germany to visit her. Enough was enough. This terrible state of affairs could not go on. Octavia simply wouldn't allow it.

She realised that Robert Young had come to the end of a speech and was looking at her expectantly. *He's a nasty piece of work*, she told herself, the thought surprising her as it drifted into her mind. 'That's fantastic, Robert, thanks,' she said, and he looked pleased.

It doesn't matter if I don't listen to every last financial detail, she told herself. *Ethan will tell me later.*

She itched to get hold of her phone so that she could send a message to Vicky telling her to start arranging the Germany trip. But it was too rude to do it now. She'd have to wait until later.

56

Somehow, Flora managed to endure her first few months of life in the *schloss*. The only consolation was the beauty of the surrounding countryside, and the kindness of Frau Gestenholtz.

Flora had seen barely another living soul since she'd come to the castle, apart from Otto and his mother. Once the building work started, she also saw brawny young builders about the place but she knew no German and the shouted comments she overheard meant nothing to her. Besides, what help could they offer? Who would believe her if she ever tried to reveal what was happening to her?

Flora knew that Otto was trying to break her spirit. She knew that he was trying to tame her. *He must think I will be easy to bring into line*, she thought to herself. *He must have known all about me from the start, how I'd lived. That made him think I'd be a simple conquest. But he's wrong.*

She almost wanted to laugh when she thought of it. Otto hadn't realised that she had long experience of captivity, of existing under watchful eyes. She had survived before and she could do it again. Hours of empty solitude were familiar to her, and she had learnt how to endure them. It would take much more than this before she was the cowering, broken creature he hoped for. And all the time she was waiting and watching for her chance, making him believe that she was the docile, obedient wife he wanted.

Of course at Homerton there had been Octavia to share it with, and now Flora was alone. That was the greatest hardship. And she also had to face the nightly activity she hated so much. That was a challenge, but she was learning how to cope with it. When the worst began, she would take herself to the beautiful gardens at Homerton, and walk among the sweet-smelling lavender there. Or she would be riding out across the green fields of Connecticut, feeling the wind in her hair and the rush of freedom in her blood. Lost in those vivid fantasies, she could almost forget what was really happening to her.

She had little talismans that gave her strength: the pearl earrings that were identical to the ones Octavia wore; a locket with a twist of her sister's golden hair entwined with her own. Flora looked at these things often to remind herself of the unbreakable bond between them, and to give her faith in the future. And she talked to Octavia constantly, in her mind and even aloud if she was sure that she was alone.

But best of all were the moments when Otto led her to the study and allowed her to speak to her sister or to Vicky. Flora lived for the phone calls as she was not allowed to see any of the emails that arrived or were sent in her name. It was hard to listen to the others asking when they would see her, or speaking of trips that had been arranged and then cancelled, but she always stuck to the script Otto gave her, even if she stumbled over the words. What broke her heart was that she could hear growing resentment and coldness in her sister's voice, and was unable to tell her the truth.

Don't hate me, Tavy, she would beg silently. *You think I've deserted you, but I haven't! I haven't. Please . . . please understand.*

The pain when the calls were over was the worst thing of all.

Otto must have heard something in Octavia's voice that made him think she would soon run out of patience because he seemed to become more aware of the need to allay her suspicion. He allowed a few more calls, and let Flora speak without a script, although he stood close by, ready to terminate the conversation if she said anything forbidden. They spent one afternoon posing for happy photographs, some taken by his mother and some by Otto himself. They showed the best aspects of the castle, where the dilapidation was least in evidence, and Flora was beaming in each one. In some, Otto and she had their arms around one another, laughing in the morning sunshine. In others Flora was the picture of happiness, lying on a rug on the lawn or sitting on an old stone wall, the forest behind her.

These Otto emailed back to London, to Vicky and Octavia, with a cheerful message supposedly from Flora.

There were other photographs too – not intended to be sent anywhere. 'Smile, my love,' he said as he photographed Flora with his penis in her mouth, or naked and with legs apart, a long fat red dildo pushed up inside her.

Every night since they had arrived at the castle, Otto had enjoyed forcing his penis in to her mouth, and she had learnt that he would come very quickly. He was rarely in her for more than a minute or two; soon his little prick would throb against her lips and then she'd receive a jet of hot spunk in the back of her throat, though sometimes he liked to pull it out and spray it over her face. He got pleasure from seeing his semen on her, and asked her to let it dribble from her mouth and down her chin. This would make him shiver with enjoyment. Once he even became hard again, pushing his penis back in her mouth as though enjoying the sensation of his own cum all over his shaft.

He didn't seem very interested in the rest of her until one night when he ordered her to strip for him. After she had sucked him for about thirty seconds, he pushed her backwards on to the bed, spread her legs wide and pressed the head of his cock to the mouth of her vagina. But the moment the tip was inside her, he pulled it out, swearing, as he ejaculated all over her.

'Ach, you stupid bitch,' he said furiously. 'Why do you make me come so soon?'

She didn't know what to say, but simply looked at him submissively, not wanting to inflame his anger. He seemed to think that this was her fault, so perhaps it was – though she couldn't see what on earth she could do about it. He came fast but was soon up again, although he faced the same problem each time he tried to enter her. Now and again he managed several

424

thrusts before it was over, and always withdrew his cock and came all over her belly.

'We don't want any babies yet,' he jeered at her one night.

'Why don't you wear a condom then?' she asked in a small voice. 'It might help you last longer as well.'

'What?' he'd demanded, eyes furious. 'What are you talking about?'

'S-s-sorry, Otto,' she stuttered, realising she had made a mistake. As far as he was concerned, he was quite normal, and if he wasn't, it was Flora's fault. Then one night he brought out the red dildo. With this, he explained, he was going to fuck her. And Flora knew at once that he was going to use the toy to do the work he couldn't do. He coated it with lubricant, lay next to her and shoved it in and out of her, breathing heavily as he did so, his rock-hard penis pressed against her thigh. It certainly helped him last longer, and gave him the pleasure of seeing his semen jet out when he did come. But it was horrible for Flora: he used the dildo so roughly, until she was raw and tender. He didn't seem to care about how she felt. She endured it because she had to.

One morning, Otto's mother, looking at her with the usual light of pity in her eyes, put a packet on the table in front of Flora at breakfast. 'Take one of these every day, starting with the first day of your period. Then follow the instructions.'

Flora took the packet, guessing these were contraceptive pills. She was sure that a doctor ought to see her and prescribe the right pill, check her blood pressure and so on, but she was grateful to have them in a way. The idea of becoming pregnant by Otto was so repugnant that she could barely stand it, though she assumed that one day soon this would happen – unless someone found a way to get her out of this place.

Surely they'll come for me. How long can he go on holding them at arm's length? How long will Octavia leave me to suffer like this? Burning tears leaked out of Flora's eyes in the darkness when she couldn't sleep. *She'll come. She has to.*

57

Vicky was in a state of high excitement. 'It's Flora on the phone!' she hissed, giving the handset to Octavia who was already packing a case for her flight to Germany.

Octavia took it. 'Flora?'

'Y-y-yes.' Her sister's voice came soft and slightly breathless down the phone. 'Are you coming over, Tavy?'

'Yes, I bloody am. I've had enough of this cloak-and-dagger stuff. What are you thinking of, sacking Vicky like that?'

'I should have talked to you first . . .'

'Of course you bloody should have!' Octavia said, indignant. 'We're not sacking her, all right? She does a fabulous job! Brilliant. You must be crazy. Listen, I'm booked on a flight tonight.'

'N-no, you can't come . . .'

'Why not?'

'W-w-we're just going away actually. For a short holiday. With friends of Otto's. We're leaving today. But he says he's planning a trip to London very soon, in a couple of weeks, and we'll come over together then.'

Octavia had been about to explode with anger, but at this news she calmed down a little. 'Really? When?'

'I'm going to give Vicky all the dates. And I'll make it up to her about the job. I don't know why I did that. It was a stupid decision. Tavy . . . I have to go now, okay?'

'Okay,' Octavia said slowly. She wanted to be reassured so badly. 'But you have to let me know the dates right away. I mean it, Flora. If you don't, I'm coming over there and waiting for you, I don't care where you are.'

'Yes. Okay. Bye, Tavy. Bye.'

The phone went down before Octavia could say any more.

'What do you want me to do about this flight?' Vicky asked. 'You'll need to go to the airport if you're taking it.'

'There's no point,' Octavia said helplessly. 'Flora won't be there.' She shook her head. 'Well, I've got plenty of other things to do, and Flora vows she's coming to London very soon. I had planned to meet Iseult tonight to talk about our plans for Noble's. And I won't be home tomorrow. Ethan's arranged a weekend away with a businessman he wants us to suck up to.' She looked down at her travel bag. 'I guess I won't need this after all.'

In Hurley's later that night, Iseult's high spirits were quite gone. She seemed to be very low indeed.

'You were so bubbly this morning at Noble's,' Octavia said, as they sipped their dirty martinis.

'My act. I'm very good at it.' Iseult sighed listlessly. 'Besides, I'd taken some happy pills. They always help. But I'm not taking any more now until tomorrow.'

'Aren't you excited by Noble's?' asked Octavia. 'Think of what we can do there.'

'Oh, darling, of course I am. But this whole project . . . we thought of it for Roddy, remember? Well, he doesn't need us now. He doesn't need *me* now.' She sighed again.

She is depressed, Octavia thought, worried. She'd never seen her friend quite like this, as though she were sinking away into a dark place where it was very hard to reach her.

'It's all right for you, Octavia,' Iseult said suddenly, an edge of bitterness in her voice. 'You have everything, don't you? Money, beauty, a gorgeous man.'

Octavia didn't know what to say. She'd always simply accepted Iseult's single state, and as her friend never spoke of it, had assumed that she was perfectly happy. 'I'm sure there are men you could go out with . . .' she said, feeling hopelessly blundering. Was Iseult even really interested in men?

'I want love,' she said simply. 'It seems remarkably cruel that it has eluded me most of my life.' Then she laughed. 'What am I saying? I'm *in* love! Have been for years. It's so cruel that the love of my life happens to be a gay designer with a heart of stone!'

'Roddy . . .'

Iseult nodded, her strange yellow-green eyes sad. 'Who else? It wouldn't be so difficult if he hadn't once led me to believe he loved me too. We had a great love affair at first, you know. Yes . . .' she said, seeing Octavia's expression. 'That too. Sex. We spent a month in bed together.

You'd be surprised how much Roddy enjoyed sleeping with me. But he soon moved on, once he'd got my heart. That's what he does.' She paused and then looked carefully at Octavia. 'I thought he was going to go that way with you at first. He seemed to be trying his old tricks. But then you got involved with that randy little Ferdy and he missed his chance.' Iseult added quickly, 'That's not to say he isn't truly fond of you. He is.'

'I know,' said Octavia slowly. 'But I've always been wary around him, no matter how much I like and admire him. He's an unpredictable beast, isn't he? You never know when he's going to turn on you.'

Iseult smiled. 'Exactly. I feel better already for talking about this, you know? You've cheered me up. And a little bird has told me that Roddy is coming to London tomorrow, to pick up some designs from his old studio. I think I might go there, take the chance of being on our old stomping ground to be honest with him. Now – shall we make some plans for this delicious new shop of ours?'

58

'So all we do is this . . . and . . .' The young man sat back, triumphant. 'You're in. Very easy, really. Basic hacking.'

'Thanks, Ricky, I owe you.' Vicky leant forward. This was Flora's old email account, the one she hadn't used since her marriage. The new *floravonschwetten* one was the only active account now, but Vicky had the feeling that it might be worth taking a look into the old one. Flora's recent emails sounded so odd, even though they were innocuous enough, and all of Vicky's instincts were telling her that something wasn't right. So she had called in her friendly computer geek to help her. Ricky hadn't minded, he hadn't even asked why she wanted to access someone else's emails.

She pressed a £50 note into his hand. 'Thanks, Ricky. Just something for your time.'

'You are most welcome,' he said, touching his baseball cap in a mock salute and then heading for the door. 'I'll leave you to it. See you soon.'

'Mmm.' Vicky was already engrossed in the email account. It was full of messages. There were several

431

hundred unopened emails, but most of those, she could see, were just the usual bits of blather from shops and services that Flora used. Some looked more personal than others, though, and she wondered if she should open those.

Why hasn't Flora checked her old account? she thought, puzzled. *Wouldn't she keep an eye on it, just to make sure? But nothing's been opened since . . .* she scrolled down . . . *since just after the wedding day.*

Her eye was caught by a message with the subject heading '**Diane Beaufort**'. She went to click on it, then hovered the small arrow over the email for a few seconds. This was Flora's private email account. Should she open a message intended only for her cousin? *But I'm her personal assistant. She trusts me with everything.* Except that she just tried to sack you, said a small voice in her head, but Vicky ignored it and clicked.

Dear Miss Beaufort,

I'm attaching a report with the initial results of the search you instructed. I haven't heard from you so I hope that was the right thing to do. I trust you got my last email, please let me know if not and I will resend it. I've attached a bill to cover the cost of my services thus far and would be most grateful if you could arrange for it to be settled.
I look forward to hearing from you.
Yours sincerely,

Nick Falcon
Falcon Private Investigations

Vicky took in the contents, wide-eyed. So Flora had been searching for her mother! But, of course, that made perfect sense. Both of the twins had been bowled over when they'd learnt that she was still alive but Flora had been particularly deeply affected. Then it seemed to be forgotten in the preparations for the wedding . . . But all along Flora had been acting on her own, setting in train the process of finding her mother and getting the answers to the questions that had been haunting her all her life.

Vicky frowned. But why on earth hadn't Flora checked her own email account for this important message? Or given the new address to this Falcon person? She read the message again then scrolled down the inbox, looking for the first message that he had referred to. It didn't take her long to find it. It was dated not long before the wedding and was untitled, but it came from Falcon. It had been opened and read. Vicky clicked. It was a short message thanking Flora for her visit and attaching a statement of costs. Falcon promised to be in touch soon with the preliminary results of the search.

But Flora had never read them.

Vicky scrolled back up and found another couple of unopened messages from the detective. She opened them. They were reminders to Flora that her bill was still outstanding and asking for payment.

Vicky sat back in her seat. *Oh my God,* she thought. *There is an email here that says where the twins' mother is.* Should she open it? The arrow hovered over the attachment, her finger poised above the mouse.

Open it or not open it? And why the hell hadn't Flora opened this herself?

59

The memorial service to celebrate the life of Graham Radcliffe was held at St George's, Hanover Square. It meant going perilously close to Noble's but Amanda had sworn to herself that she would never set eyes on it again, not while those people, those bastard thieves, were in charge. Not just thieves. *Killers.*

Hundreds of people turned out to mourn Graham: they remembered his old world charm and gentlemanly kindness. During the service, former Noble's staff came forward to speak about his passion for the shop he'd inherited from his father, his real love for what they sold and his faith in the Noble's vision. Then there was the way he had cared for his staff.

'He wouldn't let us retire!' declared one. 'Always some excuse to keep us on the payroll. We had one cleaner in her eighties . . . she never cleaned a thing. Turned up, had a cup of tea and a chat, and got paid for it.'

Dear Fa, thought Amanda fondly. *That's why those ruthless shits are in charge now.*

Afterwards there was a drinks reception at the Arts

434

Club on Dover Street. Amanda had to be on receiving duty with her mother and brother, and dutifully shook hands and reminisced about her father with a long line of well-wishers. This was a comfort too, she couldn't deny it – remembering all the wonderful things and the happy times. She didn't want to rush this moment.

'Amanda, my sweet.' It was Gerry, dapper in a double-breasted black suit, dark purple shirt and a funny little black string tie. He bent forward to kiss her. 'I don't have to tell you how deep my sympathy is. Condolences, darling. You poor bloody thing.'

'Thanks, Gerry. And thanks for coming. Can I have a word?' Amanda took his hand and stepped away from the receiving line so that they could speak in private. 'You know how this happened, don't you?'

'Of course!' He blinked his nut-brown eyes. His skin looked even more peachy and unlined than usual. He must have just had another of his refreshing facelifts. 'It could hardly be a coincidence. Your shop gets taken over, your father has a fatal heart attack.'

'But . . . you know who took us over?'

Gerry shook his head. 'Someone corporate, no?'

'Octavia Beaufort,' Amanda said slowly, with bitter emphasis. 'That's who. It's her company that arranged the buyout.'

Gerry's eyebrows climbed to his hairline. 'Astounding! Who would have thought that little child had it in her?'

'Oh, she hasn't done it alone. It's all going to be announced in a blaze of publicity. No doubt there'll be glossy spreads of her sitting at my father's desk and talking about the close of a dull old era and the launch of a brilliant new one. It makes me sick! The only reason they've kept it quiet so far is out of some remnant of decency, what with their actions killing my father.'

'Oh-oh.' Gerry put a hand on the sleeve of Amanda's black Dior jacket. 'What are you going to do, darling? I'm afraid I've shot my bolt rather when it comes to disconcerting the Beauforts. Their little court case story didn't achieve quite what I'd hoped. Made them more glamorous, if anything.'

'I'm powerless,' spat Amanda. 'There's nothing I can do against them.'

'You still own stock?'

'Harry and I will inherit Fa's stake. But it's meaningless. I can't outvote them.'

'And I suppose that hag Iseult is involved, is she?'

'On the board. Key person in the re-design.' Amanda's eyes were blazing. 'What really infuriates me is that I wanted to do amazing things at Noble's for years and no one would let me! I couldn't even buy in the stock I wanted. Iseult came to me offering me Roddy Wildblood when he was a no one, and I longed to showcase his pieces. I had an idea for a pop-up boutique within Noble's devoted to him – I could see he was a massive talent. But it simply wasn't possible. Young wouldn't allow it. I had to send them away, pretending I wasn't interested.'

'Wildblood!' Gerry laughed. 'Now there's a case of name and nature coinciding beautifully! Listen, darling, I want to help you, all right? If I can, I will. Just give me a little time. You're needed elsewhere, I'll let you go.'

He gave her a soft kiss on either cheek and wafted away into the room, in search of a glass of champagne.

* * *

436

Iseult took a taxi to the East End of London, reminding herself that now she was in a position to afford one as often as she liked without having to worry. The stipend from the Butterfly board was a generous one. Not only was her life a great deal more comfortable – the new maid had done a wonderful job of cleaning the Bayswater flat, which was sparkling in a way it hadn't for years – but she was able to start thinking about making repairs to Mabbes. Just in time. The old porch had finally fallen in during a winter storm; luckily no one had been underneath it when it collapsed.

I must be brave and strong, she told herself as the taxi rolled through the city, out towards Aldgate. The black depression had begun to pull at her again lately; the deep dark whirlpool that wanted to suck her down into its depths had started to spin beneath her. The familiar symptoms had started: a terrible lethargy, a sense of not being able to get out of bed and face the world. A desire to hurt herself had begun to float into her mind at unguarded moments. She found herself in the kitchen, looking at the knives; simply contemplating them without forming a sense of what she might do with them. She'd begun to look at high places and wonder what it might be like to sail off them, how the rush of air past her face would feel, whether she'd pass into unconsciousness before impact, or whether she'd feel it in a glorious explosion of crunching pain . . .

Can I stop this? she wondered. This trip to see Roddy was a real effort for her. But if she could talk to him frankly about the hurt she felt, and the sense of rejection, perhaps then he would understand and give her the love and reassurance she so desperately wanted. Oh, not that kind of love. She'd given up on that. She knew that their affair could never be resurrected, not in that way. The moment had long gone.

She'd sent a text to him. *Are you in London?*

Aye. Will I see you?

But she had decided to surprise him. She was sure he was going to be at the studio that morning. He needed to collect his archive of designs. It wouldn't surprise her if he finally gave up that funny old place now. He hardly needed it. If he ever came back to London, he wasn't likely to live or work in a place like that.

She looked out of the window as they passed out of the shiny, expensive City and into the grimier area on its far side. The streets became dirtier. Shops had metal grilles; walls were pasted with endless torn posters. Fast-food joints and litter were everywhere. The passersby weren't well-fed, besuited businessmen and women but more haunted-looking, in cheap clothing and with bad shoes, smoking cigarettes or pushing shabby prams. Iseult stared out and wondered if she might have been happier in this other world, where life was only about surviving day to day. But she suspected that same agony would have been waiting for her wherever she'd existed.

The taxi came to a halt by the old studio. Iseult got out, paid, and went along the dirty alley to Roddy's building. She punched in the code for the door. Pushing it open, she was overwhelmed by a noxious smell. It had always smelt evil on the staircase, a combination of urine, filth and something else, something more bestial, but this was incredible. An overpowering stink enveloped her.

'Christ!' she muttered, her face contorting. 'Roddy has to get out of here, this is unbearable.' She started to climb the stairs.

The first thing she heard as she turned the third landing and began the next flight was a terrible low growl followed by a raucous bark. Then another growl, fierce as a motorbike engine, joined it. She barely had time to register the sound above her when there was a clatter of claws on bare stone and a desperate shout from someone. Iseult raised her eyes and saw two huge barrel-like bodies flying down the upper flight, their short bow legs hardly seeming to touch the steps, then they careered around the corner of the landing and were facing her. For an instant she saw wide, slavering jaws, furious red eyes and rows of deadly teeth, heard the awful grinding snarls. Then, before she even knew what was happening, the two dogs were upon her.

60

Octavia could hardly bear the vibrations of pleasure. They made her twist and turn, clutching the pillows in one white-knuckled fist while her other hand roamed over her breasts, feeling her nipples as hard as bullets beneath her fingertips.

'You like that, huh?' murmured Ethan. She could feel his cock stiff against her thigh. He was enjoying the sight of her writhing with abandon, unable to stop herself responding to the persistent, unwavering buzz of the vibrating toy he was holding to her mound. It juddered against her clit, making waves of electric excitement flow through her body, and then he brought it down so that it throbbed inside her swollen pussy.

'Oh, yes, don't stop, please!'

'Is that good, honey?'

She gasped and thrashed as he brought the toy back to buzz on her bud. It was unbearable. She couldn't stop herself. A tumultuous climax seized her and she knew only the fierce waves of ecstasy until at last they subsided, leaving her breathless.

A moment later Ethan was in her. She was hot and smooth with the juices from her climax. He thrust his cock fast, turned on by her orgasm, until he reached a rapid peak of his own and came quickly with a stifled gasp.

Afterwards he was up immediately and heading for the shower as Octavia admired his firm body and taut buttocks. 'Gotta get to the office.' He turned round as he reached the bathroom door. 'Hey – you haven't forgotten we're going to Scotland tonight, have you, honey? Dress nice. I want you to impress this guy, okay? He's very, very rich and has talked about perhaps investing in BC. He likes the sound of what we're doing.'

'Okay.' Octavia smiled as he disappeared from view. 'But I'm sure it's going to be boring as hell,' she added, when she knew Ethan was out of earshot.

Octavia was just instructing her maid to look out the Zac Posen cream and silver evening dress to be pressed when her telephone went.

She wandered over and picked it up. 'Hi, Roddy, how are you? You in London?'

The voice that came down the line was barely recognisable. 'Octavia, you've got to get over here right now!' His voice was thick with tears and high with panic.

'What is it?' she said, turning cold.

'It's Iseult. She's been attacked. My God, it's horrible.' He choked back a sob. 'We're in the Royal London Hospital on Whitechapel Road. Get here as soon as you can.'

'I'm on my way,' she said, and clicked off her phone, her hands trembling. Iseult attacked? Who on earth would attack her? She'd talked of going to the East End – had she been mugged? Stabbed?

Octavia left everything as it was and ran out of the house, summoning Steve as she did so.

She arrived flustered in the Royal London foyer. Steve had dropped her off on Whitechapel Road just outside the hospital and she'd run in as fast as she could. She panted out Iseult's name to the receptionist.

'Ah, yes.' The woman behind the counter consulted her computer. 'I'm afraid she's in theatre at the moment. They're operating right now.'

'Operating?' gasped Octavia in horror. Just then her phone beeped. A message from Roddy. *Where are you?* She quickly typed back, *Reception. Where are you?*

'I think she'll be in some time but you'll need to go to the Trauma Centre to find out more,' the receptionist was saying as another message from Roddy came through: *Coming to you. Stay there.*

She looked about and a moment later he came into the reception area, his face ashen, clutching his phone. Octavia rushed over and threw her arms around him. 'What's happened? How is she?'

He hugged her back, pressing his face into her hair. 'It's fuckin' terrible.' He pulled away and said in a broken voice, 'Her face has been almost ripped off. Her eye . . .' He stopped, unable to say more, burying his own face in his hands.

'But how . . . ?' Octavia couldn't grasp what he was saying.

'Pitbulls. The guy in the flat opposite mine has been breeding 'em – breeding 'em to fight.'

Octavia remembered the nasty smell that had

442

permeated the stairwell near Roddy's flat, and the rat-faced man she'd seen in the doorway there.

Just then two policemen came up to them, fluorescent jackets worn over their uniforms. 'Mr Wildblood?' said one, a stolid man with a bald head covered in soft grey stubble. 'Can I have a word with you, sir?'

Roddy nodded and the policemen led them over to a seating area away from the main reception.

'We're from the Status Dog Unit. I'm Sergeant Philips and this is Constable Gill,' said the bald man, nodding to the younger one at his side. 'Did you witness the attack?'

'Yeah.' Roddy looked sick. 'I tried to do what I could to help her.' He looked down at his hands and Octavia noticed for the first time that they were bandaged. 'But it was so hard. It was like they were possessed – crazed. And they're built like heavy-weight wrestlers.'

'These are very dangerous dogs, sir, bred to be killing machines,' the sergeant said sympathetically. 'Those two have also been treated particularly harshly. They're covered in cigarette burns. It's what some people do to make the beasts angry and even more deadly. It's evil, sir, as I'm sure you understand.'

Roddy shook his head. 'But how has he had a couple of dangerous dogs in there all this time and I've never even noticed? I've never seen them before today.'

'These two have been kept hidden indoors, It's not uncommon,' Sergeant Philips said sadly.

'The place was torn to shreds inside,' volunteered Constable Gill. 'Everything ripped to pieces, dog faeces everywhere.'

443

'How can you keep a pair of dogs like that inside all the time?' Octavia said wonderingly. She thought back to her aunt's friendly bounding Labradors and their desperate need to be out and running around. It was impossible to imagine what state they would be in if they'd been kept permanently inside.

'They exercise them at night, miss. Or else – as in this case – they buy a treadmill and exercise the dogs on that.'

'What?' Roddy gave a mirthless laugh. 'Put the poor things on a running machine? That's crazy!'

'But it's what they do. It's a big problem, sir. Those dogs are status symbols round here. People will do stupid things to have one – they think it makes them look tough. Very likely our boy is in a gang and these dogs are his weapons. They're as deadly as a knife or a gun and you don't get anything like the time in prison if they kill while they're in your care.' Sergeant Philips took out his notebook and pen. 'Now I'd like to take a statement, sir, if I may.'

'Wait.' Roddy looked at him anxiously. 'What's happened to the dogs?'

'They're in our pound, and they'll be destroyed for sure. As for matey, he's in custody.'

'He helped get them off her, you know,' Roddy said sadly. 'Got pretty chewed up in the process himself.'

'The least he could do, sir, if you don't mind my saying. Now . . . let's go back to the beginning.'

Octavia listened in disbelief as the story unfolded and Roddy described the horror of seeing the two great beasts, their teeth locked into Iseult's flesh, snarling and slavering, crazed and desperate to kill, and the blood that had flowed everywhere. Once his

444

statement had been taken, checked and rechecked, and his contact details given to the constable, they were left in peace. Octavia hugged him as he began sobbing quietly.

'Oh, poor, poor Iseult. Is she . . . very bad?'

Roddy nodded, unable to describe it. 'Yes. Please God they can save her face. I think her eye is gone. I've never seen anything like it, Octavia. God, it was terrible . . .'

It was some hours later when they heard that Iseult was out of theatre. In the Trauma Centre a nurse reassured them that she was in the best possible place – the Centre was first-class, and there was an on-site plastic surgery department with incredibly skilled practitioners. Iseult was taken from theatre into Intensive Care. They would keep her sedated for now, and probably for some days yet. Octavia caught a glimpse of her friend as they wheeled her bed into ICU, but all she could see was a mass of bandages and tubes connected to bags of blood and fluid. The only sign it was Iseult were the fingertips emerging from one bandaged hand, the nails painted a fashionable beige. Octavia bit her lip and began to cry.

Her phone went. It was Ethan. 'Hi, where are you? I've just got home and your luggage is packed but you're not here . . .'

'Oh, Ethan, I should have called earlier—'

'We're due to meet Sir Max in forty minutes.' He sounded cross. 'What are you playing at? I thought we were going there together.'

'Ethan, it's Iseult . . .' She quickly told him what had happened. 'I'm still at the hospital.'

'Christ.' He sounded exasperated. 'Okay – well, you can still meet me at the heliport if you get a move on.'

Octavia froze. 'Don't you care about Iseult? Don't you think she's more important than a party?'

'Of course she is, but I don't see how ruining our weekend is going to help her. Now come on, Octavia, Sir Max is pretty bloody important too.'

'I see,' she said icily.

He sighed down the phone. 'Oh, don't get into a mood with me . . .'

Her mouth dropped open. 'This isn't about *you*,' she hissed. 'It's about my best friend who has just been savaged and is in Intensive Care!'

Roddy, standing nearby and hearing everything, put his hand on her arm. 'Don't you worry, hon,' he said softly. 'You go. There's really nothing more we can do for now. I'll keep you up to speed with what's happening here.'

'Are you coming or not?' Ethan was saying testily.

Octavia paused for a moment and then said, 'All right, yes. Because I know what this means to you. But I'm going to be late. You'll have to tell Sir Max.'

'Don't be. There's a fifteen-minute turnaround for landing and departure so get there as soon as you can. I'll bring your luggage.' Ethan cut the call.

'I'm not really in a state to schmooze a high-powered businessman,' said Octavia, putting her phone away and looking down at her jeans and casual shirt, thrown on this morning before she'd known what she'd be doing that day.

'I'd ask you back to the studio, but you know what? I never want to go there again,' Roddy said with a shudder. 'I can't bear to see the place where it happened.'

'This Sir Max person will just have to put up with me like this then,' Octavia said as insouciantly as she could, then gave Roddy another hug. 'Promise me you'll keep me up to date with Iseult? I'm back on Monday morning, okay?'

He hugged her back. 'You bet. See ya, sunshine.'

61

The days passed in a strange hazy state for Flora. Sometimes Otto disappeared on his business trips, and those times were the best. She didn't fear the nights as much then. Some of the day she spent helping Otto's mother, who was always pleasant company and obviously getting used to having Flora about. She seemed to like her new daughter-in-law, even though there was always that look of pity in her eyes.

'You're far too pretty to be shut away here!' she said once, then darted a quick, guilty look at Flora, adding, 'But as soon as you have children, you'll find you have plenty to do.'

When she wasn't with Marthe, Flora wandered about the castle and sometimes sat on one of the outside walls, watching the builders at work. Great rafts of scaffolding covered one side of the castle and the workmen swarmed over it, their yellow hats making their heads look unfeasibly large. There was no real way of escaping this place: they were miles from anywhere, the garages were locked, and even if Flora did get down the mountainside on foot, she wouldn't have the first idea where to go. Once she had walked as far away as she dared and had feared that she was simply becoming lost in the pine forest. She knew that wild boar roamed there. She'd turned back, too frightened to continue. She'd seen no one but didn't have a word of German anyway.

Although she stayed observant, so far Otto had not relaxed his guard or slipped up when it came to locking the office door or keeping his phone with him.

She had found a shelf of English books, mostly adventure stories, and began working her way through them, losing herself for hours at a time in *Twenty Thousand Leagues Under the Sea* and *Treasure Island*.

When Otto was at home, the hours of the day only seemed to exist in order to bring round another night, when she would have to endure whatever little game he had invented for her. He'd begun to ply his red dildo in other places, pushing it against her arsehole while he breathed heavily and laughed lightly in her ear. She knew it was only a matter of time before he would want to use it there and began to ready herself for the moment. *It can't kill me, can it? People do this all the time after all* . . . But whenever she felt that unyielding tip prodding at her behind, she felt sick to her stomach and afraid.

One afternoon she was reading in the sitting room, lost in *Jane Eyre*, when the door opened. Otto was standing there. He looked completely harmless in his grey trousers, white shirt and pale green tank top, his hair neatly combed, yet the sight of him filled her with terror.

'Upstairs. In our bedroom. Now,' he said curtly. Then he was gone, shutting the door behind him.

Flora got up at once. Her tactic was always to appear submissive and docile, so that he would begin to trust her. She sensed that this was the only way she would ever have the chance to escape him. Besides, if she could just hold on for long enough, Octavia would surely come, as she had promised. Only one more cancelled visit, and surely her sister would stand no more . . .

Flora put down her book and went upstairs. There was no sign of Otto on the way up, or in the bedroom once she got there, so she sat in the window seat and gazed out over the mountains. The first coppery signs of autumn were burnishing distant trees, though the pines stayed as dark as ever.

The door swung open. She turned to see Otto striding into the room. 'Ah, there you are, good,' he said, catching sight of her in the seat. 'Now. Go to the bed. Undress.'

Her heart sank. This wasn't fair. She wasn't ready. She hadn't yet prepared herself to shut down her emotions and surrender to him physically. But there was no way Otto would ever listen to protests, so she sighed quietly under her breath and went towards the bed, unbuttoning her shirt as she went.

'Come in, come in, don't be shy,' Otto said brusquely. Flora turned to see him beckoning to someone who stood beyond the door. A moment later a workman came awkwardly into the room, looking about him with bewilderment.

Flora froze.

'Now,' Otto said in a friendly voice to the workman, 'I don't speak Polish but you speak some English, don't you? So we will speak in English.'

The man nodded.

'Good. Now you see my wife there.' He gestured to Flora. 'You were looking at her the other day. I saw you. Then you said something to your friends and you all laughed.'

The workman blushed scarlet and stammered out that he apologised if he had offended the Baron.

'You have not offended me,' Otto said pleasantly, shutting the bedroom door and bolting it. 'My wife is not offended either. She takes great pleasure in fucking men who fancy her, well-built handsome young men like you. And . . .' Otto laughed '. . . here is the funny thing. I get great pleasure from watching her being taken.' He held up his hand. 'There is nothing queer in it, nothing homosexual. I only watch her cunt, you understand. But it would oblige us both if you would have her, right here.'

Flora still couldn't move as the understanding of what Otto wanted sank into her consciousness. The moment he said the words – *watching her being taken* – a terrible nausea gripped her and her fingers turned to ice. So that was it. He was one of them . . . a watcher. She wanted to sob. How had things turned out this way? How had she gone from one prison to another, from one gaoler to another of the same sort?

The workman looked from one face to the other, half laughing, half puzzled, obviously unsure how to take Otto's proposition. Was he serious? Was this a joke?

'Take off your clothes, Flora.' Otto's voice was soft but cold. She heard the iron within it. She began to fumble with the rest of her buttons and step out of her shoes. It was pointless arguing. She may as well

451

get it over with. 'And you.' He turned to the workman. 'I'm sure you enjoy your job here. You want it to continue, don't you?'

The man seemed to grasp Otto's meaning. He came forward, still uncertain but beginning to undo his fluorescent jacket. He looked over at Flora, who was now in her bra and knickers. 'If Herr Baron is sure,' he said. 'Whatever Herr Baron wants . . .'

'Yes.' Otto sat on a chair by the bed. 'This is what Herr Baron wants. Flora – lie down.'

She unclasped her bra and then slid off her knickers, stepping out of them, going to the bed and lying on its scratchy cover. She could see that the worker's prick was already stiff, thrusting upwards from a rich thicket of dark hair as he pulled down his grimy jeans. He abandoned his heavy boots, trousers, plaid work shirt and jacket on the rug, and moved towards the bed, his eyes on Flora's body.

'Open your legs, Flora, show him your wares.'

She obeyed, splaying her thighs. Otto bent over and pulled apart the lips of her pussy with his forefinger and thumb. 'She's delightful, isn't she? Have you seen a prettier little cunt? That sprinkling of fair hair . . . not a whisker round her arse. I'm sure you wish to plunge right in, don't you, my man?'

Flora shot a glance over at her husband. He was eyeing the other man's thick cock with interest, and the great bag of balls that swung beneath it. The hair that covered the man's bulky body was in contrast to Otto's own smoothness.

The man grunted but still held back a little, despite the rearing head of his penis that clearly longed to be sheathed inside Flora's depths.

'You're worried about disease? Pregnancy? She's clean, I assure you, and on the pill. Perhaps you fear she's not ready.' Otto spat into his hand and with a quick movement smeared his spittle over her labia. 'There. That will help you in. She'll be warm enough when you've started, I guarantee it.'

Flora stared upwards at the dark hangings on the bed and wondered how quickly it would all be over.

The builder approached her and a moment later she felt the bed sink under his weight and the warmth of his body as he lay next to her. One rough hand landed, gently, on her belly and stroked her. He muttered in Polish to her.

'Touch him, Flora,' ordered Otto.

She put out her hand and touched the rock-hard penis. It felt vast under her hand, hot and smooth, much larger than Otto's member. She rubbed her hand along it tentatively and heard the man groan appreciatively.

A few minutes passed as she caressed him and his hands wandered over her body, her breasts and between her legs. Then he climbed up on her, and she felt the head of his cock at her entrance. She closed her eyes and willed herself to be somewhere else, sending her spirit far away, as he pressed in. It hurt for a moment as he penetrated her, and the next moment he was fully engulfed. He began to thrust, gently at first but soon gathering speed. She expected him to come at once, as Otto did, but it went on and on, his rough hairy chest against her soft breasts, his head next to hers, his rasping breath in her ear. He didn't attempt to kiss her, and she was glad of that.

I'm not here. I'm far away. I'm walking down the path in the rose garden, the one that no one ever went to but me. It's summer. I can see bees hovering over the flowers and white butterflies fluttering over the lavender. The air is so sweet and still. I can hear the fountain playing in the middle of the garden. Shall I see if I can spot the goldfish sparkling in the depths of the pond? Yes, I will walk there now and kneel down on the cool, scratchy stone and put my fingertips in the water and see if the fish will come and nibble them . . .

The man began to gather speed, pumping harder and harder while she longed for it to be over. To help him along, she put one arm around his back and swept her hand over it. It was broad and hard with muscle, unlike Otto's soft, almost flabby body. In another second he tensed, yelped, and then thrust into her hard again two or three times as he came. She opened her eyes and saw him staring straight into her face and, to her astonishment, the expression in his eyes was tender and apologetic as if he knew that she hadn't wanted it, but that only lasted an instant before he collapsed on her. His post-coital rest was no longer than a moment, though.

Otto was on his feet, pushing the man off Flora, so that he could see the sperm dripping out of her pussy. As he looked at it, he groaned, pulled his own penis from his open trousers and rubbed hard at the short, stumpy thing. It only took two movements, before he sent his own jet of fluid over her, to mix with that of the builder who was still watching with a mixture of amazement and horror. As soon as Otto had ejaculated he recovered, tucked his now limp and tiny penis away, and turned to the man on the bed.

'Get your things on and get out,' he said sharply. 'And if you think you're going to get away with treating my wife as a receptacle for your filthy cum, you're quite wrong. I want you off my property within thirty minutes and I don't want to see you again. Understand? Any trouble and I shall tell the police you raped my wife. Now leave.'

Flora was not able to come down from her bedroom that evening, and to her relief Otto left her alone and slept somewhere else.

She spent a terrible night and in the morning emerged with her eyes red and swollen. Frau Gestenholtz looked at her with sympathy, guessing that something even more traumatic than usual had happened.

'Ach, has he treated you badly?' She shook her head sadly, passing Flora the coffee pot. 'That boy of mine. I do not understand him. I've never been able to control him, never. But what can I do? He's all I've got.'

Flora poured herself a cup of coffee and sipped at it gratefully. She looked up at her mother-in-law. It felt as though she had aged ten years since the previous day. She knew more clearly than ever that this situation could not go on. Otto had crossed a line the day before, from wickedness to evil, and she was as certain as she could be that this was simply the beginning. 'Why is he doing this to me?' she asked helplessly. 'You're my friend, aren't you, Marthe? Please, you must help me.'

Marthe looked away, her face pained. 'I cannot,' she muttered. Then she glanced back at Flora, and the sight of her obviously moved the older woman. 'Oh, he's a beast, I know it. He's very wrong, very unkind. Who knows why? It was nothing I did, I'm sure of it. And, you see, he's always had such grand plans for himself. He didn't want to be plain Otto Gestenholtz from Hamburg. He was a romantic little thing, but always bullied for his smallness and his glasses and his meekness, so he escaped into dreams of being a prince, a rich man, a lord . . . whatever . . .'

Flora stayed very still. Was she at last going to learn the truth about Otto?

'So he set out to make his dreams come true,' Marthe said with a sigh. 'He knew he had to make money. His own father was useless, a sailor, and neither of us was heartbroken when he died. He left us nothing but our poor house. Well, we sold that and Otto used the money to do a business course at Heidelberg University, and from there he moved into finance. Soon he was on a nice salary. We could have afforded a decent house and a comfortable life. But that wasn't enough for Otto. He wanted to aim very high and get there quickly. So he started to seek out rich women.' Marthe gave her another guilty look. 'You'd be surprised how many fell for him and gave him money. It seems you only have to be kind to women and they will trust you. We're such fools, aren't we?' She shrugged. 'I'm as bad as any, I suppose. Kindness will always melt my heart. Anyway, there were many of these relationships with wealthy women, some short, some long. Most ended quickly and badly – I don't know why but I suspect Otto cannot help showing his true nature sometimes, even when he tries hard to pretend he is something else.

'Then there was Wiebke – a pretty girl with lots of cash. He managed to persuade her to marry him, but it didn't last. Her father stepped in pretty damn quick and put an end to all that. He gave us a lot of money to leave. Otto was delighted. The money was the point of it all, you see. And with money he could buy himself what he wanted. His next task was to give himself a pedigree, so he scoured the internet and old almanacs of the nobility until he found what he was looking for. Baron von Schwetten was elderly, poor and without an heir. Otto came to visit him here and persuaded him to adopt him – and not only that, he offered to buy this wreck of a castle too. The Baron couldn't agree fast enough. You can imagine how delighted Otto was: with a title, and a property, and a new company he'd created that was quite successful, he could begin to search out the biggest fish of all. And that was, no doubt, how he found you. You're very rich, aren't you?'

Flora had listened to everything with a kind of horror mixed with relief. So he was a con artist after all, a skilled criminal, and she was not his first victim, though perhaps the most spectacular. Somehow she felt better, not so alone. Others had been fooled before her. He had made it his life's work. But . . . 'We met by chance,' she said in a small voice. 'He knew nothing about me.'

Frau Gestenholtz laughed. 'Oh, I doubt it! With Otto, nothing happens by chance.'

'Why are you telling me all this?' Flora asked.

'You are a sweet girl, I can see that. I hate to see you suffer. I thought perhaps it would help to know the truth. It will help you bear it. And it will be a relief to be able to talk frankly to you.' The old woman smiled. 'After all, we're going to be here together a long time, aren't we? So we may as well be friends.'

62

Octavia had arrived late at Battersea heliport the previous evening, held up by traffic. Ethan was waiting with Sir Max by the aircraft, a cherry red four-seater Gazelle helicopter, the two men talking together as Octavia approached.

'Thank God you're here!' Ethan said sharply when he saw her. 'Do you know how much it costs to have a late departure? You've cut it pretty bloody fine.'

Her eyes filled with tears and she bit her lip. She was feeling very emotional and sensitive after the events of the day.

Sir Max turned towards her. He was a man in his late-thirties, possibly early-forties, with short dark hair and a face that looked as though it had seen a few things in its time. He studied her with his bright blue eyes, and smiled. At once his rough, almost ugly face was transformed. She felt a jolt, as though she had just seen someone she knew well and had missed terribly without realising it. 'Please don't worry. You've come from the hospital, haven't you? I hope your friend is out of danger. I'm Max Northam. How do you do?'

'Octavia Beaufort,' she said, but he was already moving to the open doors of the craft. *He looks familiar, but I'm sure we haven't met before.*

'We'd better get going. Our slot is over in five minutes. Come aboard. Your luggage is stowed under the seats.'

Octavia climbed in to the small space at the back of the craft. Max appeared beside her and pulled the seatbelt straps over her shoulders and round her waist, snapping them into the central buckle. He showed her a small trigger. 'See this? Anything happens, flick it and it will release the belt. Easy.'

She found his nearness oddly disturbing. Perhaps it was his height and well-built frame that gave him his peculiar magnetism, but she had the strangest urge to reach out and touch him.

You're going mad, she told herself. *It must be the stress of everything.*

He took down a headset from the central hook and Octavia put it on, bending the microphone up to her lips. Ethan climbed into the front seat, buckled in and put on his headset while Max shut the door and then went round to the pilot's seat. He strapped himself in, pulled the door to, began flicking switches on the central control panel and talking to the tower as he put on his headset. Octavia listened to the conversation through her earphones but it made no sense to her: numbers, figures, flight times, directions . . . The propeller blades began to turn, slowly at first and then picking up speed, until they were one whirring shadow overhead.

'We're just on time,' Max said. They lifted smoothly

up into the air for twenty feet, then the nose of the helicopter dipped slightly and they soared away, making a turn over the heliport and flying over the river. Octavia didn't speak. She was exhausted by the events of the day. Instead, she listened to Max and Ethan's chat and watched the city disappear beneath them as they left it behind and headed north.

It was almost dark by the time they arrived in Argyll, the helicopter coming to rest in a field near the house where ground lanterns showed the landing spot. Staff came rushing out to meet them and unload the luggage, while Sir Max led Ethan and Octavia into the light and warmth of the house, where supper was waiting for them.

To her surprise, the table was only set for three.

'The others are joining us tomorrow,' explained Sir Max, seeing her expression. 'Just us tonight.'

'What about Lady Northam?' asked Octavia, without thinking.

'Lady Northam is currently setting up home in the Bahamas with a rather handsome young waiter she met there. The less said about her the better,' Max said, but with a smile.

Octavia's hand shot to her mouth. 'Oh, God, I'm sorry . . . I didn't know.'

'How could you? Let's have supper, I expect you're starving.'

The housekeeper brought out a delicious meal that was exactly what they all wanted: roasted tomato and basil soup followed by twice-baked potatoes with luscious cheese and chive centres, baked haddock and a poached egg. While they ate, Ethan talked away about business although Max didn't say much, listening and grunting occasionally, as though he didn't feel this was quite the time.

Octavia watched curiously. She'd thought he'd be much older. 'Sir' Max made him sound like a grizzled old man but he wasn't that. And there was something about him that spoke of experience and knowledge of the world, something in the way he held himself and in those bright blue eyes that looked so familiar.

Suddenly she gasped.

The men looked at her. 'What is it?' asked Max, concerned.

'Are you okay, Octavia?' Ethan frowned at her as she blushed a hot scarlet.

'Yes, yes. I'm fine.' She dropped her face so that she was staring into her plate of food, wishing fervently that her flaming cheeks would cool down. She had just remembered exactly where she had encountered those eyes before. She'd seen them twice, and each time they'd been frosty with disapproval. *He's the man from the after show party . . . and the one from the Templeton House Ball.* Oh, God, how hideous. He hated her. He thought she was a vile, spoilt little miss, off her head on drugs and prone to water-throwing. Octavia stole a glance at him, but he was calmly eating his supper. The next moment he had caught her gaze and was looking back at her. She swiftly looked downwards again, feeling her colour heighten. He hadn't recognised her. Surely it was only a matter of time, though. She remembered that the last time she'd seen him, she'd been in her fashion show make-up. The time before that she'd been in her ball finery. Here she was, in tatty jeans with her hair scraped back and no make-up. He hadn't realised she was the same girl.

Oh, God. I daren't tell Ethan. He'll be furious. There's no way Max will invest with us when he guesses who I am.

'He's a nice old bloke, isn't he?' Ethan said, climbing into bed after cleaning his teeth. 'Quite a charmer. You wouldn't guess he's a billionaire.'

'Is he?' Octavia was surprised. Everything here seemed to be on such a homely scale. Comfortable but not grand. Instead of a great stone Victorian mansion, they had arrived at a white-painted, black-roofed house. Large, to be sure, but still a house, warm, welcoming and cosy. The furniture was clearly good, antique most of it, but all was well used and obviously loved, chosen for beauty and comfort rather than ostentation.

The bedroom they were in was old-style country house: walls papered in a cottagey faded floral print, a mahogany desk with a mismatched chair and soft cushion, a battered walnut chest of drawers and original built-in wardrobe cupboard, an old-fashioned iron bedstead with a mattress just the right side of soft and made up with sheets and blankets.

'Yeah. He's created and sold some of the world's most famous telecommunications companies actually. He's a bit of a hero of mine.' Ethan looked enthusiastic.

'Let's not talk about him now, I'm too tired,' Octavia said wearily. She still felt cross with Ethan, a niggling sense of annoyance and sadness at his lack of interest in Iseult's plight that day. He'd met her many times after all. She was on the Butterfly board. She was one

463

of Octavia's best friends. And yet he'd acted as though she simply didn't matter, not compared to meeting Sir Max.

They went to sleep, back to back.

63

Octavia didn't know where she was for a moment when she awoke, and then she remembered: Sir Max Northam's house in Argyllshire. She looked over at Ethan, still sound asleep, a pillow clutched in his arms and his head pressed against it.

Why do I feel so low? she wondered. *Something awful's happened . . .* And then she remembered Iseult and the terrible events of the previous day. She imagined her friend in Intensive Care, bandaged and sedated. *Poor, poor Iseult.*

Octavia got out of the comfortable bed and looked through the windows. The view was of magnificent Scottish hills, clad in bronze bracken and grey-and-purple heather, a hazy blue sky above. She went through to the sweet, small bathroom off the bedroom, with its cast-iron clawfoot bath and the kind of wide-mouthed tap that looked as though it would gush rivers of piping hot water. When she was dressed, ready for country pursuits in cord jodhpurs, a cream shirt, cashmere jumper and a moss-coloured tweed jacket, she went downstairs.

The house lost none of its charm as she went into the dining room for breakfast, this time finding a sideboard groaning under the weight of sausages, bacon, Arbroath smokies, black pudding and eggs done all ways. A small pot of porridge bubbled over a gas flame, a jug of cream and a pot of sugar beside it.

She helped herself to the porridge and sat down to eat, picking up a newspaper to read. Ethan was still asleep but she'd left the alarm set for 8.30, so that he didn't disgrace himself by sleeping past breakfast. She was savouring the warmth and sweetness of the porridge and wondering if that was full-fat milk she could taste in it when Max came in. He was a tall man, well-built, his hard body obvious even under the cashmere jumper he was wearing. His hair was still damp from the shower, and he looked rested. She felt again that jolt of recognition. The air in the room seemed to become electrically charged when he walked in.

'Morning,' he said with a smile. 'Did you sleep well?'

Octavia flushed again. *I'm just going to have to get over this,* she told herself. *He obviously hasn't recognised me yet, so perhaps he never will.* She took a deep breath and smiled as brightly as she could manage. 'Wonderfully well, thanks.'

'It's the Scottish air. Better than any pill. I sleep sounder here than anywhere in the world.' He smiled. She noticed again how his smile softened his face and made its strong lines almost attractive. He helped himself to a plate of breakfast and came to join her at the table. 'Don't let me stop you reading.'

'Oh, no, it's fine,' she said, pushing the newspaper away.

'Ethan says you're an up-and-coming business-woman, making her mark on the world.' He started cutting up a sausage. 'That's good. We need more like you.'

'You're an entrepreneur as well, aren't you? In telecommunications?'

Max shrugged. 'Well, let's just say I saw my moment and invested wisely in modern technology. Now I'm looking at green technologies. It's the way forward.'

'When did you get your knighthood?' Octavia asked, interested. 'I thought you had to be really old to get one of those.'

Max shot her an amused look and burst out laughing. 'I'm afraid I'm not a knight. Very dull of me! Sorry. I'm a baronet, I inherited the title from my dad. I was Sir Max at nine years old, which made calling the register at school kind of funny, as you can imagine.'

Octavia laughed too, thinking of a little schoolboy called Sir Max.

'Talking of age,' Max said casually, buttering some toast, 'you seem very young yourself to be in charge of a company. Most girls like you are just starting out. Or still studying.'

'I'm very lucky,' Octavia replied. 'I've had some unusual opportunities. And I've got Ethan. He's teaching me the ropes. I like learning but I tend to concentrate more on the fun stuff – re-designing the look of the business, thinking about promotions and handling all marketing. Ethan's handling all the figures for me. I'm afraid I find them a bit confusing. I don't really understand the jargon.'

Max looked at her with his intense blue eyes, his

expression inscrutable. 'Ah,' he said. 'Yes. It can seem that way, can't it? But it's all important. It's the nuts and bolts of how everything works. You need to understand the basics. When I started out, I didn't have a penny to my name or even a maths qualification – I failed my exam five times. But once I was out there, trying to make a business work, I found that not only did I need to grasp percentages, profit margins and compound interest, but that I was interested in them. They had a practical bearing, you see – on whether my business would be profitable or not.'

'I've got Ethan for all that,' Octavia replied, putting her spoon into her empty porridge bowl. Whenever he looked at her with those blue eyes, she felt an electric tingle all over her skin. *It's odd,* she thought. *He's always drawn a reaction from me – anger at first, and irritation at his attitude to me. But now* . . . She gave herself a mental shake. *But now nothing. I don't know why he has this effect on me but it will all change when he works out who I am.*

'But . . . it's *your* money, isn't it? That's what Ethan hinted at.'

'Oh yes.'

'And you and he are a couple.'

'Yes. Not married or anything. Boyfriend and girlfriend.' *Why did I want to make that point?* she wondered.

'Mmm.' Max said nothing more but returned to his sausage and eggs, and then changed the subject.

Ethan still wasn't up when she'd finished her breakfast, so Octavia pulled on her boots, wrapped herself in a shawl and went outside. The countryside was ravishing, a palette of soft lavenders, blues, greys and chalky greens. She couldn't remember seeing anywhere quite so beautiful before.

She walked down to the bottom of the garden and stood by a small stream that burbled by, breathing in the clean, pure air and savouring the silence.

Suddenly, to her surprise, Max appeared beside her, arriving without a sound. She'd left him at the breakfast table with his head bent over the business pages of the paper while he munched on toast and marmalade, and now here he was, in a dark blue waxed jacket and black gumboots.

He put a hand on her arm, his gaze fixed out at a spot above the nearest hill. She felt it heavy and warm through her sleeve, and her skin seemed to burn where the pressure of his hand touched it. 'Look,' he breathed. 'Can you see?'

She followed his gaze and squinted into the pale blue sky. 'No,' she whispered back.

'There.'

Then she saw the graceful soaring shape of a bird as it caught an air current and glided effortlessly, without a beat of its wings.

'Do you know what that is?' Max kept his voice quiet, although it was unlikely the bird would be disturbed by them at such a distance.

'Yes,' Octavia replied, gazing at it. 'It's a golden eagle. Very rare. About six hundred left in this country. But nearly all of Britain's breeding pairs are found in Scotland, aren't they?'

Max looked at her, obviously surprised. Then he laughed. 'Yes, you're right. How did you know that? You're the first of my non-Scottish visitors to recognise it.'

Octavia was pleased to see that he was impressed by her knowledge. 'I saw golden eagles in America, when we holidayed there. And I found some books about birds in the library at home in England and I picked up quite a bit.' She looked about, scanning the skies. 'I wondered if I might see some kestrels out here actually. Have you noticed many?'

'Oh yes,' Max said, 'you'll see plenty. And buzzards, and goshawks and sparrowhawks. And owls, too, if you're up late enough.' He looked at her, interested. 'Shall we go and see what we can spot?'

The next minute they were wandering out over the open field together, talking easily as they looked up in the skies and over hedgerows to see what might be found. Octavia spotted a kestrel first, pointing it out to Max. 'Look at the way its wings beat so fast as it hovers,' she said. 'It's obviously found some prey, it'll dive in a minute . . . look! There it goes! A nice juicy mouse, I expect.'

'You make a mouse sound quite appetising,' Max said teasingly. 'Perhaps we should get Hilda in the kitchen to cook one up and try it ourselves.'

'Roast dormouse was a Roman delicacy,' Octavia remarked, enjoying the way she was able to undermine any ideas Max had about what a London socialite might know. 'They liked it drenched in honey.'

They walked on together, both now quite relaxed in one another's company. When she climbed over a stile, Max offered her his hand and Octavia took it. At once, she was startled by the unexpected jolt of pleasure that went through her as she touched him. She stared at him, and he looked back, his blue eyes no longer icy as she'd seen them before, but warm, friendly, even . . . even . . .

She pulled in a sharp breath. A feeling of dizziness suddenly threatened to overwhelm her, though she had no idea why.

'Are you all right?' Max said, concerned, as she swayed slightly. He put out his other hand and gripped her arm. The dizziness grew worse, and she had the distinct impression that in another moment she might fall into his arms. A loud electronic chirrup broke the spell.

'Ah.' Max pulled a face. 'My phone. Sorry.' He took it out, then started in surprise. 'My God, is that the time? The guests are at the house apparently. We'd better get back. I completely lost track of everything.' He grinned up at her. 'That's enough bird-watching for today. Perhaps we can go out again tomorrow?'

'I'd like that,' she said breathlessly, feeling her head clear. She jumped down off the stile and they made their way back, striding across the shaggy grassland towards the house.

Max, Ethan and the other guests went out shooting for the day. The four guns were all hale, bluff, well-rounded businessmen, ready to enjoy some country sports. Octavia wasn't interested in joining the shoot. Instead, she spent some quiet time in the house, reading and sipping cups of tea. This, she realised, was exactly what she needed: an escape from London and her hectic social life to a slower, quieter pace where she could stop and breathe.

After lunch, she went out and climbed to the top of a nearby hill. There she surveyed the beautiful view and tried to get a signal on her phone. A text came through from Roddy.

Iseult still sedated. Seems to be recovering from op. No more news for now.

So there really was no point in her being in London. There was nothing she could do to help Iseult until she was brought back to consciousness.

Octavia got ready for dinner that night feeling relaxed and reinvigorated after a long bath.

'Come on,' Ethan said impatiently. 'Aren't you ready yet?'

'Don't rush me. We're not late. They said cocktails at eight.'

'It's five past!'

'That's absolutely fine.' Octavia gazed at him in the mirror as she pushed an earring through her lobe. 'Calm down.' She finished her make-up while Ethan sighed impatiently, then straightened her Zac Posen dress, slipped on her Gina heels and followed him downstairs.

As soon as they walked into the dining room she realised that she was far more dressed up than any other woman there. The wives of the other guns were in safe black evening dresses with discreet touches of sparkle. Octavia stood out conspicuously in her cream and silver frock, her long blonde hair falling in soft waves over her shoulders. She noticed a few furtively admiring glances from the male guests as she went over to the cocktail table, where Max was mixing drinks for the guests.

'Ah, Octavia,' he said as she approached. 'What'll it be? Gin and tonic? Whisky and soda? Or something soft?'

He looked up at her, smiling, and the moment they locked eyes, she knew that he recognised her. His smile faded, his mouth dropped open and he stared at her with an expression of horror and bewilderment creeping over his face. Then a second later he recovered himself, turning away to the drinks again. 'I know,' he said in a voice that sounded normal but that she noticed was harder than before, 'have a vodka and tonic. I'm sure you like those. Ice? Lemon?'

She mumbled her thanks, feeling the heat crawling over her face. When he looked up to hand her the drink, his blue eyes were as icy and hard as the cubes clinking in her vodka.

Oh, God. I knew it! He hates me. Octavia felt depressed. She'd enjoyed their walk together that morning, and the way she'd responded to him. That was obviously all over now. Then her spine stiffened. *Well, sod him. He doesn't know the first thing about me. So let him hate me. I don't care.*

Dinner was not as enjoyable as she'd hoped, even though the men on either side of her were pleasant company and obviously appreciative of her charms. She was too irritated by Ethan, who was acting like a little boy with a crush, concentrating solely on Sir Max and hanging on his every word like an awe-struck fan. But, she realised, what was really upsetting her was the fact that her friendship with Max that had seemed so promising that morning was now finished. She picked up her glass of ice-cold white wine and drained it. The butler stepped forward at once and refilled it, and she took another gulp. She pushed away the plate of smoked Scottish salmon only half-touched, and instead alternated drinking her wine with making loud, over-cheerful remarks to her neighbour. Once she looked up and caught Max's eyes on her. She'd been expecting to see a chilly expression laced with that hard arrogance she'd seen in them before, but instead she saw confusion. It seemed as though he wasn't sure who he was seeing – that glamorous beauty he'd scolded in London, or the fresh-faced girl from the morning walk who'd known all about falcons, eagles and the plumage of kestrels. He hardly appeared to be hearing Ethan, who was chattering away beside him, obviously eager to impress. When he saw her catch his gaze, he looked swiftly away and did not look back.

Why did he have to recognise me? she thought dully, disappointment swooping through her. *It's all ruined now.* Though she wasn't quite sure what had been ruined. Perhaps it was the chance of Max joining the board – he never would now, she was sure of it. After all, he thought she was a vapid brat with a coke habit. He'd have less than no time for her now.

The second course was served: roasted woodcock with game chips, bread sauce and sautéed cabbage. A fine Château Pichon Lalande was poured out to go with it. Octavia drank more than she ate, and soon her head was swimming and she realised she was very tipsy. She began to slur her words and repeat herself, then giggle and apologise as she dropped a fork, and then her napkin, ducking down to get it and emerging flushed and breathless with a loud 'Whoops! Don't worry, got it!'

Ethan shot her a furious glance, but she simply smiled back and took another large gulp of her wine. She pouted at him over one bare shoulder. *They all think I'm so naughty. Well, maybe I will be. Maybe it'll be fun to cut loose up here*. But the effect of her vampish look was spoiled as she swayed forward and knocked over her wine glass with an elbow. The fine crystal hit a silver candelabrum and shattered, a large stain of red wine soaking into the white linen tablecloth.

'Sorry, sorry,' she stuttered.

'No need to apologise,' Max said smoothly, looking at her for an instant and then away again. He gestured to the butler and immediately everything was cleared away.

Ethan appeared at her side. He bent down and said through clenched teeth, 'Don't you think you've had *enough*?' He stood up and said to the assembled company, 'I hope you'll excuse Octavia, she's very tired and thinks it might be best if she went to bed.'

'No I bloody don't!' she said loudly, as Ethan gripped her arm and pulled her to her feet. 'I think it might be best if I got another glass of wine . . . if you don't mind . . .'

The table had fallen quiet and everyone was watching her uncomfortably. The butler made to pour her a fresh glass.

'No thanks, she's had plenty,' Ethan said firmly. He whispered, 'Upstairs *now*.'

She was furious with him. 'Let go of me!' she hissed, and stumbled as he manoeuvred her out from behind the table.

'Say goodnight, Octavia,' Ethan said in a warning tone that belied the big smile he still had plastered over his face.

Her last glimpse before Ethan steered her out of the room was of Max's face. It was set like stone.

Bugger it all. Why is he so bloody hard to please? she

thought to herself, aware of a great depression sinking on her. Then she let Ethan take her upstairs and put her to bed.

The next morning, Ethan was furious with her for making a scene and getting drunk.

'You've put the whole thing in jeopardy,' he snapped. 'I'm going to have to work bloody hard to convince Sir Max to join the board of Butterfly now, after your little performance last night. What the hell were you thinking of?'

Her head was thudding, her eyes were dry and she couldn't be bothered to tell him that it had been pretty unlikely from the start that Max would even dream of it. The realisation of what he thought of her now filled her with gloom. And she'd no doubt made it a whole lot worse with her alcohol-fuelled behaviour the night before.

It's everything, she thought wistfully, rolling away from Ethan and refusing to talk to him. *Flora, Iseult, the stress of taking over Noble's . . . the last thing I need is someone like Max against me too.*

Ethan was still cross and went down to breakfast without her, so she ordered up toast and coffee and stayed in her room, hoping that her absence didn't seem too rude. Well, she probably couldn't make a worse impression than she already had. When she felt up to it, she pulled on her walking clothes and escaped to wander the surrounding fields and hills again, leaving Ethan to sweettalk Max as best he could. On the way back to the house, she managed to slip crossing a stream and filled both her boots with cold, muddy water. She squelched crossly back to the house.

As she went through the gate into the garden, she saw Max walking towards her, his hands in the pockets of his shabby old trousers. 'Hello,' he called. 'I've been looking for you.'

'Oh, bollocks,' said Octavia under her breath. 'Just what I need.' Somehow she'd been hoping she could avoid her host until she could get away from here in the evening. 'Hello.'

He came up to her. 'Have you been for a walk?' He was still stern-faced, his eyes cool.

'Yes,' she said, adding silently, *What did you think I'd been doing? Skiing?*

'How are you feeling?'

She glanced down, embarrassed, and felt some of her bolshie attitude melt away. She'd been pointlessly rude the night before, made a fool of herself and broken some no doubt expensive glassware. 'Um . . . I'm fine, thanks. Listen . . . I'm sorry. About getting trashed at dinner. I should have eaten a bit more and drunk a bit less.'

'That's all right. Honestly. My dinner parties are rarely so eventful.' He smiled, although his eyes were still frosty. 'Listen, can I have a word with you? Come and sit down.'

They went over to a stone bench flecked with moss that faced out towards the magnificent hills. In the next field was the helicopter, bright red and conspicuous against the soft green background. They sat at either end of the bench, Max throwing his arm casually along the back of it. He fixed her with his intense blue gaze. 'I know who you are now,' he said at last. 'Ethan hadn't explained that his partner was one of the Beaufort twins until last night, but it all makes

sense now. I've seen you in the gossip columns . . . and
. . .' There was a pause then he said, 'and we've met
before, haven't we?'

Octavia froze. 'Yes,' she said at last.

'I didn't recognise you without all your finery. Not
until you walked into the room last night, looking like
a million dollars. You made the room stand still. Like
a girl who belongs in a nightclub in London, with a
fashionable crowd of bright young things.'

She turned to look at him. Had he just paid her a
compliment? But his expression was still grave, and
he went on, his voice toneless.

'It's hard to believe that the girl at dinner last night
was the same one I went walking with yesterday
morning. Will you tell me something honestly? Have
you been taking drugs while you've been here?'

'What?' She was outraged. 'No! For your information, I don't do drugs – as you'd know if you'd ever
bothered to listen to me.'

His expression was one of disbelief. 'But I saw you
in that club. Your friends were wasted. Everyone was
clearly on chemical highs.'

'Yes, but I wasn't,' she said furiously. 'And I got
drunk last night, that's all. Haven't you ever had too
much to drink now and then? What the hell makes
you think I'm on drugs?'

'Look, I'm only worried about you, Octavia. I know
what it's like to get in with a bad crowd, start dabbling
in things you shouldn't – I know how easily you can
be sucked in.'

'Will you *stop* making assumptions about me?'
Octavia cried hotly.

'You're getting angry,' he said, a teasing note in his

voice that only served to make her even more cross. 'It's lucky there aren't any jugs of water nearby, I suppose, or you'd throw one over me.'

She narrowed her eyes. 'Listen,' she said in a low, menacing voice. 'You don't know anything about me. I'm not on drugs. Not now, not ever. Not that I need your permission, thanks very much. I'll do whatever I please and I don't give a damn whether you're happy about it or not.' All her embarrassment and upset was turning into fiery rage, and it was almost a relief to let rip. 'Where the hell do you get off, with this holier-than-thou act anyway?'

He raised his eyebrows, his smile fading. 'I see. You're right. I don't know anything about you. In fact, I feel like I know less about you now than I did when you arrived.' His mouth hardened. 'And that makes me pretty sure I don't want to invest in your company. That boyfriend of yours is telling me some queer tales. I think the two of you might be a bit of a risk.'

'That's *exactly* what I thought you'd say. Thank you for not disappointing me. I was worried for five minutes yesterday that you might actually turn out to be all right.' Octavia stood up and put her hands on her hips. 'You know what? We don't need your invest-ment. Because *I* don't think much of *your* character! You've jumped to conclusions about me without giving me a chance, completely wrong ones. You were perfectly friendly to me before you let your own preju-dice blind you. Well, you can get stuffed. I'd like to go home now, if you don't mind.'

'Certainly.' Max gave her a cool look. 'I'll ask my pilot to take you back to London right away, if that's what you want.'

'I do,' Octavia snapped. 'I'll go and pack.'

She began to march away towards the house, but absurd squelching noises came from her boots, as though she were walking on quacking ducks. She tutted in annoyance. It was completely undermining her dignified exit, and she was even more outraged to hear Max's laughter as she stomped awkwardly away.

64

The man behind the desk really was very good-looking, thought Vicky, even though he was fixing her with an expression that seemed to be a mixture of hostility and concern. The story she'd told him had obviously affected him, but he seemed to be battling to remain disinterested. 'Have you ever heard of something called client confidentiality?' he asked in sharp American-accented tones. 'I'm not at liberty to talk about any of this with you. I'm sorry. I wish I could help.'

Vicky muttered impatiently, and pushed the print-outs towards him. 'But haven't you listened to anything I've said? Flora Beaufort hasn't received any of your emails. Here they are, I've printed them all out. Don't you think that's odd? She hadn't even opened them.'

Nick Falcon stared at her for a moment longer, the emotion in his black eyes unreadable, then said, 'I don't have any proof that you are who you say you are.'

'Well, no . . . I suppose I'm asking you to take my word for a lot.' Vicky thought for a moment and then said,

'Okay. Let's start again. Imagine I'm a brand new client. I've got this interesting case for you. My cousin Flora, who is also my employer and extremely rich, has gone off to Germany with her husband, and none of us has seen her since.'

'But she's been in touch?'

'Yes – but from an entirely new email account, and in a voice that doesn't sound completely like her own.' Vicky shrugged. 'There's nothing I can exactly put my finger on, but it's just a slightly different tone. And she's not seen her sister – her twin sister – since her wedding day. Doesn't that strike you as strange?'

Falcon frowned and moved the mouse on his desk, flicking his gaze over to his computer screen. 'Mmm. I've met the sister. For a moment.'

'Have you?' Vicky was surprised.

'Yeah, she came in here one day and I naturally thought she was Flora. I may have put my foot in it somewhat as I inadvertently gave away the fact that Flora was looking for their mother.' He looked uncomfortable. 'But no one's ever mentioned it since, so I let it go.'

Vicky blinked at him. 'But that explains the row they had! Just before the wedding. That's why Octavia hasn't tried as hard as I would have expected to see Flora.' She sat back in her chair, sighing with frustration. 'Oh, God, it's all turned out to be such a mess.'

Falcon frowned, and twisted his pen in his hands. He seemed to be struggling with himself. Then he looked up at Vicky. 'Listen, what you've said is worrying, I'll admit that. When I met Flora . . . Miss Beaufort . . . Mrs von Schwetten . . . I got the impression that she's not as tough as some of the girls out there.' His eyes softened. 'I mean, she's no weakling. It takes guts to look for a parent. But something about her made me think she'd been hurt.'

Vicky nodded. 'I know what you mean. Flora's vulnerable, probably because of her crazy upbringing. That's why I'm so worried about her. She's sweet and caring and loving, and the way she's acting just isn't like her.'

Nick thought for an instant more then fixed Vicky with a flashing dark gaze, setting his shoulders in a businesslike fashion. 'Okay. What exactly do you want me to do, Miss Staunton?'

Vicky was full of relief. He was going to help her.

'I want you to look into Flora's whereabouts and, more importantly, the man she married, Otto von Schwetten. Octavia and I looked him up before the wedding but he seemed to check out okay.'

'Where'd you look?' Falcon shot her a sardonic look. 'And don't say Wikipedia or I'll kill you.'

'Well . . .' Vicky stopped, embarrassed, and flushed.

'Oh my God.' He turned his eyes to heaven. 'You might as well have read the guy's CV. He probably wrote it himself.'

'Okay, maybe we should have looked harder. My guess is that's what Octavia had in mind when she came here, but she got distracted by Flora's search for their mother. But something odd happened recently. I was sure I'd seen Otto on the street, and sent a message to Flora asking her about it. I was instantly sacked by her – through her new email account – which is totally out of character. I'm beginning to suspect more than ever that von Schwetten sacked me, and that he is using Flora's email account. But why would he do that?'

Falcon looked concerned and intrigued. 'Okay.' He picked up a pen and jotted down some quick notes on his pad. 'I appreciate the fact that you've settled my bill, and offered to pay me to do this further investigation for you. But, you see, the thing that's bothering me is that you've opened the confidential files I sent your cousin. I don't like that very much.'

'Actually . . .' Vicky sat up straighter and fixed him with her stare '. . . I didn't open those documents. These printouts are just your emails. Flora's secret is still safe.'

Falcon returned her gaze for a long moment. Then he said, 'Okay then. You'd better give me some details. We'll get to the bottom of this in no time, I can promise you that.'

Amanda signed her name with a flourish and pushed the document back across the mahogany desk to the lawyer. 'There,' she said. 'Finished.'

She had thought that perhaps she might start crying when it was actually done but instead she felt a weird excitement and a sense of a burden being lifted.

'Thank you,' said her lawyer. 'Your brother has also signed his copies. That brings to an end the Radcliffe association with Noble's. After quite some time. A hundred and fifty years, isn't it? You're a direct descendant of the original Noble, aren't you?'

No need to rub it in, for Christ's sake, Amanda thought crossly. 'Yes,' she said briskly, putting the top back on her Mont Blanc. 'Now there's the small matter of the money.'

'That will be wired across to your account, probably within forty-eight hours of receipt of these documents.'

'Then there will be the accountant to talk to.' Amanda made a face. 'Yuk! Capital gains tax and God knows what else.'

'There'll be plenty left after all that,' the lawyer said with a reassuring smile. 'So, what's it to be? A new dress? A fast car? A holiday in the sun?'

'No.' Amanda stood up and picked up her Mulberry bag. 'None of that. Business. That's what I'll spend my money on.'

She turned on her heel and marched out.

It really was bizarre, but Vicky had dreamt about Flora all night and the same thing kept happening each time. She dreamt that she was on the phone to Flora, begging her to tell them the truth about what had happened with Otto, but all her cousin would say in return was, 'I need a new bicycle. I need a new bicycle.'

She woke up feeling frustrated and unhappy at the memory. She'd wanted so much to help. Why wouldn't Flora tell her what they needed to know? She heard the soft voice again saying breathily, 'I need a new bicycle.'

The house was almost unbearably quiet all day. The staff had their day off, and Vicky had scaled back some of the hours for the cooks now that Flora had gone and Octavia was often out. She spent the day doing some odds and ends of work, swimming and watching television, and was about to go down and make herself some supper when the front door opened and Octavia came in, hauling a couple of weekend bags and a dress bag.

'Oh, hi. Aren't you at Ethan's?'

'Obviously not,' said Octavia, puffing slightly. 'I got back a while ago and decided to get a cab from the heliport. It's just across the river.'

'Are you staying for supper? I was about to make some. Molly's off tonight.'

Octavia nodded, brushing a hand over her hair. 'Yes. I'm going to stay here for a while. No particular reason. I just felt the need to be home, that's all.' She smiled up at Vicky. 'Hope you don't mind some company?'

'Are you kidding? I'd love it.'

They sat together in the den, eating a light supper of lentil salad and cold chicken. Vicky listened to Octavia as she told the awful story of what had happened to Iseult, all the time wondering at the back of her mind if she should confess to her about the emails, the document containing the whereabouts of Diane Beaufort and the fact that she herself had put Nick Falcon on Flora's trail.

But Octavia seemed wholly taken up with the fate of her friend and her need to be on the spot when Iseult came round, even though she would probably be sedated for some days yet.

I won't tell her, Vicky decided. *There's no need to add to her worries right now. Perhaps if something comes of it I will, once Iseult is out of immediate danger.*

But the following afternoon, as she sat in the office doing some household admin, she saw an email arrive in her inbox. It was from Nick Falcon.

Hi, Miss Staunton

Could you get over here urgently? If possible I suggest you bring Flora Beaufort's sister with you. I'm available at any hour, so let me know when you can make it.

Thanks.

Nick Falcon

Vicky stared at it. The moment of confession had come sooner than expected. She jumped to her feet and went to find Octavia.

Falcon's office seemed dingier and more messy than ever, and smaller, too, with all of them in it.

Octavia was staring at the investigator with wild eyes. She'd been here once before, but had never expected to be back. Vicky had explained what she'd found in Flora's untouched email account and that Nick Falcon had discovered the whereabouts of their mother; she'd also had to confess that she had asked him to investigate Otto von Schwetten.

'I'm sorry if I overstepped the mark,' she said finally as Steve whizzed them through the London streets in double-quick time.

'Don't be silly,' Octavia replied swiftly. 'I should have done it myself ages ago. I tried to once, but nothing came of it. I wish I had now.'

They were both pale and nervous as they raced up the stairs to find out what Falcon had to say.

It was much worse than they could have anticipated.

'Wait, wait!' Octavia felt simultaneously panicked and dazed as Nick finished his explanation. 'Otto . . . he isn't a baron at all then?'

'Well, I suppose he could make a case for his being

487

a baron, as he was officially adopted by the last Baron von Schwetten. The old man died last year, so if there is anyone with a claim to the title, it's Otto Gestenholtz.' Nick looked almost as worried as the two girls. The situation clearly bothered him a great deal.

'This is awful,' cried Vicky. She gripped the desk with white knuckles. 'He's a con man?'

'Looks like it,' Falcon said grimly, glancing down at a printed sheet in front of him. 'I've traced a fair few of the women he's been involved with and I haven't been trying that hard. He's also been married at least once before. He's been before the courts too several times for fraudulent practices. No doubt his new surname helped him escape some of that record of petty theft and acquiring money through false pretences.'

'Oh my God!' Octavia was dead white. 'Flora . . . I've got to get to her!' She leapt to her feet. 'She needs me. How could I be so stupid?'

Vicky jumped up to grasp her arm and calm her down.

'Hold your horses,' Falcon told her. 'We're going to get her all right, but I'm afraid there is something worse to consider. It's clear that none of the emails supposedly sent by your sister were actually written by her. I have a pet analyst who knows about this kind of stuff and she says there's no way that genuine emails by Flora and the ones in the floravonschwetten account were written by the same person.'

Octavia moaned softly, clenching one fist and pressing it to her mouth. She was even more agonised as she realised something else. 'When she spoke to me . . . she spoke to me and . . . she stuttered. She stuttered like mad. I didn't even notice it, but I was the only person she never stuttered with.' She buried her face in her hands. 'She must have been trying to tell me something, and I was completely deaf to her.' She began to sob. 'Flora, Flora, Flora . . .'

'I need a new bicycle,' murmured Vicky quietly, thinking, then a look of amazement and horror crossed her face. 'I need a new bicycle!' she shouted.

The other two stared at her, Octavia through teary eyes. 'What are you talking about, Vicky?'

Her cousin spoke rapidly. 'When Flora and I had a secret correspondence years ago, we had a code. A silly, simple thing where one sentence really meant another. We agreed in advance a whole load of meanings – you know, "I like lemonade" might mean "I hate my teacher." That sort of simple stuff. "I need a new bicycle" meant . . . "They've locked me up."' Vicky closed her eyes and released a shuddering breath. 'Flora wanted that one in. I never needed to use it, but then I was never shut away like she was.'

'Did Flora *say* this to you?' Nick asked, his expression even more anxious.

'Yes,' Vicky said. 'I think she did. When she last called. But I never noticed at the time. I only remembered in my dream last night, and even then I didn't understand.'

Falcon looked worried but kept his businesslike air. 'Okay, so this looks to me like constructive kidnapping. I don't know if there is such a term, maybe I just invented it. Even though Flora married him of her own free will, she wasn't in a position to make an informed choice as he concealed his true identity and past from her. It's fraud, pure and simple. We can get her out of this, I promise.'

'I want her back now!' shouted Octavia, frantic. 'Now!'

'Hey, try and stay calm,' urged Vicky.

Octavia felt as though she was losing it. She could feel herself shaking all over and tears were pouring down her face.

'No, she's right.' Nick Falcon stared at them with earnest dark eyes. 'I don't want to panic you but I personally think the sooner we get Flora out of von Schwetten's control the better. We don't know what his game plan is, but I've got some financial investigators hard at work on his records and what they're telling me doesn't look at all good. It appears that he has got some kind of access to your sister's fortune – at least, he's swimming in money right now. I would advise that we get Flora back straight away.' He pursed his lips and looked serious. 'My professional advice would be to call the police and get them involved. My personal advice would be that we could maybe pull this off on our own if we face von Schwetten on his own turf and use the element of surprise.'

Octavia wiped her eyes and tried to control her tears. She shook her head as she absorbed his words and stared at him, amazed. 'You mean, turn up there? At his castle? And just take her away?'

Falcon nodded. 'Sometimes the simplest things work best. We might avoid a lot of unnecessary trouble and publicity that way. I'm sure you don't want this coming out unless it really has to.'

'Absolutely,' breathed Octavia, suddenly calmer. She saw the prospect of having Flora back very soon, of going and getting her out of that place personally.

'But how would we get to Bavaria?' asked Vicky, torn

between panic and fear for Flora, and excitement at the course Falcon was suggesting

'We'll charter a plane!' cried Octavia, suddenly energised.

'Yeah,' he said. 'I guess that's the only way. But we'll have to find a suitable landing field and have a car standing by there for us too, so we can drive straight to the castle. With local arrangements like that, there's a risk von Schwetten will somehow find out we're coming.'

There was a pause and then Octavia said firmly, 'I know what to do. Leave it to me.'

65

'You have really been very co-operative,' Otto said. He looked over the dining table at Flora and gave her what for him was a warm smile, his brown eyes less harsh than usual. 'I'm pleased with you, Flora. You've been much more adaptable than I was expecting. A good little wife.'

She smiled back, trying to look as though his praise meant something to her. Her opportunity to get away from him would come only if he trusted her. She had submitted to him in all things, letting him degrade her over and over again, asking for nothing. Now she wondered if she dared try her luck with him.

She fiddled with her fork for a moment and then put it down. 'Otto,' she said in a meek voice, 'you said that if I was obedient and did what you asked, you might let me have my telephone back.'

He stiffened, looking wary. 'Why do you want it? Aren't you content as you are?'

'Yes,' she said hastily. 'But I'd love to talk to my sister. I miss her, you know.'

Otto turned back to look at the newspaper he'd put

492

on the table beside him. 'I know you do. But I don't really want you talking to her. I've heard of the way that twins can communicate, sometimes telepathically. Only when I'm sure you completely accept your new life.' He spoke dismissively. There were to be no arguments.

Flora felt her spirits dive again. Would this nightmare ever end? How long could it go on before she would rather be dead?

'But there is some good news for you,' he said brightly. 'The work on the western side of the castle is almost complete. I thought you and I could go shopping. Christie's New York is having a sale of antique German furniture and paintings. It might be fun to go there and buy some pieces. What do you think?'

She was astonished. From months of captivity here in the *schloss* to . . . a buying spree in New York? It was ridiculous. But surely this would be her chance to escape. 'Y-y-yes, I'd like that,' she said, trying not to sound too eager. 'I'd love to s-see the castle brought back to its former glory.'

'Would you, my dear? I'm so glad.' Otto looked very pleased. 'That means you are thinking of this place as your home. I shall arrange it. We will stay somewhere nice and make a little trip of it. A kind of honeymoon, perhaps. We might have some other treats while we are there – some of the more *exotic* pleasures.' He gave her a thin smile. 'Every whim is catered for in a big city.'

She did not want to think about what that might mean.

'We will leave tomorrow,' he said decisively. 'Yes.'

He folded the paper. 'I shall go and book flights at once.'

Octavia ran past the receptionist and burst into the lavish office with its view over St James's Park. Max Northam looked up from his desk, surprised.

'What the hell are you doing here?' he demanded.

'Please,' she said, rushing up to the desk and grasping the edge of it with both hands, 'you have to help me. You're the only one who can. We don't have long.'

Max's assistant came in, red-faced. 'I'm sorry, Sir Max, she pushed right past me, I didn't have time to stop her.'

'That's all right, Bettina.' Max flicked his cold blue gaze back to Octavia, taking in her flushed face and her air of distress. 'I know Miss Beaufort. She can have a few moments to explain exactly what's she's doing, bursting in here like this.'

'Very well.' The assistant went out rather reluctantly, closing the door behind her.

'You've got five minutes,' Max said abruptly, standing up.

'Okay. Okay.' Octavia took a deep breath and tried to stay calm. She had to explain this as best she could. She knew there was only one chance. 'I know we haven't had the best start. You think I'm a spoilt coke-head – though I promise you, I don't touch drugs – and I think you are rude and arrogant, but I think we need to give each other a fresh chance. You see . . . I'm in trouble.'

'Really?' Max had walked to the window and stared out at the park opposite. Now he turned round to face her, a slight smile twisting his lips. He was wearing the most perfectly cut suit she'd ever seen. It showed off his broad shoulders and long legs. 'Well, it can't be money. You've got plenty of that already. Is it business? Has that boy you're sleeping with finally shown his true colours?'

She shook her head. 'It's nothing to do with Ethan.'

'It had better not be illegal,' said Max, his face hardening. 'You say you don't touch drugs and I very much want to believe you . . .'

'For Christ's sake, it's nothing like that!' she cried out, frustrated. 'I need you to help rescue someone – my sister – who's being kept prisoner against her will. Please, please . . .' Tears rushed to Octavia's eyes again with the force of her emotions. 'I know you don't like me, but I'm begging you. I can't think of anyone else who can help.'

He stared at her, bewildered. Then he gave a half laugh. 'Okay. This is going to be worth listening to. And, I have to admit, you have some balls coming here. Go on then. Sit down and tell me everything.'

Fifteen minutes later, Octavia had told him most of the story and explained why Nick Falcon thought a rescue was the best option.

'We've got to get her out of there as soon as possible,' Octavia finished, sounding breathless again. 'And I know you have a helicopter and can pilot it . . . and Ethan said you were in the army once.'

'That was a long time ago, but yes, I have had experience of rescue missions.' Max was sitting at his desk again. He picked up a pen and ran it idly through his fingers, frowning. 'But this sounds extraordinary.'

'It's true, I promise. Nick Falcon, our investigator,

will verify everything and supply proof. Please . . .' She leant forward, beseeching, her eyes wide. 'Please help me rescue my sister. I know you can help me.'

'This is incredible.' Max looked down at his polished desk top and laughed quietly to himself. 'I can't believe this, but I think I'm actually going to do it. Christ knows why. I must be crazy.' He looked up at her. 'Okay, you know what? This is serious. If a young woman is being held against her will, it's a matter for the police. But I take on board everything you've said. This Otto sounds like a prize shit. He might be dangerous. Is he likely to be armed or to want to hurt your sister? Perhaps you *should* consider getting the police . . .'

'No, no police, not unless it's absolutely necessary,' Octavia pleaded. 'Don't you see? We could swoop in there, surprise him, grab her and be gone before he even knows what's happening.'

'Do you intend to go in alone?'

'Nick will come too. He's used to dealing with low-lifes and violent types.'

'I'm quite handy with all of that myself, which is lucky for you,' remarked Max, getting to his feet while picking up his telephone. 'Bettina? Can you check my diary for this afternoon, please – and ask Roger to prep the helicopter, will you? I'll need it brought from the hangar to Battersea early tomorrow morning.' He waited for a moment and listened while Octavia tried not to stare at him too anxiously. 'Okay. Thanks.' He put the phone down. 'I've got an important dinner tonight, one I really can't pull out of. It's at Downing Street and can't be missed. But it does make more sense anyway for us to leave at dawn tomorrow.'

She was slumped back in with relief. She'd feared he wouldn't believe her or would accuse her of being a fantasist – but he obviously took her seriously and grasped the urgency of the situation. She was grateful and impressed by his attitude.

'All right. Whatever you say.' It was hard to wait so long when she was itching to get going, but Octavia could see his point. 'Thank you, Max, thank you so much!'

She stood up, rushed over to him and gave him a hug. His body was tough and well-muscled; he smelt deliciously of sandalwood and lemon. He stood quite still, obviously startled by her embrace, then put one hand on her shoulder. 'Well, you're obviously in trouble. I never turn down a genuine request for help.'

She pulled away, suddenly shy. *What am I doing? He can't stand my guts.* 'I . . . I . . . I appreciate it. I'll pay any costs involved.'

'Don't be silly. But I'm afraid we won't be able to take Ethan.'

Octavia stared at him, realising that she hadn't given Ethan a thought in the course of the whole crisis.

'The helicopter seats four,' Max explained, 'and we'll need a seat for your sister on the return journey. It'll be you, me and this Falcon character.' He looked amused again. 'I can't quite believe I'm saying this, but I'll see you at the helipad tomorrow morning at four-thirty. Don't worry about anything else. I'll make all the arrangements. Oh, and bring your passport.'

'You deserve a little treat, my love,' Otto said fondly, in the tenderest voice he'd used with Flora since their wedding day. 'You have been very well behaved.' He looked searchingly at her face.

497

They were lying together in bed. He had already performed his ritual with her. The blessing of it was how quickly it was over. Now she could sleep, and think about the excitement of the following day. She was leaving the castle, at last! Finally she would get the chance to see the outside world again. It was ironic how much she'd once feared going out – now she was desperate to see other people, to get some sense of life going on beyond this place. She craved some noise, some movement – anything to put an end to the desperate loneliness of being a prisoner.

She knew they were leaving mid-morning the next day to drive the few hours to the airport. From there, they would take a first-class flight to New York, arriving early in the morning US time.

Otto reached out one hand and pushed a wisp of hair away from her face. 'Please don't let me down, Flora,' he murmured. 'I wouldn't want to have to instigate harsh measures against you. You've come so far already. You really have made wonderful progress! Let us enjoy our little trip. And if it goes well, we will have many more.'

'Yes, Otto,' she replied meekly, wishing with all her heart that tomorrow had already arrived and they were in the car, making their way down the mountain and towards freedom.

66

Octavia nestled into her padded jacket. It was a cold morning and still dark, though dawn was beginning to show in the distant line of gold in the sky. She had dressed for travel and ease of movement in a pair of jeans and walking boots. She had no idea what would face them at the end of their journey, after all. Would they be able to find a landing place near the castle? Max assured her that he had scouted out the terrain on Google Maps and the satellite imagery showed a patch of bare land to the east of the castle that he estimated would be big enough to land on.

Ethan knew nothing of what they were doing. Why hadn't she wanted to tell him? Perhaps it was because he would have insisted on coming too, though she suspected that would have been more to do with being close to his beloved Max Northam than actually wanting to help Flora. Octavia could sense her feelings towards Ethan changing, perhaps because of the way he had reacted to the news of Iseult. She'd seen a different side of him then.

Iseult was still lying sedated in hospital but she was recovering well, they said, and they were going to begin the process of bringing her round soon. Roddy had been warned that she would need strong painkillers for some time and that her bandages would remain in place for weeks. But the main thing was that she had survived the operation and so far there were no complications.

'Hey.' It was Nick Falcon, offering Octavia a steaming cup of coffee. She took it gratefully and sipped the hot, milky liquid. 'Your pal is a useful guy to have around, isn't he? Always good to have your own helicopter, I guess. Plus he must have got us a flight plan into Germany and out again.'

'I expect Max can do anything,' Octavia said, as she wrapped her chilly fingers around the paper cup. 'Are you ready for this?'

Nick nodded. 'Ready for anything. I'll do whatever it takes to get your sister out. But that's all I'll say for now.'

Octavia felt a sudden stab of apprehension. This whole thing was dangerous. Someone might get hurt. *I'm not going to think about that,* she told herself. *It's all going to go just fine, I know it.* But what if Otto had guards at his castle? What if there were heavies, and what if they were armed? She had a mental vision of a bloody gunfight, bodies sprawled motionless on the floor, Flora staring up at the sky, glassy-eyed, her face smeared with . . . *No.* Octavia shook her head. *Max won't let that happen.*

At that point he came striding over to tell them that they were cleared for departure in ten minutes so should get strapped in.

Octavia and Nick crossed the helipad and she climbed up into the back seat of the helicopter. She settled herself, belted in and put on her headset.

'Let's get outta here,' Nick said, his drawl crackling through the earphones. 'It's time to rock 'n' roll.'

Max took his seat and set the propellers whirring above them. The powerful engine roared into life as the blades began to spin. Max adjusted his instruments, spoke to air traffic control through his mouthpiece, and a second later piloted the aircraft upwards. It lifted off the ground then rose smoothly until they were higher than the surrounding buildings and looking down at the grey city, still sequined with streetlights. Then, with a tiny dip, they were off, heading out towards the west and the sea.

Flora was up at first light and in the bathroom, preparing herself for the journey ahead. She looked at her reflection in the mirror. Several months of living with Otto was written in her face, she felt, along with the effects of Marthe's cooking. Flora knew she had lost even more weight despite the relentless diet of potatoes, noodles, rice and pasta accompanied by lots of heavy meats and boiled vegetables. She ate just enough to keep her strength up but her appetite, always delicate, had almost disappeared under the strain of her existence and she took pleasure in exercising the little control she had over her life, pushing away the platefuls only nibbled at while Marthe urged her to eat. Otto didn't care much either way, she suspected.

Apart from her slightly sunken cheeks, she had dark circles under her eyes and an expression of weariness.

Her eyes themselves seemed deadened, as though some kind of vital light had been extinguished.

She washed quickly, cleaned her teeth, then dressed. She needed something easy for travelling – she thought for a minute and decided on jeans and boots, along with a silk shirt and a grey cashmere tank. That should keep her comfortable. Her bag for New York was already packed, with some smart outfits suitable for the Carlyle hotel. Perhaps Otto would let her buy some things when they were over there. It had been so long since she'd done any shopping. She laughed quietly to herself. *What would Octavia think? No shopping . . . and who would ever have thought that I'd miss it?*

She took one last look at herself, bundled her hair back into a ponytail and went downstairs for coffee and a slice of toast.

The journey seemed to take forever although the lightening sky showed that time was passing as relentlessly as usual. Max kept them abreast of their position, pointing out the first glimpse of the French coast and the mountains they were passing over. Octavia knew that Bavaria was in southern Germany; it was going to be a long trip with two refuelling stops there and back that would take up precious time. With each stop, they'd have to be cleared by air traffic control, perhaps inspected by customs and have their passports checked.

Both outward stops went smoothly, and only one airfield bothered to check their documents, and even then in a cursory way. The three of them spoke very little, each concentrating on the task ahead. They

502

made good time. It was getting close to mid-morning when they flew over Bavaria.

'Only a few minutes more and we'll be there,' Max told them. The day was bright and clear and the countryside below them looked exquisite: dark forests, purple mountains and sweet little towns that seemed like something from a fairy tale of long ago.

'You okay?' Nick said, turning round to Octavia. She nodded. He was all in black including a pair of aviator shades, and looked like he might be some kind of secret agent or Special Forces member. They had sketched out a basic plan for what they would do but he said it was important to be flexible. 'Our primary aim is to get Flora,' he explained, 'we may have to think on our feet. What I want you to do is stand well back and stay out of the way. Let me handle it, okay? I'm trained for this kind of thing.'

Octavia had agreed. She'd be there for her sister once they were safely back on board.

'Right,' Max said. 'I think we've got a visual. Can you see it? Look at one o'clock.'

They peered out of the windows. Nick saw it first, patted Octavia's arm and pointed. On top of a mountain stood a sprawling stone castle, one side of it covered in scaffolding and blue plastic. It appeared to be deserted. The helicopter was approaching it swiftly and Octavia saw that Max was heading for a piece of ground that seemed both empty and large enough for them to land. There was nothing to stop them – no cars or vehicles visible. *How do they get around?* she wondered as she gazed down. *Is Flora really in there? Are we truly close to each other again?* She thought she could feel her sister's presence but it was a weak sensation, as though Flora were somehow less than herself. *We've got to get down there now,* she thought, the feeling suddenly urgent.

Just then, she saw the front door of the castle open and two people emerge carrying bags. She knew instantly that they were Otto and Flora. They walked across a stretch of concrete towards a garage, and Otto went to unlock the padlock that secured the door.

'There they are!' Octavia cried urgently. 'What's he doing? Are they going somewhere?' The next moment Otto and Flora disappeared inside the garage. 'Stop them!'

'Stay calm,' ordered Max, concentrating hard as he manoeuvred the joystick. 'I'm bringing us down now. Don't worry.' He positioned the aircraft above the landing area. 'When we land, you're going to have get out while the rotors are running. There won't be time to get them going again, so for God's sake keep your heads down as you get out!'

He began the descent. Octavia could see that it was extremely tight. On one side was the castle wall, and on the other the close-packed branches of the pine forest. Max's judgement was going to have to be centimetre perfect to land them safely. As they hovered above the stretch of ground, the pine branches waving furiously in the wash of air from the propellers, a car emerged from the garage with Otto driving and Flora in the passenger seat next to him.

As soon as they were out of the garage, Otto looked up at the helicopter, his expression angry and worried. He stopped the car, obviously unsure what to do for a moment, watching as Max gently brought the aircraft down to touch the ground with a tiny bump. Even before they'd landed, Nick had opened the door and was leaping to the ground then racing towards the car. As soon as Otto saw him coming, he revved the engine into life, roared the car forward as though he was going to attempt to hit the man running towards him, then a second later, spun a round in a right turn. It was obvious now he was going to head for the gate and the road leading down the mountain. If he made it, they couldn't possibly catch the car: it would be impossible to pursue it in a helicopter.

Octavia gasped and fumbled with her seatbelt straps, struggling to release the buckles. Max turned round and snapped them open with a practised movement.

'I'll be here ready to go,' he said. 'But hurry! Head down, don't forget.'

She jumped out of the helicopter, keeping her head low as the blades sliced the air above her, and began to follow Nick. She'd been able to catch one glimpse of Flora's shocked face as the car hurtled towards them but it had disappeared as Otto swung the vehicle towards the gate.

'Stop them!' Octavia screamed as Otto skidded the car to a halt, ready to accelerate into the road. Nick kept running towards the car, pulling a pistol from his jacket as he went. Otto put his foot down and the car wheels spun on the gravel then began to turn inexorably. Just as they gathered speed, Nick lifted his pistol, took a split second to aim and fired. A tyre burst with a loud bang and the car careered over to the right, out of control. It veered back and forth as Otto fought to correct it then hurtled straight for the side of the concrete garage.

'Flora!' cried Octavia, just as the car hit the wall

with a sickening thud. She ran as fast as she could, aware that the bonnet had concertinaed against the unyielding surface, but Nick was there before her. He raced to the passenger side, tugged open the door and checked Flora.

'Are you okay?' Octavia heard him say.

There was a pause and then: 'Y-yes.'

Tears sprang to Octavia's eyes. Just the sound of that soft stammer made her want to weep. She realised she'd been dreading never hearing it again.

'Come on, let's get you out.' Nick began to unbuckle her seatbelt.

'Otto?' Flora's voice was high and tremulous.

'He's out of it. He'll come round in a minute, don't you worry about that.' The next instant, as Octavia reached the car, Nick was helping her sister out.

'Flora!' she cried, her eyes streaming with tears, and as Flora climbed out of the car, dazed and pale, she saw her twin. She gasped but couldn't speak. Her expression told the whole story. The sisters fell into each other's arms, sobbing.

'I knew you'd come for me,' wept Flora. 'I kn-kn-kn-knew you would in the end . . .'

'I'm sorry it's taken so long,' Octavia said through her own tears. 'Can you ever forgive me?'

Nick had gone round to Otto's door. He opened it and quickly rifled through the pockets of the unconscious man's jacket. He came over to them, Flora's passport in his hand. 'We'd better go. Sonny Jim is going to be waking up any second now.'

Otto groaned loudly as if for answer.

'My bag,' Flora said anxiously, looking towards the trunk.

Nick reached into the trunk and pulled out the black holdall. 'Now, let's go.'

An old woman in a flowered apron and sensible clogs came out of the castle, no doubt alerted by all the noise. She stopped short at the scene in front of her and gazed at them all, astonished. 'Flora?' she said in a guttural German accent.

'Oh . . . Marthe . . .' Flora stared back at her, and then looked towards Otto, who was now stirring in the driver's seat and opening his eyes.

'Come on,' ordered Nick curtly. 'No time. We have to go.'

They ran across the concrete towards the helicopter, their hair blown back by the gust of the propellers. Nick pushed Flora's head down as they approached, then helped both girls in as Frau Gestenholtz watched in wonder, hands still tucked into her apron pockets.

'Quickly, please,' Max said as they busied themselves with their buckles and headsets. 'We've got to go right now if we're going to make that refuelling stop.'

Nick had just pulled the door to as the aircraft lifted off, rising gently in to the air until it had cleared the trees. Octavia looked down at the *schloss*. She saw Otto stagger out of the wrecked car and start stumbling towards them. His face was contorted and he was clearly screaming at the top of his lungs but they couldn't hear a thing over the roar of the helicopter's engine. The old woman, staring upwards in amazement, mouthed the word 'Flora' again, as the aircraft lifted away and disappeared over the tree tops.

'That,' said Max, 'was easier than we had any right to expect.'

'Not so easy,' Nick said with a laugh, tucking his pistol

back into his jacket. 'But it wasn't as nasty as it could have been if that shithead hadn't knocked himself out.'

Octavia turned to her sister, hardly able to believe that Flora was back with her again. She looked tired and thin, but her eyes were bright with happiness despite the tears she was still shedding. Their hands were clasped tightly together, as though they would never let each other go again.

Part Three

67

The day after Octavia returned to London with Flora, Roddy had sent her a message.

Iseult is awake. Come and see her.

Octavia had gone to the hospital, half fearing what she was going to find. Roddy had paid for Iseult to be moved to a private room and had hired a nurse who was with her day and night, making sure that she received the highest standards of care. Once Iseult began to eat, Roddy said, he would arrange for the finest food in London to be brought to her, whatever might tempt her appetite back. But it was uncertain how long it would be before her face would have healed well enough for her to be able to eat normal food. With bandages still covering most of her face so that she was unable to open her mouth very far, it would be purées and very soft things for a good few weeks.

The first visit had not been the worst by any means. Iseult had been very drowsy then, coming to her senses after nearly a week, still dazed on the heavy-duty painkillers that were constantly dripping into her bloodstream. 'What happened?' she asked, her voice sounding thick and strange through her swollen mouth. 'What am I doing here?'

Octavia held her hand, which was still in bandages. 'You're in hospital, sweetheart. You had an accident, remember?'

'Accident?' Only one of Iseult's arresting yellow-green eyes was visible, the other covered by a thick pad and closely bandaged. 'What was it? The car?'

'No . . . no . . .' Octavia looked up at Roddy, who was grey-faced. Neither of them wanted to tell her. 'Can't you remember anything?'

'No . . . no . . . I'm so tired.' Her eye flickered and drooped shut and she sank into sleep again.

Roddy rubbed a hand over his stubbly head. 'I don't know how I'm going to tell her.'

'Have any of her family been? Can't they tell her?'

Roddy gave her a look. 'You've never met her sisters, have you? Yes, they've been in. But, put it this way, I wouldn't want to hear about my severe trauma and disfigurement from one of them. Her mother sent a card and a bunch of flowers –' he nodded to a bouquet drooping in a vase in the corner '– and says she'll pop in when she has the time.'

Octavia gave a small laugh of outrage. 'Great! When she can fit it into her diary . . .'

'No one else knows about this yet,' Roddy said, moving closer to Iseult's side and gazing down at her. 'I've managed to keep it under wraps. I know she wouldn't want it to be gossiped about.' He looked up at Octavia. He was tired, she could tell, from his constant commuting between Paris and London. He had had to return to work but came over every other day to see Iseult. 'I'll tell her what happened. It was my fault anyway. If I hadn't kept that stupid studio in that filthy block of flats, this would never have happened.'

'It wasn't your fault,' Octavia said softly. 'It was that brute who kept those dreadful dogs.'

When she'd returned to see Iseult the following day, her friend had been much more awake, and now knew what had happened.

'I wish they had killed me, the damn things,' she muttered through her puffy lips. 'They say my eye is gone, so I shall see this half-arsed way for the rest of my life.'

'Oh, Iseult...' Octavia had almost wept for her then, horrified to think of Iseult's best, most unusual feature, that pair of slanting yellowish eyes, ruined for ever.

But that was nothing compared to the day Iseult saw her face for the first time. The surgeons had done what they could in the initial operation, but their priority had been simply to save tissue and reattach skin and muscle. A plastic surgeon had attended too, but it would only be later that they could begin work on trying to repair the aesthetic damage: the scars left by those tearing, ripping teeth.

Iseult's scream had echoed from her room and out into the corridor. The nurses on the ward desk had looked up, and then at each other, knowing what must be happening.

The dogs had taken a fair bit of flesh when they'd ripped Iseult's face from the bones of her skull, and what was left was now horribly distorted and twisted. Livid purple weals where the tears were healing covered the entire left side of her face, and it could be seen that her bad eye, although still covered, had been dragged downwards. She now had ripples of skin in ugly raised contours around it.

No one could pretend that Iseult would ever look vaguely normal again. Her face was difficult to see without gasping. The plastic surgeons came in and spoke positively about rebuilding and repairing the damage, about skin grafts and the wonderful advances in all the different types of facial surgery, and for a while they would all feel positive about her prospects. But after the surgeons had gone, they would realise that even if things could be improved, it would be a long and very painful journey.

'Is it even worth it, darlings?' Iseult would joke. 'My face wasn't exactly an oil painting to start with! Perhaps I could get used to this.'

But Octavia could hear the despair under the brittle humour. They knew that Iseult was calling on all her resources merely to face each new day, to fight the dreadfulness of her own situation.

'Whatever it takes,' Roddy said to Octavia, as they sat in the hospital café over cups of coffee one day. 'I can pay for the best in the world. If she has to go to America, wherever, it's no problem.'

Octavia smiled at him. 'We can both look after her. I'm sure it will be all right in the end.'

But it was hard to see how Iseult, fragile at the best of times, would be able to endure it.

68

Flora was utterly determined.

'I'm not going from one prison to another,' she said forcefully. 'That's been my whole life. I've got to break free. I won't let Otto win.'

Octavia and Vicky were stunned by her strength. On her return, Flora had been just as they had feared: thin, frightened, exhausted, and clearly badly abused, both mentally and physically. A doctor came to the house as soon as they got back, and said that while she was outwardly well, if a little underweight, she clearly needed complete rest.

Octavia refused to leave her sister's side, sleeping on a camp bed in her room, dashing to her when Flora wailed in the night and woke up sobbing and sweating.

'It's all right, sweetie, you're home now,' she'd soothe her, stroking her sister's hair as Flora trembled in her arms. 'You're all right. You're going to be fine.'

Flora would never say what had happened at the *schloss* to give her such awful nightmares. She spoke about her strange captivity with only Otto's mother for company and the total lack of any contact with the outside world. She said that Otto was cold and cruel to her, but she couldn't begin to describe the systematic degradation he had inflicted on her, designed perhaps to break her, but probably more to satisfy his own desires. Her horror came not just from what she had experienced but from the constant fear she had suffered of what he might do to her in the future. She had sensed strongly that he was only taking the first tentative steps in this game he enjoyed so much. He was a voyeur, that much was certain, obsessed with semen – his own and other people's – and with an interest in sadism. She was sure that he would have continued to experiment with her and that his interests would have gone from strength to strength, becoming far worse than anything she had suffered so far.

It was the realisation of her own lucky escape before the worst things came to pass that frightened Flora so much. In her dreams Otto was coming for her, finding her, locking doors and turning to smile at her with that thin cold smile, those brown eyes burning with a lust that was monumentally selfish.

'He'll never touch you again!' Octavia cried, when Flora sobbed out that he was coming, to keep him away from her. 'You never have to see or speak to him again!'

In the daytime Flora seemed to have recovered from her night terrors, and within a couple of days was keen to be outside, walking about the streets of London and relishing her freedom. *I was stupid to be afraid before,* she told herself, *what on earth did I have to be frightened of then?* Life outside still made her nervous, but now that she knew the dread of having it taken away, she was determined to overcome her fears.

Octavia came with her, though, and Steve, with his Special Forces bodyguard training, was never far away, just in case Otto tried to do something.

They all knew that however much they might wish the opposite, Flora's relationship with him was far from finished. She was married to him after all and had signed her fortune over to him. Flora's fear was that he could order her back somehow or claim control of her.

'No, that's just not possible. Besides, we'll hire the best lawyers,' declared Octavia, 'the very best there are! Don't worry, Flora, you'll be fine.'

Octavia had gone to visit Iseult. Flora was at home, alternately reading and dozing, when Vicky came in to tell her she had a visitor.

'Who?' Flora said, with frightened eyes, trying to quell the fear that automatically leapt up inside her.

'Don't worry, I wouldn't let anyone in I didn't trust.' Vicky smiled. 'I think you'll be pleased. It's Nick Falcon.'

'Really?' She felt her heart lift. 'Okay. I'll be right there.' She went to the dressing table to brush her hair. Her reflection told her that in just over a week, she was already far from the woman Nick had helped out of Otto's car that morning. She looked less haunted and gaunt, though she was still thin. The dark circles around her eyes were lifting, and the constant tremor in her hands was beginning to subside. It was wonderful to have a fresh wardrobe of clothes to wear as well – she couldn't bring herself to put on anything she'd worn in the castle. Now she was simply

517

dressed in jeans, dusky pink vest top and a light cream cardigan. She made sure she looked all right, and then went downstairs.

She opened the drawing-room door tentatively and peeped round it. There he was, in a dark suit, his black hair curling onto the collar. Seeing him was like witnessing someone in colour after knowing only black-and-white. After months spent with Otto, Nick seemed incredibly vivid, glowing with life and health and strength. Otto, she knew now, was a pathetic weakling who enjoyed exerting power over her, probably to make up for his own deficiencies. Nick, she sensed, had no such problems. He moved like a man who was confident in himself – but then, he was a good six foot tall and startlingly handsome with it, from the silver streaks in the black hair at his temples to those penetratingly sharp black eyes.

'Hey,' he said, standing up as she came in. His eyes brightened. 'How are you?'

Flora moved towards him and there was an awkward moment while they faced each other not sure whether to shake hands or to embrace. The drama that they'd been through together seemed to have bonded them even though they knew so little about each other.

'Hi,' Flora said with a smile, and went forward to kiss his cheek: it was faintly stubbly under her lips.

They stood back and regarded one another.

'You look a hell of a lot better,' Nick said heartily. 'You were kind of beat-up looking when I last saw you.'

She reached out and took his warm hand in hers, surprising herself by the action. 'I owe you such a lot,' she said sincerely. 'You saved me back there. Octavia told me it was your idea to come and get me – another

518

hour and Otto and I would have been gone. And . . .' she smiled '. . . if it hadn't been for your good aim, I could have been in that car, heading down the mountain.'

Nick looked pleased but embarrassed. 'Anyone would have done the same.' He stared at the floor and then coughed. 'Anyway . . . bearing in mind what a major situation we had there, I just wanted to come by and see how you are.'

Flora nodded. 'You know what? I'm doing so much better than I thought I would be. I just don't want to waste my time. Otto's stolen so much of my life, I'm determined not to let him have any more.'

'That's a great attitude,' Nick said, admiration in his dark eyes.

'Come on, let's sit down. I'll get us some tea.'

'Er, coffee, if you have it, please,' he said with a laugh. 'I've lived in Britain a while now, but I've never picked up the habit of drinking tea.'

They sat together and talked. Flora wanted to speak about anything but her ordeal, so she asked him about his life, and he told her about growing up in Chicago and how his mother, an English doctor, had brought the family over here when he was a teenager and he'd ended up staying.

'But you never lost your accent,' remarked Flora, thinking how much she liked his easy way of talking and the way his eyes changed from brown to black depending on the light.

'Nope.' He shook his head. 'They say that once a boy's voice breaks, he's stuck with the accent he had at that moment.'

'Really?'

He laughed. 'I dunno. It's probably a myth. Actually, I've found having an American accent useful. English people are always judging one another by the way they talk. I slip out of that net – and into a whole different one called "stupid Yanks".'

Flora laughed too. *This is bliss*, she thought. *A normal conversation with a normal man. But* – she reminded herself – *I thought Otto was normal. How am I ever going to trust my judgement again?*

After they'd chatted and drunk their coffee, Nick looked awkward and said, 'At some point, we ought to talk about the situation with your husband, you know.'

'Yes.' Flora looked down into her cup. 'But not right now.'

'Do you still want me to stay on the case?' he asked gently. 'There's going to be a lot to sort out.'

'Yes, I do,' she said at once. 'I don't want a stranger involved.'

'Because I think you've got good grounds for annulment,' Nick said seriously. 'I'm going to look into all the options for you, okay? I want to do all I can for you. I mean it.'

'Thank you. Thank you so much.'

'Don't thank me.' He smiled at her and his dark eyes softened. 'I'm going to take great pleasure in helping you get this jerk out of your life for good.'

69

'One day you'll have to meet my sister,' Octavia said to Ethan over a table in Scott's, where they were dining. 'It's weird to think we've been together all this time, and you haven't met her.'

'Yeah. How's she doing? Is she okay?' Ethan prepared to slurp down another oyster from the icy platter in front of him.

'She's fine – amazing, considering – but I think she's not really up to meeting strangers right now.'

'Fine by me. Whenever. Listen, are you coming to Shagi's party later tonight? She's giving a bash at her place. It's going to be wild, knowing her. She told me it was going to be super-classy – you know what that means?'

Octavia shook her head.

'Ah, you're getting boring in your old age,' he said dismissively.

'I'm staying in with my sister,' she said pointedly. 'Remember?' She stared at him as he ate his oysters, anointing each one with a spoonful of shallot vinegar before sucking it down.

She was beginning to realise that Ethan was fine when it came to discussing business, and very happy indeed to talk about ways of spending money and matters of style. And, of course, he was more than delighted to practise his mind-blowing sexual techniques on her. But with anything else he was less than interested. He tried to pretend that he cared about Iseult and her recovery, or about Flora's state of mind, but he was hopeless at it. He'd been more excited by the fact that Octavia had been in Max's helicopter than by the news that she'd brought her kidnapped sister home – although, to be fair, she'd deliberately kept some of the details sketchy, knowing that Flora would want her to keep things private.

Still, Ethan was always pressing her to come out with him to parties and restaurants. Most of the time she refused. Flora needed her, and Octavia was damned if she was ever going to let her sister down again. She had moved back full-time to the Chelsea house, and it had been noticeable that Ethan never visited. Shagi had taken him under her wing and introduced him to a whole new world of Middle Eastern luxury and high living, taking him with her as she partied in Dubai, lazed in Arabian palaces, or went to amazing three-day festivals of luxury in silken tents in the Kazakhstani desert.

Since Shagi had joined the Butterfly board, Ethan's appetite for luxury had grown even more voracious. Suddenly he needed more: a steel-blue limited-edition Maserati, a yet-to-be released cherry red Porsche, a long, lean yellow Lamborghini. He was constantly badgering Octavia to buy a plane – if not for herself then for Butterfly, to put at the disposal of its directors.

He had been bitten by the art bug, too, thanks to Shagi's taking him to a high-class gallery, and now talked constantly about how he needed to invest in some important pieces, and did Octavia think three million was too much for a Warhol original, considering it was only a little one and not all that famous either?

Since Flora had returned, traumatised and beaten, all these things seemed merely frivolous and pointless. Octavia began to look at Ethan with new eyes: he was still handsome and sexy, and she still enjoyed – very much – being taken to bed by him. But the mad infatuation she had once felt for him seemed to have run its course. Sometimes she felt as though she didn't know him at all.

But how can we split up? Our lives are completely entangled. I owe my companies to him, he basically runs everything. I couldn't manage alone.

There was no way Ethan could not be in her life. She needed him too much.

Later that night, after she had brushed Flora's hair for her and made sure she was asleep, Octavia wandered about her own room restlessly. She went to the window and opened it, letting the cool night air in, and sat down in the window seat, looking at the twinkling lights that stretched across the city. Somewhere over to the west, Ethan was at Shagi's grand mansion, drinking and partying with other millionaires, comparing the cut of a suit and the finish of a hand-made shoe and eyeing up what others were wearing on their wrists. She was glad she wasn't with him.

A vision of Max floated unbidden into her mind. She'd hardly paid any attention to him when they'd finally arrived back at Battersea, she'd been so wrapped up in Flora. He'd sent them straight home, guessing that they needed to be together.

I've never really thanked him, she thought with horror. *He did that for us – for me, when he didn't even like me – and I've not shown him any gratitude.*

She went to her dressing table and picked up her phone.

I'll have to put that right as soon as I can.

70

The press thought it was just another ridiculous high-fashion wheeze.

Iseult Rivers-Manners has reached a new level of English eccentricity, wrote one gossip columnist. *Her latest fad is to wear a thick black veil over her face wherever she goes. How will this one go down with the fashion crowd?*

The veil was Iseult's solution to living with her new face. She had surprised them all with her recovery, determined to be out of hospital and back at home as soon as possible. After a few more weeks, with the help of her trained nurse, a car and driver supplied by Roddy, and many different kinds of pill and tablet, she was able to return to her Bayswater flat. Once there, though, she hardly ventured out, preferring to watch the world go by from her windows, refusing all invitations and letting only a favoured few visitors come to her. When she did receive people, she wore the black veils that stopped anyone seeing exactly what had happened to her.

Iseult's friends showed their loyalty. Details of the attack were kept from the press, and her sudden absence from the social scene wasn't reported. People with influence made sure that nosy journalists on the hunt for a good story understood that any attention paid to Iseult would be most unwelcome. As a result, she was left in peace to heal.

Octavia hoped that Iseult might return to work and perhaps forget some of what she had suffered in the excitement of the Noble's re-design, but she refused even to consider visiting the shop. Octavia was allowed to bring sketches and ideas to her, or to email designs, and Iseult would comment on them, although without much enthusiasm.

'I need you, Iseult,' Octavia pleaded. 'I can't do Noble's without you.'

'Sorry, my darling,' she said with a sigh. 'I will get my mojo back, I promise. But it's hard right now. I'm sure you understand.'

One day, about eight weeks after the accident, Octavia went round to find Jasmine and Rosie and a few of the old crowd there. They were delighted to see her, asking her where she'd been and how come they hadn't met her at all the major parties, the gallery openings, film premières and the usual society round.

'I've been . . . busy,' said Octavia, but didn't go into detail about caring for Flora and working at Noble's.

They were just the same, she thought, as they whooped it up, shrieking and giggling while Iseult mixed them her famous White Ladies. She hoped the girls had cheered her friend up but the effect was almost macabre as she sat on her chaise-longue, swathed in her veil, taking her cocktail glass behind it to sip at her drink. It was usually Iseult who provided the focus of colour and style; it was awful that she was hidden away like this.

The others seemed to find it odd as well and they weren't seen much at Iseult's flat after that. When Octavia went round to visit one day, taking a folder of ideas for her approval, she had the impression that there were fewer and fewer visitors calling round.

'Do you know, Octavia,' Iseult said idly, looking through a suggested autumn range of bags, 'you have quite grown up lately. You have surprised me. You're taking this business of yours very seriously. I'm impressed.' She had taken off her veil while Octavia was there, as she had already seen the worst. Even so, it was hard to look at the raised weals and puckered skin, and to know that one of those striking eyes was gone.

'Thank you,' Octavia said, touched.

'Don't grow up too much darling.' Iseult attempted a smile that twisted oddly, pulling downwards at one side instead of upwards. 'It all goes so fast, the carelessness of youth. Oh, don't be like those other little fools with their drugs and their drink and their limitless capacity for vacuity. But don't be too serious either. Remember to have fun.'

Octavia laughed lightly. 'Of course I will. As long as you promise to have fun with me.'

'Mmm.' Iseult turned a page and said no more.

71

'Hello, Nick,' Octavia said, coming into the drawing room where he was waiting. She was simply dressed in black trousers and white Chanel shirt trimmed with black ribbon at the collar and cuffs. Flora followed behind, also in black trousers and a white top, though they hadn't planned their outfits to match. It often happened like that.

'Whoah,' Nick said, looking from one to the other. 'You two really are identical, aren't you? I didn't notice it so much in the helicopter but now you're both on home turf . . . well, it's kind of freaky.'

The girls laughed and looked at one another.

'We don't really notice it so much ourselves,' Flora said. 'I suppose we're used to it.'

Molly brought in coffee, hot milk and some plain biscuits while they settled down, chatting lightly about nothing and preparing for the real business in hand. It made sense to keep Nick on the case to do the investigative work, and meanwhile he'd recommended a firm of top solicitors who could begin to deal with the legal work needed to assess exactly what Flora had assigned to Otto, and how to get it back.

'Right,' Nick said, when they were all comfortable. He pulled a file out of his battered old briefcase. His suit looked well-worn and frayed at the edges against the immaculate backdrop of the sea-green sofa with its Icelandic-print cushions. 'So, I've continued to investigate Otto Gestenholtz and I've also kept in close touch with Sirjiwan Singh, your solicitor at Fawcett & Mather. We've come up with some interesting facts about the man who duped you.'

'He was very convincing,' Flora said suddenly, keen not to appear a complete fool. 'He even called off our engagement because I hadn't told him how rich I was.'

'A nice touch,' remarked Nick. 'Made him out to be the opposite of what he actually was. And you say he told you the pre-nup was to protect *his* interests, not yours, right?' He shook his head. 'The guy has some front, I'll give him that. As it turns out, you didn't sign a pre-nup of any kind. The so-called lawyer you went to see was probably a fake, or else Otto's employee. I'm sure he wanted to keep you a million miles from any kind of real pre-nup or lawyer. You did, though, give him carte blanche to access your money, and as you girls haven't protected your cash assets, it was pretty easy for him.'

Flora glanced over at Octavia and saw her own embarrassment reflected back at her. *What were we thinking? We've been like children in charge of a sweetie shop, playing all day long without any thought of how to manage the place.*

'So Sirjiwan is working on shutting down access to your funds. That shouldn't be difficult. The difficulty

529

will be if Otto has already removed a great deal for his personal use – we're just working on that right now.'

'Let him have it!' burst out Flora. 'I don't care.'

'That's not really the right approach to take with criminals, on the whole,' Nick said with a wry smile. 'He ought to be made to give it back and punished for taking it in the first place.'

Octavia shifted in her seat and looked uneasy. 'But it's going to be hard to prove everything isn't it? Without going to the police and so on.'

Nick coughed uncomfortably and shuffled some of the papers he was taking out of the file. 'In a word, yes,' he said. 'It's up to you what you want to do.'

The sisters looked at one another.

'If we can keep it quiet, get out of this without any more trouble, then that's what I want,' Flora said at last.

Nick fixed her with his intense dark stare. 'Are you sure? You do know that leaves Otto free to go on conning women and treating them the way you've been treated? If this Wiebke Mullinsdorf had spoken up after she was robbed by him, you might not have gone through all this.'

Flora froze. Her head whirled after what Nick had just said. She felt panicked and afraid all of a sudden and could feel the blood drain from her face. She staggered to her feet. 'I . . . I . . . W-w-w-would you excuse me?' Hardly able to see suddenly, she fled from the sitting room and out into the hall. She sat down on the stairs and put her head in her hands.

A moment later, she heard the sitting-room door open. Someone walked softly towards her, and then sat down beside her.

It was Nick.

'Hey,' he said softly. 'I'm sorry. I didn't mean to upset you. I guess I get a little . . . businesslike sometimes. I forget this is very raw for you. I just want to get that guy, that's all, and have him punished for what he did to you. Just thinking about him makes me furious.'

Flora felt him move, as though he'd wanted to reach out and touch her and then changed his mind. She lifted her head and looked at him. *He's so handsome,* she thought. *So alive.* Somehow she could only remember Otto as being half alive, as faded as old wallpaper that had been too long in the sun. 'It's all right,' she whispered. 'Really.'

'I don't want you to be hurt any more,' said Nick in a low voice. 'Understand? Just tell me when to shut the hell up.'

'Okay.' She managed to smile weakly.

'As long as you know I'm on your side. Always.'

It didn't take Otto long to show his true colours. As soon as Flora's solicitors informed him that access to their client's accounts was closed and that the return of the £50 million he'd removed from them would now be required, Otto shot back a response.

Flora, he wrote, would be well advised not to pursue the matter. He was willing to agree to the end of the marriage but his divorce terms would be not only to retain the £50 million he already had, but to acquire another £25 million. 'As this does not constitute even half of your client's assets, I consider this to be more than fair,' he declared.

That was the extent of his formal dealings with Flora's representatives.

If this is all he wants, she thought, *then perhaps we can let him have it.* But she had a feeling that he wouldn't stop there. And anyway, could she live with herself, knowing that he was still out there, preying on other women, doing to them what he'd done to her?

72

Vicky came in as Octavia was putting the finishing touches to her outfit, attaching a pearl and gold earring to her lobe.

'Wow! You look brilliant,' Vicky said admiringly. 'Are you going out with Ethan tonight?'

Octavia flushed slightly and said, 'Oh . . . no . . . I'm going out with Max Northam. I'm thanking him for his help in rescuing Flora.'

'It's okay,' Vicky said affably. 'You don't have to justify yourself to me. You can go out with whoever you like, as far as I'm concerned.'

'It's not a date,' Octavia said quickly, pushing a white resin, pearl-encrusted cuff on to her wrist. She was wearing a silk and lace evening dress, a modest knee-length style and high-cut at the neck. Somehow it didn't feel appropriate to be going out in full-on sexy mode with Max Northam – but nevertheless she knew she looked appealing, and the dress clung to her in all the right places.

'Sure.' Vicky went over and sat on the sofa by the window. 'Listen, I wanted to talk to you about Flora.'

'Is she all right?' Octavia asked quickly, spinning round to face Vicky.

'Yes, yes, she's fine. She's getting ready for a quiet night in with lasagne, some rubbish telly and me. But . . . I just wanted to know what you thought about Nick's report on your mother?'

Octavia froze momentarily and then carried on checking her make-up. 'What about it?' she asked, a slight edge to her voice.

'Well . . . it's still sitting there in Flora's email account. I guess he'll need to know what she wants to do about it at some point.'

'He can wait, can't he?'

Vicky looked at her with understanding. 'Yes, but should we tell Flora? Doesn't she have a right to know it's there?' Her tone became sympathetic, 'I know it's hard for you.'

'Damn right,' snapped Octavia. She turned to her cousin and stared at her. 'Listen, I think this whole idea is madness. We don't need more bloody trouble after everything that's happened, and I don't think Flora is equipped to deal with further trauma. The chances are that we'll track our mother down and she'll be a raving lunatic or something equally dreadful. As far as I'm concerned, we should just let it go.'

She looked back to her mirror and smoothed her dress.

There was a pause. Then Vicky said, 'As it happens, I think you're right. Flora is far too fragile at the moment. I don't think we need worry her about her email right now, she's shown no interest in looking at it. I think she's concerned Otto will try and contact her that way. I'm going to set her up a new account, one he won't have the address for.'

Octavia looked relieved. She went over to the bed and picked up a cream cashmere wrap. 'Good,' she said, obviously pleased by Vicky's response. 'And if I have my way, we'll never open that report. Ever.'

Steve took her swiftly from Chelsea to the narrow back streets of Mayfair, then up South Audley Street to Harry's Bar, a discreet members-only club in a tall red-brick townhouse on the corner of Mount Street.

Inside, the club was decorated with striking Fortuny fabrics, gilt-edged mirrors and brass lamps. The ambiance was elegant, comfortable and old-fashioned without being fusty or boring. Max was waiting to meet her, smart in a muted Richard Anderson suit, and he greeted her with a kiss on her cheek.

'Does this mean we're friends?' Octavia said, as they were shown to their table.

'I guess it means we're not enemies.' Max grinned. 'It's Italian food here,' he added, as they were given their menus. 'I hope that's all right.'

'It's lovely,' said Octavia. She was feeling oddly gauche and nervous, butterflies fluttering in her stomach. 'I adore Italian food.'

'You look very nice this evening,' he said casually. 'That dress suits you.'

'Thank you,' she said, flattered. She had the impression that he did not hand out compliments lightly.

The waiter came up. Max greeted him by name and they had a quick conversation in Italian. Max looked over at Octavia. 'Sergio says you must try the tagliatelle with butter and truffles. The truffles are the finest, from Alba, and he says you'll never taste anything else like them. If not that, he says the *prosciutto di* Parma is exquisite.'

'Well, I'll just listen to Sergio, he obviously knows what he's talking about. The truffle thing sounds great.'

She watched Max as he ordered for them both. He really had the most odd ugly-handsome face she had ever seen. His features were large and heavy, with a jutting brow and chin. His dark hair had prominent streaks of grey at the temples. And yet, when he fixed his blue gaze on Octavia, and smiled, he went from rough-looking to almost angelic. It was very strange.

The bottle of Pouilly Fumé arrived. As the waiter poured it out, Max said, 'So how is your sister?'

'She's doing amazingly well, thanks. Much better than I'd hoped. It's as though she had a choice between being broken by it all or surviving – and she's chosen to survive.' Octavia took a sip of chilled wine.

'I'm glad to hear it. She looked in quite a state when we got her back.'

'And thank you so much for your help. I mean it, it was amazing. We couldn't have done it without you,' Octavia said, in heartfelt fashion. 'I owe you so much.'

'You're welcome.' Max fixed her with one of his piercing blue stares. 'I haven't asked too much about what was going on there, because I think there is probably a limit to what I ought to know, but I'm trusting that you know what you're doing and that you're on the side of the angels.'

'Really?' Octavia raised her eyebrows at him. 'You're trusting *me*? The spoilt little rich girl? Not so long ago, you wouldn't trust me as far as you could throw me.'

'Don't tempt me to throw you anywhere,' Max said, but with a glint of amusement in his eyes. 'Listen, I admit it. Maybe I was hasty in my judgements. I don't think you are quite as flighty and air-headed as I assumed.'

'How kind,' she rejoined tartly.

'Well – you've got to admit it was an easy assumption to make. Your crowd of friends aren't exactly saints.'

'What do you know about them?'

'You'd be surprised. I know enough to be sure that I wouldn't want any girl I care about to hang around with them too long, unless she had her head firmly screwed on.'

Their starters came and they went quiet as the waiter set their plates down.

'If you must know, I thought you were very rude,' Octavia said, when the waiter had gone.

Max shrugged. 'I don't stand on ceremony. I get right to the point.'

'I know that now.'

He looked her straight in the eye. 'I'm also honest. You came to me for help, and you managed to convince me to do something I wouldn't do for just anyone. I respect your courage, and I respect what you did. I'm prepared to admit that.'

Octavia felt absurdly pleased to have his respect. 'Thank you.'

'Now, eat that thing you ordered, and let's talk about something other than my manners.'

'See?' She speared a piece of pasta on her fork. '*So* rude.' Then she laughed to show she was joking and Max joined in.

As they ate, he said, 'Your business – how is that going?'

Octavia looked down at her plate, toying with the next morsel of her starter but not picking it up. 'I suppose I haven't been giving it my full attention, what with Flora needing me so much. But I've been working on the re-design and coming up with lots of new ideas. I'm going to give it more time now Flora needs me less.'

Max chewed thoughtfully on his ceviche of sea bass, and frowned. 'Well, I can understand that circumstances have been rather difficult. But you mustn't leave your business alone for too long. They can founder without attention, sometimes irreversibly.'

'Yes, but . . .' Octavia put down her fork and picked up her wine glass, swirling it round and round until the straw-coloured liquid inside formed its own little whirlpool. 'I have Ethan for that. He deals with figures, the bits I don't understand.'

'I see.'

'If I'm honest,' Octavia said in a rush, 'it's been harder than I expected. I thought they'd welcome me there with open arms, but as soon as I walk through the door of Noble's it's like everyone hates me. I hardly get a smile.'

Max shook his head. 'An unhappy workforce is never good. What do you think is the problem?'

'I don't know.' She couldn't stop a slightly plaintive note from entering her voice. 'I haven't done anything wrong!'

'Haven't you?' Max spoke casually but there was something in his tone that made Octavia look up anxiously. 'Are you sure?'

'I don't think so,' she said cautiously. 'Not that I know

of anyway. I suppose it's been a big change for them. And it was really unfortunate that the old chairman died just after the deal was done.' She frowned. 'Do you think that's the reason the staff hate me? Because Butterfly bought the Radcliffes out?' She couldn't help feeling indignant. 'We paid them well enough!'

'That's not really the point. No one likes a hostile takeover, particularly not when the bidders seem to be a little . . . sneaky about their intentions. I've heard some things about the transaction and looked into it after Ethan talked to me about joining the board. The way that Robert Young was – as I understand it – bribed to change sides was considered a little unsportsmanlike.'

Octavia was confused. Robert Young had made a business decision, nothing more, surely? 'Ethan told me it was all completely normal,' she said, frowning. 'He said that people would be impressed by my business acumen when the deal came off.'

Max said nothing. There was an uncomfortable pause alleviated by the arrival of the waiter who cleared away the starter plates, while bantering with Max in Italian, and then their main courses arrived. It was only when everything was settled again and they were taking the first mouthfuls of their excellent food that Octavia said, 'Is this why you're not going to join the Butterfly board? Because of the takeover?'

'I'm afraid so. I haven't warmed to your boyfriend. He's not quite my cup of tea. Usually I'm a big fan of young men with ambition, drive and talent. But occasionally I meet one who gives me a peculiar feeling – the sense that I really ought not to get involved too deeply with this one. That's what I get from your boyfriend. I'm sorry to hurt your feelings.'

'No, don't worry. It's fine, really.' Octavia felt her spirits swoop. What on earth must he think of her? He seemed to think her boyfriend was both callous and dangerous. It was a wonder he wanted to be out with her at all.

'Hey, come on.' Max smiled at her. 'We just decided we were friends, didn't we? Let's talk about something else.'

He told her a little about his time in the army, and as they relaxed in each other's company Octavia talked more about her past. He was interested to hear about the long years behind the closed doors of Homerton, with no experience of the outside world, no school, no university.

'Then I was wrong about you,' he said, looking at her with that piercing gaze. 'You're not like those other girls at all. You've had to learn rather a lot in the time you've been in the world, and you've achieved more than most.'

After dinner, when they were both feeling replete and languorous, he suggested they should go to Colette's for a nightcap. 'It's the nightclub just round the corner in Berkeley Square.'

They wandered out into the Mayfair night. Max offered her his arm and they walked together through the cool air, chatting as they went. Octavia felt comfortable with him now, she realised. He didn't seem so prickly and unapproachable as he had at first. He was making jokes and smiling so often, she'd begun to think it was normal for him to wear that lighter, handsomer expression.

Colette's was quiet and elegant, with couples or small groups of people laughing and talking together over chilled bottles of champagne or vodka cocktails. 'Still early,' Max muttered, leading her to a red velvet banquette in the sitting room opposite the bar. 'The party doesn't usually kick off here until much later. We'll have some peace for a while yet.'

They drank a bottle of club champagne and he talked about Scotland and why he loved it so much. Octavia remembered the sensation of being in that cosy house and the sense of well-being it had engendered in her.

'How long have you been divorced?' she asked idly, watching the bubbles zoom to the top of her glass.

Max drank some champagne. 'I'm not divorced,' he said. 'Not yet, at least. My wife is in the process of making her demands clear.' He shrugged. 'I have a feeling she'll have quite a lot.'

'Are you going to give in to them?'

'That depends. Some fights are worth having and some aren't. I'm a fair man. I don't relish conflict for its own sake. And I have to remember I loved her once, even if I don't love her now.' He frowned, looking serious for a moment. Then he said slowly, 'Do you mind if I say something unforgivably schoolmaster-ish? It's been on my mind and I feel I have to say it. You've been very lucky, Octavia. You've been given an enormous inheritance. I admire the fact that you want to do something with it – and I think that's only right. Put it to work and make it do good things in the world. Either that, or give it away to others who need it more. But don't fritter it away. Don't let others take it from you. Don't let it be leached away and wasted.' He smiled at her, showing straight teeth. 'There. Excuse the little lecture.'

Octavia said nothing. She felt a stab of shame. She had thought of her money as there entirely for her own amusement, but the moment Max said this, she saw clearly that it was also a responsibility. She thought of everyone who worked at Noble's, from the cleaners to the sales assistants to the managers. They all depended on her for their livelihoods. No wonder they were nervous at the idea of a flighty rich girl buying the shop for a plaything. *I'll have to make sure I don't let them down.*

'And remember,' Max said softly, 'it doesn't do to rely too much on one person, or put all your trust in them. Always make sure you have plenty of advice from different sources.'

Just then a beautiful blonde girl, her hair piled up high on her head and her black evening dress discreetly sexy, came over and said, 'Max, how lovely to see you.'

He got to his feet. 'Allegra.' He kissed her cheeks. 'You look divine as usual. How are you? And how's David?'

'I'm fine, thank you, and so's David – but he isn't coming in tonight. He'll be so sorry to have missed you.'

Octavia looked up questioningly. Max said, 'Allegra, may I introduce Octavia Beaufort? Octavia, this is Allegra McCorquodale, who runs this excellent club.'

'Hello,' Allegra said with a friendly smile. 'I hope you enjoy yourself here. I'd love a few of the younger crowd like you to join.'

Octavia said politely, 'I'm having a lovely time, thank

you,' but she couldn't help the cold feeling that crawled over her skin at the sight of the other girl and her obvious familiarity with Max. She felt suspicious and protective all at once. Allegra chatted to him for a while longer, and then wished them both a pleasant evening. It was only when she had gone that Octavia was able to relax, once she had him to herself again.

It was well after midnight when Max said, 'I think we'd better call it a night. I'll get my driver to take you home.'

'I can call Steve,' she said, disappointed that their evening was coming to an end. She felt contented and a little bit high. *From the champagne, I expect.*

'Don't be silly. You'll take my car home. I like to walk late at night and it's not so far to my place from here.'

They climbed the metal staircase back up to the outside world, emerging from the cosy darkness and warmth of Colette's into the crisp night air. People passed them on their way into the club, their evening about to begin as Octavia and Max's was ending. As they stood on the pavement, he hummed a few bars of music.

'I love that song, don't you?' he said. 'I always think of "A Nightingale sang in Berkeley Square" when I come here.'

'I don't know it,' Octavia said, feeling keenly that her life was nowhere near as rich and full as Max's. She was still so ignorant of the world. Her years spent locked away from everyday life meant that hundreds of references everyone else knew simply passed her by. *I need to learn,* she thought longingly. *I need to find out what I've been missing.*

'You don't know it?' He looked surprised, then put his hands in his pockets and hummed a bit more of the melody. Then very softly, he sang a couple of lines in an unexpectedly sweet baritone:

> *And as we kissed and said 'Good night'*
> *A nightingale sang in Berkeley Square . . .*

Just then, Max's mustard-coloured Daimler drew smoothly to a halt beside them. A doorman pulled the passenger door open for Octavia. Max settled her wrap round her shoulders, smiled, dropped a kiss on her cheek and whispered, 'Goodnight.'

Then she was in the car and he was saying, 'Take Miss Beaufort home, Clive,' and they were heading away, leaving him behind. Octavia turned and saw him put his hands in his pockets and set off at a jaunty pace in the opposite direction.

I wish . . . Oh, God, I don't even know what I wish . . .

73

When it happened, it was so unexpected that she almost forgot to feel afraid. Flora had popped out alone to a café not far from the house and had just bought herself a skinny latte and was heading for the door when she felt a hand on her arm.

She turned and found herself face to face with Otto.

She gasped, eyes wide and staring, hardly able to believe that she was looking again at that face that now seemed so unbelievably hideous to her, with its greyish complexion and small brown eyes, its childish hairlessness with eyebrows so faint they seemed to have been half pencilled in and then left.

Before she could speak, he began to talk, very quietly and very fast. 'Don't be afraid, Flora, I'm not going to hurt you, don't worry about that. I don't mean you any harm, it's important that you understand that. You are still my wife, I still love you despite that ridiculous stunt you pulled. There was no need for that, no need at all. You simply had to ask to go home, you know that. But I realise you are set on divorce, and while it breaks my heart I'm willing to agree to it.' As he spoke, a long, rapid mutter under his breath, he took her elbow and steered her towards the door, walking her outside while his eyes glanced quickly about, making sure that they were not being observed.

In a second, they were on the pavement, people walking past them oblivious as Otto kept on talking. 'The thing is, Flora, I need to preserve my financial independence, as I'm sure you understand. I've worked very hard, and indeed spent a great deal of money, to get where I am. But I need more, much more. You've been kind enough to share some of your fortune with me – and I'm sure you'll not be so mean-spirited as to request its return – but I need a little more to be absolutely sure that the rest of my life will be spent in the manner I desire. People, bad people, will advise you not to give me what is only my due. I don't wish you to listen to them. I have ensured you will not.'

Suddenly she realised that he was pressing a small envelope into her hands, just big enough to hold a compact disc.

'I will contact you when you've had a chance to look at these.' With a small smile, barely more than twist of his lips, he was gone, striding off down the busy street, leaving her staring after him and beginning to feel shock crawling over her.

Flora raced home, her breath coming in short gasps and her hands shaking. Once inside she ran up the stairs to her study and sat down at her computer. She hadn't been here since her return, somehow unable to face this particular window on the world. A few moments later the system had booted up and the screen was bright with colour. She ripped open the envelope Otto had given her and put the disc inside into the drive. It began to whirr in the depths of the machine and a moment later a prompt box asked if she wanted to play the contents. She pressed yes.

There was a momentary pause and then, there they were in front of her: pictures of herself, naked, splayed on the bed, in all sorts of attitudes. There was that hated instrument Otto had used on her, protruding from her body. The photographs flicked quickly from one to the next, so that she barely had time to register one before another would replace it. In each, though, she noticed her face held the same frozen, blank expression – not the face of a woman in the throes of ecstasy but a numbed, removed look. Then another screen opened and, a second later, a video began to play.

She gasped, her hands flying to her mouth. It was herself and the builder Otto had forced her to have sex with. She was lying on her back on that awful great bed, one hand gripped around the huge dark red shaft of the builder's penis, moving it slowly up and down.

All along he had a camera on the bed!

She scrabbled for the mouse, found it and clicked the video off. Clicked again and again even after it had disappeared.

Then she ran to the bathroom, crouched down in front of the lavatory and was violently ill, heaving and heaving until there was nothing more to vomit.

74

Nick shook his head in disbelief, rubbing one large hand through his black hair. His eyes flashed with fury. Octavia and Flora sat on the sofa, huddled close together and holding hands, gazing up at him with huge, pleading eyes.

'The old ways are the best for Otto,' he said curtly. 'Good old-fashioned blackmail. You know what, I was seriously thinking about telling you to cut your losses with this guy and let him have the cash he's already got. But now he's starting to piss me off. I mean that seriously.'

'Wh-wh-wh-what are we going to do?' Flora said in a husky voice, her face pale.

'Mmm. Let me think.' Nick stood up and started to pace about the room, a frown of concentration on his face. He turned to face the girls on the sofa. 'He made sure he gave you this unmarked CD in person, right? So no electronic trail to him. My guess is that you'll have another episode of personal contact so he can tell you his demands, but to be honest it's perfectly clear. Unless you give him what he wants, he'll reveal these pictures to the world.'

Flora hung her head, her face flushing with shame. She hadn't shown anyone the contents of the disc and no one had asked to see them. She had barely been able to describe what was on there but Octavia had understood at once – she had known instantly that Otto had forced her sister into activities she had never wanted to take part in. She had been so angry that Flora had thought she might break something. Later, Octavia had gone out for a long run and when she'd returned her eyes had been red-rimmed. She had said then they must talk to Nick at once.

'I don't think I can bear it,' Flora had said, going dead white. For some reason, the idea of Nick knowing was particularly dreadful.

'You must. We have to. He'll help us.' Octavia refused to take no for an answer, even though Flora felt agonised with embarrassment, and not just that. She felt soiled and dirty and somehow complicit, as though she'd gone along willingly with Otto's desires.

'There's a video too,' Octavia said now.

Nick looked appalled. He clenched his fist. 'Christ, this guy is a fucking low-life – excuse my language, ladies.' He shook his head again, even more amazed. 'What a piece of shit! I guess he understands that the press go crazy for stories like this: wealthy, beautiful heiress in a real-life sex scandal, with the whole thing available for download.'

Octavia clasped her sister's hand even more tightly. 'Some people might be able to live this down,' she said, 'but not Flora. She's too sensitive, too delicate. This would kill her. We have to keep a lid on this.'

Nick looked over at Flora. His expression softened

'This is about you, honey. Is that what you want too? You want us to pay this guy off? We can, you know, with certain conditions and clauses to ensure he plays ball. You say the word and it's done. And you know what? I, for one, would completely understand. I would think no worse of you for it. This is a big bad choice and I'm fucking thankful I don't have to make it.'

Flora held on to Octavia for strength. Much of the resolution and determination she'd gathered over the last few weeks seemed have to melted away from her. She felt weak and helpless again, at Otto's mercy. Could she really live with those pictures in the public domain? The moments they had preserved were the worst of her life, the most desperately intimate and deeply hurtful memories she had. They'd be out there for the world to gawp over, laugh at, make jokes about, as though she didn't matter and as though she hadn't suffered.

I can't let it happen, she thought desperately. *I won't! I'll do whatever he wants . . .*

'Please,' she said, gazing up imploringly at Nick. 'Please – just make it go away!'

He stared at her for a long while, sympathy in his dark eyes. 'Okay, honey,' he said at last. 'You got it.'

Octavia volunteered to see Nick out. In the hallway, she stopped him for a moment.

'Nick,' she said urgently, 'I don't have to tell you what a state my sister is in.'

'No.' He looked down at her and she could see both compassion and anger burning in his eyes. 'She is in a bad way, and who can blame her, poor kid? I tell you what, my dream scenario is turning that shithead in to the police for fraud, false pretences and blackmail. But he's very effectively stopped that from happening.' Nick's expression became frustrated.

'It's not just this.' Octavia put her hand on his coat sleeve. 'It's that report on our mother. I want you to destroy it, Nick. Flora is so fragile, she mustn't be put through any further trauma. I want everything wiped from the file. And you have my guarantee that she will never want to know where our mother is.'

Nick looked awkward. 'You've put me in an uncomfortable position here, Octavia,' he said slowly, a furrow of concern appearing between his dark eyebrows. 'Your sister is the client, not you. I can't really destroy the work she commissioned on your orders.'

'You saw her in there!' Octavia said hotly. 'She's in no fit state to take any decisions herself! And with her in that condition, I have to act for her, don't you see?'

'I guess that makes sense.' He smiled his lopsided smile and Octavia could see how good-looking he was. She wondered if Flora had noticed it too. It was funny, but lately her own ideas of what was handsome had changed. She found a rugged, lived-in look more appealing than sugary good looks. Nick went on. 'I'm not sure . . . I've never worked with identical twins before. I'm not sure of the ethics of the situation. Can one be considered a kind of stand-in for the other?'

'Yes they can.' Octavia smiled back. 'I'm so glad you understand, Nick, thanks.'

She saw him out, relief flooding over her. Now they could put that thorny issue behind them once and for all. There was no need for the difficult and painful matter of their mother ever to see the light of day. She, for one, preferred it that way.

'Octavia?' It was Vicky, emerging from the shadow of the back hallway. 'I couldn't help overhearing what you were saying.' She came up to her cousin, her expression serious. 'I don't know if this is the right thing to do.'

'Of course it is,' snapped Octavia, irritated that she was interfering.

'Perhaps this is just the right time for Flora to find her mother. Perhaps she needs her now more than ever.'

'Don't be an idiot,' retorted Octavia. 'We don't know her! She left us, remember? How the hell could she be any use to us now?'

'You might be wrong,' Vicky said reasonably.

'I'm not wrong. And anyway it's too late now, Nick's going to destroy his records. I don't want Flora hurt even more then she is right now. Can't you see, it would kill her? I have to get back to my sister. She needs me.'

Octavia turned away, brushed past Vicky and left her standing there, staring after her.

75

I have to get my mind off everything, Octavia told herself. She was glad to be a support to her sister, and desperate to help her through her ordeal but the whole thing was exhausting for her too. She needed to get away from it and think about some of the other problems in her life – after all, they weren't simply going to disappear because of Flora's disaster. She still had a business to run.

Her last conversation with Max echoed in her mind. He was right; she should make her money do some good in the world, and she had to step up to the mark if she was going to make Noble's a success. She wanted to sort out the problems with the work-force and get the re-design going properly. Lately she'd begun to tire of the whole thing and rather regret that she'd been so hasty about getting involved. It had all seemed such wonderful fun at first, when it was her and Jasmine and Rosie – and, of course, the real creative talent, Iseult. But Jasmine and Rosie and the rest of the gang had melted away lately, not very interested in the realities of running a business when there was hard work to be done. Without the force of Iseult's personality driving them, they had lost their enthusiasm for the project. There were new parties to go to, more people to meet, more drugs to take. Jasmine was, apparently, going out with Ferdy now, while Rosie was virtually unreachable now that she had become even more hooked on ketamine, spending most of her time lost in a K-hole of oblivion.

If only Iseult hadn't been attacked and changed so much, Octavia thought longingly. *Then I would know what to do. She'd be here to help me.*

But Iseult didn't show any signs of returning to her old self. She remained locked away in her Bayswater flat, with only a select few people allowed to see her. Octavia was one of them and went round as often as she could, laden with fruit, muffins, music and magazines, hoping to reawaken her friend's interest in the outside world.

Iseult was always happy to see her, though she still remained swathed behind a thick veil now that the bandages were pretty much off. She wore an elegant black velvet patch over her blind eye which gave her a nicely piratical air, and now wore only black, her former vivid greens, yellows and purples banished to the back of her wardrobe.

'Because I'm in mourning, darling, for my poor face. It was only a plain old thing but it was all I had, and I did like it. Far more than I ever realised at the time,' Iseult would say, smiling that strange twisting leer that looked more agonised than amused, and made the scars of her face buckle in an alarming way. Her beautiful, distinctive speaking voice was changed too, so that she always sounded as though she had just had an anaesthetic at the dentist.

The strange thing was, Octavia thought, that Iseult seemed quite cheerful. She spoke about her trips to her doctors, consultants and surgeons, and the forth-coming plastic surgery operations, in tones of huge amusement. She detailed her adventures of walking about town, when she did venture out, with her damaged face and her veil, and the comments of cruel adults and innocent, uncomprehending children, and laughed hugely at all of it.

But Octavia could not persuade her to come out and resume her old life.

'People will soon get used to you, I think you're underestimating them,' Octavia said gently. 'They love you for who you are.'

'Darling Octavia,' Iseult said, her smile twisting. 'Can't you understand, my whole life has been devoted to appearances? Fashion, image – they've been every-thing to me. I'm still trying to understand how I can go on like this. It's a terrible struggle. Oh, I know I'm vain and shallow and silly, but that's how it is. I need time. Please – you won't rush me, will you?'

'Of course not,' Octavia said, feeling awful. The last thing she wanted to do was put pressure on her friend. The accident was still very recent, she reminded herself. It was early days.

One day, as she arrived, she bumped into a familiar figure, dapper in a teal cord jacket and buff-coloured flannels. 'Gerry!' she said in astonishment.

'Octavia,' said Gerry Harbord, a smile playing about his lips, nut-brown eyes sparkling. 'What a *very* long time no see. How are you, darling? Keeping shop?'

'I'm fine but . . . but what on earth are you doing here?' She could only gape at him. Wasn't this the man who had famously feuded with Iseult for years?

He bent towards her conspiratorially and raised his eyebrows towards his bouffant white hair. 'Darling, when the chips are really down, that's when we forget old antagonisms and stick together. Talking of which, my love, I'd like to come and see you some time, if I may?'

'Of course.' She still couldn't get over the shock of seeing him here. 'Any time.'

In the flat, she told Iseult who she had met by the front door. 'Did you know he was coming?'

'No.' Iseult laughed. 'It was rather a turn-up. But he was sweet. He quite touched my heart. Isn't it odd, the people who stay around – and the people who vanish? It's never quite whom one expects.' Then she said carelessly, 'Have you heard from Roddy recently?'

Octavia paused, knowing the answer mattered to her very much. 'No, he's hugely busy with the new collections and putting the finishing touches to his latest show. It's very important for him. He has to prove he has more than one season in him.'

It was the truth, Octavia knew that, but even so . . . Roddy's visits had begun to tail off now that Iseult was out of danger and on the long slow road to recovery. He had returned to his high life in Paris and showed little sign of coming back. He had finally got rid of his East End studio as well, evidently unable to face going there again.

Without Roddy himself to talk to, Iseult pored over his pictures in fashion magazines, followed his appearances at glamorous parties and critiqued any of his designs when they appeared. It was obvious she missed him very much.

She was quiet while Octavia made them coffee in the tiny kitchen. When they were sitting down, talking together, she said, 'You know, I've been working on our plans for Noble's. I think you're going to like them.'

'Wonderful, can I see them? I'm so curious!'

'Not yet, darling. Soon, I promise. But first, I have a favour to ask.'

'Anything.'

'Would your driver take me back to Mabbes? I have a sudden longing to be at home. The builders I had in have finished some of the repairs and I'm desperate to see what they've done.'

'Of course!' Octavia was delighted to hear some enthusiasm again in Iseult's voice.

'Good. I want to go tomorrow, if that's all right.'

'I . . . I can't come with you,' Octavia said, regretfully. 'Flora's at home, you see, and . . .'

'Oh, that's all right, darling, it's no problem. I'm quite used to being on my own as you well know. Just come and see me when you can, that's all I ask. One of my sisters is there, I believe, so I shan't be alone.'

And then Iseult was gone, back to Mabbes, and there was no chance that she would be coming into Noble's.

76

If there was ever a time to fall in love, Flora thought, this wasn't it. She knew she was in a delicate emotional and mental state, only just beginning to recover from her ordeal at Otto's hands and still reeling from the horror of his blackmail and the terrible decision she'd been forced to take.

But what was she supposed to do about it? She couldn't stop herself. The feelings were there whether she wanted them or not. They were there and getting stronger. She couldn't stop thinking about Nick.

She played and replayed in her mind the moment when he had rescued her from the car: helping her out of the seat, making sure she had her bag, seeing her safely into the helicopter. Since then he had been nothing but concerned for her, showing an instinctive understanding of what she must be going through.

It wasn't just that, though. Flora sighed, and twisted on her bed, staring up at the ceiling through unseeing eyes. It was everything about him. He was so beautiful to look at, so full of life and colour with that dark hair and those brown-black eyes under strong brows. He was handsome in a way she craved, as though someone had drawn a picture of a gorgeous Renaissance youth and then coloured it in with strong, vibrant colours. He was alive, he was vivid, and she longed to touch him.

After everything I've been through, I should be off sex for life! But she couldn't believe how much she craved a kiss from those full, well-defined lips or how she yearned to stroke a finger down the long straight line of his nose. She wanted him to kiss her and wipe out the memory of Otto touching her. She was sure that a kiss from Nick would be a totally different experience from those pallid, unsatisfying probings Otto had inflicted on her.

More than Nick's looks, though, it was the humanity in his eyes. He was a good man, she knew that. She'd never been more certain of anything.

She had begun to dream about him constantly and to think about him all the time. She was sure a therapist would have a lot to say about the tumultuous feelings she was experiencing and relate them to her past, both recent and distant, but that didn't make any difference. These feelings seemed real and there was nothing she could do about them. After all, did love always come when life was nice and tidy and everything was ready for it? Could you decide someone was not right just because of the moment when you met him?

She knew that she had fallen a bit in love with Nick Falcon the moment she met him in his office, before she had even married Otto. And now she was somersaulting head over heels for him.

But how on earth is he ever going to love me back, she thought, agonised, *when he knows the truth about me?*

* * *

Approaching the enormous, imposing shop that took up the entire corner of two streets, Octavia still couldn't shake off a feeling of amazement and pleasure that the whole place was hers. It was so distinctive and beautiful, with its black-and-white exterior, diamond-patterned windows and impressive brick chimneys. Among its bland, grey neighbours, it stuck out like a wildly eccentric, theatrical beauty, determined to keep her own personality while all about her subsumed theirs.

She stepped through the front doors below the heraldic shields in brilliant scarlets, azures and golds, and into a sweet-smelling porch, full of flowers. This was Noble's flower department, and the florist was hurrying about, tying bouquets with string or assembling blooms to make the perfect arrangement. She barely looked up from her work as Octavia passed through the dark-wood and glass internal doors. Now she was in the main ground-floor gallery: scarves, handbags, umbrellas and gloves were for sale here, with the jewellery room, carefully alarmed and with a security door ready to plummet down from the ceiling at the first sign of trouble, sparkling nearby. Octavia wandered through the ground floor, from handbags to stationery then through to perfume and make-up. Wherever she went, it was the same. People were polite, but they were stiff and, despite the smiles and the courteous 'hellos', their eyes were cold and their smiles empty.

She climbed the grand staircase and went up past fashion and shoes on the first floor, one hand resting on the gleaming wooden balustrade. On the second were more clothes, haberdashery, and the tiny wedding department. On the third, bedding, bath and homewares, on the fourth, rugs and lighting. On the fifth were furniture and art. Then she went up to the final floor, the attic storey that was now the offices and boardroom of Noble's. She heard a peal of laughter coming from Ethan's office as she walked down the hall towards it. His assistant must be on her coffee break as her desk was empty and she was nowhere to be seen. Pushing open the door, Octavia saw Ethan sitting behind his desk and Shagi sitting on top of it, her long brown legs swinging as she laughed.

Their amusement died away as they saw her.

'Oh, hi, Octavia!' said Shagi brightly. She was as incredibly perfect as ever, her caffe latte skin smooth, dark eyes glittering and lined in black kohl.

'Hi,' Octavia said, looking at her boyfriend. 'Ethan, could I see you for a moment, please? Sorry, Shagi, do you mind?'

'Of course not,' she said, still in that high bright voice. 'I was just passing and thought I'd look in and see Ethan. He's planning a super birthday party, really mega-glam.'

Octavia raised her eyebrows. 'Are you?'

Ethan coughed. 'Well, you know . . . got to celebrate. Sorry, Shagi, I'll see you another time, okay?'

'Sure.' She got off the desk, straightened her miniscule Gucci skirt and sashayed out, saying, 'See you around, Octavia!'

'What's *that* all about?' she asked sharply as soon as Shagi had gone.

'It's nothing,' Ethan said, getting up and coming round to kiss her. 'You're my girl. How are you, lovebug? I haven't seen you for ages.'

He wrapped her in his muscular arms and his scent

enveloped her: it was rich and musky, a dark, slightly dangerous smell. She suddenly recalled how Max smelt: light and citrusy, fresh as sunlight. *Stop it,* she told herself. *That's a stupid way to think.* But she'd been thinking of the other man more and more often. She'd downloaded 'A Nightingale Sang in Berkeley Square' and listened to it constantly, wondering why it made her feel simultaneously happy and oddly depressed. She thought frequently about those piercing blue eyes and the strong features of his face, and jealously of the beautiful blonde in Colette's he'd seemed so friendly with, and then told herself to stop it.

'I've got a lot going on,' she began, as though excusing her absence, and then stopped talking suddenly. She looked up at Ethan, at his enquiring blue eyes with their speckles of hazel and frame of dark lashes, his clean-shaven, handsome young face. He looked masculine and strong in his well-cut Prada suit, and successful with his huge Patek Philippe watch and polished Church's brogues. Everything about him breathed money. But, Octavia realised, she wasn't convinced there was anything below the surface. All that stuff was there for its own sake, and everything Ethan did was about acquiring it – the stuff he felt he deserved. All he could think about was his birthday party and the things he still craved to lay his hands on.

As she looked up at her attractive, high-powered, sexy boyfriend, one momentous thought floated into Octavia's mind.

I just don't love you any more. But how the hell am I going to get out of this one?

77

Flora never knew how Otto got hold of her new mobile number but she knew it was him almost before he spoke. Her skin crawled as the sound of his breathing came down the line and she turned icy cold.

'Have you had a chance to look at our little photo album?' he said, his voice giving away his evident enjoyment of the moment. He loved having her back in his power, that was obvious.

'Yes,' she whispered. 'How c-c-could you?'

'Oh, I very well c-c-could,' he mimicked. 'And I will. I'm capable of a great deal more too. I want twenty-five million transferred to my account by the end of a fortnight, do you understand? You've had plenty of time to think about it. I'm not prepared to play games any longer. Though I'm very happy to play other sorts of games . . . if you're ever in the mood again.'

Flora felt her stomach turn, and twisted her head away from the phone in revulsion.

'I understand,' she said.

'And an assurance that the fifty million I already have is irrevocably mine. Do you understand?'

'Yes,' she said, and ended the call. Her head buzzed, the sound in her ears growing louder and louder, she felt faint. She swayed but clung on to consciousness. Then she pulled herself together and dialled Nick's number.

He came at once. As soon as the doorbell sounded, she rushed to let him in, feeling a heady mixture of relief and excitement as she saw him.

Nick looked anxious as she opened the door to him, and the concern in his eyes made it seem perfectly natural to fling herself into his arms. He wrapped her in his embrace, holding her tightly. It felt amazing. Flora pressed her head against his chest, soaking in his strength. He put his cheek on top of her head, resting it against her hair.

Then he pulled away. 'I guess we ought to go inside,' he said, a little awkwardly, as though it had just dawned on him that their hug had gone beyond a social embrace.

'Yes, yes . . .' She led him in, already feeling stronger now that he was here.

'So Otto called you? Tell me everything the slimeball said,' Nick urged, as they sat down together on the sofa. Flora told him the contents of the short conversation, longing all the while for those arms around her again. They had felt like the safest place in the world.

Nick's dark eyes flashed as she finished. 'A fortnight, huh? That's because he knows the longer this goes on, the worse it will be for him. He wants it all tidied away before you get yourself better.'

'I don't want to be exposed!' Flora said, panicked. 'I couldn't bear that.'

'No one's going to make you go through that,' Nick said, reassuringly. He smiled at her and she felt herself melt inside. 'Don't you worry, we'll work out a way to pay him and make this watertight, so that you won't be at risk.'

'I can't bear to talk to him,' she whispered. 'It makes me sick. Literally sick.'

Nick put his hand on hers, closing his fingers around it. They were warm and smooth and she felt his strength passing to her, holding her up. She wanted to drop her head and put her lips to them. Where his skin touched hers, she burned pleasurably.

'You won't have to,' he reassured her. There was something in his eyes – a look that seemed to say he sensed the same power in their touch as she did.

'We can contact him direct now we know what his terms are. I'll handle all of that for you, along with Sirjiwan. Okay?'

Flora nodded. Then she said slowly, 'Nick . . . can I ask you something?'

'Sure, honey, anything.' He looked into her eyes, his expression honest and open.

'Did you . . . did you ever find out about my mother?'

He hesitated, obviously struggling with himself. He opened his mouth and closed it again, then looked away and muttered, 'Goddang it!'

'You did,' she said in a small voice. 'I knew you had, even though there aren't any messages from you in my email account. Deleted, I suppose. What did you find out?'

He frowned. 'Flora, I'm in a really difficult position here. Your sister has asked me to terminate the search

565

and expunge my records. She says you're too delicate to face your mother right now.'

Flora stared down at Nick's hand on hers, noticing the dark hairs on his wrist. 'Maybe she's right,' she said at last. 'Maybe this isn't the right time. If Octavia doesn't want to know our mother . . . well, I can't go against her wishes. She's so adamant that she wants nothing to do with her. There's no way I can ever look for Diane Beaufort if Octavia forbids it.'

'But you want to, huh?'

Flora looked away, then shrugged. 'I feel like I'll never be able to be whole again without knowing, that's all. I just want to know.'

There was a pause and then Nick said, 'Have you thought about getting away for a while? Maybe you should go on holiday somewhere, you know, just until these next weeks are over and you can forget Otto for ever.'

'I don't know,' Flora said uncertainly. 'I like being at home. I don't want to go anywhere strange.' *I don't want to go away from you*, she thought, staring at him.

He held her gaze and then his dark eyes softened. They were still holding hands, she realised, and the air between them suddenly crackled with suggestion. She felt him move almost imperceptibly towards her and found herself looking at his mouth, willing it to touch hers.

For a moment she thought he was going to kiss her then he seemed to remember himself. He pulled back, looking self-conscious, and took his hand away. 'Ah . . . ah . . .' he said, flushing slightly. 'I . . . er . . .'

She wished she had the courage to lean over, take

his face in her hands and turn it to hers so she could kiss him. But she didn't.

'I don't want you to worry,' he said firmly, regaining control of himself. 'I'm gonna sort this out for you, once and for all.'

Outside in the hall, Vicky, who had been listening silently at the door, turned and padded away.

'This is a crazy idea!' Ethan said, his eyes blazing. 'No. I won't let you do it!'

'What do you mean, you won't *let* me do it? How can you stop me?' Octavia demanded, one hand resting on her hip. 'I can do precisely what I want. I'm your boss, remember?'

He stared at her and growled with frustration, obviously biting back some kind of retort.

'I think it's a brilliant idea,' Octavia said obstinately. 'It's exactly what I need to do. You must be able to see that.'

'It's degrading,' spat Ethan. He went back to his desk and sat down in his hugely expensive designer leather chair. 'You're humiliating yourself.'

'I don't see how.' Octavia frowned at him. 'What's humiliating about it, anyway?'

'If you can't see it, I'm not going to tell you,' Ethan retorted.

Just like a little boy in the playground! she thought.

Then he made a face. 'Do it if you want,' he mumbled. 'I don't care. Just don't blame me when you're a laughing stock, that's all.'

'I don't intend to be a laughing stock,' said Octavia coolly. She stared at him as he played with his computer mouse, his eyes flicking to the screen. *He's a child. An immature little boy*. She knew that Max would approve of her idea. It would be exactly the kind of thing he would applaud.

Ethan made a sulky face. 'I can't believe you're acting like this. It's my birthday tomorrow.'

Just then her phone went. Octavia dug into her bag and pulled it out. The number was unfamiliar. 'Hello?'

'Hello, is that Octavia Beaufort?' It was a woman with a well-spoken voice who enquired.

'Yes.'

'My name is Elaine Rivers-Manners. I'm afraid I have some terrible news for you.'

78

Octavia didn't know what else to do, so she went to Mabbes. Steve drove her there, his foot hard on the accelerator nearly all the way while Octavia sat in the back of the car, alternating between staring out of the window, frozen in shock, and sobbing into her handkerchief.

Iseult, Iseult, Iseult . . . why did you do it?

But she knew very well why. In fact, as the reality of it sank in, she realised that on some level she'd been expecting it. Iseult had been preparing her for it, she could see that now. She'd told her quite clearly that it was too difficult to go on, that she was readying herself. Octavia had thought she was girding her loins to face life, but now she understood that Iseult had been preparing herself for death.

Elaine, her younger sister, also staying at Mabbes, had found her in the newly repaired drawing room. The chandelier had been removed for cleaning, leaving its strong brass hook extending like a small claw from the ceiling rose. It was there Iseult had hung her noose. First she had dressed herself in a wonderful sparkling vintage thirties dress, wrapped her face in a creamy bridal veil embroidered with tiny glittering crystals, put on the pair of shoes designed by Roddy that she had loved so much, and then hanged herself with a length of golden twisted rope taken from the pair of curtains at the great bay window.

'The strangest thing was what a pretty picture she made,' Elaine said to Octavia, taking her into the room where she had discovered her sister. 'She looked like an exotic chandelier herself, hanging from the fitting by her golden cord, sparkling as she swung there. And her face – well, it was covered so you couldn't see what had been done to it. Her poor face. As if it hadn't been through enough . . .'

Octavia felt tears drop from her eyes. She wept hard, mourning her friend. *Iseult. We went through so much together. Couldn't you have told me? Couldn't I have stopped you?*

'She would have done it one day, you know,' Elaine said. 'Oh, we're sad, of course . . . devastated. We loved her. But it was always on the cards for her, an end like this. We knew it and she knew it. That's why she lived so flamboyantly, I think. She was flying as high as she could, making her mark in the short time she had.' Elaine came over to Octavia and hugged her. 'You're so young,' she said, looking at her through eyes the same yellowish-green as Iseult's. Her voice was similar too – a beautiful, low, upper-class sing-song sound. For a moment, Octavia felt as though Iseult herself was speaking to her. 'You think death is so tragic, the worst thing in the world.

Believe me, it isn't always. Sometimes it's a relief, a blessing. Don't be sad for Iseult. She wouldn't want that.'

'But . . . *why?*' begged Octavia helplessly.

'Should she have lived to make you happy?' Elaine smiled and shook her head. 'That's too much to ask of anyone, isn't it? Least of all someone like Iseult. She knew what she wanted to do. We are the ones who will suffer without her. I'm sure she's happier without us. Did I show you her note?'

Octavia shook her head, still sniffing and trying to stem the tears that wouldn't stop flowing.

Elaine handed it to her. It was a piece of thick cream paper engraved with Iseult's monogram. In her flowing black handwriting, it read: '*I cannot go on being a daughter of Anguish any longer.*'

Octavia stared at it for a moment. 'What does she mean?' she whispered.

'In Arthurian legend, Iseult was an Irish princess, the daughter of King Anguish. That always tickled her. She thought it was apt.' Elaine squeezed her hand. 'You see? She'd reached the end, that's all. By the way, she left something for you. Come with me, I'll give it to you.'

Elaine led her into the kitchen. On the scrubbed pine table was a brown calfskin folder with an envelope on the front addressed to *Octavia*. Next to it was another envelope, this one marked *Roddy*.

Elaine handed the folder to her. 'Here you are,' she said. 'Would you like to stay? You can if you want to, you know. Roddy is coming any moment.'

Octavia stared at the folder in her hands. What had

Iseult left her? 'Yes,' she said slowly. 'I think I would like to stay. I feel close to her here.'

'Oh, yes, she'll always be here at Mabbes,' Elaine said. 'We won't be able to escape her. I'm sure she's going to haunt us all and enjoy it hugely too.' She smiled at Octavia. 'You're very welcome. Stay as long as you want.'

Octavia took the folder outside. It was a brisk late-autumn day. Winter would soon be upon them. Leaves whirled in the air and the trees were already bare and spiky against the grey sky. She went through the gardens to the orchard, and sat down on a wooden bench under one of the trees. The soft brown remains of rotting apples were everywhere.

She picked up the envelope and looked at it. Then slowly she tore it open and took out the letter inside.

Darling O,

You're so beautiful and special, I don't believe I ever told you enough how much. You've been a wonderful friend to me, better than anyone else in the end. You were always there for me and I love you for it. I'm sorry that our time together has turned out to be so short. I wanted to stay and help you with our grand project but, my darling, I just couldn't. I have to go, you see. I need to be somewhere that doesn't hurt me as much as this place. You're different from me: you're blessed, I can feel it. You're going to have an amazing life and know love, real love (maybe not with Ethan, my sweet, though I suspect you know that).

*So here is my gift for you: the plans that I won't be here
to see through. It's my legacy, the only sort of child I can
leave. I hope you'll like them.*

*Goodbye! Don't be sad! Do you promise, you silly thing?
All my love*

Iseult xxx

Octavia laughed, then she felt her face tremble
and distort and she sobbed again. It was a long time
before she was able to open the folder and look
inside.

When Roddy arrived, having flown into Bristol airport
and come to the house by taxi, he was red-eyed and
in a bad state. As he came stumbling through the
front door, he fell weeping into Octavia's arms and
she stroked his stubbly head as he howled. He was
quite drunk, she realised. She felt calmer now, having
come through her own initial storm of grief, and was
able to soothe and comfort him as he cried.

When he was quiet, Elaine made cups of tea in the
kitchen and then produced a supper of fish pie and
peas.

'Where is she now?' Roddy asked. He ate hungrily,
obviously needing food after drinking so much.

'She's at the undertaker's,' Elaine said. 'They took
her there after all the various official things were done.
I imagine we'll have a quiet funeral soon. But I'm
counting on you two to help me with a memorial
service for her. She'd have wanted something
wonderful, don't you think?'

Roddy and Octavia sat up together late into the night, drinking bottle after bottle of red wine while Roddy stared at the envelope in his hands, his name on it in Iseult's flowing writing, turning it over and over.

He looked up at Octavia. 'I don't want to know what she's going to say,' he said bleakly. 'Because I know what she should say.'

'What should she say?' Octavia asked, her voice quiet. She gazed at him earnestly.

'That I let her down. I didn't do right by her. I didn't repay her for everything she did for me. When she really needed me, I wasn't there for her.'

'But you were,' Octavia said. 'After the attack, you were there for her.'

Roddy looked away. 'Not as much as I should have been. But that was after. I'd already let her down. You know it, don't you? You know it and I know it. We can't pretend.'

As he got drunker, he grew more and more maudlin, berating himself for not being grateful enough to Iseult, for every time he was short or snappy or bad company. He told Octavia the story of their love affair, opening his heart and spilling out what was inside. 'I did love her, you see,' he said, tears running down his face again. 'I was so mad about her at first that I could actually make love to her – I mean, me! But it couldn't last. It wasn't meant to be. I broke her fuckin' heart, I know that . . .'

Octavia tried to comfort him but it was useless. He berated himself into the early hours, weeping and ranting. *He needs to do this,* she thought. *He has to let it all out.*

Eventually, they fell asleep, Roddy slumped in his chair and Octavia curled up on the sofa with an old, moth-eaten rug over her for warmth.

Roddy left early the next morning, white and shaky from the force of his hangover, more subdued now but still obviously in shock. He had to go, he said, he had so much work to do.

Octavia summoned Steve, who had been having a comfortable stay at a local pub, thanked Elaine and asked her to let them know as soon as the funeral date was decided. Then she climbed into the car and they headed back to London. She wanted to read over the things inside the folder again – the contents hadn't yet really sunk in.

As they left the village behind them, Octavia called Ethan.

'Hey,' he said. 'How's it going? How was everything at Mabbes?' She'd told him the news the day before, as soon as she'd heard it herself.

'It's okay. Pretty sad. Horribly sad, actually. But I'm sure you can imagine it.'

'It's tragic. Really. Poor Iseult.'

'But she's left me something amazing.' Octavia opened the folder again as she spoke. 'She's written down the most incredible plans for the future of Noble's – how it can be redone and all the brands she recommends and hundreds of ideas for designs, the website, a beauty department, pop-up shops, which brands we should co-operate with . . . it's an absolute treasure trove. It's everything we need . . .'

'Hey, that's fantastic. Good old Iseult. What a brilliant legacy.' Ethan sounded delighted.

'I'm so glad you think so,' she said happily. 'If we follow this, we'll be absolutely made.'

'Uh-huh.' There was a long pause and then he said, 'Haven't you forgotten something?'

Octavia frowned. 'Have I? What?'

'It's my birthday, hon.'

'Oh!' She put a hand to her forehead and scrunched up her eyes. 'I'm sorry. Happy birthday. I forgot – I'm sure you understand, with everything that's happened?'

'Of course, but you've got a present for me, right?' He spoke teasingly. 'I mean, you would have bought it before all this, right?'

She was taken aback. 'Well . . . yes . . . I do have a gift for you.'

'Cool. And are you going to be back in time for my party?'

'Your party?' She was astonished.

'Yeah.'

'Your party . . . tonight?'

'What other party is there?'

Now she was horrified. 'But, Ethan, you can't have a party tonight! A friend has just killed herself! It's so disrespectful! It's like dancing on her grave.'

'Hey . . .' Ethan sounded upset. 'What am I supposed to do? I can't cancel now. It would be a huge waste of money. And anyway, I didn't know Iseult that well. I'm sure she wouldn't mind.'

'She was a member of your board. She died the day before yesterday. For crying out loud!'

'Look, you don't have to come.'

'Oh, big of you,' said Octavia, furious. 'Were you really expecting me to dress up and drink and laugh and party as though nothing had happened? As though the fact that my best friend couldn't see the point in living and has hanged herself from the ceiling means shit? Fuck off, Ethan!'

'Fuck off yourself,' he said brusquely, and hung up on her.

Octavia seethed all the way back to London.

79

When Octavia got home, Vicky told her there was a visitor waiting in the drawing room.

Octavia went in, still clutching her folder, wondering who it could be. To her surprise Gerry Harbord was sitting there, resplendent in a bottle-green velvet suit. He was leafing through one of the coffee-table books and looked up as she came in.

'Ah, Octavia my sweet.' He stood and went over to brush her cheeks lightly with his lips. 'What a very sad time. I never wanted to see you in circumstances such as this. A desperate day. Poor Iseult.'

'Thank you, Gerry. Sit down.' She sat down too. 'Strange to think how long you couldn't stand each other.'

'We were two bright birds who would fight to the death for their chance to display their plumage,' Gerry said mournfully. 'That was the problem. But people like Iseult and me are a vanishing species. You can't afford to lose us.'

'No.' Octavia smiled at him. She couldn't help being fond of him. 'So what is this visit in aid of?'

'Ah.' Gerry sat back and crossed his legs. 'Two words. Amanda Radcliffe.'

Octavia blinked at him in surprise. 'What about her?'

'She's sent me to pass on a message. Not a very nice message, I'm afraid.'

'Why didn't she come herself?'

'Because – not to put too fine a point on it – she hates your guts.' Gerry smiled. 'She thinks you and Ethan Brody killed her father with your takeover of Noble's.'

Octavia gasped. 'But . . . that's not fair! I was horrified to hear about his death, but I don't see how we can be accused of causing it.'

'Well, darling, he dropped down dead the minute he heard the news about Robert Young changing sides. In front of Amanda's eyes,' Gerry said tartly. 'So I suppose that's why.'

Octavia stared at the floor, absorbing this, full of confusion. 'That's terrible,' she said at last in a small voice. *Are we really to blame?*

'I'm sorry,' Gerry added ruefully. 'But that's how she sees it. One can hardly blame her. It's Brody she thinks most culpable, if that's any comfort, though she believes you went ahead with the whole purchase of Noble's as a personal vendetta against her.'

Octavia blushed. It sounded so appallingly childish when it was put that way. She wished that she'd never started all this.

'And that's why she's decided to make sure Noble's is in safe hands, knowing the kind of methods employed to take it off her. So . . .' Gerry looked uncomfortable again '. . . it's my unpleasant duty to tell you that her investigations have uncovered something rather . . . rather disturbing.'

'Yes?' Octavia sat suddenly very still. Her instinct told her something serious was about to happen.

'It's come to our attention,' Gerry began, not quite able to meet her eyes, 'that Brody, your boyfriend, is not all he's cracked up to be.'

Octavia went cold.

'You need to know that Ethan Brody is a thief. He invents companies, uses them to make as much money as he can and then dumps them, owing hundreds of thousands. He's been very clever, he's done it all semi-legally, so as not to arouse suspicion. But there's a difference between going to the wall because you can't help it and letting your company implode on purpose, and it's a game you can only play so many times. Ethan was previously based in New York and got out just before the Securities and Exchange Commission and the Federal Business Regulators started investigating him seriously. He operated there as Ethan Johnson, but an Ethan Brody was fined by the Australian authorities ten years ago for financial misconduct.

'After New York he came here, took up his former name and started the same old tricks – a made-up venture capitalist company this time, which is very amusing considering he had zero capital and relied on the slightly less able of the City boys to introduce him to some. And then he met you. Hallelujah, the heavens open in glorious light and the sound of trumpets! Pay day.'

Octavia could only stare at him, fighting the awful sick feeling that was rising in her stomach. 'Is this true?' she whispered at last, through dry lips.

'Of course.' Gerry gave her a pitying look. 'I wouldn't bother spinning lies about something like this, and nor would Amanda. Anyway –' he picked up a manila envelope from the table '– it's all in here. I'm afraid you'd better look swiftly into what Ethan Brody's been doing with your business affairs. I just hope it's not too late, that's all.' He stood up. 'Don't bother getting up. I'll see myself out.'

He turned to go and then stopped and looked back at her. 'By the way, I don't know if it helps but Amanda had big plans for Noble's, you know. It was Young who stopped her instigating any of them – including her wish to stock your friend Wildblood's designs. Goodbye for now, darling. And sorry to be the bringer of bad tidings.'

80

The helicopter blades whirred overhead. Max looked over at Flora encouragingly and smiled. She smiled back, grateful he wasn't talking today. He seemed to sense that both sisters needed their peace. Octavia was in the back, clearly still in shock after the events of the last few days.

It seemed strange suddenly to discover themselves leaving London far behind and heading for Scotland, but as soon as Octavia said that Max had offered them his Argyllshire house, it had made perfect sense. They needed to get away.

The only bad thing is that I'll be so far from Nick, she thought to herself, staring at the countryside, a patchwork of dull green and grey as it spread out below them. *But we'll keep in touch.*

Nick was still busy working with the lawyer at Fawcett & Mather to come up with the solution to the Otto problem: how to guarantee that he would destroy the recorded material in his possession and ensure that it could never be found, and that he would never bother Flora again once he'd been paid off. The one good thing was that Nick had promised to come to Scotland to inform her personally of any major developments. She hoped it was because he cared about her enough to want to make sure she had the support she needed if the news was bad. Time was running out and every hour was precious now.

'As long as you're sure that you've made the decision you really want to make. Handing over seventy-five million to a low-life dick makes me a touch unhappy,' he'd said to her. 'But I'll do whatever you want me to, you know that.'

Flora couldn't help thinking that he wished she would turn and fight Otto, make him give up the money he'd stolen and pay for what he'd done. But the price was too heavy; the idea of her most private self being revealed to the world was too much. Besides, she needed her strength for something else now.

She glanced over at her sister, who was looking pale and drawn. *Octavia.*

Octavia was enjoying the thudding of the engines. She wanted the world to be blanked out for a while. How much more could she cope with?

The loss of Iseult was still acute. And on top of that, she now had to live with the awful sense of being duped.

Is this how Flora feels? We've both been such idiots. Maybe we are the same person, just split in two. We've certainly both been taken for a ride.

As soon as Gerry had left, Octavia had run to her room and put on the first party frock she could see and a pair of silver heels. Then she'd hastily applied some make-up and brushed her hair in the car as

Steve drove her to Quaglino's, which Ethan had booked for the night to celebrate his birthday.

She strode past the security guards on the door and down the staircase into the restaurant. The first person she saw was Shagi, in a tight metallic Delphine dress, bopping away while she chatted to an admiring gaggle of men. Then she saw Ethan holding court in the middle of the gathering, accepting birthday wishes and directing people to put their expensive-looking packages on the gift table at the side. He was dressed in a hand-made Kilgour suit with a purple silk shirt and a Gucci tie. He looked good in them. When he'd caught sight of Octavia walking towards him, pushing her way through the crowd, his face had split into a massive grin of pleasure. 'Octavia!' he'd called. 'You made it – fantastic.'

As she reached him, he said in a sexy voice, 'So what are you going to give me for my birthday?'

'This,' she said, drawing back her hand and delivering a stinging slap across his cheek. The room fell silent and everyone turned to look at the unfolding drama. 'That's for Iseult,' she said as he stared at her in astonishment, his face flushing under her blow. She whacked him again on the other side. 'And that's for me.'

Ethan's face turned steely and he clenched one meaty fist. 'What the fuck are you doin'?' Then he turned to the people round them, forcing out a laugh as he said, 'She's kidding. Carry on, people, carry on. Just a little lovers' tiff.'

'I don't think so,' Octavia said in ringing tones so that the whole room could hear. 'Why didn't you tell me the truth, Ethan? All those nights when you whispered your secrets to me while we were in bed together . . . You could have told me that you're not much more than a petty criminal. Someone who's built a life for himself on other people's money. How many people have you left in the shit? How many pensions and life savings have you stolen, you bastard? And me? Have you stolen from me too?'

The room was deathly silent as everyone stared at Ethan, waiting to hear his reply. He went paper-white under his tan.

'Octavia, I-I-I . . .' he stammered. 'I can explain, sweetheart. Let's talk about this somewhere else, huh?'

'No. Right here. Right now.' She folded her arms across her chest and waited.

Ethan stared at her, panic-stricken, and then a moment later he was elbowing his way through the crowd and making for the door as fast as he could. No one stopped him. They were all too stunned to see the birthday boy exiting his own party.

Octavia had pulled out her phone and dialled Nick. 'I think I've got an urgent case for you,' she'd said, 'but you might need the police to help on this one.'

Auditors had been brought in immediately and given access to the entire company structure, not simply the British companies. Their first perusal of the records had been enough for the police to be called in immediately and for an arrest warrant to be issued for Ethan Brody. He wasn't at his house when the police entered to cart away his computer and hard drive and any files in his study. No one knew where he was.

Nick called Octavia over the weekend to tell her that it looked as though Ethan had been building a complex series of companies that allowed him to keep restructuring loans, essentially lending money to himself. The cash that had come from the sale of the

Noble's freehold was supposed to have paid back the bank loan. It had repaid some of that loan but the rest of it had been 'lent' to another company founded by Ethan and, supposedly, Octavia. That money had duly disappeared into other loans, but it was a fair bet it had ended up buying the Notting Hill house, the yacht and all of Ethan's various toys.

'I think anyone else would have been suspicious of how Brody could afford all this stuff on his salary,' Nick said to her. 'You weren't paying him a fortune – a generous salary but not enough for some of the baubles he's got. That Lamborghini alone must have cost over a hundred grand.'

'I thought he was independently rich,' Octavia said lamely. 'He told me he was.'

'I'm afraid he was lying.'

'Am I ruined?' she asked despairingly. 'Has he taken everything?'

'Not quite,' replied Nick. 'He used the investment company as his main vehicle. That means your losses are limited. But others will have lost out too.'

'I'll make it all good,' Octavia said immediately, but Nick cautioned her to wait and see the extent of the whole situation before taking any decisions.

Then she had called Max.

They arrived at the house in the late afternoon and it was almost dark. There were no streetlights here to lighten the gloom, just lanterns to show the helicopter where to land. Max brought the aircraft down gently. Once the propellers had slowed to a stop, they climbed out. The butler waited nearby to unload the luggage and the housekeeper held another lantern to lead them over the cold field to the back door. They stepped into a warm, welcoming country kitchen radiating heat from an old iron range cooker, with a kettle already whistling on the hot plate.

'You're very welcome here,' Hilda said in her soft Scottish accent, smiling to see Octavia again. 'Now, I've got some hot scones in the oven, so sit yourselves down and we'll have them.'

While Godfrey the butler took the luggage up to the bedrooms, Hilda put out a pot of tea, a plateful of scones, some jam and a big dish of thick yellow cream.

The girls sat down gratefully and tucked in. Max had stayed outside to finish up with the helicopter but a moment later he came in.

'Bit colder than London,' he said, rubbing his hands. 'Thanks for this, Hilda. It looks wonderful, as usual.'

Octavia was looking at Flora with a smile. She wondered if her sister felt the same way she did. As soon as the helicopter had landed and she'd breathed in the cold air and seen the lights shining out, the same sense of peace and calm as last time had come over her. *What is it? I feel like I belong here! But how could I? I'd never even been in Scotland before I came here, as far as I know . . .*

'See?' she said quietly. 'Didn't I tell you? Isn't this place like home?'

'Like a home from a book,' Flora answered. 'I can hardly believe it's real.' She turned to Max. 'Thank you so much for letting us stay here.'

'Not at all. I like to share this place,' he said, sitting down at the table. He smiled at them. 'Every time I come here, I feel all the pressures lift away.'

As soon as Octavia had told him what they were

both facing, Max had said, 'You two need a refuge. Glachach is the place for you. It's completely removed from everything else in your life. It's my solution for a troubled soul. Please, consider it yours as long as you need it. I'll happily take you there, but I'll be leaving the next day for meetings.'

Octavia had been overwhelmed by his generosity, but absurdly disappointed that he would not be staying with them. *Don't be silly,* she told herself. *He's a very busy man. Why would he drop everything to stay with us?*

But she longed to be with someone with experience and knowledge, someone who'd be able to teach her about the world. *It's because we know nothing that we've got into all these problems,* she thought. She remembered the way Iseult had always had interesting things to say about what was going on, the way her flat had been crammed with books, magazines, pictures and ornaments. She knew so much – and now Octavia too felt a hunger to know more and more about life beyond the narrow existence she and Flora had been restricted to all their lives. At first she'd been dazzled by everything on offer to her that she'd previously been denied: beautiful clothes, shoes and bags, as many as she wanted. But now she was ready to begin devoting herself to something more serious.

She looked over at Max as he talked quietly with Flora. She was drawn to him with a force more powerful than she'd known before. It wasn't the teenage lust she'd shared with Ferdy, or the overwhelming sexual attraction she'd felt for Ethan. This was about the man himself.

Oh, my goodness. So it's him.

* * *

That night, for the first time in ages, the sisters climbed into one bed, snuggling together under the sheets, blankets and old-fashioned pink satin feather-filled eiderdown. They had had a delicious dinner with Max, who had told them silly stories that made them laugh and forget their worries. Then it was an early night – a hot bath, pyjamas, and now these crisp, clean sheets.

'Didn't I tell you how perfect it is?' Octavia asked, smiling.

Flora nodded. 'It's real bliss. I love the way we're so far from everything here. I feel properly safe. For the first time in ages.'

Octavia reached out and took her sister's hand. 'I'm glad. Goodness, we're a pair, aren't we? What a mess we've made of things!'

'Are you very upset about Ethan?' Flora asked softly.

'Well . . .' Octavia rolled on to her back and stared up at the ceiling. 'Of course I'm upset. I thought I loved him once. But, if I'm honest, I suppose I stopped loving him a while ago. I guessed he wasn't the one for me. Iseult said so too in her last letter, and I knew she was right. I already knew, before the letter, but it crystallised it for me. The money . . .' She turned to look Flora in the eye. 'He shouldn't have stolen from me and the others. But sometimes I think it would be better if we didn't have any at all. Look at what it's done to us. We never would have attracted such awful men without it. But if we hadn't been so sheltered from the world we would have been able to judge them better.'

'Tavy . . .' Flora said tentatively. 'I sense that you feel something for Max . . . am I wrong?'

There was a pause, and then Octavia said seriously, 'I think he's amazing – because he plainly is. You know, he wasn't bowled over by me when we met – quite the opposite. He had no reason to like or respect me, but now he's changed his mind. You've no idea how good and strong that makes me feel. As though I have something to recommend me beyond my money and my clothes and all the trappings.'

'You know you do,' Flora insisted. 'You're clever and spirited and determined.'

Octavia sighed. 'Really? I hope so.'

'Tavy, he'd be crazy not to adore you. If you want him to?'

Octavia turned to her sister and gazed into her wide blue eyes. 'You know . . . I have a feeling you're mad about Nick.'

'Oh, dear.' Flora blushed scarlet and began to fiddle with the edge of the eiderdown. 'Is it very obvious?'

'Only to me. He is unbelievably nice and extremely gorgeous. And he's a real hero, a proper one this time.' Octavia smiled mischievously. 'It's no wonder you've fallen for him.'

'It's probably just a crush,' Flora said hastily. 'It's a terrible time to fall in love.'

'Maybe it's just the right time. You're due something wonderful. Why shouldn't you forget Otto as soon as you possibly can, and begin to love someone?'

'But it will only mean more heartbreak if he doesn't love me back!'

'I don't see how he couldn't.'

'You're biased!'

'Yes, I am.'

Flora gazed at her sister. 'I'm so glad I have you, Tavy. We're the only family we've got, aren't we?'

Octavia nodded. 'We're all we need.'

81

Amanda was eating her breakfast when the phone rang.

Gerry's voice came down the line without preamble. 'I take it you've seen the news?'

'Not yet. The paper's on the mat, I think.' She wandered out to the hall with the phone, picked up the paper and turned it over. She gasped.

'Yes, darling,' Gerry said, triumph in every note. 'Brody's done for.'

She scanned it quickly. The headline halfway down read: *Top businessman on the run following fraud allegations*, and the article below went on to outline the bare bones of the situation. Amanda read aloud: 'It's unknown at this point how this will affect the fortune of Noble's, the hundred-and-fifty-year-old emporium purchased by Brody's Butterfly Limited, a company he co-owned with heiress Octavia Beaufort. Beaufort was not available for comment.'

Gerry said, 'We were right, he *was* up to his tricks. Can you believe that men like him are allowed to operate the way they are?'

'He's a slippery bugger,' said Amanda. She pushed her short dark hair behind her ears as she wandered back to the breakfast table. 'I just hope this isn't going to destroy the old place.'

'But Octavia's fabulously rich. I shouldn't think he made a dent in that.'

'We don't know how much he's taken, or how he's done it. She might be down to her last few mill and decide to let the shop go. Or he might have compromised the business so badly it can't go on.' Amanda bit her lip. 'I'm glad Fa didn't live to see this. It's a bloody disaster.'

'Well, you wanted to get back at her,' Gerry said lightly, 'and you have. Congratulations.'

Amanda sat down at the table and stared again at the headline. 'We've done her a favour. God knows how long he'd have stayed there, milking them all dry, before he did a bunk or whatever it was he planned.'

'Just imagine,' said Gerry, clearly enjoying the mental image, 'he's probably sitting in a Holiday Inn as we speak, wondering how he's going to get out of the country.'

'That's what I don't understand – how did he ever think he could get away with it? The thing with all these schemes, magicking money out of nowhere and spending it, is that one day they get found out. It's inevitable.'

Gerry said, 'It must be like a drug habit. He just couldn't stop himself. Well, no doubt he'll be caught soon. I wonder how little Octavia is feeling today!'

'Yes.' Amanda looked out of the window at the bright winter sunshine. 'I wonder.'

* * *

Vicky sat at her computer screen, contemplating what kind of arrangements the twins might want her to make for Christmas this year. Usually they were away for the holiday, sometimes on a hot beach or else in an Alpine chalet surrounded by snow. Last year, Flora had been in Germany and Octavia had been whisked away to Thailand by Ethan for one of their no-expense-spared luxury breaks, spending time in a fabulous decked house with a vast private beach. Now the girls were both in Scotland. They'd been there a week and there was no talk of their coming home yet.

I think it's the right thing for them, thought Vicky, clicking on to the Fortnum & Mason website to start looking at Christmas hampers to give as gifts to the staff. *They need to get away from all the stress round here.* They'd both been through extraordinary events after all.

Her desk telephone went and she picked it up, saying crisply, 'Vicky Staunton.'

'Hi, Vicky, it's Nick.'

'Hi, Nick, how are you?'

'Good, I'm good. Listen, I thought I'd better let you know that the police have picked up Brody in Dover. He was trying to leave the country by ferry, slipping on as a foot passenger. I've tried to call Octavia but her phone is off or hasn't got reception. Do you have the number of this joint in Scotland where she and Flora are staying?'

'Sure.' Vicky opened her address book and looked out Max Northam's details. 'Here you are.' She dictated the number to him. 'I'm so pleased they've got that piece of shit.'

'Yeah. It's going to be a long and arduous process, though. This is just the beginning. See ya later, Vicky.'

'Yeah, see you.' She rang off and then looked down at the numbers she had for Max, carefully written in the address book in her neat hand. As she stared, Vicky frowned. A thought came into her mind and she froze. Then she got up and began to walk about the room, thinking hard. A few minutes later, she sat down and prepared to make a call.

The news that Ethan Brody had been picked up by the police came as huge relief to both Octavia and Flora. One of the sources of tension that was making them so stressed was partially resolved. Ethan was now in custody. When Nick called, he told Octavia that there would be an initial hearing and then a long preparation period while the lawyers gathered their evidence for the prosecution and the case for the defence. 'This won't be over any time soon,' he warned, 'but you can make a start.'

'What about Butterfly and Noble's?'

'You better talk to a business advisor about that,' Nick said, 'it's not my area of expertise. Hey, is Flora there? Can I talk to her?'

Octavia passed the phone to her eager, bright-eyed sister, knowing that Nick had been impatient to speak to her all along. She heard Flora say, 'Hi, Nick,' in soft tones that were full of romantic longing, even if she wasn't aware of it herself. Octavia smiled and left her to it, going off to think about Ethan and everything that had happened.

Both the girls were enjoying relaxing at Glachach: some of the strain of the past few weeks began to lift. They were sleeping better, eating well and going for long walks together across the cold hills, well wrapped up in fleeces and stout boots. They were talking properly for the first time in a long while, and at last Flora was able to confide some of the things that Otto had done to her, although she could only refer to them obliquely. Octavia was almost too horrified and outraged to listen, but she managed to cap her own emotion and let Flora tell whatever she needed to tell, without interruption. Each discussion left them happier and more at peace.

The only thing that Flora couldn't tell her sister was that she still yearned to find her mother. Now more than ever. But Octavia had made her own feelings on the subject plain and there was no way that Flora would go against her wishes.

Perhaps when the whole situation with Ethan and the court case was resolved, it might be the time to raise the issue again. But that would be a long way into the future, she knew. Until then, she'd have to keep her longing to herself.

82

Iseult's funeral was held at the small village church near Mabbes. She was buried in the graveyard there, not far from a honeysuckle hedge and the cool spreading branches of a yew tree.

Octavia left Glachach to go to the service. It was immediate family only attending, along with Iseult's closest friends. Her wide circle of work colleagues, acquaintances and admirers would be invited to a big memorial service done Iseult-style, with lots of lavish touches, fun and laughter. The funeral was more solemn and heart-wrenching, though Iseult's love of drama had not been forgotten. The coffin came into church topped by a glorious dome of cream roses, at least forty fresh blooms, and her favourite pair of lime green python-skin platforms. Octavia knew that inside the coffin, Iseult was wearing the fabulous shoes designed by Roddy that she had once declared she wanted to be buried in. Now she would wear them for ever.

Roddy stood by Octavia in the second row from the front, subdued in a black Yves St Laurent suit and black tie. He was shaking constantly throughout the ceremony and his face was thinner than usual. He didn't look at all well, in Octavia's opinion, and she held tight to his hand all the way through the service.

Elaine read Donne's 'Death, where is thy sting?' in beautiful ringing tones, and Octavia couldn't help weeping. Iseult's other sister, Ettare, gave an address that perfectly captured Iseult's personality and why they would miss her so much. 'She left us far too soon,' Ettare said towards the end, 'I'm sure there was so much more we had to learn from her, not least how to dress as magnificently as she did.' Ettare looked over at Roddy. 'She loved fashion and she loved Roddy with all her heart. Those two things made her happiest.'

Octavia felt his hand shudder under hers. When she looked at him, he was pale, the tears running down his cheeks.

He wasn't able to witness the burial itself. As they prepared to put Iseult's coffin into the deep hole that had been dug for it, Roddy went away to stand by the honeysuckle hedge, staring out over the cold Somerset landscape, drawing hard on a cigarette. Octavia stood next to Elaine. Opposite them on the other side of the grave was a hard-faced old lady with a heavily lined face, a turned-down mouth, and steel-coloured grey hair. She wore a plain black coat and supported herself with a walking stick.

'Who's that?' whispered Octavia to Elaine, who was magnificently dressed in a vintage black suit and who still reminded her eerily of Iseult.

'Oh, that's our mother. She wasn't going to come but Ettare persuaded her.'

Octavia stared over at the old woman and a wave of intense hatred passed through her. It was so strong that for a moment she thought she might fall over, She clutched at Elaine for support.

'Are you all right?' Elaine asked anxiously.

'Yes . . . I'm fine.' Octavia couldn't quite explain how she felt, but it was as though she wanted to rush over to Iseult's mother and scream at her, asking how she could hurt her daughter the way she had. The impulse made her heart race and her breathing quicken. It was some time before she was calm again.

At the wake at Mabbes she tried to talk to Roddy, but he was glassy-eyed and strange, staring about him in a nervous way.

'Roddy, what's wrong?'

'Dunno. Dunno. I . . . feel like . . . she's here. Like she's round the next corner, you know?' He was ashen as he dragged compulsively on a cigarette. 'Christ, I've got to get out of here.'

A few minutes later, pleading an engagement in Paris, Roddy headed off to where his car was waiting for him. He hadn't said goodbye to Octavia. He obviously couldn't wait to leave, but Octavia felt that whatever or whoever it was he was trying to escape was going with him on that plane to Paris.

She said goodbye to Elaine.

'Don't forget us, keep in touch,' said Iseult's sister, kissing her. 'Are you going back to London?'

'Oh, no,' Octavia said, 'I'm going home. I mean . . . I'm going to Scotland, where I'm staying.'

And then she left.

83

Flora stayed at Glachach on her own while Octavia went to the funeral, with only Hilda and Godfrey for company – not that she minded. It was only a few days until Otto's deadline was up. After that, surely, she'd be free of him and able to move on. Up here at Glachach she could go on long wanderings, dreaming of her future and conjuring up Nick's face, indulging in happy fantasies.

It was a bitter day outside as she sat in the breakfast room, enjoying Hilda's hot porridge with Scottish heather honey and toasting her feet by the fire. The house seemed to have an endless supply of cosy socks and blankets so that whenever she was chilly, there was something to snuggle under.

She was reading a novel she'd picked up in the sitting room and sipping coffee when Hilda came in.

'I've just had a call from the boss,' the housekeeper said, looking surprised. 'He's on his way up here. I wasnae expecting him so I'm going to have to send Godfrey out for some extra supplies. He's bringing your cousin too, apparently, and someone called Mr Falcon.'

'Vicky? And Nick . . . Oh!' Nervousness flickered alongside pleasure. Why on earth were Vicky and Nick coming here? Did that mean there was bad news? Had Otto decided he couldn't wait any longer and revealed his cache of material to the world? She knew that formal negotiations went through the lawyers' office but when it came to his truly dirty work, Otto communicated directly with Nick. Flora put down her coffee cup, suddenly feeling she didn't want anything more.

'They'll be here quite soon, I think,' Hilda said, turning to go back to the kitchen. 'I do wish he'd let me know more in advance . . . I hate it when he springs these surprises on me!'

Flora went up to her room and brushed her hair. She could see from her reflection that her eyes looked frightened. There must be some nasty shock in store or else why hadn't they called her? She changed into a pale blue silk shirt printed with tiny stars and pulled on a lavender ballet cardigan, wrapping the ties loosely at the side of her waist in a looping bow. Her jeans were fine. She dumped her thick socks and put on some tan leather boots. As she was applying some lip gloss, she heard the thwuck-thwuck-thwuck of the approaching helicopter and hurried downstairs, picking up a jacket as she went and letting herself out of the back door, passing Hilda who was rushing about preparing more lunch.

The cherry-red Gazelle came quickly over the trees towards the open field and then began its descent. Flora felt her hair whipped back hard from her face. The noise was almost overwhelming after the usual silence. She could see Max in the pilot seat, in dark glasses and headphones, and Vicky next to him. Nick must be in the back. She tried not to feel nervous as the helicopter came in to land, touching down with a slight bump. The engine began to die away and the propellers slowed. The doors opened and Nick got out first, protected from the cold by a black sheepskin jacket. Her stomach jittered; no matter what news he brought, it was wonderful to see him.

When Nick had climbed down, he turned and put his hand up to the craft to help someone else down. A slender black-gloved hand took it, held it tight, and a dark head with streaks of grey appeared. The next moment a woman had emerged from the helicopter. She was wearing a smart long coat in plum-coloured wool, with a black shawl wrapped tightly about her shoulders. She began to walk towards the house, still holding on to Nick as she crossed the rough ground. Behind them, Max and Vicky were emerging.

Who's that? wondered Flora, and frowned as she watched the woman coming towards them. She was in her fifties perhaps and there was something about the face that was familiar, as if she had known it once, a long time ago when it looked different. But the eyes seemed to have remained the same . . . where did she know them from?

Then an image came to her mind with the force of a blow: it was a picture of a bride, with short dark curly hair and a wreath of flowers, her lips glossy and her dress billowing out . . .

Flora gasped. Her hand went to her heart and her mouth dropped open. She knew who this was. The woman walking towards her was her mother.

She wanted to go forward and meet her, but she

couldn't move. All she could do was stand there, thinking, *This is her, this is my mother, she is here at last* . . . over and over.

As they reached her, coming through the gate in the fence and into the garden, Diane Beaufort smiled. 'Flora?' she said in a soft voice.

'Yes,' Flora replied. But although her lips moved, no sound came out. She was too overwhelmed by the sight of her own flesh-and-blood mother coming towards her that she couldn't do anything at all.

Then Diane opened her arms and suddenly she could move. Flora raced forward and an instant later was wrapped in her mother's embrace for the first time she could ever recall in her life. The wool coat was scratchy under her cheek, but she didn't mind.

'You're here!' she breathed, her eyes tight shut as she felt the reality of her mother's arms around her. 'At last.'

'I think that went all right,' said Vicky to Nick as they sat in the kitchen over coffee and Hilda's home-made flapjacks.

'It was a hell of a risk,' Nick said. He smiled. 'But I think, just maybe, you did the right thing.'

'What do you make of Diane?'

Nick looked thoughtful as he nibbled on a piece of sticky flapjack. 'I thought she seemed okay. Kind of reserved, but maybe that's nerves. You can sure see where the girls get their looks from. She may be getting on, but she's still a beauty.'

Vicky nodded. 'It must be completely strange for her too. She's been living in isolation for years.'

'But you managed to persuade her to leave?'

'It took a while,' Vicky said. It was easy enough to slip away for a few days while the girls were in Scotland and she had made the first trip to the Pyrenees on her own, using Nick's information to locate the mountainside cottage on the outskirts of a remote village. There, Diane Beaufort was living alone, with only a collection of animals for company, almost entirely cut off from the outside world except for a satellite phone in case of emergencies. It was a bare, beautiful place to live, where the only passersby were hardy mountain goats and the occasional goatherd. Vicky's arrival had clearly been a great shock and Diane's first reaction had been hostile, but Vicky had persisted and gradually won the older woman's trust. The temptation to learn about her daughters and their lives was too much for her. Eventually she'd allowed Vicky in to talk to her for hours about what had happened to Octavia and Flora.

Diane had listened hard, much of what she was hearing causing her obvious pain.

'Flora wants to see you,' Vicky had said at last. 'More than anything, she wants to know her mother.'

Diane thought and then said, 'But not Octavia?'

'Well . . . not right now. She's turned her back on the past. She only wants to move forward.'

'I see.'

'But I know how you can see Flora alone. And I hope you'll decide to do it. I don't think you'll regret it.'

'I need to think about this,' Diane had said, sighing. 'I'd resigned myself to never seeing my daughters again. If I'm to step back into the world, I need to be sure it's the right thing to do.'

When Vicky had returned the next day, Diane had said, 'No one else needs to know about this, do they? If I go and see Flora, I mean?'

'No, no one. It can all be done privately. You needn't so much as book a ticket,' Vicky said eagerly.

'If that's true, then I'll come. But there's one condition. I have to be allowed to leave when I say, and after that I must be left strictly in peace. I don't want a stream of visitors coming here, trying to understand me and my life. Understand?'

'I understand,' Vicky said, trying to hide her jubilation. She'd done it. She was about to make Flora's dream come true. All she needed was Max to help her, just as he'd promised.

84

Flora and Diane sat alone in the sitting room. At first Flora had hardly known what to say to her mother, but only wanted to look at her in amazement.

'You've grown into a beautiful girl,' Diane said, staring at her. 'I knew you would. You were a gorgeous baby. You both were. I suppose that, looking at you, I'm getting a glimpse of Octavia too.'

'Yes,' Flora said, wanting to blurt out the question that was hanging over them both: *Why did you leave us?*

'Vicky has told me something of what you've been through recently. I'm so sorry, Flora. It sounds as though you've suffered very much.' Her mother's voice was gentle and sympathetic. With all her heart Flora wanted to reach out to her, confide in her, tell her everything, but this woman was a stranger. And until Flora knew why she had left her two young daughters, it didn't seem possible to understand her.

'Yes, and it's not over yet.'

'Vicky said this man you married has some hold over you?'

'He's . . . he's blackmailing me with private photographs. If he made them public, the scandal would be . . . terrible.'

'Ah, yes. Well, I know something about that. Your aunt made sure that every salacious detail she could dig up against me was used in the custody case. There was almost no part of my private life that didn't become public knowledge, and the pain of it was awful.' Diane's eyes darkened at the memory. 'But let's not talk of that now. I want to hear about your life . . . what it was like growing up with Frances.' Her mother looked at her, questioning, something like vulnerability in her eyes. It seemed that a lot hung on her answer.

Flora stared at the floor for a minute. Where did she begin? With the strange, restricted lives they'd been forced to endure? With the rigid diets and severe punishments? With the string of governesses and the finishing school that might as well have been a prison? With the things she'd had to suffer in those huge but mostly empty houses? 'It was . . . happy,' she said, unable to bring herself to begin to tell the truth. How could she? Perhaps when . . . if . . . they ever got to know her. 'We were well treated by Aunt Frances and she looked after us. It was a bit eccentric, perhaps, but at least Octavia and I had each other.'

'Ah, yes . . . Octavia. Who doesn't want to see me.'

'Yes. She'll be angry. She thought we should leave things as they were.'

'But you didn't agree.'

'No.'

Diane Beaufort sat back in her armchair. 'Tell me

more about growing up,' she said. 'What games did you play?'

It became easier after a while to talk about the happy things, the holidays and Christmases, the silly things that had happened. And it seemed important to reassure her mother that she had done the right thing in leaving the girls, even though the question of why they'd been left at all remained hanging in the air. Hilda brought them sandwiches at lunchtime, and tea at four o'clock, and still they talked on. Eventually, Vicky knocked discreetly at the door and told them it was almost dinnertime.

'Aren't I going back tonight?' Diane asked, surprised.

'Max says the flying conditions aren't terribly good this evening, and anyway you've talked for hours. It's probably best to stay here tonight and leave tomorrow.'

Diane cast a worried look at Flora. 'But isn't Octavia coming back?'

Vicky said, 'Not until later tomorrow. I'm sure you'll miss her.'

'Won't you stay and see her?' asked Flora. 'I think it would be terrible if she missed her only opportunity to meet you, even if she believes she doesn't want to.'

Diane shook her head. 'I don't want to force myself into her life. She thinks she'd be better off without me and she very well may be.'

'Come on,' Vicky said. 'Max is waiting for us.'

Dinner was surprisingly enjoyable. *My mother,* Flora kept thinking in a daze, wanting to pinch herself to check she was awake. *My mother is here.* Max, Vicky

607

and Nick kept discreetly quiet during the meal, speaking just enough to keep conversation flowing, but letting Diane and Flora continue their exchange of memories.

Flora realised with surprise that on one side of her sat her mother and on the other was Nick. *If only Octavia were here, it would be perfect,* she thought.

While they were waiting for the pudding, Diane looked about and said, 'This reminds me a little of the house I first lived in with Arthur. You girls were born there. It was your first home.'

'Really? Where was that?' Flora asked, interested.

'A house in the countryside just outside Edinburgh, where Arthur was doing a Master's in engineering. It was when he planned to go into the family business eventually.' A wistful look passed over Diane's face. 'We were so happy then. Before it all went wrong.'

There was a pause and then Vicky said, 'And you've lived in France ever since you left England?'

Diane laughed. 'Oh, no. We lived all over the world. Africa, for years and years. And then in the Far East. I only turned up in France about six years ago.'

We? Flora thought. *We lived all over the world. But only I turned up in France.*

Dinner finished and Diane said politely, 'Thank you for a lovely meal. I haven't been to a proper dinner party like this for longer than I can remember. It was most enjoyable. But, if you don't mind, I'd like to turn in now.'

Max stood up. 'Let me show you upstairs to your room.'

When they'd gone, the other two looked at Flora, both with concern in their eyes.

'How did it go?' Vicky asked.

'Fine, fine . . .' Flora sighed. 'It was all very friendly. And she hasn't disappointed me – she's what I expected: gracious and dignified and all of that. But we haven't really talked about what happened, why she went away.'

'There's still tomorrow,' Nick suggested, with a sympathetic smile.

'Only an hour or two. I don't know how I'll ever ask her,' Flora said sadly. 'But it will be hard to say goodbye to her without knowing.'

'Let's see what happens tomorrow.'

As they were all about to go upstairs to bed, Nick put out a hand to stop Flora. 'Can I speak to you alone?' he said in a low voice.

She nodded, a flutter of excitement in her stomach. All day the knowledge of his presence had been disturbing her, tingling within her, even when she was lost in conversation with Diane. She had been longing to see him by herself. Perhaps he'd been thinking the same thing.

She followed him into the sitting room, lit only by the glowing embers burning in the grate. He stood close to her, his face illuminated by the half-light so that his perfectly straight nose was even more pronounced. Her heart began to race and she felt a light and delicious fizz in her belly as her body responded to his nearness.

'Did everything go okay? I hope it was all right, springing this surprise on you. Vicky thought it was the best way.'

609

'It was fine.' Flora smiled at him. 'Thank you for helping.'

'That's all right,' he said gently. 'I want to help you.' His expression became sad and he hesitated before saying, 'I hate bringing bad news.'

The pleasurable tingle turned to a swoop of fear in Flora's chest. 'What is it?' she asked. 'Otto . . . ?'

Nick nodded. 'I'm afraid so. I wish I didn't have to say this to you. He's been in touch to let me know that he's demanding an extra five million a year. For life.'

She gasped. 'But he already has more money than he could ever spend!'

'He's greedy, Flora. It'll never be enough, not until he has everything you own. My guess is that he considers you to be his property, and what's yours as his.'

She put her face in her hands and closed her eyes. 'Why won't he leave me alone?' she cried out in anguish. 'I only want to be free of him. God, I wish I'd never laid eyes on him. If only I hadn't been so stupid . . .' She burst out crying.

'Hey, hey.' Nick reached out and put his arms round her, pulling her close to him. 'Don't blame yourself. Older, wiser and more sophisticated women than you have fallen for nasty little conmen before now. You were targeted. You weren't to know. You didn't have a chance against an operator like that rat.'

She huddled into his arms, comforted by the smooth warmth of his cotton shirt and the sound of his heart beating. She stopped sobbing, sniffing slightly instead as her tears subsided. No matter how dreadful Otto was, his power over her receded when she was with Nick.

He pulled back from her, a sweet expression in his eyes. 'Better?'

She nodded, looking up at him, her face tilted towards his. *Kiss me, kiss me,* she was begging him silently, desperate to have the touch of those full lips on hers.

'Oh, God,' he muttered. 'I want to kiss you. This is crazy.'

'No, it's not,' Flora whispered. Her fear and anguish had disappeared and she was filled with yearning for him. Nick gazed down at her; his eyes were a melting brown in the soft glow of the embers.

'You're so beautiful,' he said in a wondering voice. 'What did I do to end up in a house in the middle of nowhere with a gorgeous girl in the firelight like this? I must have one hell of a fairy godmother.'

'Please, I wish you would kiss me,' said Flora, unable to bear the tension any longer.

He bent down and with exquisite gentleness, put his mouth on hers and kissed her lightly. His lips were as soft and gorgeous as she'd expected. Something in her melted further second by second as he kissed her, over and over, each kiss a little harder and lasting an instant longer than the last. It was a delicious, delicate tease, until she was longing for him to take possession of her mouth. Then, at last, his lips opened and his tongue brushed her lips. She opened her mouth to him, savouring the sweetness of his taste, putting her hands round his head to pull him to her, digging her fingers into his thick black hair.

611

This is a kiss, she thought dizzily. *The first perfect kiss of my life.*

They kissed for what felt like a long time, her desire for him growing with every moment. She had thought, in those terrible encounters with Otto, that he was killing her, destroying her capacity for love and desire. The instant Nick touched her, she felt as though something was put back into place, as though he had somehow fixed her. And as they kissed, a sense of joy that Otto's power over her was being vanquished grew and grew, along with the wonderful sensations shooting all over her body like delightful fireworks. She wanted to kiss all of him, explore him, feel his skin, discover his body . . .

'Oh my God, Flora,' said Nick, pulling away from her at last and looking down at her in astonishment. 'That was . . . beautiful.'

'Nick . . .' she said, gazing up at him, her eyes shining, 'Nick, I—'

The door opened and Max came into the room. He stopped short when he saw them standing so close to one another. 'Oh. I'm sorry.' He seemed disconcerted. 'I didn't realise you were in here. I just came to get my paper.'

'Not at all, we were just discussing . . . er . . .' Nick said uncomfortably. He looked at Flora and his gaze became tender as his voice trailed off.

'Please, please, don't mind me, I'm just going,' Max said, picking up his newspaper.

'I . . . er . . . I guess we'd better all go to bed maybe.' Nick turned to Flora. 'You must be tired.'

'Yes, I am.' She smiled at him. The spell was broken for the moment, but she could still feel the imprint of his lips on hers and taste him in her mouth. For now, she wanted to savour it, treasure it and think about it. 'I'll go up now. Goodnight, Max. Thank you for everything. Goodnight, Nick.'

'Goodnight,' he said softly, looking as though he wanted to kiss her again. 'I'll see you tomorrow.'

'Goodnight, Flora,' Max said, as she headed out of the room, feeling as though she were floating. 'Sleep tight.'

85

Octavia sat back in the taxi, feeling pleased with herself. Once the funeral was over, she'd wanted to return to Glachach as soon as possible and in the end had managed to get a dawn flight from Bristol to Glasgow, then a taxi to the village near the house, and from there another local taxi with a driver who actually knew how to find the house, as she had no idea where it was unless she was coming by air. She had a feeling that 'by some mountains, not far from a loch' wouldn't cut it as directions in Scotland.

As the battered old car bounced along the unmetalled track that led to Glachach, Octavia thought how much she was looking forward to eating a proper breakfast with Flora, and was idly wondering if she could get Hilda to teach her how to make porridge in that particularly sublime way when suddenly she sat up straight. There was the cherry-red helicopter in the field by the house.

'Max,' she breathed with excitement. 'Max is back!' She leant forward. 'Can you hurry up, please?'

The taxi driver muttered something under his breath

and they carried on juddering up the track until at last they came to a halt in front of the house.

I'll surprise him, thought Octavia, paying the driver and then hurrying round to the back of the house where she could let herself in. Hilda was in the kitchen when she came in, topping up a large pot of coffee.

'Hello, miss!' she said, looking surprised as Octavia skipped past her. 'We weren't expecting you back till later.'

'I know, don't say anything!' she said mischievously, and darted out of the kitchen down the hall and flung open the breakfast-room door. 'Da-dahhhh!' she announced, flinging her arms into the air. Then she stopped short and stared. Around the table were Max and Flora, as she'd expected, but also Vicky, Nick, and an older woman with blue eyes and short dark hair. 'Oh,' she said.

'Octavia!' gasped Flora, looking scared. She immediately glanced over to the stranger at the table. Octavia followed her glance and at once she knew. Fury rushed through her.

'No!' she shouted. 'No! No!' She stared round at them all. 'How could you? How could you after what I said? You're traitors, all of you!'

Then she turned and ran out of the room.

There was a horrified silence as they all looked at each other, then Flora leapt to her feet and raced off after her sister, calling out, 'Tavy! Tavy, please!'

'Oh, dear,' Diane Beaufort said. 'That didn't go well at all.' She put her napkin on the table, obviously no longer wanting her breakfast. 'I should never have come, not when Octavia didn't want it.'

'She'll come round,' Max said.

'How do you know?'

He put down his porridge spoon. 'Because she does want it. She might not know it, but she does.'

Flora found Octavia sobbing in Max's study.

'How could you, Flora?' she shouted furiously, tears running down her face. 'After what we talked about? Everything we said!'

'But I didn't,' she said, pleading. 'It wasn't me. Vicky arranged it. Nick tracked her down, Vicky found her and she got Max to bring her here in the helicopter. She did it for me . . . she knew how much I wanted it. You weren't supposed to know. Vicky planned to get her out of here before you got back. I wasn't part of it, Tavy, I promise.'

She went over to her sister and sat next to her, struggling to put her arms around her despite Octavia's trying to shake her off.

'I don't want to see her!' Octavia felt the same wave of hatred as when she'd seen Iseult's mother at the graveside. 'I don't want her in my life.'

'But why?' asked Flora, her voice beseeching. 'She's just a person. She's not a devil or anything. She's just a woman who made mistakes.'

'She left us, Flora!'

'But we don't know why . . .'

'I don't care. I don't need to know why. All I know is that she had her chance and she ballsed it up!'

Flora thought for a moment while Octavia cried a little more quietly. Then she said, 'She told me we used to live in Scotland when we were little, in a house like this one.'

'Oh?' Octavia looked up, her attention caught. 'Did we? Where?'

'Why don't you ask her?'

'I see, I see – you want to trick me into talking to her!'

'No, I don't. I just want to show you that she can tell us things we don't know. She's the only one who ever will.'

Octavia took a handkerchief out of her pocket and blew her nose. 'If we talk to her, it will be like we forgive her.'

'You don't then?'

'I can't,' Octavia said, her eyes welling up again. 'Not after what we've had to go through.'

'But we can never know what other life we might have had. It might have been worse.'

Octavia laughed hollowly. 'I'd like to know how it could have been worse.'

'Well, you don't know.' Flora put her hand on her sister's arm. 'All I'm saying is, you don't even know what you won't forgive her for. You don't know why she left us.'

Octavia stared at her, wiping her eyes and reddened nose, and then said suddenly, 'You know what? You're right. We *don't* know why she left us. And I want to find out. Right now. Right this goddamned minute.'

She got up and strode out of the study, Flora following behind, breathless. At the breakfast room, Octavia stopped in the doorway and said with cool politeness, 'Would you mind excusing us? Not you, Diane. Flora and I have some questions for you and we'd like some answers.'

Once the others had gone, Octavia and Flora went in and shut the door behind them.

Octavia put her hand on her hip. 'Now, if you don't mind, *Mother*, we'd like you to answer us.'

Diane Beaufort got up and went over to the window. She stared out at the bleak countryside, the way the wind was swaying the branches of the trees. At last she said, 'I should have known this would happen. Somehow I convinced myself that Vicky was right – a quick, friendly meeting and that would be it. Finished. I should have guessed you'd never leave it there. Perhaps I did know, in my heart. I must have wanted this, I suppose.'

Octavia went to the table and rested one hand on it. 'We only have one question. Why? Why did you do it? Why did you leave us?'

Diane Beaufort turned back to face her daughters, and sighed. 'Why? Because I loved you, of course. That's why.'

They all sat round the table, poured out tepid cups of coffee from the cooling pot and listened as Diane told her side of the story.

'Your aunt was determined to take you from me and I was equally determined to keep you. It was true that our marriage was virtually over when Arthur died. We'd been living separate lives for months but that was largely because of his alcoholism. We were both party animals when we were younger, there was no denying it, but it took its toll on Arthur. He always went at it harder than anyone else and ended up hopelessly addicted. He was charming to the end, but not safe to be around. I've always believed that he was drunk at the controls of that plane, but it was never proved. We'd lived in a louche crowd, I must admit. Arthur's money attracted all kind of sybarites and hangers on, people determined to party at his expense. We were both . . . somewhat debauched, and enjoyed all the freedoms of youth.' She looked at her daughters. 'I mean sexual freedoms. AIDS didn't bother us then, it was for junkies and gays and we thought we were immune. Life was a free-for-all. A crazy roundabout.

'But then I had you, my gorgeous daughters. Arthur adored you too and our lives quietened down for a while, we were almost normal. We had our little Edinburgh house and Arthur had decided to study, and make a career for himself. For a while he seemed to be better, but then the drinking came back worse than ever. He was constantly drunk, unable to study, and his old friends found us again, ready to tempt him away from his family. And then . . .' Diane took a deep breath and traced her finger along the pattern in the white damask tablecloth. 'Then I fell in love.'

The sisters looked at one another, wide-eyed and almost holding their breath as they took in every detail of the story.

'Arthur and I were, in effect, separated when he died. Frances couldn't believe that anyone could leave her darling brother, let alone a woman she'd always considered a trollopy little golddigger who was no better than she should be. As soon as he was killed, she began her bid to get you for herself and she wasted no time in recruiting Arthur's old friends to give her the evidence she needed, no doubt paying them well as she went. They obliged with plenty of stories about my moral degeneracy. Nevertheless, the courts weren't about to take you away from me, not when I could show I was a perfectly good mother and that my wild days, such as they had been, were long behind me.'

Octavia spoke up then. 'They said you had practically won the case,' she said quietly. 'But on the morning of the judgement, you took us in, handed us over and went away for ever.'

Diane looked at her. 'I was forced into that position. You see, your aunt discovered something about me and threatened to use it. The man I loved – he wasn't any man.' She stared at the table for a while then said, 'I promised myself I would never tell you. That you would never know. And here I am, about to say it.'

They gazed at her, waiting.

'The man I fell in love with was my own brother. Or, at least, my half-brother, the product of a fling my father had in his youth. I hadn't known him while I was growing up . . . I hadn't even known he existed. But he found me when we were adults, and we simply couldn't help ourselves. We fell passionately in love. No one knew he was related to me – we had different names and no obvious link. But in the course of digging up the dirt, Frances found out. She must have been so jubilant when she did. She must have realised she'd won.' Diane smiled sadly. 'She came to me with a bargain. If I gave you up, she would leave me in peace in my incestuous filth, as she put it. If I refused, she would expose me to the world. I would be considered unnatural and repellent, my lover would be forced to leave me . . . and if he did not, I would lose my daughters anyway. Whatever happened, you girls would be stigmatised by association with me.

'And then she played her trump card: she would

claim that I was having sex with my brother before you were born. That you were possibly children of that union. It was a lie, of course. A court case and blood tests and DNA would have proved all that. But we both knew that the scandal would taint you girls for life, and that wasn't a price I was willing to pay. If I left you with her, you'd be safe, untouched, pure. If you came with me, you'd be ruined. I couldn't spoil your lives. So I left you with her. It broke my heart, but I trusted she would do right by you. She loved her own brother so much, you see. I sometimes wonder if her terrible anger towards me came from a subconscious jealousy. I got to sleep with my brother. She could only adore hers from afar.'

Diane got up and went back to the window, staring out at the countryside again.

'I agreed to leave Britain and the States for ever. My lover and I went to live in Africa, where we were anonymous and very, very happy. We had eight years of bliss together, and then he died. After that, my life was pretty much over. I travelled for some years then went to France, to settle in the mountains by myself, to see my life out there.' She turned back to her daughters. 'I thought about you every day. But I forced myself to let you be and never contact you. Frances's threat always hung over my head.'

'So . . .' Flora spoke up for the first time, her voice tremulous 'So it was fear of this scandal that made you give us up?'

Diane nodded. 'Public outrage is a terrible thing. It can blight an existence.'

'But she didn't keep us pure and safe,' Flora protested. 'She didn't.'

Diane looked at her, her face fearful. 'She . . . didn't?'

Flora shook her head. 'N-n-n-no.'

The three women emerged from the breakfast room some hours later, all tear-stained and obviously shaken by what they'd been through, but with an air of catharsis. Something had been exorcised. There was a feeling of peace in the air, the kind of calm that comes after a fierce storm of crying, when all passions are spent.

'Max,' Diane said. 'You said I could go home. Is that possible? Can you take me to the airport, please?'

'It's late to start,' he said uncertainly. 'Perhaps best stay another night.'

'No. There's a late flight to London. I have to go now. I haven't spent this long with other people in many years. I need to be alone.'

'Very well,' he said. As Diane went to collect her things, he turned to Octavia and said quietly, 'It's only twenty minutes to Glasgow. And then I'm coming straight back, so don't you go anywhere.'

Nick was waiting for Flora in the upstairs hallway, pacing about anxiously. As she came up, he strode over to her. 'Hey, are you okay? I think you girls have had quite a day of it.'

She nodded. 'It's been hard. But, yes, it's been good too. It was what we needed.'

'I'm glad. I know how much you wanted to find out the truth about your mom.' He hesitated then said, 'Listen, I think I'll hitch a lift to the airport and catch that ride back to London. We've only got a day or two

622

left to deal with Otto, and I'd better make the arrangements for that annual payment. If that's what you want?'

'Actually . . .' Flora stared up into his black eyes and took a deep breath. 'I've changed my mind.'

He frowned. 'You have?'

'Yes. I don't want to give him a penny. I intend to seek an official annulment of our marriage and pursue him through the courts for all the money he's stolen from me.'

Nick looked astonished, then his face creased with anxiety. 'But, Flora, I gotta warn you . . . You know what this means. He'll put those pictures and that film up on the internet and you'll be splashed all over the papers, probably all over the world.'

'I know.' She straightened her shoulders. 'It will be horrible. But I'll live it down. You see, I've discovered what happens when you live your life afraid of what the world will think. You become the prisoner of all your secrets, and so does your family. I need to be free, and I'll do whatever it takes.'

He gazed down at her with shining eyes. 'Flora, you're amazing.'

'Am I?' She laughed. 'I don't feel very amazing.'

'Well, you are.' He put his arms around her and hugged her. 'And very brave. I'm in awe of you.'

They pulled away and gazed at one another for a moment, and there was a strange, excited awkwardness between them as they both remembered the kiss of the night before but couldn't mention it, like embarrassed teenagers.

'You've done the right thing, I know it,' he said softly. 'I'm so proud of you.'

'Nick?' Max was calling from downstairs. 'We're making tracks, if you're coming?'

'I'll be right there!' he called back, not taking his eyes off Flora. 'Take care,' he said, dropping a kiss on her cheek. 'I'll see you very soon.'

86

When Max returned, Flora and Vicky had gone to bed but Octavia had waited up for him, a bottle of his favourite Scotch ready.

He came in, cold and tired, raising his eyebrows when he saw her, sitting in the dimly lit kitchen. 'I thought you'd be asleep,' he said.

She shook her head. 'I'm not sleepy. But it was a hell of an emotional day.'

'I can't begin to imagine what you've been through.'

'I've got some supper for you.'

'That's thoughtful of you. Thanks.'

They took a plate of sourdough bread, ham and cheese, and the Scotch, through to the drawing room, sat on the comfortable old sofa and Octavia watched Max while he ate his late supper.

'Did you help Vicky bring our mother here?' she asked softly.

Max shot her a quick look. 'Well . . . yes. I lent her the Gazelle and my pilot, and they collected her and your mother from France. I hope you don't mind?

I was under the impression that was what you and Flora wanted.'

'It was very kind of you. Thank you. I didn't want it – but I'm glad now.'

He munched thoughtfully. 'She's quite a woman, your mother. I can see where you get your strength.'

When the plate had been put aside and the glass refilled, he took his Scotch in his hand and observed the orangey-brown liquid and the way it changed colour with the light from the fireplace. Then he looked up at her, his eyes serious.

'I've been wanting to have a talk with you, Octavia. I've heard about what happened with Ethan. It's very bad news. I don't have to tell you how sorry I am.'

'It's a mess,' she said frankly. 'I've got to appoint a business advisor to help me sort it out.'

'You're lucky in a way that Brody used the investment company for his main fraud. That can be put in abeyance until the court case without too much trouble. Noble's pays BC Investments for the lease of the property, doesn't it? Well, that can go on as before. Butterfly can continue as long as Brody is voted off the board immediately and a new chief executive is appointed, ideally someone who knows the company very well.'

'A little bit easier said than done,' Octavia said with a sigh. 'I've never done anything without Ethan before. I guess this is my chance to step up to the mark.'

'Anything I can do to help . . . you can count on me.'

'Thank you, Max.' The sense that he was there to help had filled her with quiet happiness. But she

626

didn't want to rely on him. She needed to prove herself too.

He leant back on the sofa and sipped his Scotch. His expression was solemn. 'Money is a very serious thing. It's not your fault that your father didn't put your inheritance into a safe form. Perhaps he meant to, who knows? But the reality is he left you entirely unprotected and that has attracted these terrible fraudsters. Money can do amazing things in the world but it also brings out the very worst in the human character: meanness, venality, greed. It's sad, but true.'

'I know. I'm not going to let anything like this happen again. I'm going to hire the best lawyers, the best advisors, and make sure I protect what I've got – and the jobs of everyone who works for me. I'm never letting a criminal get near me again.' Octavia looked at him sadly. 'Ethan frittered it away on nothing. On himself. It's the waste of it that makes me so angry. That's not going to happen again.'

Max stared at her intently. 'I believe you,' he said simply.

Octavia found she couldn't meet his gaze, even though his faith in her filled her with pleasure. *His opinion matters to me. I feel better about myself when I'm with him. And this place feels like home.* She looked up at him, into that strong face with the force of his personality shining from its eyes, thinking how amazing he was. Suddenly the air crackled with the tension between them.

Max, she realised, was staring back at her, a fierce light in his eyes that she'd never seen before. 'What a beautiful girl you are,' he said. 'You're not like anyone else I've ever met. You're passionate, unusual – so much older in some ways than your years . . .'

'Max,' she whispered, an intense warmth growing in her stomach and spreading out all over her.

'You do something to me, Octavia. You make me feel alive again . . .'

She pulled in a breath. So it wasn't her imagination, that curious magnetic force between them. He felt it too.

'It's the same for me,' she said, her eyes shining. 'It's been there from that start hasn't it? From the very first time.'

He nodded, a smile curling about his lips. 'From the moment we met.' Then his eyes darkened. 'But . . .'

Her heart swooped. 'What?'

Max frowned almost helplessly. 'It's not as simple as that. I'm somewhat older than you are. And I'm married.'

'You're getting divorced,' she said hurriedly.

'True.' He seemed to be struggling with himself. 'But shouldn't you be with someone closer to your own age?'

'I've tried that,' she said. 'It's no good. I need someone like you, Max. I'm not the same as girls like Jasmine and Rosie. And it isn't about age. It's about who you are, who I am . . .' She looked at him beseechingly. 'Is it because you still think I'm hopeless?'

'God, no.' He frowned into his whisky and his voice was gruff. 'I think you're anything but hopeless. And I like you very much. Too much. But I have to think of you. If we were together, people would talk.'

'They talk about everything! And let them,' cried

Octavia hotly. 'I don't care about that! There are worse things, believe me. We . . . *like* . . . each other. We can't pretend that's not the case. Max . . . please . . .' She moved across the sofa towards him, took his face in her hands and kissed him hard on the lips. After a startled instant he began to respond to her, putting his hand to her head and pressing her to him. The moment the kiss began, they were both possessed by fierce desire and the kiss quickly became wild. She unbuttoned his shirt, suddenly possessed by an over-whelming lust. She wanted to possess him now as much as possible. This might be her only opportunity. She straddled him, one thigh on either side of his, and pushed her groin towards him as his tongue probed her mouth and they panted together between deep kisses.

'Max . . .' she whispered as his hands followed the curve of her waist, down over her hips and round her buttocks.

He moaned. 'My God, you're gorgeous you're irre-sistible . . .'

She had his shirt open and his hands were under hers, cupping her breasts, his thumbs rubbing her nipples, when suddenly he pulled away from her mouth and said, 'No, Octavia, we can't do this.'

'What do you mean? Why not?' She reached for his mouth with hers but he turned away.

'I can't do it. I can't take advantage of you.'

She looked down at their bodies. Max was lying underneath her, with her legs on either side of him, his shirt unbuttoned to the waist. 'Does it *look* like you're taking advantage of me?' she asked.

He looked down as well, and then laughed. She could

sense his desire for her burning through him. 'When you put it like that . . . I appear to be your prisoner.'

'Max . . .' She bent down and nuzzled his face. She kissed his jawline, gently licking the slightly stubbly skin, until she got to his ear. She pulled on his lobe with her lips for a moment and then whispered, 'Max, I want you to make love to me . . . *please.*'

His eyes filled with a passionate light. 'How can I refuse an invitation like that?' And he pulled her mouth back to his.

They made slow, intense love by the fire. Max was strong and passionate, well practised but full of amazement at her, delighted by her body and able to show her new ways to enjoy it. But when, finally, he was moving inside her, it was so perfect that she understood that the feeling she'd had of coming home when she was with him was only a pale shadow of the rightness she felt when they were joined together.

When she came, Octavia realised she was crying and crying, and he kissed away her tears, stroked her hair and held her in his arms till she fell asleep.

Octavia woke in her own bed, not remembering how she'd got there but not caring. The events of the previous night came back to her and she smiled happily, stretching and luxuriating in the feeling of the sheets on her naked body.

'Max,' she said, savouring his name in her mouth. 'Mmmm-max.'

What does this mean? Are we together? Surely we must be. He was so wonderful last night . . . That delicious hunger rippled through her body. She wanted him again. She couldn't imagine not wanting him.

She rolled on to her back and looked up at the ceiling. Yesterday had been truly momentous, even in light of the days that had gone before it. She had met her mother and heard her story. She had learnt the secret of Flora's unhappiness. She'd realised that nothing was worth giving up just because you were afraid of what people might say. And then there'd been Max . . .

It was time to leave Glachach, she knew that. They had done what they needed to here, and there was work to do at home. She had to get back and see how things were with her business. She was going to learn more about the world; begin to understand how to read people; to protect her money, and all the good it could do, from people who wanted it for their own selfish ends. She was going to prove to Max that she was worthy of his love.

And now it's time to face what Ethan's done to me.

87

'Come on, Flora, come on!'

She puffed behind him up the hill, her cheeks pink from the chill winter air and the exertion of the walk. 'I'm coming!' They were approaching the graceful eighteenth-century building that stood at the top, Nick a few steps ahead of her and well wrapped up in a dark overcoat and woolly hat.

'What is this place? It's beautiful.' She stopped for a moment and turned to look back at the view. She could see down over parkland, over the museum and university buildings below, to the river. Beyond that was the city of London, grey and magnificent.

Nick stopped, panting for breath. 'This is the Royal Observatory. Do you know what's special about this place?'

'Of course.' Flora started walking again, eager to get to the top of the hill. 'We're in Greenwich, aren't we? This is where they keep the time.'

Nick laughed. 'Yeah, I like the way that sounds. Like it's in a little box in there. But it's true. Did you know that every day, every year and every millennium is measured as starting from here?'

She shook her head, then put out her hand. 'Come on, slow coach, I'll help you.'

He took it and let her pull him up a couple of steps, and when they were together he didn't let go but said, 'Come on,' and they held hands all the way to the top. 'There's something else here too,' Nick said. 'The meridian line.' They walked into the courtyard in front of the Observatory and he pointed to a shallow, metal-lined trench passing through the ground. People were wandering about, some inspecting the trench and standing on either side of it. Nick led her over to it.

'This is longitude zero. Has been ever since Greenwich won the right to be the starting point of all navigation and time in 1884 – I studied it in high school. And if you stand with one foot on either side . . . come on . . .' Flora obediently stood astride the line, and so did Nick '. . . then you're simultaneously in the eastern and western hemispheres. This line cuts right around the earth and comes back to this exact spot.'

'Wow!' Flora laughed. 'How amazing. But why did you bring me here?'

He smiled, making his face look even more hand-some. 'Because I wanted to show you how powerful you are – you can stand on top of the world if you want to. And also because we might not be able to turn time back or slow it down, but we can, as the poet said, seize the day.'

'Yes,' she said, laughing. 'That sounds good.'

'Flora.' He grabbed her hands and came up close to her. He stared down into her eyes, smiling softly.

Her stomach turned in a leisurely but most enjoyable somersault, and her pulse quickened. 'I've got some news.'

For a terrible moment her happiness dropped away and she feared the worst. Had Otto carried out his threat? Did the world know her secrets? *I can't bear it. But I'll have to.*

'Oh, sweetheart . . .' Nick's dark eyes looked apologetic. 'I've frightened you. I'm so sorry. It's not bad news, I promise. I've had a communication from Germany.'

She closed her eyes and swallowed hard, trying to quell the dread rising in her. 'Yes?'

'I think you'd better look for yourself.' He took something from his pocket and pressed it into her hand. She looked down. It was a jiffy bag, already torn open, addressed to Nick in strong black writing. At least, the address was Nick's. The name on the bag was Flora von Schwetten. Seeing it written down like that, in thick black pen, made her feel even more ill.

'It arrived this morning. Look inside.'

She peered in. There were a dozen or so silver CDs or perhaps DVDs, all marked in German with Otto's handwriting, and several photographs. She had expected to see awful images of herself in that bedroom, the place where she found herself in her nightmares, trapped by the suffocating curtains around that hellish bed. But these photographs were not of a person. She fished one out and looked at it. It showed Otto's study – and the place had been ransacked. More particularly, the computer on his desk had been smashed to smithereens, its innards spewed everywhere, clearly never to be reconstituted.

Flora frowned, confused. 'I don't understand . . .'

'This note was inside.' Nick took a piece of paper from his pocket and unfolded it, holding it out so she could see what was scrawled across it:

Flora, Machen Sie sich keine Sorgen. Otto wird Sie kein mehr Ärger machen.
Marthe Gestenholtz

Flora stared at it. 'What does it say?'

'Basically, don't worry, Otto won't be making any more trouble for you.'

She looked up at Nick, realisation dawning. 'Otto's mother did this!'

Nick nodded, a huge smile spreading over his face. 'My guess is that she found out what his game was, and it was just a step too far for her. She obviously wanted to protect you.'

'Oh, my goodness, this is fantastic!' Flora's face softened. 'Marthe was kind to me, in her way. I think she grew fond of me.'

'She obviously did.'

'Does this mean . . .' The implications started to sink in as Flora gazed at the pictures of Otto's wrecked computer. She began to smile as well. 'Does this mean that he hasn't got any of that material left? He can't publish it?'

'Well, it's hard to say. It might be that his hard drive is salvageable in some way. He might have put a disc into safe storage somewhere, or even used an internet file service to store a backup. But we've got about twelve identical discs here. I'd say these are probably his backup.' Nick gestured to the jiffy bag. 'Otto is a cautious guy. He's clearly tried to protect his stash, but I'd guess that probably means he didn't want to store anything anywhere else. I'd bet good money that this is the real deal.'

Flora pressed one hand to her face, her eyes welling as she began to realise that she might be free from the threat of exposure. 'Oh my God ... Marthe ... she did this for me.'

'She did something else too.' Nick took another piece of paper out of his pocket. 'The icing on the cake. It's a marriage certificate, proving the marriage of Otto and Wiebke Mullinsdorf.'

'Why would she send that?'

'My hunch is that he probably neglected to get himself a divorce or official annulment from Fraulein Mullinsdorf. Which would make your marriage illegal and thus he'd be in line for no divorce settlement at all, and probably more likely to be arrested for bigamy.'

Flora giggled. 'Oh, dear. All his careful plans! Everything ... it's all over for him, isn't it?'

'He's certainly left without much of a hand to play. It's going to be a pleasure re-opening negotiations with him. I think we're going to find the balance of power has shifted.' Nick looked at her, his eyes bright. 'You did exactly the right thing, Flora, in calling his bluff. He must have confided his decision to expose you to his mother, and for her it was the final straw.'

'We'll never know exactly, I suppose, but ... how can I thank her?' Flora murmured softly. She looked up at Nick. 'Can we make sure she's looked after? I don't think Otto was ever kind to her, he treated her like a servant. It would make me happy to know she was free of him at last.'

Sure. I'm certain I can sort that out. Leave it to me.'

She laughed again with happiness. 'Thank you! I'm so happy!' She flung her arms round Nick and kissed his cheek.

He leaned back and looked into her eyes. 'Hey now . . . I don't know if this is the moment, but we never did talk about that night in Scotland.'

Flora smiled. 'I loved it,' she said quietly.

'Yeah, me too.' A confused expression crossed his face. 'But, you know, you're kind of my boss . . . I work for you.'

'So you're not allowed to kiss me?'

'Not really.' He looked longingly down at her lips, obviously pulled in two directions on the matter.

'If I'm your boss, doesn't that mean you have to do as I say?' Flora said, tilting her face up to his.

'Within certain prescribed boundaries,' he murmured. 'Actually, what am I saying? I'm my own boss. You're paying me but that's different. I can stop working any time I want.'

'How about you stop for now and start again later?' suggested Flora. She slipped her hands inside his coat and wrapped her arms around his waist. It felt blissful and his flesh was tantalisingly close.

'Hmm, interesting suggestion . . . yeah, that might work.' Unable to resist her a moment longer, he bent his lips to hers and kissed her gently then less gently until they were lost in the pleasure of one another's mouths. Flora became aware that people around were clapping and cheering as they saw the beautiful young couple locked in a romantic embrace.

They broke slowly apart, both breathless and a little

dazed, smiling at all the good cheer around them as tourists applauded.

'Be happy!' called one in a windcheater and back-pack.

'Shall we? Be happy?' Nick asked, holding her tightly to him.

'Yes,' she whispered, full of joy. 'Let's.'

He smiled down at her, and she hugged him tighter, never wanting to let him go.

88

Octavia came out of the meeting with her new financial advisors with her head spinning. They had explained the position to her in simple terms but it was still hard to grasp. All she knew was that Butterfly remained safe, as long as she was prepared to plug the financial gap left by Ethan's fraud. BC Investments was a different matter, but there was nothing to be done about that until the extent of Ethan's activities had been unravelled and his case brought to trial. At least, even though he'd stolen millions, she was still a very wealthy woman and able to keep the business going. She intended to make sure that any defrauded investors were recompensed. There were to be more meetings in the New Year with the accountants, to go through her entire financial situation.

The yacht's going, that's for sure. What a waste of money! I'll have to look over my entire portfolio, see how much of a stake I have in Ethan's possessions. Whatever's left over after creditors are paid, I'll give to charity.

As she walked, Octavia made a resolution. She would begin to learn about business and money management.

It was true she had no qualifications, but she was educated up to a point and surely would find a way to learn whatever was necessary.

She felt suddenly excited. *I could go to university. Maybe to business school . . .* The world seemed full of possibilities. But, best of all, she already had a business, and a blueprint from Iseult for how to rebuild it. Up until now she had relied on Ethan to help her, but he was in custody, in the process of applying for bail although his attempt to flee the country wasn't going to help that particular cause. She couldn't yet go it alone. And besides, there was still the problem of Noble's staff and their resistance to the new regime.

But Octavia had an idea for a solution to all that. She checked her watch. In fact, her solution ought to be waiting for her right around now.

'Let me get this straight.' Amanda Radcliffe, smart in a charcoal-coloured Dior suit and high black shoes, her dark hair neatly arranged, crossed her legs elegantly and looked over at Octavia as they sat in the elegant foyer of Claridge's, a pot of tea on the small table between them. 'You want me to come back to Noble's as chief exec?'

Octavia nodded.

Amanda stared at her without speaking for almost a minute then threw back her head and laughed heartily.

'Is that funny?' Octavia asked, a little confused.

'Well, yes, it is a bit! Talk about mixed signals. I was under the impression your family wanted my family out of Noble's – you certainly managed to pull the rug from under our feet pretty effectively.'

'I know. And I have to apologise to you for that, Amanda. I was appalled when I heard about your father's death and I'm horrified to think that the takeover might have caused it. I didn't fully understand what was happening at the time.' She looked the other woman straight in the eye. 'I'm so sorry.'

Amanda stared back at her sombrely. 'It was a terrible time. I realise you weren't personally responsible. And I guess I had my revenge, destroying Brody.'

Octavia gave a small smile. 'I ought to thank you for that, really.'

'Is that why you want me on the board?'

'It's a mixture of things. I want to make amends – but I also happen to think you're the very best person for this job. And I found out that you wanted to do new things, including stocking Roddy, but couldn't.'

'Yes.' Amanda picked up her china cup, took a sip of tea and put it back. 'You may have overreached yourself but I did the opposite. Gave in too much. Tried to be accepting and didn't fight for my personal vision. The result was that it was all taken away. I don't want that to happen again, which is why I've decided to start my own boutique, funded by my own money. I want to be my own boss.'

'Oh.' Octavia was crestfallen. She had become set on the idea of Amanda coming back on board. It had seemed the perfect solution. 'But . . .'

'It's all going ahead, I'm afraid. I'm not prepared to pull out now.' Amanda shook her head then smiled across at Octavia in a way that was almost friendly. 'If you'd come to me a little earlier then maybe . . .'

'I've brought something to show you,' Octavia said, taking a calfskin folder out of her bag.

'Oh?' Amanda raised her eyebrows inquisitively.

'Look at this.' She passed it over.

Thirty minutes later, Amanda closed the folder. She frowned and looked a little surprised for a moment. Then her face cleared and she laughed softly. 'So these were Iseult's ideas. Extraordinary. She truly was a talent. I love these plans. The shoe boutique is gorgeous, especially those cabinets. I adore the display ideas for the women's clothes, and the list of designers she's suggested is just right. In fact, I can think of several ways we can build on this. She's suggested a couple of pop-up boutiques and I'm sure we can do loads more of those, teaming up with famous brands. I love the idea of having pop-up famous restaurants on the fourth floor – a mini-Caprice and a Hix oyster bar and so on. And her idea for getting celebrity rock stars and artists to do their own riff on famous Noble's fabrics is brilliant.' Amanda patted the folder. 'It's all great.'

'You just said "*we can*",' Octavia pointed out.

'What?'

'We can build, we can do . . . It sounds like you really want to be a part of it.'

Amanda's face grew solemn and she pursed her lips for a moment. 'Of course I do. But I also want to express myself with my own boutique, do my own thing.'

'But . . .' Octavia stared at her intently, trying to convey the strength of her conviction that Amanda had to come back to the store her family had founded. 'You can do all that as well, if you want! Why don't you start a Noble's diffusion line? Or a luxury goods line?'

Amanda tapped her fingernail on the folder, thinking hard. 'Oh, God,' she said at last, 'I can't believe you're making this so difficult for me. Listen, let me think about it.' She put her head on one side and looked Octavia in the eye. 'Could we work together? That's the question. There's a lot of water under our particular bridge.'

'Well, you won't get much interference from me on the management side, if that's what you're worried about.' Octavia smiled over at her mischievously. 'I'm going to have a rather different role, as it happens . . .'

89

Octavia left Claridge's satisfied that she was in with a fighting chance of persuading the other woman to come back to Noble's. She had promised that Amanda could appoint four new board members of her own choosing and have full executive power over business decisions, although Octavia would retain her voting power and be consulted on all moves.

She walked out into the wintry Brook Street sunshine, making her way down the broad pavement, feeling smart and businesslike in her outfit of pencil skirt and belted jacket under a Dries van Noten coat. Her telephone went and she saw Max's name come up on the screen. Her mouth dried and her heart pounded. He hadn't been in touch since that night in Scotland just over a week ago and she'd begun to worry that it had meant nothing to him. 'Hello?' she said breathlessly.

'Octavia? Where are you?'

'In Mayfair,' she said, smiling at the way he got right to the point as usual.

'Can I see you?'

'Yes, of course.'

'Good. My driver will be in touch. You can give him your exact location so he can collect you.'

Five minutes later Max's driver was bringing the enormous Daimler to a halt next to her. He jumped out with a grin and opened the door for her.

'Afternoon, Miss.'

'Afternoon, Clive.' She climbed on to the buttery leather seat and sat back, putting her briefcase next to her. 'Where are we going?' she asked as he got back behind the wheel and pulled smoothly away from the kerb.

'Sir Max's house, madam,' he said, and they were off, moving through the London traffic, heads turning to look at the magnificent car as they went.

The Christmas lights that were hanging everywhere were already sparkling, she noticed. Despite the fact that it was early afternoon, it was getting dark.

It wasn't far to Max's impressive Holland Park house, on a quiet back street in a row of other substantial mansions, although his was notable for being painted a pale blue. The front door was opened as Octavia came up the steps and a maid took her coat then led her to a drawing room. It was like Glachach, cosy and inviting, with evidence of its owner's cultivated, international taste everywhere, from the ancient Buddha statues to the antique Chinese porcelain, the Graham Sutherland oil on the wall and the prints of Japanese ladies holding silk parasols. There were books and photographs, and heaps of international newspapers in five different languages.

Octavia wandered over to the mantle and examined some photographs of Max with heads of state and important-looking businessmen. She put out a finger to touch his face, missing him suddenly and desperate to be reunited.

A moment later there was the sound of a familiar voice in the hallway and then he was in the room with her. He smiled, and held out his arms to her.

'Max!' she cried joyfully, and ran into them. As she pressed her face to his chest, Octavia said, 'Oh, I've been so worried.'

'Worried? Why?' He hugged her tightly.

'You haven't been in touch.'

His expression became grave. 'I can't pretend that I haven't had a few sleepless nights over what happened between us. I've also been to South Africa and back, so please forgive me. I needed to sort some things out before seeing you. Now, have you had lunch?'

They had a delicious late lunch together of borscht and then baked stuffed sea trout, and Octavia told him about her business meeting and her plan to tempt Amanda back to Noble's, which he liked very much.

As they were drinking coffee, he said idly, 'I expect you've noticed that Christmas is the day after tomorrow.'

'Yes . . .' She felt rather surprised. She'd been so caught up in her business affairs lately that she hadn't given it much thought. She had never had to make any kind of preparations for the holiday, except for a little present-buying the last two years, so it didn't seem to affect her very much. She hadn't given a thought as to what she'd be doing this year.

'I wondered if you'd like to spend it with me. I have

a little place in France. We could have a very quiet time there together . . . if you'd like to?'

Excitement bubbled up inside her. 'Oh, yes! I'd love to! But when will we go? Tomorrow?'

'Oh, no.' Max smiled at her, his blue eyes intense. 'I thought we'd go right away.'

'Right now? But . . .'

He laughed at her expression. 'Don't worry it's all taken care of. If you're ready, we'll leave.'

Clive was waiting outside with the Daimler, already packed, and he drove them swiftly through the rush-hour traffic. London was busy with Christmas shoppers, wrapped up in coats and hats, carrying bulging bags and hurrying past brilliantly lit shop windows. They passed Noble's with its angel-themed displays shimmering out into the darkening afternoon, and Octavia was pleased to see how busy it looked. Soon it would be the main focus of her life, but right now she was going to forget about business and enjoy herself.

She'd expected that Max would pilot them to France in his helicopter, but this time they boarded a tiny aeroplane instead and sat opposite one another in large, comfortable seats, enjoying their privacy. A stewardess brought them drinks and Octavia gazed out into the inky sky as they left Britain behind. The journey was swift. In only an hour and a half they were landing at Bergerac airport, and being taken quickly through passport control. To Octavia's surprise, Max had her passport, and her luggage appeared on a trolley ready to be loaded into the dark green Mercedes waiting for them at the exit.

'A little help from Vicky,' he explained with a grin, and then they were in the car and heading out into the countryside, his hand holding hers.

This is like a dream, Octavia thought happily. The whole thing became even more fantastical when they passed between a pair of wrought-iron gates and approached a beautiful house, lit by floodlights so that it shone out against the night sky.

'Here we are,' Max said, with a smile.

Inside the house was quietly luxurious, full of paintings and antique furniture and opulent fabrics. It was the richest-looking house of Max's she'd yet seen, but it was also intensely comfortable, like being in a superb private hotel. It was toasty warm and when Octavia went up to her room to change for dinner, there was lashings of hot water for her bath.

'This is very romantic,' she said, when she came into the salon dressed in a ravishing floor-length black silk Dior gown.

Max turned and drew in a breath at the sight of her. 'My God, Octavia, you're stunning.' He went over and kissed her, his hand touching the bare skin of her back and sending delicious tingles all over it and down to her groin.

This is bliss, she thought, wanting only to make love to him right there. But she was also starving, and they had all night . . . and the whole of the next day . . . and the day after . . .

She sighed happily. There was no need to hurry.

90

It had been a wonderful evening, but it was the night that raised the whole experience to truly magnificent heights.

After dinner at Corrigan's in Mayfair, they had come back to the Chelsea house and at last, Flora's longing for Nick had been assuaged. They had undressed each other very slowly between long kisses, taking their time as they revealed themselves to each other. He was perfect in every way to her, with the most delicious scent to his skin that she longed to inhale forever. When finally they were both naked, and breathless with longing for each other, he had laid her down on the bed and very gently made love to her, first paying homage to every part of her body with feather-light kisses, telling her how much he wanted her. With every loving kiss and every gentle murmur, he restored something that had been taken away from her. She'd worried that she wouldn't want him to enter her, after everything that had happened, but instead she was desperate for him to possess her. Where Otto had been ugly, he was beautiful. Where she'd once been revolted, now she fell passionately in love with every part of a man. She wanted to touch and caress every inch of his body, his skin and his cock.

'Is it all right? Do you want to?' he'd asked softly as he'd put his hands between her legs and touched her.

'Yes, please . . .' She'd pulled him to her and then guided him inside, so that he knew for sure it was what she wanted. Then he'd made love to her, so carefully that she had felt renewed by him, as though he was beginning to erase all the terrible things Otto had done to her, and show her that love could be healthy and healing.

When he called out her name, told her he loved her and fell on her breast, spent, Flora kissed his face and neck and hair, almost hurting with the delight she felt in his pleasure and the depth of her love for him.

Afterwards they lay together in each other's arms, their fingers interlaced, talking quietly.

'Everything with Otto', Flora said, feeling as though they were so close, so intimate, that she could say anything, 'was made worse because of what happened to me as I was growing up. You see . . .' She struggled for a moment, but then continued, determined to finish. 'We grew up almost completely shut off from the world, with only our uncle and aunt for company. My aunt was a strict, unbending woman, and my uncle . . . well, he . . . he . . .'

'Oh, honey.' Nick bent his cheek down to her shoulder. 'What happened?'

'That's the funny thing,' she said, 'because he didn't abuse me. I mean – he never touched me.'

'So what did he do?'

Nick lifted his head to look at her and Flora gazed back into his eyes.

'He watched me,' she said simply. 'All the time. I knew he was constantly observing me, sometimes as though I was a creature in his personal collection, and sometimes with a different kind of intent. I felt watched all the time, and sometimes I found holes drilled in strange places in my bedroom or in my bathroom ceiling . . . peep holes. Once I discovered a tiny camera inside a cupboard in our schoolroom, fixed on my desk and filming me while I worked. The sense of being observed constantly was terribly oppressive and I developed an awful stutter. As I began to grow up, he seemed less interested in me. It was from the age of about twelve to sixteen that it was at its worst.'

'Didn't Octavia notice?' Nick asked.

Flora shook her head. 'He was only interested in me. I don't know why. So when Otto turned out to be . . . a watcher . . . it was awful. I thought I was going mad. I couldn't understand why I attracted men like that.'

'Flora.' Nick propped himself up on one arm and gazed at her seriously. 'Those men, both of them – they're sick, in their own way. They're voyeurs. I don't care what people get up to if they're consenting adults but exploiting others, especially children, against their will, is abuse at best. No one should have made you suffer like that.' He kissed her face. 'It's a wonder you're as amazing as you are, considering what you've been through.'

'Nick,' she said softly, 'will you . . . will you stay with me? Not just tonight. For a couple of days. I want us

651

to be together, to get to know each other properly for a while.'

'Hey, it's Christmas, you know. I have plans.'

'You do?' Her heart sank. She had been hoping she could persuade him to spend Christmas with her.

'Yeah, I had planned to stay in on my own, maybe see some pals, drink some beers and swear at bad television.' He looked at her with amusement. 'You're not going to make me give all that up so I can spend a romantic day with a beautiful girl, are you? What kind of trade is that, for God's sake?'

She laughed.

Then he looked serious, holding her hand a little tighter and stroking her other palm with one fingertip.

'Don't you think', he said quietly, 'that you need to be with someone rich? That way you know they're not after your money.'

'No . . . I need to be with someone whom I trust. Someone whose heart I know. I know yours. You're a good man, Nick Falcon.'

'I'm a man with about six cents in the bank.'

'That's the lucky thing, you see. I've got enough for both of us.'

'Hey, I don't want that money of yours, understand?'

'I'm not giving you money – although I don't mind doubling that six cents. But . . .' Flora hesitated, feeling shy again. Then she went on in a rush: 'I do want you to love me, with the money or without it. Do you think . . . you might be able to?'

He stared at her and then said earnestly, 'How could I not? You're the most loveable person I've ever met in my life. It's not just that you're beautiful, it's what's shining out of your eyes. I want to make everything rotten in your life good again.'

Tears sprung to her eyes but she was smiling and laughing as she hugged him. 'Oh, Nick. That's exactly what I want too.'

Octavia woke in Max's magnificent bed on Christmas morning. She was wearing nothing but a stunning diamond necklace that he had given her as a Christmas present the night before. She hadn't got a gift for him, as she'd come away at such short notice, but he said that her divine body was present enough as far as he was concerned, and they'd made passionate love until they'd fallen asleep in one another's arms in the early hours. Now it was late, the morning already well advanced.

Max was not there so she got up, showered and dressed in a bright red jersey wrap dress, which she thought was suitably Christmassy, and put her diamond necklace back on. She went down to breakfast feeling wonderfully sexually sated, but a little depressed as well.

'Hello, darling,' Max said, getting up as she came in so that he could kiss her.

She was thrilled to hear him call her 'darling'. This man, this wonderful man, really cared for her.

He hugged her tightly and murmured, 'Happy Christmas! How are you? You look gorgeous.'

'Thank you. Happy Christmas to you.' She sat down to a bowl of fruit and yoghurt, and a cup of coffee. 'I'm . . . I'm missing Flora, I suppose. We didn't spend Christmas together last year, and I promised her that we would this year.'

'Yes. It is sad to be apart from loved ones at this time of year, isn't it?' Max's eyes sparkled with amusement in a way she'd never seen before. 'Look out of the window.'

She got up and went to the huge window that looked out to the front of the house, with its ornamental fountain and sweeping circle of gravel. It was a chilly day outside and frost sparkled on the iron railings and the lawn. Then she noticed the Mercedes that had met them at the airport was purring quietly up the drive towards the house.

She turned back to Max, who was obviously delighted at the way things were working out. 'Another Christmas present,' he said.

The car pulled around the fountain and came to a stop outside the house. The driver went to open the passenger door, but it had already been opened and out stepped Nick Falcon.

'Nick?' Octavia said wonderingly, watching as he turned and put his hand out. The next minute Flora was climbing from the car and looking up at the house, evidently impressed.

'Oh, Max!' said Octavia in a choked voice. 'Oh, thank you!' She raced to him and covered his face in kisses, then ran to the front door, opened it and hurried down the front steps to greet her sister and hug her happily.

Just as they were all talking and wishing each other a Happy Christmas and laughing about the surprise, they realised that another car was coming up the driveway, another dark Mercedes just like the first.

They all glanced at each other with questioning looks. Then Max came out, saying, 'Ah, here's the second part of your Christmas present, Octavia. And it's for you too, Flora.'

The car drew up behind the first, the driver got out, opened the passenger door, and suddenly there was Vicky, grinning delightedly. 'Hello!' she shouted. 'Happy Christmas!'

The driver opened the other door and there, standing on the far side of the car, was Diane. The twins stared at her, their mouths open in astonishment. Their mother came around to the front of the car and looked up at them.

'I hope you don't mind,' she said, 'but I rather thought I'd like to spend Christmas with my daughters, and Max was kind enough to arrange it.'

The three women stared at one other, the two younger ones looking at their mother with stunned expressions. Diane smiled at them, her face expressing love and apology as well as something else – it looked like a silent request to be forgiven. She opened her arms. There was a long moment when no one stirred and then the girls moved together as one, going quietly, almost solemnly, to their mother, who wrapped them both in her embrace. They all stood together like that for a long time.

The others watched, moved by the scene of reconciliation.

Then mother and daughters pulled apart, smiling and blinking back tears.

'Now,' said Max, 'time for a drink. And then, I don't know about you but I'm already looking forward to our goose.'

He put his hand out to Octavia who took it, still wiping away tears, and led her into the house. Nick put his arm around Flora and the two of them followed Max and Octavia inside. Lastly Vicky gave her arm to Diane, and they walked together up the worn old steps into the light and warmth of the welcoming house.

Epilogue

Roddy Wildblood sauntered into the magnificent old shop, walking through the double doors and straight into the handbag department. He looked about at the fantastic display of designer bags, with all kinds of luxury labels displayed, from well-known brands to more cutting edge up-and-coming names. He nodded with approval at the imaginative displays. A miniature golden spiral staircase climbing from a counter in the centre of the room had a beautiful bag displayed every few steps. He noted a Noble's own-brand luxury bag line, with handsome leather pieces lined with Noble's fabric or blind-stamped with famous patterns.

As he went through the shop he noticed that the customers included many stylish, well turned out women who clearly knew the best places to shop. He saw them handing over pretty dark green loyalty cards as they did their shopping, selecting delightful silk scarves from a little counter that looked like an ice-cream parlour. He glanced into the jewellery department where a Cartier pop-up store had a lavish display of watches, some with straps lined with Noble's prints.

He wandered, admiring everything he saw, negotiating the crowds until he came to the scent department. He looked about him for a while and then went over to one of the counters where a shop girl was doing a careful inventory of her stock, frowning with concentration as she did so. He leant on the counter next to her.

'Hello, I wonder if you could recommend a nice scent?'

The girl jumped, looked at him and burst out laughing. 'Roddy! How lovely to see you!'

'Octavia.' He bent over the counter and gave her a smacking kiss on the cheek. 'Lovely to see you too. I never thought I'd see you in the role of shop assistant. Aren't you the owner of this place? I was certainly under that impression when I agreed to let Noble's become the only stockist of Delphine outside our own boutiques.'

'Of course I'm the owner, but I have a magnificent chief exec in the form of Amanda who's doing an amazing job.'

'Mmm, she certainly drives a hard bargain. She got my prices down, and she's got you working down here while she's in the best office! Unbelievable.' Roddy grinned at her.

'This was my idea actually,' Octavia said proudly. 'I need to learn the business from the ground up, so I decided to start on the shop floor. Now if you'd like to buy a scent, how about this gorgeous one from Trevellyan? They've just relaunched some of their historic men's colognes. This one is Albemarle, and it's delicious. Guaranteed to drive Didier wild.'

Roddy turned his eyes up to heaven. 'Oh, forget Didier.

I have. It's Luca now. And whoever else is available – which is pretty much everyone.'

Octavia looked at him with concern. 'Are you okay, Roddy? You do look tired.'

'Ach, I'm fine. Always working, but what would I do without it? Whenever I think about stopping or taking a break, I can hear Iseult telling me not to be so silly, to crack on and get things done while I can.' He gazed about the room. 'I can see her touches everywhere here. It's nice. It's like this is her memorial.'

'I think about her all the time too,' Octavia said softly.

'She'd be proud of you,' he said sincerely. 'You're all grown up. And I hear you're finally with a man who's worthy of you.'

'Max,' Octavia said happily. 'Yes, he is pretty wonderful. He's helped me as Ethan's trial gets closer. It's going to be painful and horrible but I know he'll be a big support to me.'

'Ah, that's great, honey.' Roddy glanced down at his watch. 'Shit, I can't stay. Meetings here, there and all over the place. But I wanted to pop in and see you. Maybe come and party with me soon? In Paris perhaps?'

'Of course, darling, sometime soon.' Octavia gave him a goodbye kiss. 'You'll look after yourself, won't you, Roddy?'

He smiled at her. 'Course I will, sweetheart. And you too. Bye, darlin'. Bye.'

Octavia watched him as he sauntered away, out into the busy London street and off to wherever his meeting was. There was an air of melancholy about him that bothered her. *I hope he'll be all right. I'm sure he's become even wilder since Iseult died.* She couldn't help thinking that Roddy and Iseult were two of a kind, and wondered what his eventual fate would be. Perhaps he'd escape the sense of hopelessness that had eventually destroyed her. But she feared for him.

Julie, another shop assistant, came up and said, 'Octavia, you're on break. Twenty minutes off.'

Octavia nodded and put her inventory down. The work was quite tiring and the regimented hours had taken a lot of getting used to, but she was learning a great deal about how the shop worked, how the sales force could be motivated and what targets they needed to achieve. More important than that, the staff had softened in their attitude towards her. They appreciated what she was doing and respected her willingness to get down to some hard work. Once she'd proved that she expected to be treated like anyone else, they'd actually started to like her. Bringing Amanda back had also helped.

And the store was doing brilliantly now. The revamp had worked very well, and they'd been featured in just about every magazine aimed at fashionable women. The result was that people had come to have a look round, been impressed, and come back. The whole place felt modern, stylish and desirable, but with its magnificent setting still in place, it remained linked to its history. Noble's had been reborn, under the aegis of a Radcliffe and a Beaufort – unlikely allies but growing stronger every day as they learnt to trust each other.

Yes, she thought. *The future is looking bright even if I have this trial to get through. But once it's over and Ethan is sentenced, we can start to move on.* She thought of Max then and smiled happily.

'Octavia,' Julie said warningly, 'you'd better get a move on. You've wasted four minutes of your break already.'

'Okay,' she said cheerfully, heading for the back stairs and the staff room. 'See you later.'

'Don't be late back.'

'I won't. Don't worry.'

Flora read the letter through twice. It was over then. Her marriage to Otto was void. It had never happened. He had never owned her. He had returned all but £5 million of the money he'd stolen, and that had all been spent. She had to decide now whether to take criminal proceedings against him.

She folded the letter and went to the window, staring out as she thought about him. He had lost his power over her the day she'd decided he couldn't hurt her even if he did his worst. And she'd come through it all, and found this mind-blowing, heart-exploding love with Nick in the process.

Most miraculously of all, they'd found their mother. Diane had been through her own trial of fire and hadn't been able to stay strong in the face of the world's opinion. They'd all paid a high price for that. Now the first tentative steps towards forgiveness had been taken. Diane still lived in her remote French cottage but there were dates in the diary for holidays together, and over Christmas at Max's, they had started to form a bond and get to know one other. It would be a long time before there would be a natural mother-daughter relationship between them, if ever. But the biggest questions were answered now and Flora felt she could at last begin to move forward into her future.

The door opened and Vicky came in.

'Nick said there's been good news. Otto . . . It's all over?'

Flora nodded happily, smiling at her cousin. 'Yes, all over. Nick's coming soon to celebrate.'

Vicky came over and hugged her. 'I'm so pleased. I wish you'd never laid eyes on him.'

Flora gazed at her cousin, her blue eyes candid. 'I'm not so sure. Sometimes it's the troubles in our lives that lead us to happiness. I'd never have fallen in love with Nick if I hadn't married Otto.'

'Maybe not,' Vicky said. She laughed. 'And he's a very good thing, isn't he?'

'The best,' Flora said with a happy smile.

'I brought you this,' her cousin said. She held up the marriage certificate that had Otto and Flora's names on it. 'And this.' She held out a box of matches. 'It seemed appropriate somehow.'

Flora laughed. They took the certificate to the grate and Flora held it up while Vicky struck a match and set light to one corner. The flames quickly licked up the paper, consuming it in seconds. Flora held it as long as she could, then dropped it into the grate where it melted into soft grey ashes.

'Goodbye, Otto,' she murmured, staring at the remnants.

'Come on,' Vicky said, 'Molly's just made tea. Let's go and get some.'

Acknowledgements

Huge thanks to everyone who helps me write my novels.

To James, who is endlessly supportive, and ensures I have the time and space to work. To Barney and Tabby, who make me laugh and love so much.

To the indefatigable Lizzy and Laura at David Higham Associates. Lizzy is the dream agent; lovely to me, terrifying to everyone else, and with fiendishly good ideas. Laura is always on hand to provide a sympathetic ear and amazingly speedy help.

To my family and friends, who are always prepared to step in at deadline moments to help out, and tireless at spreading the word.

To the people who helped with my research: Colin Bodill, record-breaking pilot, who took me on my first helicopter flight and explained all I needed to know;

the Murray family for their generous hospitality; Jane Mackenzie for her friendship and enthusiasm.

To Paul Laikin, for a very helpful first draft read-through, and to Lynn Curtis for her splendid copyediting.

To the wonderful team at Random House: Gillian, my editor, who's given so much time, suggested so many excellent ideas and boosted morale wonderfully well; Kate, my publisher; Amelia, my publicist, and all the fantastic people in sales and marketing; plus the unsung heroine Helen in production, without whom the book wouldn't ever be printed.

And I would like to acknowledge the talents and personalities of Isabella Blow and Alexander McQueen, who helped to inspire some of the events in this book, although this is not their story. They burned so brightly and were extinguished far too soon.

ALSO AVAILABLE IN ARROW

Midnight Girls

Lulu Taylor

From the bestselling author of *Heiresses*

From the prestigious dormitories of Westfield to the irresistible socialite scene of present-day London: everywhere Allegra McCorquodale goes, scandal follows her. And in Allegra's shadow are her closest friends since school, the Midnight Girls.

Romily de Lisle: super rich, brilliant and bored. She's as blessed as Allegra when it comes to looks, but she's a force to be reckoned with. And Imogen Heath: pretty, timid and hopelessly drawn to Allegra's reckless charm. She longs to be a part of the glitzy high-society world where her friends move with such ease.

Once free of the cloistered worlds of school and university, greed, tragedy and sinister passions threaten the girls allegiance and each of them stand to lose what they love most . . .

Praise for Lulu Taylor's *Heiresses*

'Addictive, decadent and sexy' *heat*

'This is such great escapism it could work as well as a holiday'
Daily Mail

'Pure indulgence and perfect reading for a dull January evening'
Sun

arrow books

Heiresses

Lulu Taylor

They were born to the scent of success. Now they stand to lose it all . . .

Fame, fashion and scandal, the Trevellyan heiresses are the height of success, glamour and style.

But when it comes to . . .

. . . WEALTH: Jemima's indulgent lifestyle knows no limits; Tara's one purpose in life, no matter the sacrifice, is to be financially independent of her family and husband; and Poppy wants to escape its trappings without losing the comfort their family money brings.

. . . LUST: Jemima's obsession relieves the boredom of her marriage; while Tara's seemingly 'perfect' life doesn't allow for such indulgences; and Poppy, spoiled by attention and love throughout her life, has yet to expose herself to the thrill of really living and loving dangerously.

. . . FAMILY: it's all they've ever known, and now the legacy of their parents, a vast and ailing perfume empire, has been left in their trust. But will they be able to turn their passion into profit? And in making a fresh start, can they face their family's past?

arrow books